THE CRY OF THE BANSHEE

THE SEQUEL TO "THE LAMENT OF THE LEPRECHAUNS."

ALLAN C. HOWARTH

*FOR MUM AND DAD,
FOR ALL THEY DID
FOR ME*

*AND FOR MOM, FOR
GIVING ME LIFE
AND INSPIRATION*

Prologue

The sound seemed to emanate from somewhere deep within the very bowels of the earth. A rolling, rumbling growl, that oozed malice and malevolence as it slowly seeped and slithered into the dark corners of the mind. A resonance that swiftly grew in volume and intensity until it became a crashing tidal wave of noise; a deafening roar that filled the ear, saturated the senses and paralysed the brain. It was, quite simply, the most frightening thing that young Wayne Higginbotham had ever heard in his life.

Wayne's breath caught in his throat as his mouth dried up, and his stomach suddenly seemed to become vacuously empty. He crouched down and closed his eyes tight as he heard the sound, just a few feet away from his hiding place.

"And just what do you think you are doing there, BOY?"

Wayne could almost hear his teeth clashing together uncontrollably, as they chattered in fear. It was difficult to believe that a human being could emit such a sound, a sound that engendered an instinctive degree of terror in others of the same species. Yet Dai Davies - the big, bald and Welsh deputy headmaster of Wormysted's Grammar School, Shepton, Yorkshire - possessed a voice that could reduce even the very hardiest of boys to little more than quivering lumps, with just a single word.

Dai Davies: the scourge of the unkempt, the untidy and unruly pupils of Wormysted's. The scion of the righteous, the rule-abiding, and the rugby first fifteen. Dai Davies: the very name itself had set bowels churning amongst more than one generation of Wormysted's schoolboys.

Annoyingly, Wayne had only himself to blame for putting himself in his current predicament, at risk of incurring the full and terrible wrath of Dai Davies. All for the sake of trying to get in with the Wormysted's 'in crowd'... all because he had wanted to just appear cool, for the very first time in his life.

Wayne looked up and saw Dino Giardano's feet swiftly disappear through the window of the chemistry laboratory as he was yanked unceremoniously into the adjacent corridor.

"What were you doing in there, boy?" Dai Davies' voice boomed.

From the volume, Wayne could imagine that Dai's face would be less than one inch from Dino's and his breath would have seemed like the blast from one of the hot hair dryers in the changing rooms.

"Nothing, Sir!" came Dino's timorous reply.

"Nothing?" Dai's voice thundered incredulously. "NOTHING?" he repeated sarcastically, a full octave higher.

"No, nothing, Sir." Dino almost whispered.

The sound of a sharp intake of breath shot through the open corridor window to Wayne, as he trembled behind the window in the chemistry lab. From what he had seen previously, Wayne knew exactly what would be happening. Dai would have grabbed Dino by the lapels of his blazer and yanked him up into the air, letting his feet dangle uselessly inches above the ground.

"No, nothing, Sir!" Dai's voice mocked the plaintive alto of the dangling schoolboy.

"Please Sir, not me Sir! I'm a good boy, I am, Sir."

Wayne bit his lip. What if Dino cracked and told Davies why he had sneaked into the chemistry lab through the open corridor window? What if he admitted that he hadn't acted alone?

Dai Davies stopped shouting and began to growl, quietly and even more ominously.

"I catch you red-handed, climbing out of the chemistry laboratory, boy - and you have the bare-faced cheek, the sheer audacity, to tell me you weren't doing anything! Do you think I am a bloody idiot, BOY?" The question ended in a deafening bellow.

"No, Sir," Dino squeaked.

"Do you think that I am some sort of half-wit? A moron? Is it your impression, boy, that I am a sandwich and a packet of crisps short of a picnic?"

"No Sir, course not, Sir."

There was a brief silence, broken only by the shuffling feet and the muffled whispering voices of a crowd of boys gathering in the corridor, watching Dino Giardano's public humiliation.

"It is a sad fact of life these days, boy, that some people don't seem to believe in corporal punishment," Davies growled. "There is a wet, liberal, female-dominated elite within the teaching profession, who seem to believe that enforcing discipline is a bad thing. Indeed, some do not seem to like discipline at all."

There was the harsh cracking sound of flesh hitting flesh as Davies slapped Dino's face.

SLAP!

Wayne winced.

"It is your misfortune..."

SLAP!

"...that I am not..."

SLAP!

"...one of those..."

SLAP!.

"...people!"

SLAP!

"Giardano!"

The sound of Dino's feet hitting the wooden floor as Davies released his throat reached Wayne, who looked frantically around the chemistry lab for a means of escape by any means.

"And I suppose you were alone in this enterprise, Giardano?"

Wayne's eyes widened.

"Yes, Sir," panted Dino, as he tried desperately not to sob.

"Yes, Sir," Davies repeated sarcastically. "Honour among thieves, is it? Well, let's see then, shall we, boy? Let's see if anyone else believes that they are superior beings. That they are above school rules."

Wayne's heart was surely about to stop beating; nothing could stand the battering it was giving the inside of his ribcage. Beads of sweat burst out all over his forehead. He was going to die, and it was all because of Dino's stupid idea that they 'borrow' some sulphur to make stink bombs to celebrate the end of term and the fact that they, the fifth form, had finished their 'O' levels. They hadn't even planned it. It had been a spur of the moment thing, as Dino had noticed that the corridor window of the chemistry lab had been left open as they had been passing.

"Come on," he had said to Wayne. "Are you in, or are you still one of the nerds?"

Wayne had glanced around nervously; the corridor and adjacent labs were empty. He had hesitated, but Dino had already slipped through the window into the lab and had disappeared into the darkness.

"Come on Higgs, you wet!" Dino's dismembered voice had urged in a whispered hiss.

Wayne had clambered swiftly through the window, and had pointed out the chemical that Dino had wanted on a shelf full of bottles of powders and potions of various colours and sizes.

"Cool!" Dino had whispered, stuffing the bottle into his blazer pocket. "Anything else we can nick?"

Wayne had shaken his head vigorously. "No come on, let's just go."

Dino, the coolest bad boy in the fifth form, had sneered.

"Not scared, are you? God, Higgs, you're wetter than a spring bank holiday Monday in Morecambe!"

Wayne - who had never in his five years at Wormysted's had so much as a telling off or even a detention, let alone a caning - hissed back, "I'm in here, aren't I?"

Dino had shaken his head dismissively.

"Ooh, you are a naughty boy, aren't you? Come on, then. Let's go before little goody-two-shoes Higgybotts wets his pants."

Dino had just mounted the bench by the window and had started to squeeze back through the gap into the corridor, Wayne just behind him, when they had first heard the chilling sound of Dai Davies' voice. Dino had immediately frozen, half his body still in the lab, the other half dangling out in full view. Davies had sprung like a panther and been on the unfortunate Dino in seconds.

Wayne had just had the time to duck under the bench below the window without being seen; but it seemed like his luck had now run out, as he heard the sound of the key turning in the chemistry lab's door. He looked around desperately one more time, trying to see if there was anywhere to hide, anywhere at all.

Wayne took a last deep breath as the door handle twisted. Maybe, instead of bolting for it, he should just stand up and coolly face the deputy headmaster, like a man, and calmly take whatever punishment that came, or...

The door swung open and Dai Davies marched purposefully into the lab, dragging behind him a dishevelled-looking Dino Giardano by the collar of his blazer.

"Let's see who your accomplices are, shall we then, boyo?" Davies fumed, glowering around the dark shadowy lab. He reached for the light switch.

Wayne took the third of his possible options.

He promptly disappeared into thin air..

One

Wayne Higginbotham ran up the dark and narrow staircase in the middle of his small terraced house, as though the very hounds of hell were on his tail. He burst through his bedroom door, dived on his bed, and kissed the blue envelope that his father, Frank, had given him just a few moments earlier.

Wayne stared at the spidery handwriting that conveyed his name, care of his old teacher, Mrs Ball's, address. The lettering was just so beautifully neat and feminine. He studied the exotic stamps topped by the abbreviation USA, and the price in cents. Each stamp showed a different picture of the American wilderness. How cool was that?

He turned the envelope around and kissed the sender's name and the return address. Oh, that address:

2145 Coldwater Canyon Drive,
Beverley Hills,
California, 91241,
USA

Could anything in the world sound more sun-kissed, warm and awe-inspiring than that? The very words Beverley Hills, California, sent images of cars the size of canal barges, unfeasibly tall palm trees, languorous surfing dudes and huge snow-capped mountains cascading into Wayne's mind. He fell back onto his pillow and closed his eyes, clutching the envelope and hugging it tightly, close to his chest.

One day he would go to California and see it all for real. One day he would see all those famous sights that he'd seen so frequently on television and in the movies. One day he would be able to act like the son of a movie star, instead of just being a nobody; living anonymously in a terraced back street, at the back end of a small town, at the absolute back end of Yorkshire.

One day he would visit his real mom and stay with her. But for now, the sound of the seemingly incessant rain hammering against his bedroom window forced Wayne to open his eyes and acknowledge grim reality. One day!

The envelope looked and felt surprisingly thin, compared to the usual vast tomes that Wayne had been used to, especially in the halcyon days immediately after their initial reunion. Even so, he was overjoyed at having received some word from his mom at long last.

It had been absolutely ages since her last letter. Wayne had been so upset by that one. It had made him feel incredibly jealous, but also very guilty. His mom had said that she had fallen in love and was going to marry the man who had helped her get the part in her last movie. She was so deliriously happy. Her fiancé was a really great guy and could really help her career. He had been her agent and then manager for some time, but now he was going to be her husband.

Wayne didn't understand why she needed this bloke's help. His mom was already famous. She'd been in at least three major movies and even the lads at school had heard of her after her last starring role, although Wayne had not been able to tell them that the gorgeous Terri Thorne, star of the disaster movie Tornado, was his real mother. The boys at Wormysted's Grammar School would have laughed him out of class had he even attempted to tell them the truth.

He had been quite cross when they'd all agreed that they fancied her, especially when they kept going on about that scene where she had ended up dressed only in her bra and pants; but he had also secretly swelled with pride when one boy had said she was "as fit as Debbie Harry." Everybody loved the lead singer of Blondie and one guy had compared his mom to her. Wow!

Not one of the lads at Wormysted's knew that Wayne had been adopted - not even his best friend, Paul Harland. None of them knew that he was anything other than plain, fuzzy-haired Wayne Higginbotham, who lived in one of those tiny, little terraced houses in the middle of the Yorkshire Dales market town of Shepton.

Wayne 'Goody-Two-Shoes' Higginbotham. The kid with the thick brown curly hair that covered his ears, like a pair of furry earmuffs. Wayne 'Swotty' Higginbotham. The only son of Doris Higginbotham, the hot-tempered, red-haired barmaid at the Junction Inn on the corner of Cavendish Street, and boring old Frank who worked in a factory.

They would have died in shock had they known that his natural mother was actually a real life movie star in Hollywood, California.

Wayne himself had been totally and utterly gobsmacked when he had found out five years earlier. Until then, he hadn't even known that he had been adopted. The careless whispers of a passing doctor, whilst Wayne was pretending to be asleep in a hospital bed, had been the first time he had ever heard of it. Adopted? Him? No way!

A search through his parent's private papers, however, had furnished him with the proof that he needed and also provided him with an address in London that could have been his home. The address was on an old immunisation record card:

24 St. Joseph's Road,
Hammersmith,
London

It didn't ring any bells with him, but then it wouldn't have. He'd been adopted as a tiny baby.

For a few weeks, Wayne had not been able to take in the fact that he was not really Wayne Higginbotham, the only son of Frank and Doris Higginbotham, but some kid called Michael Sean O'Brien. He had been so traumatised by the discovery that eventually he did something quite out of character. Shy, mousy little Wayne had run away. Well, not run away, exactly...more set out on a voyage of self-discovery.

The eleven-year-old Wayne had travelled all the way to London in the hope of finding his real mother, and that had only been the start. The journey had taken him to the very far West of Ireland; an incredible odyssey that had eventually reunited Wayne with his real grandfather, two of his aunts, an uncle, a cousin and, yes, eventually, his real mother. His beautiful actress mother, who had been just about to move from New York to Los Angeles to take her first movie role.

She had dropped everything to fly to Ireland as soon as she had heard that he had turned up at her father's farm. He had only seen her once since then, when she'd been in London for a premiere, but she had written to him at least once a month. At least, that was until she'd gone and met Dean, just over a year ago. Dean Vitalia, who had started out as her agent, but who had then become her manager and was now her fiancé. What a smart Alec he was!

Wayne didn't want to deny his real mom happiness, but this Dean guy... he just sounded so greasy and slimy and generally yuk! Her letters had almost dried up over the last year, since she'd gone and gotten engaged to him.

Doris would have gone totally mad had she known that Wayne was in touch with his 'birth mother.' Doris Higginbotham was a very jealous and insecure woman who would never have understood Wayne's need to know his roots. She would have hated Terri on sight, just out of principle. That was why Terri's letters had to be mailed to Mrs. Elizabeth Ball, Wayne's old primary school teacher, so that Doris remained blissfully unaware that he had ever met his real mom. Mrs Ball passed them on to Frank, Wayne's adoptive father, who then slipped them surreptitiously to his son.

Both Frank and Mrs Ball had been in Ireland when Wayne had been reunited with his real mother, having followed his trail to London and then across Ireland. Frank had saved Wayne's life when some mad priest had tried to kill him, just before his reunification with his mom. Now, that really would have blown the lads at school away! They all thought they knew his dad. Boring old Frank.

Sad, old, Frank Higginbotham, who put thingummys onto widgets at a factory and then put them into boxes; who couldn't afford a car and went to work on a decrepit, old Honda 50 moped, who couldn't afford decent clothes, so he looked like a tramp most of the time - and who was much older than the other lads' middle-class, professional, fathers. They had no idea that Frank Higginbotham was a hero, and not just because he'd saved Wayne's life. No - he really was a hero, and had medals from the Second World War to prove it. Yes, that would have shocked them alright!

"Wayne!"

Wayne heard Doris shout from somewhere downstairs. He kissed the letter again and hid it under his pillow. He would read it later, when he had more time.

It was strange how little time he seemed to have, even though he was on holiday from school. The long summer holidays were almost at an end though, and soon he would be in the lower sixth form.

"Wayne!" Doris shouted again, with an edge to her voice. Wayne sighed, and climbed off the bed.

It was still nearly two weeks before Wayne would be back at school, but only two days until he would find out his 'O' level results. Would he be able to match his cousin Cedric Houghton-Hughes, who had passed seven of the eight subjects he had taken?

"Wayne!"

"Coming," Wayne shouted distractedly, staring out of his bedroom window at the rain-washed back street and the expanse of the town's cattle market beyond.

Maybe if he did pass all eight 'O' levels and beat Cedric, Doris would finally forgive him for running away all those years ago. Beating the Houghton-Hughes' was the entire meaning of Doris' life.

Margaret Houghton-Hughes, Cedric's mum, was Doris' younger sister. The Houghton-Hughes' lived in the posh part of Shepton, because Stanley Houghton-Hughes was a bank manager. Everything they did, or had, Doris envied.

Yes; maybe if he did get more 'O' levels than Cedric, she might even finally forgive him for not being Trevor, her first attempt at adopting a child. He had supposedly been absolutely perfect, until he had been returned to his real mother when he had contracted meningitis. Doris had always maintained that he had died. It made the pain of losing him more bearable.

12

"WAYNE!" Doris bellowed.

Hearing that Wayne's dad was a hero would certainly have shocked the lads at school. They would have been much, much more shocked, however, to discover that - just as Doris wasn't his real mother - Frank Higginbotham wasn't Wayne's real dad at all.

Wayne's real dad had been a shapeshifting, Irish, immortal. Wayne's real father was no less than a Prince of the once mighty Tuatha De Danaan. Now that would have really shaken them up a bit. Once he'd explained who the Tuatha De Danaan were, of course.

"Coming, Mum," Wayne sighed, as he opened his bedroom door and began to trudge downstairs.

A grin crossed his face as he remembered Dino Giardano's expression when Wayne had nonchalantly walked past him in the corridor some two months earlier, as Dai Davies had been frogmarching the unfortunate boy to the headmaster's study after the Chemistry lab incident.

"How the hell did you get out of the lab, Higginbotham?" Dino had asked him a few days later, after he had served a short suspension.

"I was just lucky," Wayne had grinned. "Old Davies obviously isn't as sharp as he used to be."

Giardano had shaken his head in disbelief.

"There was no way you could have gotten out of there without being seen. No way at all."

Wayne had shrugged, and his grin had grown even wider as he had turned away from the other boy.

"You didn't know I was magic, did you, Dino?"

He could still see Dino's mouth hanging wide open, incredulously. If only all those cool bad boys knew that invisibility was one of the least of his abilities...

When Wayne thought about it, he could really shake those Wormysted's lads up a lot, if he wanted to!

Two

James Malone ran his hand through his long dark hair, and smiled. The warm California sun kissed his well-tanned cheeks, and it felt good to be alive. He slung the guitar bag over his shoulder and stuck his arm out, thumb raised. Jimmy was on the road again and all his troubles seemed like just so much ancient history.

It had been just over five years since James had fled his native Ireland and the priesthood. Five years in which he had been constantly on the move; always looking over his shoulder, just in case some shadow of the past should sneak up on him unaware and remind him of the horrors that he had seen. Five years of lies and half truths, five years of running, five years of loneliness.

Five years since...

A cold shiver ran down his spine and chilled him to the bone, despite the rapidly-climbing temperature of the morning. The road surface of Highway Number One was already hot enough to fry an egg and the brown, parched hills, away to his left, shimmered lazily in the haze.

If the Order hadn't found him in five years, it was likely that they had forgotten all about him by now. After all, what could they possibly want with him now anyway? Father James Malone was long gone. Now he was just plain Jim, or Jimmy Malone; vagabond, troubadour, and wandering minstrel.

A pick-up truck slowed down as it passed James, but as soon as he picked up his rucksack and began to run towards it, the driver stuck a tattooed arm out of the window, made a rude gesture, and accelerated off.

James stopped, shrugged, shook his head and grinned.

"Thanks buddy," he mouthed sarcastically. "Like you're the first one who's ever pulled that stunt."

He looked to his right as he ambled slowly along the sidewalk. Between two new apartment blocks and through a small thicket of palm trees, the brilliant blue of the Pacific Ocean came into view. Sunlight flickered silver on the waves, like a million carelessly scattered diamonds. James sighed contentedly. It must have been the luck of the Irish that had led him to such a beautiful place. After all, he could have ended up in the back streets of New York, or Boston, where he had relatives; or even London, where his lawyer brother, Dan, practised and where most of his schoolmates had settled.

Yet, in his desperate flight into anonymity, he had landed initially in San Francisco and had then moved up to Portland, Oregon and then latterly, back down the West Coast to Santa Barbara. It was on the edge of that town where he now found himself, searching for a ride on down to Los Angeles.

He had gotten too comfortable in Santa Barbara. There had been too many questions.

A Ford Mustang passed at speed, followed by a large truck, both of which ignored James' outstretched thumb. He dropped his arm, shrugged again, and began to whistle as he walked.

The fleeting thought of Dan had reminded him of home, and a familiar feeling of loss and regret ran through his mind. He hadn't contacted any of his family since he had left Ireland so suddenly. What must they have thought? Did they think he was really dead? That was what he had intended when he had faked his suicide. Only death would have prevented the Order from hunting him down.

Jimmy took a deep breath. The road was quiet, so he sat down on a low wall and swung the guitar off his shoulder along with his rucksack. A sudden twinge of pain in his arm made him wince. It was where his right arm had been broken on that fateful night, five years earlier. Dark images began to run through his mind.

"Come on, Jimmy, not all this stuff again," he whispered and stood up sharply, just as a red T-bird convertible appeared over the brow of the hill behind him. He stuck out his thumb and, much to his surprise, the car pulled to a halt.

James swiftly picked up his belongings and ran to the car. A stunningly beautiful young woman smiled up at him from behind the wheel.

"Going far?" she asked, cheerily.

"All the way to L.A.," James replied, his Irish brogue still recognisable even after five years in exile, "but I'd be more than grateful for a lift that takes me anywhere nearer."

"Jump in," the girl replied, with a grin and a toss of her long blonde hair.

James tossed his rucksack and guitar onto the back seat of the car and had hardly taken his seat and slammed the door when the girl accelerated sharply away.

"I can't take you all the way to L.A.," the girl stated as she glanced into her rear view mirror, "but I can take you as far as the Valley."

"The Valley?" James frowned quizzically.

The girl peered through her shades into her mirror as she sped round a palm-fringed corner.

"Yeah, the San Fernando Valley - it's just to the North of L.A. It's where all the movie stars live."

James smiled mischievously. "And is that what you are?"

The girl glanced at him with a look of amused admonishment.

"Oh yeah, right. Typical Irish, sounds like you sure got the gift of the blarney," she laughed.

"What's your name?"

"Malone, James Malone; but most people call me Jim, or Jimmy," James replied, wondering in the same instance why he had introduced himself using his real name for the first time in years. It had just seemed the right thing to do.

The girl took her right hand from the wheel and proffered it to her passenger.

"I like James, it sounds sort of dashing, you know? Bond, James Bond. I'm Caroline Horden, but you can call me Carrie - everyone else does."

James shook her hand and grinned at her, as she flashed him the sort of perfect, gleaming white smile that only Californian girls seem capable of.

"And I'm in real estate, not the movies, sadly," she gently chided the Irishman. "What do you do, besides attempting to flatter and take advantage of innocent young women?"

James blew out a long, deep sigh.

"Anything I can," he shrugged, "but sure, it's not flattery when I'm only for telling the truth, and I would never take advantage of anyone."

Carrie snorted quietly, and smiled as she accelerated up the slip road onto the Freeway.

"You have nice eyes," she said, glancing at James. "You should be in counselling, or something. You look sort of real sympathetic. You have a positive aura, kinda spiritual, you know? You look like a good guy and trust me there aren't many of those left, these days."

James grimaced and bared the teeth he'd had whitened a few weeks earlier.

"Yeah, I used to have a sort of...well, I guess you could have called it a spiritual counselling job...but that was a long time ago." His look became wistful.

"A different time, a different place, far, far away," he whispered.

"Do you believe in auras?" Carrie asked, as she glanced in her overtaking mirror and pulled out to pass a truck that seemed almost as long as a football field.

"I dunno, maybe. I suppose so." He shrugged and shifted a little uncomfortably in his seat.

"You mean no, not really!" Carrie laughed. "Don't worry, I won't throw you outta the car just for thinking I'm a bit kooky; all my friends do, you know? It's just that you have such a kind, peaceful presence, real soothing. Like a priest, or something. I feel like I oughta be giving you my confession."

She laughed again, an infectious, easy giggle that invited you to laugh along, but James didn't. He looked away from her, out at the burnt, brown hills, just in case she noticed the panic in his eyes.

"Yeah," he muttered eventually. "Something like that."

The car sped along in silence for a few moments, only the rumble of the tyres and the rush of the wind disturbing the peace. James hadn't realised how tired he was, as his eyelids began to flicker. Carrie's elbow hitting his arm woke him sharply.

"Hey, come on, Irish Jimmy," she reproached her passenger. "I picked you up for some company, you know?"

James rubbed his eyes and stuttered an apology.

"Sorry, Carrie, I guess I was more tired than I thought...and what with the car's motion and the sun..."

"Hey, don't apologise," Carrie interrupted him, breaking into her easy laugh. "I was only fooling with ya."

She glanced at him again, concern creasing her features.

"You've been through some bad stuff, haven't you? I can tell."

James shook his head, and sighed. "Hey, let's not talk about me. I'm boring. Let's talk about you."

Yet there was something persuasive about the American girl and, before long, James Malone found himself telling her most of his life story; all except for that fateful summer night over five years earlier. He told her about his life in Ireland, about having been a priest and about not having seen any of his family since 1974.

"See, man, I just knew you were a spiritual sort of person!" Carrie squealed when James told her his past profession.

"So what happened, you know? Isn't it 'once a priest, always a priest' in Ireland?"

James loved the way she said Ire-Land as though it was two separate words.

"It was meant to be, I guess, but..." He shrugged.

Carrie lifted her sunglasses off her nose and turned to her passenger. For the first time James saw her clear, light blue eyes. He gasped and choked on the words in his throat. He had known she was beautiful, but her eyes were beyond conventional concepts of beauty. They were so clear, so caring, but strong; so unutterably perfect. They seemed to burrow right through his own eyes, as though she could see straight into his troubled soul.

James Malone decided at that moment, for the first time in over five years, to tell another person what had happened on the night that he had decided to run away from everything he had ever known. James knew that somehow this girl - this person who had been a total stranger only half an hour earlier - would believe him. Carrie would believe the whole story, even the bits that Jimmy still couldn't quite believe himself.

"Did you run off with the collection plate?" Carrie teased him, "Or maybe with the prettiest boy in the choir?"

James smirked sarcastically.

"Ha Ha. Very funny, Carrie Horden."

Then he took a deep breath.

"Would you be promising to keep it totally to yourself, if I was to tell you the whole story? Something happened five years ago that I haven't told anyone about, because it was just, well, so unbelievable."

Carrie cast him a quick glance, her face now serious.

"Sure!" she said. "You've got my word and my attention."

James nodded, and looked at the black snaking freeway as it twisted into the shimmering, hazy mountains ahead. He took a deep breath, and began.

"It all started nearly six years ago. I was a young priest in a rural part of County Mayo, Ireland. One summer day, while out cycling in the hills, I bumped into an old farmer and, just by way of conversation, I happened to mention the fairy folk…"

By the time Carrie's Thunderbird wound off the Freeway up onto the Santa Susanna Pass, high above the suburban sprawl of the San Fernando Valley, James had told her the whole story.

He told her about the clandestine sect operating deep within the inner sanctums of the Catholic Church: The Sacred Order of St Gregory. He told about their mission to stamp out all of the 'Magical Fairy folk', believing them to be demons out to stop the impending second coming of Christ.

He told her about the strange Spanish priest who had used the name of the Conquistador Francisco Pizarro, but who had really been an immortal assassin, on a mission of revenge against the people that he felt had cursed him with immortality.

He told her about his friend and colleague in the priest house in Finaan, who had perished in the events leading up to 'that night.' He told her about the Tuatha De Danaan, the mystical race, who had supposedly inhabited Ireland before the Celts had arrived and who were

18

the basis of the stories of the 'little people' of Ireland. He told her about the old, eccentric "farmer" Mickey Finn, who really had turned out to be a shape shifting, immortal, Prince of the Tuatha De Danaan.

Eventually, he told her about the things he'd seen on that last night of his priesthood, such as the Order's assassination attempt on Mickey Finn, which had culminated in a battle of immortal shape shifters. An unbelievable battle, which had seen Pizarro blasting energy bolts from his open palms, only to be matched by Mickey Finn, now transformed into his true shape; a tall, stately warrior, straight out of the pages of Irish legend, or pulp fantasy fiction.

He related the tale of the strange intervention of the young British kid who had also seemed to have magical powers, and then the kid's father, which had seen Pizarro finally destroyed...but only at the cost of Mickey Finn's own life.

Finally, he told her about his own disgust at the actions of the Order and his flight from Ireland and the Church, and his pain at not being able to see his family or his friends.

Much to James' surprise, Carrie did not seem to think he was totally insane, but had listened to his tale in rapt attention. Every mile of their journey had been punctuated with her gasps at the tale he told her. She had continued to glance at him, often open-mouthed, even after they had turned off the freeway and sped down the narrow, winding, canyon road. James had even paused at points so that Carrie would hopefully concentrate on negotiating the seemingly impossible tight bends ahead.

James was even more surprised when she had gripped his hand tightly, leaned over and planted a kiss on his cheek at the conclusion of his tale.

"I've always believed in magic and the existence of powers that we don't understand," she exclaimed, tears rolling down her cheeks from under her black shades. "What you tried to do was just so wonderful."

She was referring to James' retelling of his futile attempt to stop Pizarro and his sidekick Burke from murdering Mickey Finn. Burke had been killed in a car crash, fleeing from the scene of the battle, but Pizarro had blasted James with an energy bolt and had very nearly killed him. A twinge of pain ran up his arm, which had been badly broken in his fall, at just the memory of that night.

"James, you have just got to come in and tell me more," Carrie pleaded as she rounded a bend with a squeal of protest from her tyres, taking a sharp right turn up a steep road.

"I've got lots of ice cold beer in the fridge, just in case you're tempted, and we're just about there."

The Thunderbird pulled to a stop outside a small Mexican hacienda-style house. James and Carrie climbed out of the car. She lifted off her shades again, and her eyes implored James to stay.

"Please James. I've just gotta know more, you know? All about these Tuatha dudes and the immortals and shape-shifting and all that stuff?"

"Now, how can I be refusing such a kind and generous offer?" James grinned. "It's not like I have to be anywhere soon, but will your husband - or your boyfriend, - not mind you bringing a stray old ex-priest home?"

Carrie raised her eyebrows as she locked the car door.

"He," she hissed, "my ex-boyfriend, that is, moved out last fall, so that he could continue his affair with my ex-best friend. They can both kiss my...well, you know! Sorry, Father."

James shrugged. "Well, I suppose if I quickly rearranged my diary, cancelled all my non-critical appointments and rang a few people, who will just have to find me new spots in their agendas...I guess I might be able to spare you a few minutes. Oh, and Carrie - I'm not a priest anymore."

Carrie cast him a sceptical glance and walked towards her house. James picked up his rucksack and guitar and followed her. An unattached, beautiful, woman had not only listened to his long and incredible tale, but had actually believed it. Now that had to be the luck of the Irish.

It was at that moment that James Malone realised that he'd gone and done something that he'd been trying to avoid doing since he had landed in America all those years earlier. James Malone had fallen in love, somewhere down the 101 interstate.

Three

The long, shiny black Mercedes limousine pulled to a stop outside the ornate marble façade of a huge office building. The road surface seemed to shimmer in the blistering heat of the Italian summer afternoon, as a perspiring uniformed chauffeur jumped out of the car, carefully placed his cap on his head and strolled around to the kerbside rear door. He opened it and stood to attention while an old man in flowing crimson robes and matching skullcap struggled to get out. Eventually, with the aid of a stick, the old man stood on the pavement. Without so much of a glance at the chauffeur he shuffled off towards the building, climbed painfully up the marble steps, and disappeared into the cool, dark interior.

Bishop Donleavy - one of the most important Catholic priests in Ireland and secret head of the Sacred Order of St. Gregory in that country - was very, very nervous. It had been many years since he had been summoned to Rome, to the Vatican City, on official Order business.

His wrinkled throat rolled slowly, as he tried to summon sufficient liquid lubricant to soothe the cloying dryness in his mouth. Why now? he thought to himself. Surely our business is now complete, and all we have to do is wait for the glorious day when our Lord declares his resurrection...?

His slow footsteps echoed in the empty marble-floored corridor, as he made his way towards the office of the Cardinal who was the worldwide head of the Order.

The Sacred Order of St. Gregory was a covert, secretive clique within the Roman Catholic Church, which had been founded nearly fourteen hundred years earlier by the Pope whose name it bore. The Order was dedicated to rooting out and destroying Satanic forces on Earth; and by Satanic forces, it meant anything that defied the natural order of things, especially anything that could be described as immortal.

It had long been prophesised that the second coming of Christ could only be prevented by "A child no mortal man shall sire." Supposedly, only the head of the Order knew the entire prophesy, although most of the organisation knew the key lines. It had been rumoured for many centuries that the prophecy made it clear that 'God's Assassin' would be a Jew.

Over the years, the Order had taken many liberties in exercising their mission to destroy any and all supposed "immortals," as well as being a major driving force behind the persecution of the Jewish people. Later they had been responsible for inciting many of the excesses of the Spanish Inquisition. Anyone described as a witch, a werewolf, a vampire, a warlock - or anything else out of the ordinary - was considered fair game. In more modern times they had had to be much more discreet in their operations, but had still managed to whittle down those they considered 'threats' to the Second Coming to a few solitary individuals, clinging to existence at the edges of the civilised world.

Of these individuals, very few were truly immortal. Most were just strange and different, outcasts from normal society, but that made them no less of a target to the Order's assassins. Yet there were some true immortals left, hiding in the bogs and mountains of the far West of Ireland. The remnants of what had once been a mighty race: The Tuatha De Danaan.

The Tuatha had been a noble, civilised and advanced people while mankind had still been hanging from the branches of trees; gibbering, screeching, and competing for bananas. They had been tall and graceful with olive skin, finely pointed ears, and piercing eyes. They had worn their shining hair long, and dressed in fine robes, woven of a cloth of such quality that it would be beyond the imagination even of modern man. Aging and disease had no dominion over them. Only by suffering savage and serious wounds could they be killed, and they had such enormous powers at their disposal that few natural forces could pose them any threat. They could change their shape at will to match any living creature, and becoming invisible was as easy as taking breath to them.

They could throw out bolts of concentrated energy from the palms of their hands, capable of immobilising most species at short distance. Their sight was so keen that they could fire an arrow virtually through the eye of a needle. For many millennia, the Tuatha De Danaan had been the Lords of the Earth. However, they were so powerful that complacency had set in, and they had not bred in any great number for many centuries.

Eventually man stopped fighting over bananas, came down from the trees, and multiplied, becoming like a plague of locusts to the Tuatha.

Early man had worshipped the immortals and had been taught many skills in the arts and sciences in return. The written word and mathematics had been gifts of the Tuatha, as was medicine, astronomy and the building of cities. Mortal man soon became jealous of the

Tuatha's powers, their beauty and immortality, and wanted the secrets behind such assets. Secrets such as the great Stone; a mysterious, unearthly orb that amplified the powers of the Tuatha from its place on a plinth in the city of Falias, and glowed with a green light whenever magic was used.

Wars broke out. Battles were fought. The warriors of the Tuatha, in their arrogance, refused to use their magical powers to defeat man. They considered such advantages would render their victories dishonourable, and so they relied on the same weapons as men; sword, spear, and arrow. Even so, men were slaughtered like cattle.

Yet mortal men breed quickly. Man's number kept growing and growing, and after uncounted centuries of conflict, the Tuatha were finally forced to flee their homes in the warm and fertile lands. The great Stone of Falias was smashed as the capital city was sacked, and only a number of broken shards were retrieved after the ensuing conflagration. Even then, the immortals refused to use their magical powers against the lesser beings.

The Tuatha fled to the north and to the west, their number in perpetual decline. Finally, the last remnants of this once mighty race reached a cold, dark and misty island on the very edge of the known world, and found that there was nowhere else to go.

So it was that the Tuatha De Danaan settled on the island of Ireland, defeating the primitive indigenous Fir-Bolg in battle. There they lived peacefully for many years, until a new race of men eventually discovered them: the Celts.

The ensuing wars between the Celts and the Tuatha De Danaan were long and bloody. Although by now few in number, the Tuatha's fighting skills still served them well and the Celts were often pushed back into the sea; returning sullenly to the island of Britain, where they brooded and plotted and planned their next attack. Again and again, the war-like Celts invaded Ireland, like countless waves rolling onto a sandy beach. Celtic legend tells of the mighty warriors and the Kings who would eventually triumph over the Tuatha, legends familiar to the children of Ireland to this day.

The Tuatha De Danaan were whittled away, until they were finally exhausted and ultimate defeat and extinction stared them in the face. Only then did they decide that their magical powers should be used to preserve the race.

The few remaining souls of this once great and mighty people took to the caves and barrows, the mountain peaks and the bogs of the Wild West coast of Ireland. They changed their shape at will and would disappear into thin air whenever mortal men challenged them. So arose the legends of the 'little people,' the 'fairy folk' who could do such magical things.

The Sacred Order of St. Gregory heard tales of these beings in the Middle Ages and had immediately ranked the surviving Tuatha alongside witches, werewolves and vampires in the assemblage of evil. No true child of God could perform magic, and, being immortal, they could be the source of 'God's Assassin' - the one who it had been prophesised would kill God made flesh! For nearly five hundred years the Order had searched out the remaining immortal Tuatha De Danaan and exterminated them, often in the most heinous of ways.

So the slaughter continued, until, by the early twentieth century, it was believed by the Order that they had achieved what the Celts had never managed, and finally eliminated every last single one of the so-called 'fairy folk.' However, in 1974, it came to the Order's notice that a simple Irish peasant farmer, calling himself 'Mickey Finn,' bore all the hallmarks of being one of the immortal Tuatha De Danaan.

The careless words of a local village priest had alerted a bishop, who just happened to be a member of the Order. An assassin was promptly despatched from Rome to expunge the Earth of what was presumed to be the very last of the Tuatha De Danaan, for once and for all.

Bishop Donleavy had been inordinately proud when he had heard that the mission had been successfully accomplished; and accomplished under his tenure as the head of the Order in Ireland. The only downside had been the lack of solid evidence of the demon Finn's demise, and the amount of media attention generated by the amount of casualties that had ensued in the operation.

A local priest had perished in a car crash, while another had committed suicide just before the event, and another supposedly immediately after. A visiting Spanish priest, Father Francisco Pizarro - who was, in fact, the Order's chief assassin - had also seemingly disappeared off the face of the Earth.

The supreme head of the Order in Rome had been far from happy with the high rate of attrition and the ensuing publicity, which had threatened to finally expose the existence of the Sacred Order of St. Gregory. Although he had been sufficiently satisfied with the overall result of the operation, he had postponed Donleavy's promotion to Archbishop. That had been five years earlier.

While no disbanding of the Order had been announced, it had generally been assumed by its membership that its sacred task had been completed. The path to the second coming was presumed clear. Bishop Donleavy had been most surprised, therefore, to be summoned to Rome by the supreme head of the Order during the summer of 1979. He had been even more surprised that he had been told to maintain an operational degree of silence.

It was with a due sense of foreboding that he rang the bell outside the office of the Cardinal who had ruled the Order with an iron fist for the last twenty-five years.

The ornately carved wooden door swung open silently as a small bespectacled man in a business suit, sweating profusely, beetled out.

"His Eminence is expecting you, Your Grace."

The small man bowed as he passed, gesturing that Bishop Donleavy should enter the sumptuous office, all the while dabbing his forehead with a white handkerchief. The aged Irish bishop shambled slowly into the room and crossed the wooden floor to kiss the hand of his superior, who proffered a red-gloved hand from behind his desk.

"Thank you for coming all the way to Rome, Bishop Donleavy," the Cardinal whispered. His voice was heavily accented. "I know it is not easy for a man of your advanced years to make such a strenuous journey."

Donleavy waved his hand dismissively.

"The journey was not a problem, Your Eminence."

His undulating, wrinkled throat rolled. The Cardinal rose from behind his desk and beckoned for Donleavy to follow him. He walked slowly to a door in a sidewall of the office, which he opened, allowing Donleavy to pass through before him. The Irish bishop squinted in the darkness of the chamber.

"In here we can talk freely, away from the prying ears of the uninitiated," the senior clergyman whispered, closing the door behind him. "It is now five years since we dealt with the last of the Irish demons, is it not?"

Donleavy nodded. "Indeed it is, Your Eminence."

"Do we yet have any tangible evidence that the demon did indeed perish with all those poor priests?" the senior churchman enquired, rubbing his hands apprehensively.

Donleavy shook his head, his mouth dry. He grimaced painfully.

"I still have people in the area. There has been no sight of the Finn demon, since our late colleague Pizarro set out to deal with him."

The Head of the Order grimaced and frowned, disappointment etched into the lines on his brow.

"And what of the young priest who disappeared in the aftermath? Do we yet know if he truly committed suicide?"

Donleavy grimaced and shook his head.

"We have not been able to find any trace of him, Your Eminence. The Gardai - the Irish police, that is - believe that he committed suicide in the aftermath of the tragedy, but no body has ever been found."

The supreme head of the Sacred Order of St. Gregory pursed his lips.

"I am afraid, Bishop Donleavy, that you must re-double your efforts in this matter. Do what you have to, but find that priest...even if you only find a rotting corpse. If there is any chance that he does live, that he still draws breath, we must speak to him. He is the only one who can corroborate what actually did happen that night. What was his name...Mahone?"

Bishop Donleavy's eyes opened wide.

"His name was Malone - Father James Malone - but why are you so concerned about the events of five years ago, Your Eminence? Surely the Order's mission was accomplished?"

The supreme head of the Order nodded sagely.

"Ah yes, Your Grace, the mission. The war against the unnatural. That particular costly battle is long over, my old friend, but it seems the war is not yet won. The stones have shown us that the magic is still being used, somewhere."

Bishop Donleavy looked aghast. "How can that be, Your Eminence?"

The Cardinal shook his head and sucked in his cheeks.

"I believe we might have been, how do you say...hoodwinked. There has never been any tangible proof that Finn did, in fact, perish that night. It is possible that he has just been very careful over the past five years. These creatures are very resourceful."

Bishop Donleavy shook his head as vigorously as he could.

"There must be another. I am absolutely certain Finn met his end at Pizarro's hand. Pizarro never failed."

The supreme head shrugged. "Come, my friend. There is someone you ought to meet."

The Cardinal opened a door at the far end of the chamber. The light was bright in this room. Sunlight poured through the windows, and a courtyard could be seen beyond. Grey robed figures scurried across the cobbles, hurrying between the imposing Vatican structures. Donleavy had to shield his eyes in the brightness.

A young woman stood and murmured apologetically, standing as though to attention. Behind her, a small blonde-haired boy with huge blue eyes sat on a small chair. He turned and appraised the visitors.

"This, Bishop Donleavy, is Maria," the Cardinal announced, vaguely waving his hand in the direction of the woman.

"She is the mother of this...beautiful child."

The Irish bishop slowly and painfully bowed as low as he could, and kissed the hand of the girl. The Cardinal then kissed her hand in turn.

"You may see, my son, but briefly. Do not tire him," the girl whispered, suddenly assuming an imperious air.

The Cardinal nodded his agreement.

"Thank you, my Lady."

The girl smiled, nodded, and strolled out of the room. The Cardinal took a very deep breath.

"Five years ago, Maria was a junior novice in a remote convent in central Sicily. She is still a virgin, Bishop Donleavy, yet she is the mother of this child you see before us. He is a miracle."

He cast a furtive glance in the direction in which the girl had departed.

"And now she begins to act like Our Blessed Lady herself," he whispered, with a shrug.

The boy stood up from his small chair. Donleavy noticed he was clutching a small plastic toy soldier.

"So this is Bishop Donleavy?" the boy asked, his voice sounding totally confident and assured, yet still appropriately high in tone. It was undeniable that the child was stunningly beautiful. His skin glowed pink and cherubic, his blond hair shone and tumbled about his head in perfect curls. His eyes were large and vividly blue. Yet, there was something else about them; something that Donleavy couldn't quite place. He heard the Cardinal speak.

"Yes, my Lord. This is His Grace, Bishop Donleavy, all the way from Ireland."

A slow realisation began to dawn deep in the dark recesses of Donleavy's aged mind, and the Cardinal's strange statement about the girl's virginity suddenly began to make sense.

Donleavy looked up and saw the child staring deep into his eyes.

"Why have you failed me, Bishop Donleavy?" the child asked, sounding more curious than cross.

Donleavy frowned and leaned towards the boy.

"I, failed you? I don't know what you mean, my child." His voice was soft but condescending in tone.

"I am not your child, Bishop Donleavy," the boy stated scathingly. "I am your saviour."

Donleavy flinched, almost as though he had been struck. He straightened and took a step back. He knew now what it was about the child's eyes. They were devoid of emotion, so empty and icy cold. The child sniffed and pouted.

"I was told it was now safe for me to me born. That 'God's Assassin' was dead," he stated sulkily. "I was told that there was no more evil magic on Earth. I was told that nothing could hurt me anymore. I was assured that the ancient prophecy could not be fulfilled." The boy glared at the Cardinal, who bowed his head and slowly knelt down before the child.

Bishop Donleavy's mouth dropped open as he finally realised who the boy believed himself to be. He could see that the Cardinal's lips were quivering with fright. The ancient bishop struggled to kneel himself, his bones creaking with every move, yet his mind was so full of awe that he did not notice.

"I am sorry. I have done my best, My Lord." Donleavy stammered.

The child sniffed again, then glanced at the Cardinal.

"And you - bearer of lies and falsehoods - will please show my Momma the respect that she deserves in future!" Donleavy was aware of a strange gurgling sound coming from the Cardinal's mouth.

The senior Churchman fell to the ground and rolled onto his back, clutching his throat; his face white, his eyes wide and terrified. The gurgling sound had become a gasping noise as he struggled desperately to breathe. The small boy cocked his head to one side, smiled, and carefully studied the choking priest.

"I hate being let down by those who supposedly serve me. It makes me very, very cross indeed. I mean, I'm supposed to be very important...am I not?"

Donleavy, his mouth hanging open, nodded urgently in agreement.

"Very, very important, my Lord."

"I am a miracle," the child declared. He began to laugh; a humourless, menacing giggle.

The smell of burning, melting plastic filled Donleavy's nostrils. The plastic toy soldier was now a liquid pool bubbling and steaming on the wooden floor. The boy stopped laughing, turned away, and stared petulantly out of the window.

"Please don't fail me again, Bishop Donleavy, all the way from Ireland. Go and find this wielder of magic, whether it is the Finn creature, or another. Bring him to me. Dead or alive, it matters not."

The Cardinal turned sideways onto his elbow and gulped in great gasps of air. He struggled to his feet, and then gripped Donleavy's elbow to help the old bishop back into a standing position. Both Churchmen bowed before the child, who was now staring blankly out into space, before turning quickly and beginning to scurry out of the chamber.

"Wait!" The child's voice brought to the two men to an immediate halt.

"Y-yes, my Lord?" Bishop Donleavy stammered.

The child frowned in concentration, then looked up and smiled beatifically.

"Thank you both for coming. Bye bye!" he whispered, sarcastically.

The Cardinal and the bishop bowed meekly again, then exited the room as quickly as their legs would carry them.

The young woman was sat in a corner of the Cardinal's office reading a fashion magazine. At the sight of the bedraggled clergymen, she stood and rushed back into the room where her son had wreaked such havoc.

"I do hope you haven't upset him," she hissed, with a toss of her luxuriant brown hair as she passed, slamming the door behind her.

The cardinal slumped into his ornate chair while Donleavy leaned on the other side of the desk, his mouth agape, his eyes wide and bulging.

"And how old did you say he is?" Donleavy finally croaked.

"Just four," came the gasped response.

"And you are absolutely certain that he is who we believe him to be? For he is not quite as I had imagined."

Donleavy's question caught the Cardinal by surprise. He didn't answer at first, but looked away despondently and took a deep breath before whispering, "For all our sakes, I pray that he is. The alternative is simply too awful to contemplate."

The supreme head of the Sacred Order of St. Gregory, Cardinal Vittorio D'Abruzzo began to recite a poem that he had learned by heart, many decades earlier.

A child no mortal man shall sire
By mother's blood Royal line acquire,
Shall suckle he no milk white breast,
Shall rise in exile, unwelcome guest,
Shall learn to change his form at will
His shape, his face, his ways to kill
Unseen, unheard, his telling blow,
His doom to lay The Messiah low,
Shall tears then flow and kings shall fall
And darkness take us, one and all...

He took a deep breath, and put his hand on Bishop Donleavy's bony shoulder.

"I think you will need help, Your Grace. There is a priest in Brussels who has served the Order extremely well in the past. His name is Father Pierre de Feren. He is very dedicated and - if I may say - totally ruthless. Let us say his motivation is fired by the fact that he owes me a considerable debt. Use him, my friend, Donleavy. Use him to find out what really did happen in Ireland, five years ago. Find out if Father Malone really did perish that night, or indeed, if he still lives. Find out if Finn survived, or if there is some other possible 'God's Assassin'. Do it quickly, my friend; for I fear that this incarnation of 'The Light of The World', Our Lord, is more like the merciless Old Testament God of the Israelites than our new more modern, liberal interpretations. If we fail him, I fear we are all doomed. Doomed for all eternity."

Four

Wayne Higginbotham was fed up. All he wanted to do was read the letter from his real mom, but Doris had been on his back all afternoon.

First he'd had to go to the 'Co-Op' supermarket in town to pick up a few groceries that Doris had listed on a piece of paper. Then he'd had to take a pile of pressed and ironed clothes upstairs...then empty the bins...then tidy up the living room. Then he'd had to sit and eat his tea of fish fingers, chips and peas, with Doris. At this rate, Wayne was beginning to despair of ever getting to the Youth Club on Westmoreland Street, let alone passing a quiet ten minutes in his room, reading his real mother's letter.

It was hard to believe that a kid who was supposedly the last of the Tuatha De Danaan - the special one, known as the Slanaitheoir Mor, who could change his shape and disappear into thin air at will - could be plagued by such trivial and annoying mundanities.

Wayne Higginbotham was a direct descendent of Kings, both mortal and immortal. It had been prophesied that he would save the world.

Yet here he was, listening to Doris drone on about the state of the country under that useless, new Prime Minister, Maggie Thatcher and then on and on about Aunty Margaret's latest holiday in Spain. Hell, had he really blasted fire from the palms of his hands less than six years ago?

The spirit of Wayne's real father, Aillen Mac Fionnbharr, had appeared to him several times over the years, since his untimely demise at the hands of Pizarro; always through that familiar haze of green-tinged mist. He had warned Wayne that danger was around every corner and to always be on his guard, that he should try and avoid using his magical powers except in times of real need. Wayne, or Michael Sean O'Brien to give him his real name, had protested, saying that he would never be able to use his powers well if he didn't practice. Aillen had said that he would be able to use his powers instinctively and more than adequately, when such need arose. He also said that all the remaining pieces of the stone of Falias glowed when someone used magic. That meant that until all the pieces were found and reunited, someone else could be aware of his existence.

Aillen's last appearance had been the night after the disappearing act that Wayne had performed in the chemistry lab at school during the summer term, to avoid Dai Davies' wrath. He had appeared somewhat cross, but also slightly amused when he had materialised in Wayne's room that night.

"I thought I had told you to only use the magic in times of great need," he had gently chided his son.

"If you knew Dai Davies, Dad, you would have done the same thing," Wayne had replied, with a nonchalant shrug.

Aillen had smiled knowingly.

"He is a Celt?"

Wayne had nodded.

"Mmm," Aillen had nodded in return. "They are fierce warriors, the Celts. Perhaps you were right."

He had smiled at his son.

"You have grown tall since last I saw you, Michaeleen. How is your mother?"

"Okay," Wayne had replied hesitantly. It had been ages since her last letter and he wasn't really sure how she was; happy with her new husband and having far too much fun to write to someone as insignificant as her son, he supposed.

Aillen had grimaced.

"Her life moves on a different path to yours, my son, but you and your sister are very much in the centre of her heart."

"Yeah, I suppose," Wayne had sighed, sounding totally unconvinced.

Wayne had discovered, when he had been reunited with his blood relatives, that he was a twin. His sister had been adopted at the same time as him, but as they had been separated he had no way of finding her, and neither had his real mother, Terri.

"And how is the Northman warrior?" Aillen had asked, referring to Wayne's adoptive father, Frank, who had saved his son in spectacular fashion on the night of Aillen's demise.

"Fine," Wayne had shrugged.

Aillen had nodded and shook his head, smiling.

"You have truly reached the age of the warrior when your own father's words ire you."

Then he had stepped forward and put a ghostly hand on Wayne's shoulder.

"It was foretold that three trials would be put before the Slanaitheoir Mor. You have already passed one such test. Now you are of an age to be a warrior. What the form of the next two trials will be, I know not, but your boyhood is about to end. Succeed in these trials and you will become a true Prince of the children of Danaan, and the Slanaitheoir Mor."

Wayne had pondered Aillen's words for a second.

"And if I fail?"

Aillen had smiled reassuringly. "You will not fail, you are my son. It is your destiny to be the Slanaitheoir Mor."

Then, with a barely discernable wave, he had disappeared back into the mist, which had thinned and evaporated like a puff of steam.

"Great...thanks, Dad. I'm going to be something I can't even pronounce!" Wayne had groaned, as the last wisp of green mist vanished in the darkness of his bedroom.

That had been several weeks ago. Did the warrior trials that Aillen had referred to include doing the shopping in the Co-Op? Did they include having to sit at the kitchen table listening to Doris' jealous drivel about her rich sister, Aunty Margaret?

Wayne eventually escaped from the table and found himself with a few minutes to himself in his room, so he pulled his mother's letter out from under his pillow. He stared at it again for a while and was just about to rip it open, when he heard Doris' footfall at the top of the stairs. He quickly stuffed the letter back under his pillow. His door opened, and Doris peered in inquisitively.

"What are you doing?" she enquired.

"Nothing!" Wayne responded, guilt etched across his features.

Doris looked very suspicious, but didn't press the matter.

"Are you going to the Youth Club tonight?"

Wayne shrugged and nodded. "I suppose so."

Doris twisted her mouth and scowled.

"Your dad's not going to be back from work 'til late, he's on double shift. I suppose I'll be all on me own tonight, then."

Wayne shrugged again. It wasn't his fault if the only night he went out, Thursday, just happened to coincide with Frank's double shift at the thingummy factory. Anyway, he wouldn't be too late. The Youth Club closed at nine-thirty.

Doris turned with an exasperated sigh and clumped back downstairs, muttering darkly. Wayne fell back onto his pillow. He would read the letter before he went to sleep. Now he had to get ready to meet his mates and, with a bit of luck, the beautiful Stephanie Fleming...who he just happened to really, really fancy.

Girls were a total novelty to Wayne. Wormysted's Grammar School was an all-boys establishment, and over the years he had sort of forgotten about the opposite sex. Until, that is, he had set eyes on the gorgeous Stephanie. She reminded him of a girl he had met in London, years ago, when he had set off to find his real family. He couldn't quite remember her name, although 'Mandy' seemed to ring a bell. She had been tall, with long golden hair, blue eyes, and legs longer than Wayne had believed possible. Without her help his adventure would have been very short and fruitless, so she had held a special place in his heart for five years; a place that Stephanie Fleming was now rapidly beginning to occupy.

Wayne had first noticed Stephanie at the Youth Club, where a few of the lads from Wormysted's had started to congregate on Thursday evenings. It wasn't the most exciting place in the world - a couple of pool tables, three table tennis tables and a temperamental old stereo - yet it was more fun than staying in with Doris, watching rubbish on the telly.

Wayne had hardly noticed the regular girls at the Youth Club before Stephanie arrived. They were mostly fourth and fifth formers from the town's Girls High School, who seemed to spend most of their time sipping from straws in coke bottles, gossiping and giggling annoyingly. Worst of all, one or two of them kept casting furtive but critical glances at all the boys. Then, a rather plain girl with black-rimmed glasses called Anne Ducket, had brought her best friend, Stephanie, along. Wayne and most of his mates had fallen instantly in love.

Whereas most of the girls were either frumpy, wearing clothes that could have passed for their mother's, or were kitted out in the baggy, black shapeless uniform of the post-punk era, complete with the compulsory Doctor Martens, Stephanie dressed like a fashion model. Her pencil skirts and jumpers were always tight, showing off her slim long legs and the sort of figure that sixteen-year-old boys dream of. Her hair was long and sandy blonde, while her eyes were big and very blue. Her skin was flawless, not a spot in sight, and her lips were as red as the proverbial rose. Wayne just couldn't stop thinking about her.

Unfortunately, he had heard on the grapevine that she fancied some guy who had just left the upper sixth and had a car and was probably going to Oxford; but Wayne hadn't seen her with him, so maybe that was just somebody's ruse to put rivals off.

Wayne checked himself out in the mirror. His unruly, curly hair had been brushed as flat as he could get it, although it still resembled waves crashing towards the seashore. At least it was now long enough to cover his large, pointed, ears. He splashed on some cheap aftershave that he had seen a boxer promote on the television, pulled on his best checked jacket with its fashionably narrow lapels, and he was ready.

Tonight was the night.

Five

James Malone stared out at the incredible panorama spread out below him. The entire San Fernando Valley was bathed in early morning sunlight. Long, straight boulevards crossed the valley floor, like lines on a checked bed cover. Huge office blocks and sprawling malls dotted the landscape, looking like tiny doll toys. In the distance he could see the San Gabriel Mountains as they curved around in a huge wall, and beyond them the pointed peaks of the San Bernadino range. Directly below him stood the empty bed of the old Chatsworth reservoir, derelict since an earthquake in the early Seventies had persuaded the local authorities that the reservoir presented a huge risk of flooding to the entire valley.

He took a sip from his steaming mug of coffee and breathed in the cool morning air. By mid-morning the heat would be almost unbearable, and James could already see small smoggy clouds gathering at busy points down in the valley. Now, however, the air in Box Canyon was fresh, clear and fragrant, as the scent of bougainvillea filled his nostrils. The soothing splash of Carrie's gurgling ornamental fountain, the warmth of the sun on his back, and the coffee in his belly soon began to eclipse the empty feeling of dread that had chilled his stomach.

"Are you out there, James honey?"

He smiled, and the best bit of his recent Irish good fortune appeared from the house behind him. Carrie smiled sleepily.

"Why did you get out of bed, honey?" she asked, as she tucked her arm around his and snuggled into him. James grimaced.

"Ah, I woke up, and decided I needed a coffee and some sunlight."

He turned to the American girl and kissed her fondly on the forehead.

"Why don't you go back to bed, babe? You'll catch your death out here, wearing nothing but that T-shirt."

Carrie kissed the side of James' neck.

"Was it another bad dream?" she asked sympathetically. Malone nodded.

"Pizarro again. It's like...no matter how far I run he's still there, staring at me from the flames of that burning cottage with his black eyes. Accusing me. Threatening me."

James Malone sighed deeply. "It's like there's someone else too. Someone I can't see, but I know that he's there. It feels like he's looking for something...looking for me."

"Come on back to bed, honey," Carrie whispered soothingly. "I'll make the nasty men go away, and I've got a nice surprise for you later."

"What sort of surprise?" James asked, raising a quizzical eyebrow.

Carrie giggled, then ran her tongue over her lips and mouthed, "It won't be a surprise if I tell you, will it?" Then, with another giggle, she disappeared back into the house.

James shrugged, took a long last look at the view over the valley, put down his coffee cup and followed her.

It had been some six weeks since Carrie had picked James Malone up from the roadside in her T-Bird, and they had hardly been apart since. Carrie had begged him stay with her and tell her more about the strange people and creatures he had encountered in Ireland. One night had turned into two, and by the second night he was sharing her bed as well as her house.

Life in Box Canyon suited James just fine. He took a gardening job at the house of a recently retired actress in nearby Chatsworth and contemplated settling down at last. Carrie continued to sell real estate and began to wonder, just in passing, if their children would inherit her blue eyes and blonde hair, or his dark Celtic features.

"So, what's the surprise, honey?" James asked quietly some twenty minutes after returning to bed. Carrie raised her eyebrows mischievously.

"Well..." she teased, looking away from the puzzled face of the Irishman. "I've spoken to a friend of mine who thinks that, as an ex-priest, you would make an ideal bereavement counsellor down in the valley."

James scowled, albeit good-naturedly.

"But I quite like being a gardener," he moaned sulkily, pouting like a naughty little boy.

"A counsellor paid at a rate of twenty bucks an hour," Carrie breathed, rolling her eyes in mock exasperation. James smiled and kissed her.

"So, when I do start counselling?" he laughed.

"Oh, when Dan goes home, I guess." Carrie looked incredibly pleased with herself.

The air left James' lungs in a long deep gasp, and his forehead creased in disbelief.

"Dan? Dan who?" He managed to whisper, incredulously.

Carrie stopped smiling when she saw the look of sheer panic in his eyes.

"Er, duh, like your brother, Dan. It's okay, honey. I told him you were okay, but that there were some guys out to get you, so he had to be real careful. He was just glad to hear that you're alive and well after all this time."

James face had gone quite white. He pulled himself up and sat on the edge of the bed, breathing in short gasps, as though struggling for air.

Carrie knelt behind him on the bed.

"I'm sorry, Jimmy baby, I thought you'd be pleased."

James tried to smile reassuringly. "I am, Carrie, I am. I guess I'm just, just...terrified. Confused."

Carrie put her arms around his neck and kissed the back of his head.

"How did you find him?" James whispered.

"It was just so simple, honey," Carrie gushed. "You'd told me about Dan, and finding an Irish lawyer in London called Dan Malone was no harder than ringing a friend of mine over there and getting her to look him up in a phone book. Man, he nearly died when I told him I was ringing about his long-lost brother."

James coughed and laughed at the same time. "What did he think had happened to me?"

Carrie shook her head. "He had no idea. He said your mom and dad had just, like, freaked when you disappeared without a word. They all thought you were dead at first, but when no body was found..."

James nodded, tears rolling down his face.

"When's he coming?" he asked, quietly.

Carrie kissed the top of his head, jumped out of bed, and slipped on a robe.

"Saturday," she chirped gaily, as she skipped towards the bathroom. "You are pleased, aren't you, James?" she asked hesitantly, glancing back at him.

"Sure," James smiled wanly. "Sure I'm pleased."

"I knew you would be," she beamed, as she closed the bathroom door.

James fell back on the bed, a torrent of negative images flooding his mind.

What if the Order followed Dan? What if they'd persuaded Dan that he was involved in some scandal? What if they'd pinned the deaths of Father Pizarro and Father Burke on him? What if they'd set him up for the murder of Mickey Finn?

37

His stomach felt empty, and his heart was beating so quickly he thought it would either stop or simply burst right out of his chest. Over five years of running and hiding and pretending to be someone else; and now as soon as he'd gone and let his guard down and let someone get under his skin, all his pigeons were coming home to roost.

He could hear Carrie singing in the shower.

Should I just run? he wondered. Now's my chance...I could throw on my T-shirt and jeans and be down in the valley before she even comes out of the bathroom. When will it end? Will I have to keep on running forever? I love her. I love Dan. I love me ma and da.

Conflicting emotions fought a pitched battle in his head. In one way, he was delighted that she had taken the initiative and contacted his family. At least now they all knew he was alive and would hear his side of the story at last, irrespective of what they had been told - if they had been told anything at all. No, they must have been told something. Three priests had died in quick succession, and another had disappeared. The Gardai must certainly have suspicions about him, having never found a body after his apparent suicide.

At least he would know now where he stood. Maybe he'd been running for no reason; maybe the Order had been satisfied with the elimination of Mickey Finn and hadn't given a thought to the fate of the insignificant village priest, Father Malone of Finaan. That last thought seemed mildly reassuring. If the Order were satisfied that the 'Fairy Folk' had been finally removed from the face of the earth, then maybe he had nothing to fear. The Order might even have been disbanded. He had been on the run for over five years and probably, by now, no one was even chasing him.

James Malone began to laugh; quietly at first, then louder. The fear seemed to evaporate. He could see sunlight streaming through a gap in the drapes. He could feel the warmth of the Southern Californian morning. He could hear the birds singing in the lemon tree outside the bedroom window.

"Are you okay?" he heard Carrie shout from the bathroom.

"Yeah, never better," he shouted. "Never better."

He shook his head, still laughing, and padded barefoot into the kitchen to pour himself another coffee.

"Oh Danny Boy..." he began to sing as he ambled back towards the bed, before spitting a mouthful of coffee back into his mug.

"Saturday?" he exclaimed. "But today's Saturday!"

Carrie's head peered around the corner of the bathroom door.

"Uh huh," she nodded sarcastically. "Sure looks like you got them days of the week sorted out, Jimmy boy!"

Six

Bishop Donleavy chewed nervously on his bony fingers as he sat behind the enormous oak desk. The room was almost dark. Every pair of heavy velvet curtains had been tightly drawn, to prevent any daylight from seeping surreptitiously in and damaging the invaluable artworks which covered the walls. A few candles flickered in a huge crystal glass chandelier, suspended from the ceiling in the centre of the room.

Donleavy stared at the ornate carving which decorated the edge of the desk. It seemed to dance in the flickering candlelight, as though shifting in a gentle breeze. Had the artisan who had laboured over such work worried about the sorts of things which now plagued Donleavy's imagination? Donleavy doubted it. Lesser mortals never worry about the more important matters, especially those whose minds are preoccupied with supplying a daily crust for their families. The bishop ran a finger over the smooth surface of a leaf carved in the wood.

"No, my friend," he whispered aloud. "All you had to worry about was whether this leaf would look good or not, and whether there would be bread and meat on your table." He laughed, but it turned onto a racking cough.

There was a knock at the door of Bishop Donleavy's office. The bishop composed himself, sat upright, and smoothed out his black robes.

"Enter!" he barked as best he could, his ancient voice capable of little more than a loud croak.

A nervous young priest shuffled into the room, approaching Donleavy's desk with his head down and his eyes fixed firmly on the floor.

"Bishop O'Leary is here, Your Grace," he whispered.

"Send him in then, Logan. Send him in," Donleavy croaked, making a loud swallowing noise in his throat, before repeating his instruction.

The young priest bowed and quickly scurried back out of the room. Donleavy clasped his hands together, and waited for the rotund Bishop O'Leary to appear through his office door.

He didn't have long to wait. Bishop Desmond O'Leary bumbled into his office almost as soon as Logan had left. His forehead gleamed in the candlelight. as beads of sweat ran down his face.

"I am so sorry I am late, Your Grace," he mumbled as he approached the senior Bishop's desk. "The Dublin traffic is a veritable nightmare these days." He took Donleavy's proffered hand, and kissed the ring.

"You may sit." Donleavy waved his hand, indicating an ornate chair next to the bishop. O'Leary took a white silk handkerchief from a pocket in his cassock, dabbed his forehead, and sat down.

Donleavy watched the podgy bishop scowl as he tried to focus in the gloomy twilight of the Bishop's office. His pink cheeks wobbled as he shook his head slightly, and his small beady eyes twinkled in the reflected candlelight.

"And how is Africa?" Donleavy asked, disinterestedly.

"Hot, Your Grace," O'Leary replied, vigorously wiping his forehead. "Very, very hot."

"Do you remember young Father James Malone?" Donleavy asked, his voice low and muffled. His Adam's apple bounced up and down as he tried to moisten his dry mouth.

"Malone?" O'Leary asked, unsure that he had heard correctly. The bishop inclined his head in a slow, affirmative, nod.

"Why, yes, of course, Your Grace. He was the young village priest from Finaan. He was the one who initially brought the demon Finn to our attention, was he not?"

The senior bishop pulled his hands up to his mouth, looking almost as though he was in prayer. He nodded slowly again.

O'Leary gabbled on.

"Yes, it was five years ago or so, was it not? We lost some good men that day: Father Callaghan, Father Burke, and the special Vatican Emissary, Father Pizarro; as well as young Father Malone, an almighty tragedy for the Order and for Mother Church. At least the creature Finn was destroyed in the process."

Donleavy fixed O'Leary with a steely glare.

"Was he?" he croaked. His hands dropped onto his desk, and he leaned forward. "Are you absolutely certain of that fact, Bishop? Would you swear on your life?"

Bishop O'Leary's mouth dropped open and his eyes widened, until it looked almost as though they might actually pop out.

"I, well, we...yes," he bumbled, wringing his hands together.

Bishop Donleavy slumped back in his chair. The sound of gurgling in his throat echoed in the eerie silence of the darkened room.

"That is what you reported at the time, Bishop," Donleavy whispered. "You assured us - quite categorically, if I remember correctly - that the Finn creature had been destroyed. Yet you failed to deliver the piece of stone that most of these demons seem to possess."

Even in the sombre office, Donleavy could see that O'Leary had gone quite white as the colour drained from his round chubby face. Donleavy leaned forward again, quite threateningly.

"It took months for the Finaan scandal to quieten down, Bishop O'Leary. One priest committing suicide in his own church, one killed in a road accident, and two missing, presumed dead. The Order had to use every last piece of its influence on the media to smooth things over. It cost us a great deal, I can assure you. It is still mentioned in the corridors of power in Armagh, and even in Rome."

The ancient bishop's throat rolled, the loose skin under his chin swung, and spittle gathered in the corners of his mouth. "There are those who have said that it was the greatest disaster in the Order's long and illustrious history."

Bishop O'Leary shuffled in his seat. His mouth had dried up and his more than ample stomach felt like it was trying to squeeze up through his throat.

Bishop Donleavy sighed deeply and sank back into his seat.

"Yet, at the time, I must confess, it all seemed worth it. It was seen as our final and greatest victory. The Sacred Order of Saint Gregory had taken fifteen hundred years to do it, but finally we had eliminated the very last of the heathen immortals. Fifteen hundred years and we had cleared Satan's spawn and the possibility of 'God's Assassin' off the face of the Earth. Or so it seemed. You know the Prophecy, of course?"

O'Leary nodded nervously, and began to recite a poem like a fourth former stumbling over a piece of English Lit homework:

A child no mortal man shall sire
By mother's blood Royal line acquire,
Shall suckle he no milk white breast,
Shall rise in exile, unwelcome guest,
Shall learn to change his form at will
His shape, his face, his ways to kill
Unseen, unheard, his telling blow,
His doom to lay The Messiah low,
Shall tears then flow and kings shall fall
And darkness take us, one and all.

Donleavy smiled and nodded his approval. A small hint of relief began to trickle into O'Leary's mind. Donleavy leaned forward again.

"A holy war lasting a millennium and a half, Bishop, and it ended in your very own diocese. Wine?"

Bishop O'Leary allowed himself a huge sigh of relief. The Sacred Order of Saint Gregory had been known to be quite ruthless to those who had failed it, or who had betrayed it in any way. Individuals were regarded as totally expendable, as long as the Order's Divine objectives were achieved.

Since he had received the summons to appear before the senior bishop, O'Leary had been terrified that he might have stepped out of line, or had somehow failed in his duties. Ever since he had been sent, in shame, to a remote part of Kenya, he had believed that he would eventually have to face the full wrath of the Order for his part in the 'Finaan debacle.'

As Donleavy stood slowly and poured two goblets of wine from a crystal carafe, O'Leary began to imagine that maybe his audience might not be so bad after all. Donleavy passed one of the goblets to the bishop.

"Have you any idea what happened after the supposed demise of the last of the Tuatha demons?" Donleavy almost spat the last two words.

"No, Your Grace," O'Leary mumbled, before taking a large sip of wine.

"Only a handful of people in the world know this, Bishop O'Leary. All of them in the Vatican, of course."

Donleavy sat down slowly, as though every bone in his body was racked with pain. He took a small sip of wine. O'Leary watched as Donleavy's Adam's apple bounced up and down, and then as the older man licked his lips and put down his goblet.

"As soon as it was known that Satan's spawn had been defeated and that 'God's Assassin' would never come to pass, the Second Coming took place."

The old bishop raised an eyebrow and arched his hands on the desk in front of him expectantly. O'Leary's mouth dropped open, much as Donleavy had anticipated it would.

"Yes, you did hear correctly, Bishop. Our Lord and Saviour walks among us once again!"

O'Leary's mouth opened and closed like that of a goldfish in a bowl.

"Our Lord returned because the Sacred Order of Saint Gregory assured him that it was safe to do so. He would be able to be born of the womb of a woman and grow as a child in safety, until he was ready to redeem the world and announce that the Day of Judgement was upon us."

Donleavy's voice had grown in volume as he spoke, and the spittle gathered at the sides of his mouth.

"So, Bishop O'Leary, how do you think it felt to have to tell Our Lord that the Order was, in fact, wrong? That we have not eliminated all of the demons, yet. That 'God's Assassin' - the child no mortal man shall sire - could still be lurking somewhere, even in a corridor near him, right now?"

The cold, empty feeling returned in the pit of O'Leary's belly. He took a large swig of wine, as Donleavy continued his rant.

"The stones that you failed to recover from Finn's cottage have been used to amplify the use of magic by somebody. It can only mean that Finn is, in fact, alive and well."

Donleavy was shaking with rage. O'Leary also found himself trembling, but his tremor was a manifestation of terror. Donleavy held up his hands.

"So...Our Lord is here. A helpless babe, while his most dangerous, immortal enemy still stalks the earth, intent on his demise - and with it, the end of all hope of eternal salvation and the everlasting Kingdom of Heaven."

There was a long silence as O'Leary pondered the old Bishop's words. The enormity of what he had heard made it difficult for him to think rationally.

"Malone called me, before he threw himself in the river," he mumbled eventually. "He was quite unhinged, but he clearly said that he had seen Finn perish, as well as Pizarro and Burke. He swore he had seen the demon die. He told me that was why he was going to leave the priesthood - that, and how evil he thought the Order was."

Donleavy did not move or respond for several long seconds. Then he leaned forward and smiled, a thin, mean, humourless smile that boasted of superior knowledge.

"And yet, my dear Bishop, magic is still being performed somewhere out there. The fragments of the magic stone are giving their power to someone; someone with the ability to draw on that power. Only a demon such as one of the cursed Tuatha De Danaan has such power. As Finn was deemed to be the very last of that race, we must presume that Malone was either mistaken...or lying."

O'Leary drained his cup. "What would you have me do, Your Grace?" he stammered.

Donleavy smiled again.

"You shall return from your extended 'holiday' in Africa, Bishop O' Leary. I have a nice little role for a loyal bishop here in Dublin, complete with a small, but comfortable office on this very corridor. Whilst here, you will do what you should have done five years ago. You will find Father James Malone; whatever it takes, and whatever resources you need. Find Malone, dead or alive. If he is alive, as I suspect, we shall find out whether Finn still lives or not. If Malone did cast himself into a river, then we have more of a problem. One thing is for certain; we must destroy whosoever it is, whoever is using the accursed stones. We must find God's assassin...or prepare for the Dominion of Hell for the rest of eternity."

Seven

"Wayne? Wayne? Are you alright?"

The sound of Paul Harland's voice snapped Wayne out of his reverie. The image he'd had in his mind - of crystal-clear water gently lapping a sun-kissed white sandy beach, with Stephanie Fleming lying on the sand, sunbathing in the briefest of bikinis -evaporated. Instead of the somnambulistic crash of the surf, the sound of The Buzzcocks' "Ever Fallen in Love" filled his ears again, along with the laughter and chatter of a Youth Club full of teenagers.

"What?" he uttered impatiently, attempting to avert his eyes from the distant figure of Stephanie Fleming at the opposite end of the old church hall. Strange, she was now wearing a tight roll neck sweater and jeans, instead of the tiny black bikini. Oh yeah...that had been in his daydream.

Paul looked perplexed. "Are you okay?" he repeated.

Wayne raised his eyebrows."Yeah, sorry," he grinned. "I was miles away."

Paul nodded knowingly. "Oh yeah...and everybody knows who with!" He gestured towards Stephanie. "Are you going to ask her out, then? Peter Fletcher tried last week, and she told him to beggar off."

Wayne looked concerned.

"I didn't know that," he stated flatly.

Peter Fletcher was one of the coolest members of what was, come September, to be the new lower sixth form at Wormysted's. He'd spent some years at a private school and had tons of confidence, as well as being from an extremely rich family. If she'd turned him down, what chance did Wayne stand?

 Paul ambled off towards the kitchen area, where the volunteers who ran the Youth Club had thoughtfully provided large jugs of orange squash.

"Yeah, but you know what Fletch is like," Paul laughed over his shoulder as Wayne, his hands shoved deep and disconsolately into his jeans pockets, shuffled after him. "She'd probably heard that he only wanted to get in her pants."

"No, really?" Wayne gasped, feigning shock and incredulity. Not that he'd thought of anything as sordid as that himself, of course.

"Anyway," Paul continued, "she's supposedly going out with that Martin Berenger. You know...that smart Alec guy in last year's Upper

Sixth, the captain of the rugger first fifteen. He's going to Oxford, I hear."

"Oh!" Wayne sighed despondently.

Paul passed him a cup of orange juice.

"And he's got a new Mini Cooper 1275 GT. Still, if I fancied her like you seem to, I'd have a go. What've you got to lose?" Paul raised an eyebrow at his friend, who looked incredibly sheepish all of a sudden.

"Yeah, but..." Wayne groaned.

"Or," Paul suggested mischievously, "I could whisper into Anne Ducket's ear and let her know that you've got the raving hots for Steph."

Wayne grimaced. "That sounds like the sort of thing you do when you're twelve," he groaned.

Paul shrugged. "Desperate times call for desperate measures, as they say. Come on - I'll hammer you at table tennis." Paul laughed. "Let's see if we can get your mind off the opposite sex for a while. Anyway, we get our 'O' level results tomorrow. Does that not concern you a little bit more than some girl?"

Wayne grinned.

"No! There's nothing I can do about my O Levels, but I can do something about Stephanie Fleming...and anyway, she's a lot more than just some girl. She's a dream! A dream, on long, lovely shapely legs. Legs that go right up to the best bum God ever sculpted." He sighed and shook his head. "And then, from her slender waist up, it gets even better..."

"Oh , for God's sake..." Paul pretended to put his fingers down his throat, and the pair strolled over to a vacant table and began to play table tennis.

Over the course of the evening, Wayne cast several furtive glances towards Stephanie. In fact, he lost two games of table tennis because Stephanie simply moving around the hall had distracted his attention.

"Poetry in motion," Wayne sighed under his breath.

"Hah!" Martin Taggart, another of Wayne's friends, exclaimed, as he hammered the ball past his, suddenly inept, opponent.

"Yes! Another victory for the coolest dude in Shepton!"

Wayne smiled, and accepted defeat with more than a hint of ambivalence. Martin glanced at Paul Harland, who jerked his head in the general direction of Stephanie Fleming, and Martin grinned and shook his head.

Wayne was staring at her again, like a moonstruck calf. She always seemed to be smiling. When she smiled, her blue eyes lit up and she showed her teeth. They were so white, so straight, so absolutely, unbelievably, film-star perfect...

"Wayne?"

This time it was Liam Riley's deep sonorous voice that brought Wayne back to earth.

"We're going to get some fish and chips from Eastwood's. Are you coming?"

Wayne looked around and noticed that Paul Harland, Martin, and his old mate from Gas Street Primary school, Richard Hebden (who had failed his eleven plus exam and gone to Shepton's Secondary Modern School) had put their jackets on, and were heading off in the general direction of the exit.

"Er, yeah, okay," he stammered as he looked at his watch. Nine-twenty-five; the end of yet another night at the Youth Club. His heart was beating violently against his ribcage and his stomach seemed to be filled with manic butterflies, which were all doing aerobatics.

"I won't be a moment."

Wayne turned in the direction he had last seen Stephanie Fleming. This was it! He was going in. It really was now or never.

Wayne walked over towards the object of his affection in the way he'd seen actors walk in the movies; a sort of arrogant rolling gait that suggested he'd just climbed off his horse. His manner oozed nonchalance, his gaze wandering anywhere but towards Stephanie Fleming.

"Hi!" he breathed, when he finally reached Stephanie.

Anne Ducket began to giggle, while Wayne couldn't help but notice that Stephanie was desperately trying to keep a straight face.

"Hi!" She whispered back, her smile a picture of barely controlled mockery.

Wayne's confidence began to evaporate faster than the air bursting out of a freshly holed balloon.

"Ahem," he coughed. "I, er, wondered if..."

Anne Ducket snorted loudly.

"Told you!" she exclaimed, as she burst into delirious laughter.

Stephanie did her best to keep a straight face, but had to turn away as her eyes began to water.

"I, er...well, I..." Wayne gabbled, his startled eyes flicking between the laughing Anne and the barely-controlled Stephanie.

"Ha!" Anne wailed, almost doubling up in mirth.

"Don't be rotten, Anne!" Stephanie giggled, gently chiding her friend. She looked sympathetically at Wayne.

"Oh, okay, look...she's been going on all night about how you've been staring at me, and she said it was really obvious that you fancied me and that you would probably ask me out before the end of the night."

"Ha ha!" Anne continued to roar with laughter. "No, I didn't," she gasped, after taking a deep breath to try and regain her composure. "I said he fancied you like mad, but wouldn't have the bottle to ask you out."

Stephanie shrugged.

"I bet her a quid, anyway, and you did - so well done, you've made me a pound. But look...I'm sorry. I've got a boyfriend and he's a bit older, you know. Although it is very sweet of you and..."

Wayne stepped back.

"Oh no, no, I wasn't, you know, going to ask you out...not as such. I just wondered if you, er, wanted to join us to get some chips?"

"Ha!" Anne Ducket exploded again. It looked to Wayne as though she was going to wet herself. In fact he hoped she would - that would serve her just right!

"Anne, stop it!" Stephanie hissed crossly, then she looked back at Wayne. "No thanks, but it really was nice of you to ask. It's a nice compliment."

Wayne grimaced what was meant to be a smile.

"Maybe...maybe some other time, then," he stammered, doing his best to hide his disappointment.

"Yeah, perhaps." Stephanie smiled sweetly. The mockery had left her eyes. She was now obviously embarrassed by her friend's behaviour and felt somewhat sorry for the curly-haired guy, whose name she wasn't sure of, but who had such kind eyes. There was something about his eyes that she couldn't quite explain, but he definitely had lovely eyes.

A deflated, defeated and utterly humiliated Wayne beat a hasty retreat across the club's wooden floor, to the mocking sound of The Buzzcocks' 'Ever Fallen in Love' again and the fading sound of Anne Ducket's amusement. He grabbed his jacket and ran to catch up with the other lads, who were in the process of disappearing through the Youth Club's front door, out onto Westmoreland Street.

Somehow, the fish and chips didn't seem to taste quite as good that night; and despite a display of macho bravado in front of his friends and of total normality in front of Doris, he had to admit to himself, as he got undressed for bed, that he was upset. Very upset indeed!

Oh well, at least he had his mother's letter to read. He collapsed into bed, turned on his bedside light, and pulled the envelope out from under his pillow.

Terri Thorne
2145 Coldwater Canyon Drive
Beverley Hills
Ca, 91241
USA.

My Dear son, Michael,

This is the hardest letter I've ever had to write, but I think it's for the best for both of us. As you know, Dean and I were married in Las Vegas in June, and I am now carrying his baby. Dean thinks it would ruin my career if the press found out that I already had children; they seem to think we're the perfect couple at the moment, and the baby announcement will only add to that.

My career is very precious to me, darling, as I'm sure you understand. I really couldn't stand it if it all ended before it has even really begun.

Dean also says they would ruin your life by putting you at the centre of a freak show. You know what the British tabloid press is like, and you have such a lovely family there. Your dad, Frank, is a very fine man and your mom has done so much for you. If the press did find out about us and published pictures, all over the papers, it would break your mom's heart, wouldn't it?

It therefore seems to be for the best that we don't contact each other for a while, maybe until you leave home and I stop acting. After all, I've only got five years or so left before Dean says I'm past it.
Maybe things will get easier.
I love you.

Your mom,
Terri.

No matter how many times Wayne read and re-read the letter, it still said the same thing: A simple, big fat goodbye. He just couldn't believe it. Being humiliated and rejected by a beautiful girl at the Youth Club was one thing, but being rejected by his real mother; now that was quite a different matter. She'd gone and got married - without even telling him at the time - and had then gone and got herself preggers!

Wayne just wanted the entire world to end there and then. He didn't even realise that tears were pouring down his cheeks, as he screwed the letter up into a tight little ball.

The television downstairs was on pretty loud, so Doris didn't hear the racking sobs that burst from Wayne's bedroom. She didn't hear him open his bedroom window and throw the ball of paper high into the August twilight sky. Nor would she have believed that the paper burst into flames just from the power and venom of Wayne's stare and plummeted three storeys to earth like a spent firework.

Wayne threw himself back onto his bed face down and howled into his pillow until he heard the television downstairs go quiet. Then he did his best to compose himself. The last thing he wanted was a major inquiry and Doris' cloying sympathy. He heard Doris huff and puff laboriously up the stairs. She opened his bedroom door slightly when she got to the top.

"Are you asleep, Wayne, love?" she whispered.

Wayne breathed deeply, pretending to be fast asleep.

"Goodnight love, sleep tight." Doris whispered, closing his door quietly.

Wayne opened his eyes, and sighed. Aillen had said there would be two more tests. It seemed that the two had happened on the same night. Wayne's heart wasn't just broken; it was smashed into a million tiny little pieces. How could things possibly get any worse?

Then Wayne remembered: the next day, he would find out his 'O' level results. If he had failed them all, or even only managed to get as many as six, then Doris would go insane at her humiliation in front of her sister, Margaret Houghton-Hughes, whose son Cedric had passed seven. There was still plenty of room for more humiliation, but nothing could be as bad as losing his real mum. Nothing!

Eight

A long thin line of brown smog hovered over the sprawl of the San Fernando Valley, as James Malone emerged from Carrie's house for what seemed like the fiftieth time. He glanced nervously at his watch, before biting his lip and sucking on his teeth. He strolled across the yard to peer down the Canyon road to see if there was any sign yet of the cab bearing his brother from Los Angeles International Airport. James sighed heavily as the road remained stubbornly deserted.

The afternoon was now hot and uncomfortably sticky. The sandy rocks that hung precariously from the Canyon walls shimmered in the haze of unrelenting heat. The grass and bushes were all dry; burnt, brown and skeletal. Yet the heat seemed to have brought the Canyon to life. The sound of crickets was almost deafening. A humming bird hovered momentarily by a heavily-laden lemon tree and then busily skimmed away, defying the very laws of gravity in its amazing aerial agility. A huge wasp buzzed past James' ear, and somewhere high above he heard the eerie cry of a buzzard split the somnambulant atmosphere, just before the roar of a jet heading for Van Nuys brusquely drowned out the sounds of nature.

"James, honey, would you please relax? You're even making me nervous," Carrie's soothing voice whispered as she carefully crept up behind him, bearing yet another steaming, unnecessarily hot, mug of coffee. "More caffeine is probably the last thing you need right now, but at least you can chew on the mug instead of your nails," she chided, sympathetically.

James quickly pulled his fingers from his mouth and gave his well-bitten fingernails a cursory, guilty glance.

"Do you know...I've never bitten my nails before." He grinned, sheepishly. Carrie put her arms around his neck and kissed him.

"I love you, James Malone, and I promise I won't let your big brother bite you!"

"Here, watch my coffee!" James laughed, as she pulled his head down to kiss him gently on the lips.

Both turned at the sudden scrunch of tyres on loose gravel. A yellow cab pulled into the wooded area near the house, and after a few moments a large figure climbed awkwardly out of a rear door.

Carrie took her arms from her boyfriend's neck. James Malone had gone very pale; indeed, his eyes reminded her of a rabbit caught transfixed in the beam of a car's headlights.

"It'll be okay. Trust me," she whispered.

James nodded gravely, turned to her, and gave her a fleeting glimpse of a smile. "Here goes nothing."

He grimaced, and set off to walk towards the figure struggling across the dry grass towards the house, dragging a small, but apparently heavy, suitcase.

"James? Jimmy? Is that really you?"

Daniel Malone's mouth dropped open as he stared at the long-haired figure strolling laconically towards him. He dropped his case and ran towards the brother that he had last seen six years earlier.

"Jaysus Christ, Jimmy! We all thought you were dead and buried, so we did."

Dan threw his arms around his little brother and hugged him so tightly that James almost struggled to breathe.

"Hi, Dan," he gasped, his eyes welling up with tears.

Daniel pulled back and stared into his brother's eyes, but continued to clutch his arms.

"Would you look at you?" he gushed, tears rolling down his cheeks. "Whatever happened to that starched white little priest fella? You look like a bloody rock star. Jaysus, you're all hair, tan and teeth!"

James grinned. "And you look like a very well-fed, successful, affluent Lawyer, our Dan."

He couldn't help but burst into loud sobs at the sight of the first friendly face from his old life. The first member of his family he'd seen in more than five long years. The brothers pulled each other together and hugged tightly, as though nothing would pull them apart again.

"Ahem!" Carrie coughed politely.

James gently pushed Dan back and wiped his eyes.

"I'm sorry, honey. Dan, may I introduce you to Carrie - my girlfriend, I guess." He laughed through his sobs.

Daniel looked towards Carrie, and then sceptically at his younger sibling.

"So now I see you went into hiding, you jammy bugger; trying to keep such a beauty all to yourself all these years, were you?"

He held out his hand towards the beautiful, well-tanned blonde. "Hi, Carrie...it's a great pleasure to be able to put such a very fine face to such a melodious voice, at last! I'm the older, richer, far more intelligent and much better-looking brother, as I'm sure you can now see."

Carrie laughed as she took the proffered hand and leaned over to receive a kiss on the cheek. "Well Dan, I can certainly tell that James wasn't the only one who kissed the Blarney Stone. It must be a family trait."

Dan slapped his brothers back. "I just can't believe that this hairy, hippy-looking fella is that stiff little priest that I remember."

James coughed and shook his head. "James Malone the priest is dead, Dan. He died a long time ago."

The gravitas in his voice dampened the atmosphere momentarily. Dan nodded with a slight grimace, and then walked to the fence at the back of the yard.

"Would you be looking at that!" he exclaimed in wonder. "You must be able to see fifty miles from up here."

James nodded. "Right across the entire San Fernando Valley. You can see Old Baldy Peak on a clear day."

Dan turned and admired the canyon walls behind the house.

"And that looks like cowboy country."

James grinned. "They say they used to film Roy Rogers movies up here."

"I love all that stuff." Dan enthused. "Hi ho, Silver, away!" he shouted. James shook his head.

"Still a dingbat, Dan. That was the Lone Ranger. Roy Rogers had Trigger."

Dan laughed. "Oh well...they both wore white hats."

James patted his older brother's shoulder. "If you're not careful, I'll send you up there. We get coyotes and rattlers in those rocks."

Dan looked surprised, and more than a little worried.

"Real live rattlesnakes?"

James nodded gravely.

"And tarantulas!"

Dan's mouth dropped open.

"James Malone, you are so mean. Let's go inside, where it's a bit cooler," Carrie suggested, taking Dan's arm, while casting James an amused, scalding, glance."I'm sure you two have a million things to talk about and catch up on and I've just made a fresh pot of coffee - or maybe you'd prefer an ice-cold beer?"

"Sounds marvellous!" Dan agreed, grabbing his bag and following Carrie through the Spanish-styled doorway, glancing around nervously just to make sure that no rattlesnakes or tarantulas had climbed onto his case. "An ice-cold beer would be marvellous, so it would."

"Mmmm," Carrie grinned, "you two really are brothers, aren't you?"

The initial conversation across Carrie's kitchen table concerned Dan's journey and a series of amusing anecdotes about his fellow passengers on the British Airways flight from London.

Dan turned out to be a natural raconteur and a talented mimic. Carrie could imagine him holding a courtroom spellbound as he presented the case for the prosecution, or defence. It was his first visit to California, so he enthused about the weather and the landscape. He joked about how he would have to avoid Hollywood, as he didn't want to be mistaken for Al Pacino and get mobbed. As for the coast - well, that would have to be avoided, as he didn't want to embarrass the body-builders on Muscle Beach! Daniel Malone was every bit as gregarious, as James was introverted and serious.

Carrie noticed that the brothers laughed easily and were obviously very close. From his body language, it was patently apparent that James adored his older brother. He seemed to bask in his sibling's glow, almost like a member of an audience, a fan in awe of a performer. Yet Carrie also noticed that both seemed to be avoiding something. The conversation was all very superficial and light; Dan holding court, James laughing.

It was Dan who eventually broached the subject that James seemed to be too embarrassed to even mention.

"You haven't asked about Ma and Da, yet, Jimmy," Dan stated, after a long sip of his beer and a momentary silence. "I thought it was him you said you could see when you mentioned old baldy peak - but I knew you couldn't see all the way to Dublin, even from up here."

James looked down into his lap.

"How could I ask, Dan?" he mumbled. "You might be having bad news for me."

Carrie noticed James' accent had suddenly broadened, his Irish brogue becoming much more noticeable.

Dan nodded knowingly, and put his glass down on a mat.

"They took it bad when you disappeared, you know. You were their pride and joy so you were, a real live priest in the family. They thought you'd save us all!"

James looked up at his brother, his forehead creased in a confused frown.

"No, Dan, you were the one they were proud of. You were the one who was for going off to Trinity College and becoming a rich fat lawyer in London. I just sort of fell into the priesthood, because theology was my best subject at school. It was certainly the easiest. Ma and Da were never that big on religion."

Dan laughed. "Less of the 'fat', young fella. You're not too big for me still to be giving your ears a proper boxing!"

James smiled. Dan raised his eyebrows and shook his head.

"What might surprise you, Jimmy boy, is that they were very proud of what you did, because they were always terrified that you might just run off and become a hippy or something. Now is that ironic, or what? Just because they aren't big on forcing religion down our throats doesn't mean they aren't devout. They are Irish, remember."

James looked chastised. "Oh!" he gasped, quietly. Dan nodded.

"They just didn't - couldn't - understand why you left without explaining what had happened. I mean the, Gardai were like flies buzzing around dog-do for months. They said one priest had been killed, one had gone and hung himself, and another one had seemingly disappeared into thin air. They said that you'd probably gone and done yourself in. It was your phone call to the bishop that had made suicide the most likely option. What conclusion was anyone going to come to? They even found your collar and cassock, abandoned on a river bank."

James bowed his head low and grimaced as though in pain. Dan shrugged, and sighed heavily.

"It nearly killed Da; he had a heart attack about four years ago and then another last year, Jimmy. He was in St. Brendan's for weeks. I've never seen a happier man, when I told him that Carrie had been in touch and that you were alive and well and slumming it in California. He was desperate to come with me when I said I was coming to see you, but he's not well enough to travel. We don't know how long he's got."

James looked up, his expression a mixture of guilt and sorrow.

"And Ma?"

Dan smiled reassuringly. "She's fine! Tough as old boots - you know Ma. She never really lost hope that you'd turn up like a bad penny, one day."

There was a long, awkward, silence; and then Dan asked the inevitable question.

"So, go on...what really did happen back there in Finaan, James?"

His voice had taken on the authority of his profession, and his use of James' given name only emphasised the seriousness of his interrogation. "What made an ordinary young village priest, of a fine and honourable background, take off overnight, leaving absolutely everything that he'd ever valued in ruins?"

Carrie coughed and stood up, picking up the empty glasses as she left the table.

"I guess I better leave you boys to it." She winked at James, and walked over to the sink.

James took a deep breath and looked up at his brother sitting on the other side of the round table.

"Am I in the dock now then, is it, Dan?"

Daniel Malone shook his head sympathetically.

"Jaysus, Jimmy. I just need to know what really happened. Why my little brother would do something so, so totally and utterly out of character."

James shook his head.

"Dan, I can tell you this. You couldn't even begin to believe the truth of it, if I told you."

Dan screwed up his mouth, pursed his lips, and shrugged.

"James, I have heard stories that would make your hair turn white overnight. I have defended people in court who have told tales taller than the Empire State Building in New York City. I am sure I can believe my own kid brother. So go on...try me. We've got plenty of time."

James grimaced again.

"Carrie, honey?" he shouted. "Would you be getting that bottle of whiskey out of the cupboard? I think the pair of us might be needing a proper drink before long..."

Nine

The tall, thin, priest climbed out of the Ford Cortina minicab, and proffered a fifty-punt note towards the driver. He walked away from the car without waiting for change and put up an umbrella to ward off the gentle drizzle as the taxi sped away, and looked around at his surroundings with an evident air of disdain. Even in summer, when the trees are leafy and green and there are flowers in the hedges, parts of Limerick can look pretty miserable and grey, especially in the rain. Not even the huge edifice of King John's castle by the nearby River Shannon impressed the priest

He turned towards a pair of huge black wrought-iron gates set in a tall, grey, stone wall. An intercom system was mounted on the wall by the gate, so the priest pressed the appropriate button and waited. After a short delay, an electronically distorted female voice answered.

"Saint Brigid's Convent. Can I be helping you?"

The priest sniffed

"I am Father de Feren. I believe your Mother Superior is expecting me." His heavily accented voice had an air of superiority that almost verged upon caricature.

The gate swung open automatically, and the priest swept imperiously up the oak-lined gravel driveway. A nun in a black habit and white wimple met him at the door.

"Ah, Father de Feren!" she twittered, taking his umbrella and ushering him inside. "We have been looking forward to your visit. Terrible weather for the time of year, isn't it? I hope the journey wasn't too trying for you at all?"

The priest handed the nun his cloak."The journey was as tiresome as expected. No more, no less."

He removed his wire-framed round spectacles and officiously wiped them with a black cloth. He looked disparagingly around at the sparsely furnished room with its bare, dark, oak-timbered walls.

"Mother Maria will see you shortly, Father. Please, would you be taking a seat?" the nun suggested, her voice little more than a nervous whisper. De Feren sniffed contemptuously.

"I prefer to stand. I find that it galvanises people into action. Whereas my sitting would give the impression that I have time to spare. Your Mother Superior will be here very shortly, I hope. I am not used to being kept waiting."

The nun scowled, nodded, and scuttled hurriedly off with the damp cloak and umbrella.

Father Pierre de Feren was, on the contrary, quite accustomed to waiting. He was a very patient man. Hunters had to be patient. Patience wasn't just a virtue for Father de Feren; it was a necessity. He had been patient during the time he had held a minor administrative role within the Order. A role he had taken when the Order had taken him into their service after he had ceased being a village priest, back in Belgium.

The Sacred Order of Saint Gregory had been very good to Father Pierre de Feren, and he was more than grateful. They had not only managed to cover up the true depth and nature of the scandal that had forced his sudden flight from his parish, but had kept him in the employment of the church.

Father de Feren, a natural apparatchik, had begun to study the history of the supernatural - Demonology, myths, and ancient legends - while carrying out his menial tasks. The Order soon came to regard him as something of an expert and often questioned him on key issues. The more he found out, the more powerful de Feren became, especially when he began to study herb lore and potions, in order to better expedite the Order's numerous assassinations. It was only a matter of time before the Order asked him to use his newfound knowledge and skills to help eliminate not only the entities that the Order regarded as evil, but anyone who stood in their way.

Soon Father de Feren had worked his way up to being the heir apparent of Father Francisco Pizarro, the Order's chief assassin. When Pizarro had disappeared 'on active service,' some five years earlier de Feren had been initially mortified, but had then swiftly and gladly stepped into his shoes.

De Feren had been extremely sceptical about the Order's declaration of final victory over their 'unnatural' enemies. He had felt it premature to celebrate and had engrossed himself in the study of the demonic fairy folk of Ireland, from whose stock it was rumoured 'God's Assassin' would arise. By sheer happenstance, whilst beavering away in an obscure library in the Vatican he had chanced upon a major discovery. He had found out that something had been locked away in a remote convent, at the back end of Ireland. A discovery that could prove crucial, should any more of the Tuatha demons be found to exist.

An unmarked door opened near where the priest stood, his arms behind his back and his foot tapping impatiently. A middle-aged nun stood in the doorway and appraised him from over half-moon spectacles perched precariously on the end of her nose.

"Father de Feren?" she enquired, pleasantly.

"Indeed!" the priest replied, with a slight bow. The nun nodded nervously.

"I am Mother Maria. This institution," - she waved her hands around to show that she meant the entire building - "is my responsibility, for my sins. Do come in."

The priest followed her into her spartan office and closed the door behind him.

"Would you like tea, Father?" the Mother Superior asked, as she beckoned the priest to sit at her large and imposing desk.

"No, thank you," the priest replied haughtily. "I would rather that we got straight down to business, if you do not mind. Bishop Donleavy himself has sent me from Dublin to verify forthwith the existence of 'Item 741', in this, this, institution, as you call it."

The Mother Superior leaned back in her chair, her mouth open. She rustled some papers on her desk and carefully avoided the priest's penetrating stare.

"Well, I..." she blustered, "well, I must say, that, I...I..."

"Does the item exist or not, Madame?" De Feren asked, his voice flat and devoid of all emotion. The Mother Superior cleared her throat, and composed herself.

Mother Maria had been the Mother Superior at St. Brigid's Convent for over twenty years, and had never been intimidated before. She had received Bishops, Archbishops, Canons, Cardinals and politicians of every hue and persuasion and had treated them all as equals, tempered with varying degrees of respect; relevant to their position, of course. Never before had she been so taken aback by the rudeness, arrogance and pomposity of a single individual.

"Well, I am going to have tea, Father!" she asserted, with a withering glower. "Are you quite sure you do not want any?"

She picked up a small brass bell from the corner of her desk and gave it a small shake. Father de Feren raised his eyebrows.

"Madame, I have travelled from Dublin. I am to report back immediately to Bishop Donleavy, as soon as I have verified the existence of the said item: 741." His voice was still flat, but bore an edge of impatience.

The Mother Superior leaned forward, her stance now aggressive.

"And what, may I ask, does his Grace, Bishop Donleavy know about this 'Item 741', as you call it?"

She had had enough of this tall, weedy twerp. She matched his stare and the two glared into each other's eyes. De Feren did not flinch.

"As the head of the Sacred Order of Saint Gregory in Ireland, he knows all there is to know about the subject. I personally have fully briefed him, having researched the history of the said object, 741. We now seek full verification of its existence and of its capabilities. We need to know if it is...how do you say? Usable."

"Usable!" squealed the now almost incandescent Mother Superior. "USABLE?" she repeated, louder and more incredulously. "You talk about..."

There was a knock on the door.

"Come in!" the Mother Superior almost-squealed again. A young novice in a blue wimple entered the room and glanced nervously at Mother Maria.

"You rang, Mother?"

Mother Maria took a deep breath and nodded.

"Yes, Sister Concepta. Tea, please. Tea for one...unless our distinguished visitor from the continent has changed his mind?"

The priest shook his head slowly. The nun curtsied.

"Yes, Reverend Mother," she simpered, and left as quickly as possible, aware of the incredibly tense atmosphere that pervaded the room. As soon as the door slammed shut, Mother Maria stood up behind her desk.

"Usable? 'Item 741'? Father de Feren! You talk about her as though she was an object."

The priest's thin lips curved into a sneering smile.

"So it does exist," he murmured.

"It? It?"

The Mother Superior turned her back on the priest and looked out of her window at the convent courtyard and the heavy-leafed trees outside, dripping in the steady Limerick drizzle. The convent grounds looked like a small, beautifully tended park, surrounded by the high, grey stone walls; an oasis of green in the bleak, concrete, Limerick cityscape.

"I will have you know, Father de Feren, that 'Item 741', as you call her, is as fine a servant of Our Lord as you will find anywhere in all of Ireland; or anywhere else, for that matter. She dedicated her life to the service of the church a long, long time ago and is now one of my charges here - not just some object at the Order's beck and call. I am sure Bishop Donleavy's superiors in Armagh might have something to say about this."

The priest rose, his chair making a horrible scratching sound as it scraped back along the wooden floor.

"Armagh is irrelevant. This is Order business, Madame. As you have 'Item 741' here, I presume you know all about the Sacred Order of Saint Gregory and its holy mission and importance. We could discuss this all day and waste even more precious time. I will see it now, please." His demeanour had reverted to the same bland emotionless state, as when he had entered the room.

Mother Maria turned brusquely towards him.

"Oh no you will not!" she growled. "I really do not think that you have been listening, Father. Sister Bernadette will be seen over my dead body."

The priest cocked his head on to one side and raised a quizzical eyebrow.

"You would deny the Order access to its own property?" he asked, threateningly. "I thought that in your position, Reverend Mother, as custodian of the item, you were aware of its history? It is also my belief that you are fully aware of the...how can I put it delicately...reputation of the Sacred Order of St. Gregory."

The last sentence was delivered slowly and with evident relish; the woman slumped back into her chair, her eyes and expression betraying her impending defeat.

"She is no-one's property. She is a nun, a good nun - and she answers to no-one but me."

The tall priest leaned forward menacingly, and laid his hands on the Mother Superior's desk.

"On the contrary, Madame, 'Item 741' answers to the Order. It has no soul. It is a demon. It was given to this convent for safe-keeping. Not for its own safety, but the safety of all the good Catholic, Christian souls in Ireland. It is the property of the Order, and I act not only upon the authority of Bishop Donleavy in Dublin, but also of Cardinal D'Abruzzo in Rome itself. I think you will find my superiors outrank your Archbishop and Cardinal in the peasant-village cesspit that is Armagh."

He reached into a pocket inside his jacket and placed a small white envelope on the Mother Superior's desk. The envelope was adorned with an ornate wax seal, which Mother Maria slowly and reluctantly cut with a paper knife.

There was a knock at the door and the novice entered, bearing a tray of tea which she placed apprehensively on the corner of the Mother Superior's desk, before glancing at both the priest and Mother Maria and then scurrying away as fast as her legs would carry her. Neither seemed to notice her.

Mother Maria exhaled a long deep sigh and stuffed the letter she had just glanced at, back into the envelope. She looked up at the hard-faced priest, contempt etched on her own face.

"You had better come with me, then," she whispered dejectedly.

The Mother Superior's face had gone quite white and she had seemed to age almost ten years in an instant. She even struggled to walk as she left her office, shuffling with an arthritic gait. The tall gaunt priest walked out by her side, bearing an expression that could only be described as smug. It took several minutes for Mother Maria and Father de Feren to walk down the convent's numerous austere dark corridors and through several locked doors, before they reached a plain brown, wooden door.

Mother Maria fumbled with several hanging keys on the sort of chain that prison warders wear, before she found the one that seemed to fit the lock. The door opened outwards, only to reveal another door directly behind it - this one bearing a grille, which the Mother Superior opened.

"Sister Bernadette," she whispered. "I have a visitor for you."

She fumbled for another key while Father de Feren stood behind her, his impatience quite perceptible. Eventually, she placed a key in the cell door and it swung open with a slow, groaning creak. Mother Maria swept into the small bare room, followed by the priest.

"Sister Bernadette, this is Father de Feren. He has come all the way from Dublin to see you," she announced, in a barely audible whisper. A nun was kneeling by a small desk in the plain white-walled cell, her back facing the priest and the Mother Superior. She stood up silently and turned, slowly.

Father de Feren stepped past Mother Maria and duly appraised the young nun standing demurely before him. She wore the full black habit of the Order of Saint Benedictine, but her beauty shone out from under her wimple, even in the gloom of the single-candle-lit cell. The priest gasped as he appraised her perfectly unlined face, with its white porcelain skin and her large, clear, emerald green eyes, with which she shyly glanced up at him as she curtsied.

"How long have you been here, er, Sister Bernadette?" he asked, his voice strained, as his mouth dried up.

The young nun glanced up at her Mother Superior, who gave her a slight nod of reassurance.

"Sister Bernadette has been here - and I know this is hard to believe - but she has been here one hundred and thirty five years, Father," the Mother Superior whispered, as the nun glanced up at him again from underneath her thick black eyelashes.

The priest couldn't help but close his eyes for a second. He had been celibate for many years and had never found any woman a temptation before; yet the legends that such creatures could tempt and seduce even the most devoted, most modest, most chaste servant of the Lord, seemed to be true. He took a deep breath; his hauteur seemed to have momentarily evaporated.

"You have been here a long time, Sister. I hear from the Reverend Mother that you have become the model bride of Christ."

The nun shifted awkwardly and glanced up at the priest again, a slight smile on her lips.

"She tries her best, Father," the Mother Superior whispered.

"Are you ready to do the bidding of Our Lord, Sister Bernadette?" Father de Feren asked the blushing girl.

The nun glanced again at the Mother Superior, who, barely perceptibly, nodded again. Sister Bernadette nodded her agreement, keeping her eyes averted.

The priest nodded and gave a satisfied grunt. "Bon - most excellent!"

He turned to Mother Maria, his composure regained.

"She is a credit to you, Reverend Mother. I would like that tea now, if you please, and I would like Sister Bernadette to be ready to accompany me when I leave." He turned, and marched off down the corridor.

The Mother Superior turned to Sister Bernadette.

"Please be ready to leave as soon as you can, my child. The Lord will watch over you. Have no fear."

She turned quickly, and followed Father de Feren.

"How do you expect her to cope outside?" she hissed, as soon as she caught up with him at the first set of locked doors. "She has not been outside these walls for a hundred and thirty five years!"

The priest smiled. "We shall look after it well; after all, we have great need of its powers."

"And when you have finished with her...what then?" Mother Maria ushered the priest through the door into an adjacent corridor. The priest turned to her, and smiled benignly.

"I cannot predict the future, Reverend Mother. By the way, can it speak at all? It did not utter a single sound in there."

Mother Maria looked annoyed.

"She is not a number, an item, or an animal, Father. She is a Bride of Christ, and a very good one at that. She speaks little. I have only heard her voice in prayer and song, but it would charm the thingummy birds from the trees, I can tell you. You were about to tell me what would become of her?"

Father de Feren shrugged.

"Reverend Mother, I am a very busy man - be pleased that it has been blessed enough to be chosen to carry out some very important work. Hopefully it will be returned to you in an unharmed condition. Now, I must use your telephone...if you don't have any objection, of course?"

Mother Maria opened another locked door. Father de Feren shook his head.

"Who would have believed it? You and your predecessors have done well, Reverend Mother. Your part in what may transpire may be small, but it may be very significant. I assure you that your good work here has not been in vain."

Mother Maria ignored the priest's rambling. She was concerned about Sister Bernadette. She knew that Bernadette would react badly to being exposed to the modern world, and - worse than that - she had heard rumours of just what Bernadette was capable of. The thought of Bernadette's reputed abilities made Mother Maria suddenly stop in her tracks, the sudden realisation chilling her to the bone.

"You want to use her as a weapon, don't you?" she demanded of the priest. "The Order want to use her as a weapon against someone?"

The priest smiled his smug, sarcastic smile, and it was all Maria could do to stop herself slapping him across the face.

"The Order's need is the Order's business" he replied impassively. "However, I can assure you that the Order's ultimate victory is close at hand, Mother Maria. Prepare ye for the way of the Lord, Madame, for he will soon walk amongst us again and the cry of the banshee will herald the demise of his one true enemy on this Earth."

Ten

The last thing Wayne Higginbotham wanted to do on that Friday morning was to get up out of his nice cosy bed. He was so tired; it seemed to him that he had spent most of the night tossing and turning. Twice he had been forced to get up and put the new-fangled duvet back on the bed. Doris had recently bought it to replace his comfortable old bobbly orange nylon sheets, and the ancient blankets that he'd had since childhood.

His mind had seemed to see-saw between crushing sadness and overpowering rage. How dare that woman do this to him? How dare she abandon him, find him and then go and abandon him again?

He castigated his real mother in his mind and imagined what he would say to her when he saw her, if he ever saw her again. Then his attitude would soften towards her. No, it wasn't her fault. It hadn't been her fault when she'd had him adopted at birth and it wasn't her fault that she was casting him aside now. It was that slimy toad Dean Vitalia who'd done this. He was now her agent, her manager, her husband, and the father of her new baby. He didn't want anyone else in the picture. All of this was his fault!

But how could she be so weak? How could she put him first? By the time his alarm clock rattled, announcing it was time to get up, Wayne was totally and utterly confused about his reaction to the letter.

He opened his curtains, and sighed. The sky was blue and clear and the sun was already burning brightly in the morning sky. Another beautiful summer's day in the beautiful Yorkshire Dales. So bloody what!

His mother had abandoned him! Stephanie Fleming didn't fancy him! He'd probably gone and failed all his 'O' levels!

"I need to talk to someone," he whispered to himself in his dressing-table mirror as he attempted to brush his wiry hair straight - but who?

His dad, Frank? No; although Frank had been there when Wayne had been reunited with Terri, he wasn't the sort of man that one talked to - not about emotions, anyway. Frank Higginbotham was a Yorkshire man, and Yorkshire men didn't do emotions. Yorkshire men just grinned and bore it!

Wayne loved his dad, but had found him more and more remote as he had got older. He hated to admit it, but Frank embarrassed him. The fact that Frank had saved Wayne's life, in the battle against the evil immortal Pizarro, didn't mean that they could discuss deep emotional issues. The only thing he'd ever said to Wayne about his relationship with his real mother was that he would help him to keep it a secret because it was Wayne's right to have that relationship; but he warned Wayne that it would kill Doris if she ever found out.

So - who else could he talk to? His mother, Doris? Er, no...not really. Aunty Margaret? Doris would know within seconds, so no again. Aillen Mac Fionnbharr; his real father and Prince of the Tuatha De Danaan?

Aillen was responsible for the situation, in some ways. After all, he was the one who had gone and got Terri pregnant, and Wayne didn't feel like listening to any ancient homespun wisdom and philosophy, no matter how sensible it might be. So no - Aillen would not be called for on this occasion.

Wayne wanted to talk to someone who would be as shocked and disgusted by his mother's behaviour as he was. The sad thing, Wayne realised, was that there was absolutely no one he could talk to.

Adoption was a freaky enough subject at the best of times, especially when you had been re-united with your real family. All those secrets and lies, all that watching every word; all the acting and pretence. For Wayne Higginbotham, it was even worse. Half his real family weren't even human. How weird was that?

He was more alone than he had ever been, even when he'd been that lonely little kid at Gas Street Primary School. He was the last member of a magical race, doomed forever to be alone. He was also the secret son of a Hollywood star, doomed forever to remain incognito.

In the meantime, he had the little matter of his 'O' level results, and had to be at Wormysted's Grammar School by nine-thirty that very morning. He looked at his digital watch: nine am. He had better hurry, but first...what was wrong with his nose?

He peered into the mirror and scowled in concentration at his reflection. What he saw made him even more miserable.

"Great!" he muttered out loud. A humungous red spot was growing right on the end of his nose, of all places! That was all he needed. If Stephanie Fleming hadn't fancied him last night, then she would hardly fancy him the next time she saw him, complete with an enormous festering carbuncle smack on the end of his nose, would she?

"You're not going out without breakfast, are you?" Doris had called from the kitchen as he had hurtled noisily down the narrow staircase that divided the Higginbotham's little house.

"Yeah - I'll be all right!" Wayne had bellowed, as he grabbed his favourite leather jacket and slipped it on over his white T-shirt and jeans. "I won't be long."

"Good luck, love!" Doris had shouted after his disappearing back as he slipped out of the front door.

The walk to school seemed to take forever. To get there Wayne had to walk the length of Cavendish Street and then cross a main road, before taking a short cut along a narrow lane between a pair of huge, dark and imposing Victorian Mill buildings. A quick climb of a cobble-stoned hill, over the canal bridge and then along two more residential streets, and he was there. Wormysted's Grammar School, Shepton, founded in 1492, the year Columbus 'sailed the ocean blue.'

The walk up the long, tree-lined drive seemed like the march towards his own funeral. The results were to be found by the school office, just inside the main doors, which Wayne entered with an increasing sense of foreboding.

A huge crowd of boys was gathered by the notice board, upon which sheets of computer paper had been pinned. Some were turning away with solemn faces, failure etched all over their features. Some had tears streaming down their faces. Others turned away, punching the air, jubilantly shouting "Yes!" or "I don't believe it!"

Oaths of varying degrees of obscenity permeated the air, as Wayne pushed his way through the cacophony of noise to the front. He studied the alphabetical list, noting the grades and total scores of his friends as he scoured the names.

Booth, Andrew: Biology: A, Chemistry: A, and so on, leading to total of eight straight A's.

Fletcher, Peter: Biology: A, English Language: B, English Literature: C, also resulting in eight passes.

Harland, Paul: Biology: B, English Language: A, English Literature: A, a total of eight. Was no one going to join him in the ranks of miserable failures?

Higginbotham, Wayne: Biology: B, English Language: B, English Literature: B History: A. The rest faded into insignificance as he stared at his total; eight passed at grade C, or above.

Suddenly, Wayne didn't mind the constant jostling. His breath came in short, sharp bursts, and he turned away, fists and jaws equally tightly clenched. He'd done it. He'd passed every single one! For a few brief seconds, Wayne Higginbotham forgot all about Terri Thorne and about Stephanie Fleming. For a few brief seconds, Wayne Higginbotham was actually happy again.

"Yes!" he hissed triumphantly.

He felt a friendly slap on the back as Paul Harland appeared and congratulated him. Paul had also achieved eight passes, but with superior grades to Wayne. Wayne didn't mind. He was pleased for his friend, and the pair laughed like idiots as months and months of academic pressure was finally released in a flood of irrational hilarity and undisguised glee.

It was only later as he slowly ambled home, still feeling quite pleased with himself, that a huge dark cloud began to roll over the bright morning sun. As if in response to the worsening weather, Wayne began to sink back into his dark and dismal mood, and by the time he got home, he was feeling thoroughly miserable again.

The last thing he wanted to do was to talk to Doris. Yet there she was, waiting for him expectantly in the living room, as he entered the Higginbotham's small terraced house on Cavendish Street.

"So, come on - how did you do, then?" Doris asked eagerly, even before Wayne had closed the door behind him.

"All right," Wayne shrugged dismissively. Doris scowled.

"What's all right?" she demanded, her voice taking on a more aggressive tone. "How many did you get?"

Wayne began to enjoy making her wait.

"A few," he mumbled, wiping his hand over his mouth so that Doris had difficulty hearing.

She looked woebegone.

"What do you call a few?" she almost wailed.

"Eight," Wayne sighed. "I passed them all." He carelessly tossed his prized leather jacket on to a nearby chair.

"You passed all eight?" Doris asked incredulously.

"Yes!" Wayne muttered impatiently. "I passed all eight, and only one was a C grade." C was the minimum good pass mark and anything below that was deemed to be something of a failure, even though D and E were technically accepted as passes. Cedric Houghton-Hughes, Wayne's cousin, had got four C's in his seven passes, and no A grades at all. Doris positively beamed.

"Did you get any A's?"

Wayne slumped into an armchair and rubbed his forehead, as though he was suffering from a huge, debilitating headache.

"Just one - History," he mumbled.

Doris put her arm around his neck and kissed him on the top of the head.

"Nay, don't be upset, love," she cooed. "It's nowt to be ashamed of, only getting one A. Clever dick Cedric didn't get any."

Wayne shrank into his seat. Doris rarely displayed sentiment, and Wayne found it embarrassing on the rare occasions that she did show affection.

Doris had mistaken Wayne's miserable mood for disappointment with his 'O' level results. Yet she could not have been happier. The very meaning of her life was her competition with her younger sister Margaret, and Wayne had given her a victory that would really annoy her posh sibling.

"I'm just going to pop to the phone box to let our Margaret know how you got on," Doris gloated triumphantly. "This'll show her that the Higginbotham's are just as clever as them. Them as thinks they're sommat. Aye, this'll show 'em!" She bustled hurriedly out of the front door, a grin as wide as the River Arne splitting her face.

"Won't be long, love," she called, as the door swung shut with a bang. Wayne muttered something incomprehensible.

He was beginning to really despise Doris. Frank embarrassed him, which was bad enough, but Doris made him seethe inside. Had she adopted him just because her sister was going to have a baby? The only thing that seemed to mean anything to her at all was competing with her own sister. How pathetic was that?

She was always on his back, always comparing him to the perfect baby, Trevor, who the Higginbothams had tried to adopt before he had come along. Once the secret of his adoption had been inadvertently exposed, five years earlier, it seemed like Doris felt free to make him as uncomfortable as possible. She had threatened many times to send him "back to where he had come from," especially if Wayne had been in any way cheeky or disrespectful in her opinion.

"Please do!" Wayne had often muttered under his breath.

The prospect of being able to run off to California, to his real mother, because his adopted parents had kicked him out, had been Wayne's dream scenario ever since he had first been reunited with Terri. So much for that, now!

"Cow!" Wayne almost spat.

He rolled his eyes at the prospect of a weekend alone with Doris. Frank was due to work two twelve-hour shifts at the 'thingummy' factory on Saturday and Sunday, so Wayne would hardly see him. Wayne wondered why the world needed so many 'thingummys.'

"Oh well," he sighed. "I'm sure I'll be kept busy...going to the Co-op, vacuuming, or whatever!"

Wayne sighed disconsolately again, and picked up a newspaper. Frank always bought one of the tabloids on his way to work. The tabloid papers were little more than gossip sheets in Wayne's eyes. This one was the previous day's edition. It was full of the usual rubbish: photos of semi-naked girls (which wasn't too bad) and an article about a pop star that young girls seemed to find irresistible. Wayne shook his head in disgust, and turned the page.

"Girls must be really dumb if that's the kind of guy they fall for," he muttered scathingly. Yet by the time he had turned to the football on the back page, the germ of an idea was beginning to take root in his mind. He turned back to the photograph accompanying the article about the pop star.

"So girls like guys who look like him, do they?" he muttered, stroking his chin thoughtfully. "Hmm...I wonder!"

When Doris got back from the phone box, Wayne was nowhere to be seen.

"Wayne?" Doris shouted. There was no response. "Wayne!" she bellowed again.

"I'm up here!" The muffled response came from upstairs, from behind Wayne's closed bedroom door. "Won't be a minute."

Doris went through into the kitchen, and started to prepare lunch. When Wayne did bound downstairs a few minutes later, he seemed considerably happier.

"Our Margaret wasn't happy," Doris grinned. "She said she were, like, but I know her. She was as jealous as hell."

"Really?" Wayne smiled sweetly. "I've just got to pop out, Mum."

"Why? Where are you going?" Doris demanded, disappointed that Wayne did not seem to want to join in an extended gloating session.

"Er...I thought I might go and buy a bar of chocolate to celebrate," Wayne stated unconvincingly. Doris nodded.

"Aye, all right. Don't be too long, love - your dinner'll be ready by about twelve o'clock."

Wayne nodded, slipped on his jacket, and breezed out through the front door.

Doris Higginbotham breathed a contented sigh. For once, Wayne hadn't let her down. He had beaten Cedric, and for once she had something to crow about. She began to sing; it was a spontaneous outburst of joy, and it didn't matter one jot to her that she was massacring one of her favourite pop songs from the fifties. As far as Doris Higginbotham was concerned on that August morning, life didn't get much better than this.

Eleven

James Malone couldn't quite believe it. After five years in exile here he was, strolling up to the passport control desk in Dublin Airport, his brother Dan beside him.

"I can't stay long," he repeated, for perhaps the hundredth time since they had boarded the Aer Lingus flight in Los Angeles the previous afternoon. "I just had to see Da, you know...in case anything happens at all. I couldn't leave it any longer; not if he's as ill as you say."

Dan smiled reassuringly. "For goodness sake; will you stop panicking, Jimmy. It'll be doing Da a power of good to be seeing you. You'll be fine, you'll see."

The queue shuffled forward slowly, a long line of scruffy jet-lagged tourists and businessmen, who wanted nothing more than to escape the airport and find somewhere to sleep for a while and freshen up. A priest behind James coughed, causing him to nearly jump out of his skin. With each step forward he expected to feel the clamp of a hand on his shoulder; yet nothing happened.

James nervously flashed his passport at the immigration officer, who gave it little more than a cursory glance.

"See - what did I tell you?" Dan whispered, as they approached the baggage carousel. "This is the free world; it took me a good twenty minutes to get into the States. The fella wanted to know why I was visiting, how long I was staying, and so on. I even had to fill in a form saying that I had never been a member of the Communist party, or a bloody Nazi, for God's sake!"

James laughed, but his demeanour was still one of extreme anxiety. His head swivelled from side to side as though he was expecting someone to jump out on him at any moment. The passage through Customs was the longest sixty second walk in James Malone's life, and it was only when he was actually walking out into the main terminal building that he allowed himself a long sigh of relief. It was then that he heard the scream.

"JAMES!"

James looked up to see his mother rushing towards him, arms outstretched. He barely had the time to drop his case before he was engulfed in an enormous hug that nearly crushed his ribcage.

"Oh my God - James, my boy, my baby! I was for thinking I'd never be seeing you again," his mother bawled, before peering up at him through teary eyes, just to make sure it really was him. "Look at you, all tanned and handsome and with such nice, white teeth," she gushed through floods of tears, "but it's such a shame to be seeing you without your nice white collar, and you so thin and all. Oh, and you'll be needing a haircut, by the way." She pinched his cheek to demonstrate just how skinny he'd become.

"Hi, Ma," James gasped, struggling to breathe due to the ferocity of his mother's embrace. "It's good to see you too. You haven't aged a day at all - in fact, if anything it's looking younger you are."

Mrs Mary Malone pushed her son back playfully.

"Ah get away with you and your blarney," she laughed before grabbing him again. "I can't believe you're home, James, after all this time. Why oh why did you go and disappear like that? Not a single word in all these years."

"Ah Ma, I had my reasons, good reasons. Trust me."

"Were you involved in all those poor priests dying?" she implored, looking into his eyes. James smiled sadly.

"I was there, Ma...but I swear to you that I had nothing to do with poor old Father Callaghan, or the Canon Burke's demise."

Mrs Malone hugged her son again, seemingly satisfied with his assurances.

"Come on, you two," Dan called, as he strode away across the terminal building. "We've got to see a man in a hospital bed."

"See!" he muttered later, as the rental car sped away from the airport. "I told you it would all be okay."

James shook his head, and began to laugh.

"Jaysus, who would ever have thought I'd be so relieved to be driving through Dublin in the pouring rain? Will you look at this weather? You forget what real rain is in California. For God's sake - it's meant to be a summer afternoon, and it's not even proper daylight!"

Dan laughed. "Ah, you've been away too long, Jimmy boy. You're beginning to sound like a real Yank, with all your moaning."

"You never used to complain about the rain," Mrs Malone grumbled from the back seat. "Anyway, all that sunshine isn't good for you, James. It gives you wrinkles and cancer, so they say."

James Malone laughed, and watched the rain-washed grey terraced streets pass by. It seemed like a hundred years since he had last been in his native town.

It didn't take the brothers and their mother long to get to the hospital, and their father was more than overjoyed to see his youngest son after so long. He asked all the usual questions, and James did a good job in keeping the conversation on the subject of Carrie and his new life in California. He was desperate to avoid the dramatic events of five years earlier and his subsequent disappearance and ensuing silence. The elder Malone, Tomas, was not so easily diverted, however.

"So... come on, James," he asked softly, after James had just delivered a particularly long eulogy about the pleasures of Box Canyon life. "What happened? Why did you leave the way you did, giving up on the priesthood, your family and all? Leaving us all to think you were dead, so you did. What happened to those other priests over in Finaan? Come on, James. I need to know the truth before I die."

James looked at Dan, and took a deep breath. Tomas Malone was in a private room at the hospital and so prying ears were not a problem.

"If I was to tell you what happened, Da, you would have me locked up. Not because I did anything wrong, because believe me, I didn't... but because of what I saw."

James' father rose up in his bed a little. He reached out and took his younger son's hand.

"Tell me, son, whatever it was that happened. Tell me, so that when Our Lord calls me, I can be dying in peace."

"You're not going to die, Da," Dan stated sarcastically. "You'll probably be back in the pub on Sunday, knocking back pints o'porter!"

James' father's gaze did not move from his younger son's eyes. "Tell me!" he implored.

So James did. He told his father the whole story; from his initial meeting with the strange old man 'Mickey Finn' out in the wild Partry mountains beyond Tourmakeady, to the eventual battle outside 'Mickey's' remote cottage. He described the confrontation in which 'Mickey,' a Spanish priest called Father Pizarro, and Father Burke had perished; the latter in a car crash in flight from the scene.

The elder Malone was spellbound, frequently exclaiming "Jaysus!" when James related anecdotes about the Order, or the Tuatha De Danaan.

"So the fairy folk really do exist!" he gasped, at the end of James' story. "And you left because you were afraid of the murdering priests in this Order of Saint whatshisname?"

James' mother seemed less impressed, however.

"James, have you been taking them drugs while you've been over there in California?" she asked, her face a mixture of incredulity and concern. "I've heard they get up to a lot of that sort of stuff over in America. I mean, I have heard some tall tales...but secret societies within Mother Church? Leprechauns and the like, firing bolts of fire right out of the palms of their hands? I've never been hearing the like of it in all me life. You'll be telling me next that you went and got the crock of gold."

James shook his head and smiled. "I know what you're saying, Ma. It's been just as difficult for me to believe it all, I can tell you."

Dan stood in the background with his arms folded, one eyebrow raised sceptically. Tomas Malone groaned.

"You leave him alone, Mary. If our Jimmy says that that is what happened, then that is what happened."

Mary Malone folded her arms.

"James Malone - look me in the eye, and swear to me on my life that this is all true." James grinned and nodded.

"Every last word, Ma! I even swear it on Johnny Giles' life. The greatest Leeds United and Ireland player that ever there was. By the way, Dan - how are they doing?"

Dan relaxed from his earlier stance, grinned, and shook his head.

"Not good, Jimmy, not so good!"

Mary Malone let out a long exasperated snort.

"Don't you go changing the subject now, James Malone! Okay...so if all this is correct, why did you not tell us five years ago? We'd have believed you every bit as much then as we do now."

James sighed. "I don't think you realise how evil the Order is, Ma. They would stop at nothing to wipe out the Tuatha De Danaan, and anyone and everyone in league with them."

Dan Malone coughed. Tomas shuffled uncomfortably to try and get higher up on his pillow.

"Will you let the boy be, Mary Malone? He's home now and he's told us why he went away. If I believe him, so can you. For five long years we've been thinking he was dead, and all we had was hope. Now we've got him back, let's enjoy it!"

Mary shook her head.

"It is good that he's back - I would have given my life for that - but I cannot be believing in fairies and all that stuff. I'll hold my peace, though. Our James will be telling us the real truth of it all when he's good and ready, I'm sure."

James raised his eyebrows and cast a glance at Dan, who was pretending to stare out of the window. He turned and subtly shook his head, indicating that his younger sibling should not try and prolong the argument. A knock at the door of the private room terminated the discussion anyway, as a doctor and a clipboard-bearing nurse entered.

"And how are you today, Tomas?" the doctor asked jovially. "Looks like you've got quite a family turnout here."

"It's a trial run for me wake, so it is," Tomas Malone moaned, and then coughed. The nurse busied herself pulling back his bed sheets and sticking a thermometer in his mouth.

"How is he, doctor?" James asked. The doctor turned from his examination of the clipboard, which the nurse had handed him, looking somewhat perplexed:

"And you are?" he demanded.

"His - his younger son, James," James stammered.

"Ah yes, of course." The doctor turned back to the clipboard. "Well, he's as well as can be expected." He looked around the room, and raised his voice. "He really could do with some rest, though."

Mary, Dan and James all nodded and said their individual goodbyes to Tomas before filing out of the room. Just before leaving, however, James turned back to the doctor.

"Will he be okay, doc?" The doctor glowered at him.

"We are doing all we can. You are the priest, Father - have some faith!" The doctor turned brusquely back towards his patient, and James nodded ruefully.

"A priest...yeah, right!"

He turned and followed his mother and brother down the long blue-floored, white-walled corridor that stank of antiseptic, towards the lift, which opened just as they got to it.

Two men in raincoats stepped out, carefully appraising the brothers as they stepped into the lift. The men turned and stepped back in just as the doors closed. The larger of the two - a sandy-haired, well-built middle-aged man - cleared his throat.

"Would I be correct in assuming that you are Father James Malone, sir? Recently arrived in from America?"

James looked at Dan and then his mother, and grimaced.

"I am no longer a priest, but yes; I am James Malone."

The man appeared pleased with himself, and puffed out his chest.

"James Malone, I am Detective Inspector Neeson. I am afraid it is my duty to place you under arrest. I have to warn you now that anything you say may be taken down and used in evidence against you, and I am going to have to ask you to accompany me to the station. We have some questions to ask you about some suspicious events that occurred in the West of Ireland a few years ago, and the subsequent disappearance of some ten thousand pounds of Church funds."

Twelve

Bishop O'Leary' eyes were nearly popping out of his head as he stared at the young nun standing in front of him.

"Goodness!" was all he could manage to say, as Father de Feren introduced him to Sister Bernadette. The incredibly young-looking nun gazed around, marvelling at the opulent office of the bishop, just as she had been astounded by the sights of the modern world that had assailed her every view in the journey across Ireland, from Limerick to Dublin. The world had certainly changed in the one hundred and thirty five years she had spent in the convent.

"And you say, th-that...sh-she is a bone fide banshee?" the bishop stammered incredulously. "She looks no more than a fresh young novice! I...I had heard that such things as banshees existed when I was in Knock...but I never for one moment imagined that I would ever actually see one in the flesh, as it were."

The young woman stopped gaping at the room, and regarded him impassively. Father de Feren sipped from the glass of wine that the bishop had given him.

"The old tales tell of the banshees being monstrous hag-like spirits, whose mournful keening was a harbinger of death. As you can see, Your Grace, Sister Bernadette is certainly no hag."

De Feren strolled impassively around the extremely attractive woman, who glanced at him uneasily, her vivid green eyes mainly downcast.

"Sister Bernadette's real skill is not her wailing, however. Sister Bernadette's most valuable skill, according to my research, is being able to sniff out other immortal beings. Isn't that right, Sister?"

The nun nodded, only slightly perceptibly. Father de Feren smiled.

"This Finn, as you call him, or whoever it is who performs magic in his place, will soon be ours, Your Grace."

Bishop O'Leary managed a small, nervous, smirk.

"And you are certain that we can trust this Sister Bernadette?" he asked.

Father de Feren opened his mouth to speak, but was interrupted by a soft, melodious female voice.

"It is rather impolite, Your Grace, to be speaking about someone as though they themselves were not present before you at all."

The sound of the voice made both men shiver. It was like the sound of the sweetest harp, or that of the water of a mountain stream gently trickling over rocks. The mouths of both churchmen dropped open.

Father de Feren was the more surprised of the two. He had talked almost ceaselessly to the nun whilst they had been driven across the middle of Ireland, and had not heard her utter a single word.

"So...you can speak?" he gasped.

Sister Bernadette shrugged, and the edges of her lips curled in the slightest of smiles.

"When I wish so to do, Father," she whispered.

Father de Feren frowned and glanced at his superior, whose mouth flapped open and closed, like a fish out of water gasping for air. Sister Bernadette stepped forward, and both churchmen unconsciously stepped back at the same time.

"It has been long since I uttered words in this, your tongue. You need not fear me." Her voice almost sang. "I am as one with Our Lord."

Father de Feren was the first to recover some measure of composure.

"It is true, what I have read, is it not? That you can find others; other immortal inhabitants of the fairy world?"

Sister Bernadette nodded.

"As long as they are close, Father. If they have travelled far, or crossed the great waters, then there is little that I can do. Pray, tell me, Father...what it is that you have you read about me and my kind?"

Father de Feren took a deep breath.

"I read that you are a banshee. I read that you renounced your evil ways when you came into the church in the year of our Lord 1844. I read that a local priest had found you starving with a family of mortals during the great potato blight. The mortals all died, but you, although too weak to survive in any natural way, lived on. The priest suspected that magic was at work and you confessed to him your immortality and your wish to be accepted by Our Lord. I read that you proved your worth and integrity by identifying a number of other immortals to the Order, and that in gratitude and at the behest of the priest who found you, the Order allowed you eternal sanctuary in the convent where I found you." Sister Bernadette smiled sadly, and Father de Feren continued.

"In my studies on behalf of the Order, I have read that because fairies have access to the netherworld, they can trace other immortals, if they have a mind to do so. It is as if they can sniff them out. I read that banshees are related, in some way, to those who call themselves the Tuatha De Danaan."

77

Father de Feren was stopped in mid-sentence by a sarcastic bark of laughter. Sister Bernadette suddenly looked furious. Bishop O'Leary took another step back, and almost fell over his desk.

"Related, you say, Father? Related, is it? We are of the Tuatha De Danaan!"

She sighed deeply, and calmed herself. "I should say I was of the Tuatha. Shall I tell you my tale, Your Grace? Father de Feren?"

The men looked at one another, then eagerly nodded their assent.

"Once I was but a simple maiden, a woman of the fair people, the Tuatha De Danaan. Aoibheall was my name, and I was regarded as being as fair as any maid of my clan, or any other clan for that matter, in the whole of Erin's Isle. I was betrothed to a Prince, but I did not love him, for he was arrogant and aggressive. I did not believe that he would have made a good king of the Tuatha. It was my doom to fall in love with one of our enemies; a mortal man, a Celtic chieftain, who bore the name Culhainnein."

Sister Bernadette laughed softly and sadly.

"Culhainnein was all I cared about. He was as strong as an ox and as tall as any warrior of the Tuatha De Danaan. He had eyes as brown as an autumnal chestnut, and in the art of love he was as gentle and tender as a forest deer, yet he was wild and terrible to behold on the field of battle. He loved me, and I loved him."

She snorted dismissively.

"They said that I had betrayed my people by being with him. I did not care for such talk. I hoped that they would eventually come to recognise our love, and that by such love the Tuatha and men might stop fighting, and live in peace. Yet, deep in our hearts we both knew that our happiness could last only as long as the life of a spark, a spark that leaps crackling from the fire and swiftly fades into darkness on the cold of the hearth. Our love was no more than the naïve dreams of children. Yet, we did not care what they said, nor what they would do, for love addles the minds even of the wise. Love intoxicates the heart more than the waters of life paralyse the mind."

The nun snorted derisively, and her mouth twisted in an ironic smile.

"Of course, the fighting did not stop. The Tuatha Prince, who had been my betrothed, was wounded in battle by Culhainnein himself. Many of his warriors and two of his brethren were killed. I cared not, for my love was returned to me unharmed, but bitter are the tears of fools.

Fionnbharr, the High King of the Tuatha De Danaan and the father of he who had been my betrothed, swore vengeance. There has never been a greater warrior on this earth than Fionnbharr, mortal or immortal, for he was a direct descendent of Nuada. So, it came to pass, that my Culhainnein was ambushed by my own people, even as he was on his way to our wedding. Someone had betrayed me. He confessed his love for me before Fionnbharr himself; then he was mercilessly cut to pieces, and his sweet body cast as meat to the dogs.

Instead of my love arriving in the woodland glade to be married to me, it was Fionnbharr and his warriors who rode in. I was exiled and banished from the halls of the Tuatha De Danaan forever, along with my mother and her mother, who had been in attendance at the ceremony. My father and my brother challenged Fionnbharr, in defence of my honour, and were executed on the spot for their treachery.

The misery of the widows was such that we wept like mortal women. We wept like no one has wept before or since, and in our misery we tried to find solace and sanctuary amongst the tribe of the mortal man I had loved. They would not accept us and cast us out as fairy women: the bann sidhe, they called us. They blamed me for bewitching their Prince and hero, Culhainnein, and for bringing him to untimely death. That is why the legend arose that the cry of the bann sidhe - or, as you call me, the banshee, the fairy woman - was a harbinger of death, and some mortals have assumed to this day that our cry can kill."

"Your cry can kill, can it not?" Father de Feren interrupted the girl. Sister Bernadette, the Banshee Aoibheall, shook her head.

"I could drive you to insanity with no more than a scream, but no. Even if my voice could kill, I would not do it, for my fidelity to Our Lord forbids it."

Father de Feren went quite red in the face.

"How dare you declare what you would and would not do? We, The Sacred Order of St. Gregory, saved you from certain death and have given you safe sanctuary for over a hundred and thirty years. Would you not do our bidding if we so asked?"

"Your Order wanted to burn me alive, Father. It was the good Father Lydon who saved me," Sister Bernadette snapped back, before bowing her head. "Anyway, what sort of Christian would be asking a sidhe to kill for him?"

Bishop O'Leary held up his hand.

"No matter; it is no longer of consequence." His fat face broke into a wide leering grin. "Now, my child, I have heard that you have been the model Christian since your conversion, all those years ago."

"Thank you, Your Grace," Sister Bernadette whispered. "I apologise for losing my temper."

The bishop stepped forward and gently lifted her chin, licking his lips as he did so.

"Such beauty. Such eyes. I have never seen eyes so green. I can quite understand how all those primitives were so spellbound by your beauty. Bishop Donleavy will be delighted to meet you. Do tell me how you came to join us in the mother Church, Sister Bernadette, before Father de Feren and I take you to see one of the most important men in the whole of Christendom?" Father de Feren smiled faintly, and nodded.

The bishop turned from the nun and poured a goblet of wine, which he offered to her. She shook her head.

"No thank you, Your Grace. A glass of water would suffice and be most welcome."

She took the glass of water that Bishop O'Leary handed to her gratefully, and drank deeply. It had been very many years since Aoibheall had talked so much. It had been very many years since she had talked at all. She wiped her mouth, took a deep breath, and continued.

"You asked how I came into the Church. It was as the good Father said - during the great famine. My mother, my grandmother and I had hidden in the caves and the mountains for many years. We saw the Celts finally take the whole of Ireland, and I am ashamed to say that we lived on our reputations as wicked fairies to survive over the long years. Hatred drove us. We hated our own kind for casting us out and killing our men. We denounced them to the church at every available opportunity and laughed when we watched them burn. Yet we came to detest mortal men for their lack of sympathy, their greed, their whining and weakness. We did all we could to terrify them.

My mother and grandmother were both killed, in due course, by mortals in fear of their own lives. Once they were gone, I began to use my looks to seduce mortal men, and I survived by living the short lives of mortal women. I would move on before suspicion was aroused by my immortality.

I was living as a mortal wife, with a widower, in the County of Mayo in 1844. I was looking after him and his nine children when their crops failed, and they all slowly began to starve to death. I wanted to die too, but immortality is a curse beyond all reckoning, and though I wanted to take a knife to my breast, I found that I could not do so. I am ashamed to say that I had not the courage.

I begged for forgiveness from the Tuatha De Danaan, yet heard nothing, but even as I prayed to the figure of Jesus Christ on his cross that my man had hung on his wall, Father Lydon found me. The rest you know. Once I took the Lord into my heart and he forgave me all of my sins, I stopped hating."

The bishop took a large slurp of wine and wiped his hand across his blubbery lips, looking the figure of the nun up and down, and sighed.

"Ah, the miracle of forgiveness, 'tis a wonderful thing. Did Father de Feren tell you why we wanted you here?"

Sister Bernadette nodded her head. "He said that there is now but one other of the Tuatha De Danaan left on the face of the Earth. This immortal has dedicated himself to the service of Satan. Father de Feren told me that only he has prevented Our Lord from returning to Earth, because of an ancient prophecy that states that no son of man can kill Our Lord in his second coming."

"Exactly!" The bishop exclaimed, with a clap of his pudgy hands. "And do you know of this immortal?" he asked. Sister Bernadette shook her head.

"Well, could you help us to find him?" The bishop had stepped nearer to her, and was breathing heavily. "We thought that we had killed him some years ago, but we now know that he, or someone like him, is still using his magical stones, so we must have failed. If you truly love Our Lord, Jesus Christ, please help us find him!"

Sister Bernadette took a step back. The Bishop's breath was hot, and stank of sour wine.

"There is a way, Your Grace. We immortals are not blessed to enter the Kingdom of Heaven upon death, but exist in a netherworld that is neither of earth, nor of hell, but is in-between. It is our gift to be able to talk to those in the in-between world. I will help you, as long as you promise that I can return to the convent to live in peace when I have helped you to find this servant of Satan. I, myself, will not be responsible for any death, however."

The bishop shrugged impatiently.

"Yes, yes, of course! You have my word." He glanced at Father de Feren, who nodded his head encouragingly. Sister Bernadette closed her eyes and began to rock backwards and forwards on the spot, murmuring quietly.

Bishop O'Leary was convinced that he saw a greyish mist begin to envelope her. He crossed himself and stepped back towards his desk. He thought he saw two other women's faces appear in the mist. They were vague, but they were definitely there. He felt cold, yet he began to sweat profusely. A voice could be heard praying, and the bishop suddenly realised that the voice was his own. Then, as quickly as it had appeared, the mist evaporated and Sister Bernadette opened her stunning green eyes. They were filled with tears.

"The once mighty and immortal race of the Tuatha De Danaan is no more. Save me," she whispered. "The very last warrior passed from the mortal realm some score of seasons ago."

Her voice was flat and sounded tired, instead of being sweet and melodious as before.

"What? Impossible!" the bishop shouted. Sister Bernadette didn't seem to have heard him.

"I, Sister Bernadette, once known as the Banshee Aoibheall, the exile, the fallen, am the very last of the mighty Tuatha De Danaan. I have outlived them all. All of them. I am alone."

The bishop mopped his brow with a white silk handkerchief.

"So if there are no more of these damned immortals, then who is performing the magic?" De Feren raged, as he paced the room.

Sister Bernadette closed her eyes.

"The pure Tuatha may be gone, save me, Your Grace. Yet...it seems that there may be a half-breed child."

"A half-breed? Who? Where?" the bishop blustered, sounding something like an excited owl. His eyes were almost popping out of his purple face, and his jowls wobbled like jelly.

Sister Bernadette closed her eyes; the mist descended, and enveloped her again.

"The son of Aillen, son of Fionnbharr. One who is half Tuatha De Danaan and half of mortal blood, a descendent of a line of men that has..."

The bishop interrupted her.

"Yes, yes, yes, very nice, very interesting - but where is he?" he barked. "Where is this half-caste demon?"

Sister Bernadette wiped a tear from her eye. "That I cannot tell you, Your Grace. He is too far away."

"What!" the bishop shouted. "De Feren said that you would be able to find such demons!"

Sister Bernadette shook her head. "Not if they are no longer on this island, Your Grace."

The bishop banged his desk with his fist, cursed and turned towards De Feren.

"Well, my Belgian friend, so much for your pet banshee! Take her and make her comfortable somewhere. I am sure we will be able to find some suitable use at some point for our tame demon, even if she cannot lead us to this half-bred abomination." He heard Aoibheall gasp, as he turned his back on her and the Belgian Priest who had wrested her from her sanctuary.

De Feren winced at the abrupt dismissal and the lack of gratitude that the bishop had displayed. Sister Bernadette had told them a great deal more than they had previously known. He bowed in the Bishop's direction, and motioned for Aoibheall to follow him.

"Your Grace!" he whispered quietly, as he nodded a curt bow.

The pair left O'Leary's office just as the bell of the telephone shattered the awkward silence. The bishop grabbed the receiver impatiently.

"Yes?" he bellowed. Then his round face broke into a wide smile, and he punched the air in triumph.

"Really? You are quite certain. Praise the Lord! I will be there as soon as possible! It is a church matter, Inspector, unless you have proof that he committed murder."

Bishop O'Leary carefully replaced the receiver, and grinned.

"Indeed, Our Lord does move in mysterious ways."

Thirteen

The last days of the long summer holidays seemed to drag on for an eternity for Wayne Higginbotham. A seemingly endless procession of monotonous, featureless days, which Doris tried to fill with irritating little tasks that only served to drive Wayne almost to distraction. His humiliation at the Youth Club had resulted in him avoiding the place for the remainder of the vacation, and as that was his only real chance of meeting any of his friends, he remained cut off from just about everybody. The Higginbothams didn't even possess a phone, so it wasn't even as if he could ring his mates.

Wayne's isolation made him brood more and more about his mother. How could she abandon him when they'd only just got back together? Was it her new husband? Or was it her? Was he not good enough for her?

The only thing that kept Wayne going was the little experiment that he had started to carry out in his bedroom, the morning after his humiliating knock back from the beautiful Stephanie. Wayne had been staring into the mirror, wondering exactly which bit of him it was that Stephanie hated the most.

Was it his hair? His thick brown, wiry curls, which he brushed flat in a desperate attempt to look reasonably cool, but which bounced back into a series of tight waves? Was it his ears? His large, sticky-out, pointed ears which he tried to keep covered most of the time under his brushed flat hair, which bulged out over them, giving him the appearance of wearing ear muffs? Was it his freckles? Not as numerous now as they had been, but still more than enough to be noticeable. Was it his spots? Wayne wasn't massively spotty but when they did appear they always managed to materialise in the worst possible places, like right on the end of his nose, or slap bang in the middle of his forehead. It sometimes felt like he had a large neon light flashing in some prominent part of his face, like the signs in stores that flashed up the latest offers

"Hey, look at me, I'm spotty!"

"Hey, look at me, I'm freckly!"

"Look at me, I'm ugly!"

"Look at me, I'm uncool!"

Was he not tall enough? Was he just too skinny? Was he just too young?

Most people have to live with whatever shortcomings they are born with, or make the best of them. Wayne Higginbotham wasn't like other people, though.

Wayne could do something about it; or at least, he presumed he could. His real father had been a shape shifter and could change effortlessly from his natural Elven appearance to look like the grizzled old Irish peasant Mickey Finn, or the jolly, rotund farmer Dan Joyce. He could even do animals, and had told Wayne that he had first set eyes on him whilst in the guise of a black and white Border Collie.

So, morning after morning, Wayne experimented with his shape-shifting powers. At first he had really struggled and what he had managed to change bounced straight back to normal as soon as he stopped concentrating, but he kept on practicing and practicing.

Firstly, his eye colour. They were usually a watery blue-green, but Wayne found that, by visualising a deep brown and then by just thinking of his eyes, he could make them turn into the exact colour he envisaged. His nose could be grown longer, or wider, or it could shrink smaller and neater. His eyebrows could grow and become bushy, or they could retract and look almost girlish.

Then, his hair. Just by concentrating on it he could make it look like Johnny Rotten's ginger spikes, or make it long and blonde, like that of the lead singer of the Sweet. He could make it curl, like Brian May's, the guitarist in the rock band Queen, or he could even make it disappear altogether.

His freckles and spots could be just wished away, and his pale Irish skin given a deep natural tan that made him look like a Californian beach bum. The only problems were his ears, which he could not change and which most hairstyles exposed, but he did find that he could hold them back and minimise their impact.

Day after day, hour after hour, he practiced changing his appearance. One moment it was Wayne Higginbotham staring at himself in the mirror, the next moment a young Roger Moore was staring back at him.

"The name's Bond...James Bond," he laughed.

Then it was Luke Skywalker standing in Wayne Higginbotham's bedroom.

"The force is strong in you, Wayne, you must concentrate. Reach out with your mind. Feel the force flow through you." He pulled a toy light sabre from his dressing table and waved it around while making a strange buzzing noise.

Wayne then changed his face to look like Mr. Spock, his favourite television character from Star Trek.

"I find your behaviour illogical!" he said out-loud, raising one pointed eyebrow quizzically.

Now there was a character that Wayne did not have to pull his ears back to imitate; the likeness was quite uncanny. Even so, the appearance of Mr Spock on Shepton High Street on a market day might be a bit much for the small Yorkshire market town to take.

Clint Eastwood screwed up his eyes and asked if Wayne if he wanted to "make my day, punk!"

John Wayne told him, "The hell you will…"

Sean Connery grinned and hissed "Shertainly, Mish Moneypenny."

Tony Curtis jumped up and declared that he was Spartacus, before Elvis appeared and in his finest Mississippi accent declared, "Uh, no, boy! Ah'm Spartacus!"

Wayne Higginbotham collapsed, giggling, to the floor.

"Are you alright in there?" Doris' concerned voice emanated from behind the locked bedroom door.

"Fine," Wayne chirruped, in a voice that didn't quite sound like his own. He cleared his throat.

"Fine," he repeated, coughing and straightening out his clothes.

Wayne even discovered that he could make himself look passable as a girl.

"Just wait until my next visit to the swimming pool!" he thought to himself. "It's the girls changing room for me…"

Wayne continued chopping and changing his appearance, until by the very last day of the summer holidays he realised that he could make himself look like almost anyone or anything he wanted, and that he could maintain that change for ages.

Indeed, one morning, Doris had shouted "What the hell are you doing in that bedroom, Wayne Higginbotham? Get yourself down here, now!"

Wayne had panicked so much that he had left the bedroom as Elvis Presley, until a sudden mental alarm had seemed to go off half way down the stairs and he had dashed back into his bedroom just to check in the mirror that it was actually Wayne Higginbotham who was going to be putting out the bins and not the late King of rock and roll.

Wayne was somewhat surprised that his father hadn't made an appearance during his shape-shifting experiments. After all, he had materialised after the invisibility trick he had used at school. Maybe he was just leaving Wayne alone and letting him get on with it. That certainly suited Wayne!

The first day of the Michaelmas, or Autumn term, back at Wormysted's Grammar School, Wednesday fifth September, came as a merciful release for Wayne, despite his newfound skills. During the dog days of the holidays, Doris had excelled herself in finding meaningless tasks for him to do. She was getting more than a little bit suspicious about the amount of time Wayne was spending in his room, and was doing all she could to keep him busy.

It was good to be back amongst his mates and to hear their tales of exciting summer holidays in far-off exotic places. The sort of places that he could only dream about visiting: France, Spain, Majorca, Greece. They all sounded so exciting and different. Wayne could picture swaying palm trees and warm beaches covered in bikini-clad beauties.

Pete Williams had even been to America. Everyone was in awe of that, especially when he had said that American girls had loved his English accent and that he had done "everything." Wayne had been careful not to ask Pete any questions. He was wrapped up in his own jealousy, and the very last thing he wanted to hear about was Pete's adventures on the beaches of California with some tanned blonde bombshell!

The Higginbotham family holidays had always been taken in Blackpool, Morecambe, or even exotic Scarborough - although they hadn't been on holiday for two years, because money was extremely tight in the Higginbotham household. The fortune that Wayne had found in Ireland had been put into a secret trust fund by Frank, and Wayne couldn't touch it until he hit twenty-one. Frank had refused to use any of the money, declaring that it wasn't his to use. The one jewel that Wayne kept secreted in a pouch in his drawer was for emergencies only, he told himself.

Wayne had entertained visions of visiting his mom in L.A. one day; now those dreams seemed to have evaporated into thin air. Even France seemed like a million miles away, so California might as well have been located on the dark side of the moon. As for girls, they were just a total waste of Wayne's time. Stephanie would never go out with him now. He'd totally gone and blown it!

Term had started on a Wednesday, so the Thursday night Youth Club meeting was a cause of much excitement amongst the boys of the lower sixth form. Paul Harland had asked Wayne if he would be going almost as soon as the bell went for the first break.

"No, probably not," Wayne had muttered.

"Why?" Paul had demanded incredulously."Not because of Stephanie Fleming, surely?"

Wayne had shrugged.

"Oh, come on, Wayne, there are plenty of other fish in the sea," Paul had said.

"Yeah but I don't fancy kissing a kipper, thank you very much," Wayne had snapped, a little spitefully. "Anyway, we've got visitors," he had lied unconvincingly, and slunk off to the cloakroom to sit and sulk on his own for a while. He had hardly started his sulk, however, when an idea began to form in his mind.

What if the Higginbotham's did happen to have visitors? What if one of those visitors happened to go to the Youth Club instead of Wayne, because Wayne was ill, or something? What if that someone was an awful lot cooler than boring old Wayne Higginbotham?

Someone much better looking than Wayne? A little bit older than Wayne...a lot more experienced and sophisticated? Someone who looked a little bit like that pop star he'd seen in the paper...?

By the time the bell rang again and Wayne left the cloakroom, he had planned his Thursday night activities almost to the letter. It was a much happier, brighter figure who entered Jimmy Hartley's French class than the boy who had left Paul Harland only fifteen minutes earlier!

Fourteen

Doris Higginbotham was worried. Doris Higginbotham was very worried. In fact, Doris was more worried than she had been in many years.

Not since Wayne had run away from home over five years earlier had she felt like this, and she found it incredibly difficult to discuss the matter with him. She found it almost impossible to discuss anything with Wayne nowadays. The boy had become so arrogant - "bigheaded," as Doris would say. He was so opinionated about absolutely everything, especially since he had gone to that grammar school.

Well, what had she expected? Wormysted's was where all the posh kids went. Her own nephew Cedric had gone there and done quite well. Margaret had even suggested that he might go on to university and get a proper profession. Doris had simply sneered. There was nothing wrong with a good steady job, like a plumber, or a joiner, or even a builder. There was money to be made in a proper trade. That's what Trevor would have done. He wouldn't have got any lofty ideas, so above his station. At least if Wayne got a proper job then he would be of some use around the house - unlike Frank, who was the most useless man on the face of the planet.

It wasn't Wayne's future career that was worrying Doris, however. Nor was it his arrogance. What Doris was worried about was the amount of time he was spending alone in his bedroom. It just wasn't natural!

Why was he hiding in there so much? Was he being bullied, or was he a strange, reclusive, introvert? Was he doing the sorts of things that she had heard that some teenage boys do? Drugs? Smoking? Looking at filthy magazines with those brazen naked women in?

Whatever Wayne was up to, Doris Higginbotham was determined that she would find out. She had tried to discuss the matter with Frank, but he had just shrugged and said that if the boy needed time alone then that was fine with him. But Doris didn't think it was fine. She didn't think it was fine at all.

She had asked Margaret if Cedric spent much time alone in his room. Margaret had said that Cedric did, but only to do his homework; and Wayne did his homework on the kitchen table, so that wasn't the explanation. No...something was going on. Something suspicious.

And Doris Higginbotham was not the type of person to allow something suspicious to be going on under her roof without knowing exactly what it was.

Fifteen

"So you see, Father, it is a simple choice...and it is all yours." Bishop O'Leary's voice was no more than a barely-audible whisper as he leaned over the police interview room table, his nose a matter of inches from James Malone's.

"Theft, and maybe even a murder charge. I'm sure you are aware that these carry severe penalties in Ireland, even for a previously reputable man of the cloth," O'Leary continued to hiss. "However...tell me exactly what happened in Finaan, and this misunderstanding could be cleared up very quickly. Confession is good for the soul, as you above all people know, Father."

"Please do not call me Father, Your Grace," James replied. "I am no longer a priest."

O'Leary lifted his head, sat back, and sighed.

"In the eyes of Our Lord, you will always be a priest, James." He smiled. "Only you are blind to that fact; and, as you know, Father, Our Lord can forgive even the most heinous of crimes."

He leaned back towards James, and through clenched teeth hissed, "Tell me what happened on the night that Pizarro and Burke died and what became of the demon's stones - and all the charges against you will be dropped."

James simply stared at him, his eyes betraying his contempt for the fat bishop and everything he stood for. Bishop O'Leary paused, and wiped his greasy forehead.

"Your misguided attempts, James, to protect the enemies of the church and their offspring, augur very badly for the passing of your father into the kingdom of heaven."

For the first time since the Gardai had vacated the interview room to allow Bishop O'Leary to interview James, some twenty minutes earlier, James face betrayed emotion. He visibly flinched. His eyes widened and his mouth opened, as though he was about to respond, but he controlled himself quickly and took a deep breath.

Too late, however; O'Leary knew that he scored a direct hit. He sat back again and smiled condescendingly.

"Oh yes, James, we know all about the boy. The half-breed son of the late 'Mickey Finn' - or should that be Aillen Mac Fionnbharr?"

He smiled again as James' eyes betrayed shock at the veracity of O'Leary's statement, and rubbed his hands together. He was beginning to enjoy himself now.

"We know he has the stones. We know he is not now in Ireland. We just need to know where to find him," he continued. "In California, perhaps?"

It was a total bluff on O'Leary's part. He had taken what Aoibheall had told him and invented a scenario that seemed to fit the situation. Even so, he was taken aback by the impact that his suggestion had on James Malone, who sagged in his chair and covered his face in his hands. O'Leary shuffled his ample backside in his seat and closed in for the kill.

"Tell me again exactly what happened that night, Father, and we can all go home. I know you are jet-lagged and tired. Did you really think that you could sneak back into a Catholic country as devout as Ireland and not have customs inform the Gardai as soon as you showed your passport? Tell me where this half-breed spawn of Satan is, and you might be absolved of your sins after all."

Malone sighed heavily, and uncovered his face.

"Very well. I will tell you what happened that night at Mickey Finn's cottage, but I cannot tell you where the boy is or where the stones are, because I really, really, do not know, and that I swear on my father's life."

O'Leary grinned smugly.

"Excellent, Father! I am glad you have seen some reason. Let us not discuss such important matters, however, in such an uncomfortable place, where prying ears might get the wrong ideas. You shall relate your tale in my office, where your memory might even improve." He stood abruptly.

"Officer!" he shouted. A Gard appeared through the interview room door, closely followed by the two detectives who had arrested James at the hospital.

"Father Malone has explained what happened to the funds and I hereby state that he is innocent of any wrongdoing. All charges on that account are dropped. I am afraid the suicides that occurred in Finaan were more closely related to the matters we have discussed. The church has no charges to press against this young man on that matter either."

The older and more senior detective looked confused.

"So you are saying that you're not after pressing any charges at all, Your Grace?"

"Correct!" O'Leary replied pompously. "Young Father Malone here has explained what happened in Finaan and how his running away was merely the misguided reaction of youth and inexperience to entirely natural events. It was a great shock to him and a great test of his faith to discover what unholy deeds were being carried out by his senior colleagues, Father Callaghan and Father Burke. Both men were held in very highest esteem by young Father Malone."

James stared straight down at the table. The insinuation that his dear friend Father Callaghan had been involved in any criminal activities sickened him to the stomach, but he was in no situation to argue now. Should Bishop O'Leary choose to, he could condemn James to charges of theft and possibly insinuate murder, no matter how untrue and impossible to prove the allegations would be. It was all the word of a well-respected bishop and the entire Catholic hierarchy against a renegade priest who had ditched his collar and run away from a crime scene.

James felt totally trapped; his mind buzzed. What could he do to ensure that the Order did not find the boy that he had seen battle Pizarro that night?

"Come on then, Father," he heard a distant voice say. "Looks like the bishop will be taking you home tonight."

He stood mechanically, and pulled on the jacket that he'd draped over the back of his chair during his earlier questioning by the detectives.

"Can I be suggesting, Father, that you don't leave the country until we are totally satisfied that there are no charges to answer? I suppose your brother will be acting as your lawyer?" the younger detective asked threateningly, his voice betraying his disappointment at the inconclusive end to what had seemed a relatively straightforward case. At one point during the interview he had bluntly suggested that James Malone and his colleague Father Callaghan had been stealing church funds and that Callaghan had committed suicide when Father Burke had discovered the deception, and that James had murdered Burke and fled when he had realised that the game was up.

James had realised that this must have been the story that the Order had fed to the Gardai to ensure that their search for him was serious. He found it bizarre that there had been no mention of Father Pizarro or Mickey Finn in all of this. It was almost as if both of the immortals had never existed. For a brief moment, he shook his head. Maybe they hadn't existed. Maybe he had committed some horrendous crime and had gone mad in the aftermath. Immortals, shape-shifters, people firing power bolts from the palms of their hands. He shivered, and all of a sudden longed for the warmth of the Californian sun and Carrie's tender touch. He could almost smell the bougainvillea and hear the trickle of water from the fountain that stood in Carrie's front yard, looking out over Chatsworth and the San Fernando Valley.

"Sir?"

He looked up. A Gard was holding the office door open for him, as the bishop disappeared down a long corridor illuminated by glaring, buzzing fluorescent tubes.

James stood wearily.

"No, Dan will not be my lawyer. He operates in England. I don't need a lawyer." He sighed heavily. "It's been a long day."

The Gard remained stone-faced.

What had O'Leary meant by saying that his memory might improve in the Bishop's office? James knew the Order was capable of murder, so torture was certainly not beyond them. Indeed, did their colleagues in the inquisition not perfect the art of extracting confession by torture?

James Malone pondered for a moment whether it would be better to face the theft and murder rap. After all, they couldn't prove what he hadn't done. He was an innocent man. As he shuffled off into the corridor and then out of the police station, however, James Malone realised that he was in the hands of - and totally at the mercy of - The Sacred Order of St. Gregory. They could prove that black was white, if it suited their purpose. There wasn't a lawyer on earth who could protect him from the Order.

If he was ever going to get back to California, to Carrie, he was going to have to make one of two choices. Either tell them exactly what they wanted to know, everything he knew, and probably condemn that British kid to death. To wash his hands of the whole damn thing and get back to Box Canyon as soon as possible. Or, to tell enough for them to believe that he had divulged his entire knowledge, then somehow find the kid and warn him that the Order knew of his existence, before escaping back to L.A.

No. The more he thought about it, there was only one real choice, after all.

Sixteen

The scent of bougainvillea was almost overpowering, and sunlight sparkled on the surface of the water. A palm tree swayed slightly in a gentle breeze and in the distance, just below the shimmering brown mountains, the slight buzz of Highway 101 could be heard. Terri Thorne stared at the glistening surface of her swimming pool, and felt the warmth of the Californian sun kissing her skin. A hummingbird skimmed the surface of the water, leaving a faint ripple.

Yet Terri's mind was thousands of miles away. She was back on a bleak windswept Irish moor, being charmed by an exotic young American with strange pointed ears. The face of the young American was not the one she remembered, however; it was that of her son Michael. How could she have done that to him? Found him after so many years, and then gone and pushed him away.

True; he did look like his father, and that made a cold shiver run down her spine, despite the heat of the late morning. Her son's father had been a cool American kid called Danny Finn, who had been like a breath of fresh air in her boring rural Irish home. However, Terri had suffered a sort of breakdown when she found out she was pregnant, and had dreamed or imagined that Danny had said that he was a sidhe, a shape shifter, one of the fairy folk that she had believed belonged firmly within the pages of children's story books.

Had it been a dream; had he really been not human? Had he tricked her in order to violate her and leave her pregnant?

No, that was all just part of the shock and sickness. Her therapist had said it had been a real breakdown; that she had just simply, totally freaked when she had found out she was pregnant and unmarried at sixteen. None of that was the boy's fault, was it?

True, the boy's twin sister was still missing, and she felt a pang of guilt that she had been developing a relationship with one of her offspring and was the leaving the other one out. But that was no one's fault, was it? If the media did get hold of the story of the children that she had given away to be adopted then her career was likely to be over before it had really started.

But that was true anyway, wasn't it? Terri Thorne was already in her early thirties and despite what Dean, her husband, agent and manager said, the movie business was a young girl's game.

She pushed her sunglasses back up her nose and reached out for her glass of iced water, which was on the table by the sun lounger.

"Ouch!" she squeaked, as she felt a sharp kick in her swollen belly. A sharp reminder that not only was she no longer one of the bright young things, but also that she was pregnant with Dean's baby. It would be a couple of years before she was in any shape to get back in front of a camera again, by which time she would be in her mid-thirties and definitely past it. Terri sighed. So the high point of her movie career had been a bit part in a second-rate disaster movie called Tornado which had involved her running around screaming and losing most of her clothes.

Was that it? Was it for that that she had sacrificed her son? Was that what she had worked her butt off for since she had arrived in the USA?

Terri sipped her water. Why had she sent that letter? How could she have been so stupid? How could she have been so...cruel?

Terri took another sip and put the glass back down with a bang. She snorted derisively. She knew damn well why she had done it. She had gotten into a row with Dean about her career and the fact that, since she had gone and gotten pregnant, Dean seemed to be spending more and more time with his younger clients. He had bragged to her about a marvellous prospect in her twenties and about how he was going to get her on his books. When Terri had complained he had been brutal about what she would have to do to get her career back on track, and that had involved ditching her son. In a tequila-fuelled fit she had taken Dean's advice, and then regretted it as soon as she had sobered up. By then, her letter had been mailed.

Terri climbed off the lounger and strolled over to the pool. She sat down - with some difficulty due to the advanced stage of her pregnancy - on the side of the pool, and dipped her feet in the cool water.

She looked down her sweeping drive at the gleaming silver Porsche 924 that Dean had given her as a wedding present. Not bad for an Irish country girl; yet was she prepared to sell her soul for the nice house in Beverley Hills, the pool and the car?

No, she was not!

Terri Thorne clambered to her feet and marched off briskly towards the house, picked up the first pen she could find, and sat down to write another letter.

Seventeen

Wayne Higginbotham couldn't get home from school fast enough on that Thursday evening. He almost broke into a run several times as he hurried between the huge Victorian mills that still scarred the, otherwise pretty, Yorkshire market town of Shepton. Thursday night was Youth Club night, and despite the recent humiliation he had suffered at being rejected by the gorgeous Stephanie Fleming, he knew that tonight things were going to be different.

Wayne charged through the front door of the Higginbotham's little terraced house and tossed his battered brown leather briefcase to one side.

"Hi Mum, I'm home!" he shouted, before charging up the narrow staircase in the middle of the house to his room. Doris was sat at the kitchen table, a cigarette in the corner of her mouth with a long drooping line of ash ready to fall.

"Wayne!" she bellowed. "What do you want for your tea?"

The ash fell onto the tablecloth, sparking a muttered curse from Doris. A muffled voice came from behind the bedroom door upstairs, and Doris stood and frowned.

"What?" she shouted. She heard the bedroom door open.

"Anything!" Wayne's voice drifted downstairs.

"Oh, that's useful," Doris muttered. She felt extremely frustrated, having meticulously searched Wayne's room that afternoon and found nothing. She had been expecting to find a stash of dirty magazines, or love letters, something that might explain Wayne's apparent reluctance to emerge from behind his bedroom door for anything other than meals. She had found nothing, apart from a few old stones in a drawer that she had put in Wayne's waste bin. What was he doing, keeping junk like that?

Wayne ripped off his uniform as soon as he got into his room. It was still only half past four and the Youth Club didn't start until seven–thirty, but he wanted to practice his new persona and perfect his accent and mannerisms. Stephanie Fleming was going to be blown away. He had just removed his tie and hung up his school blazer, when he noticed the pieces of the mystical stone of Falias in the waste bin. He gasped in horror, dropped the tie in a heap on the carpet, and picked up the bin and emptied it on his bed. All five of his stones were there. Wayne sank onto the bed, and emitted a huge sigh of relief.

The biggest stone had belonged to his real father, Aillen Mac Fionnbharr, a Prince and the last of the immortal Tuatha De Danaan. It was really a crystal that somehow amplified the magical powers of the Tuatha and enabled them to shape-shift, or become invisible for much longer than they could otherwise manage. The stones also gave them the ability to concentrate and emit powerful bolts of pure energy from their hands. The four smaller stones had belonged to the treacherous priest: Francisco De Pizarro, also the half-breed son of one of the Tuatha. He had gathered them from some of his Tuatha victims. Wayne had discovered that he could perform some magic without the stones, but not as powerfully, nor for as long.

He stood, and marched indignantly to his bedroom door.

"Mum!" he yelled indignantly down the stairwell. "Mum...have you been in my room?"

Doris Higginbotham scuttled to the bottom of the stairs.

"Yes, love," she answered, "I was just cleaning."

"Why did you throw out my stones?" Wayne asked, his voice unusually angry. Doris pursed her lips.

"Well, I don't know what you want to be keeping a load of dirty old rocks in your drawer for? I thought I was doing you a favour."

She turned huffily, and marched back into the kitchen. "Your tea'll be ready in five minutes," she sniffed. Wayne closed his bedroom door.

"She's been going through my drawers!" he whispered aloud.

He pulled open each drawer on his chest and dressing table in turn. Everything seemed in order. The jewel was still in its pouch, untouched. He then took a chair and opened the airing cupboard, which was in his room. He pulled the chair up to the cupboard, stood on it, and groped around the side of the hot water tank. He felt a pile of paper, and heaved another sigh of relief. His real mother's letters were still there, undiscovered.

He jumped down, replaced the chair where he had found it, and stood in front of the mirror. The face looking back at him was that of an older boy with long, straight dark hair, brown eyes, and a deep golden tan. Wayne Higginbotham's Californian alter ego would sweep Stephanie Fleming right off her feet.

"What am I going to call you, buddy?" Wayne asked quietly. "I'll use my own real name - Michael - but what then?" Wayne looked around, hearing Doris' voice somewhere far away.

"Wayne, your tea's ready!"

Lying on his dressing table was a book he'd been trying to read for a while, but hated. James Joyce's Finnegan's Rainbow.

"That'll do!" Wayne smiled.

"Wayne, come on - it'll get cold!" Doris shouted again.

"Michael Finnegan. No, Mickey Finnegan."

The words had hardly left his mouth when he realised what he had done. His father, Aillen Mac Fionnbharr's alter ego had been Mickey Finn. Well, so be it; so would Wayne's, too. Mickey Finn disappeared back into Wayne's imagination, and he stared at his own pale, freckled face in the mirror.

"WAYNE!" This time, Doris sounded angry.

"Coming, Mum!" he shouted.

Eighteen

Aoibheall was also staring at her reflection in the mirror. It was the first time she had done anything quite so vain in nearly one hundred and forty years. The face that stared back at her was virtually flawless; she looked no older than a girl of around twenty.

Her eyes were the colour of emeralds, her hair was jet black, and long. Although she had never used shampoo or conditioner, it managed to shine as though it had been freshly washed in the most expensive salon in Ireland. Her skin was like new porcelain; clean, clear and white. The Banshee Aoibheall was still undeniably beautiful, even to herself.

She managed a faint, but sad, smile. What use was beauty, when she could only ever be alone? As far as she could tell, from her wanderings in the in-between worlds realm of passed immortals, she was the last of the Tuatha De Danaan on Earth. The Tuatha's time had finally passed, although many had said that had happened when the Celts had arrived in Ireland and stolen the last refuge of the once mighty race of immortals.

When she had entered the convent, there had still been quite a few of the 'fairy folk', as the mortals called them. Now they had all been hunted down and destroyed by this Sacred Order of St. Gregory. All except her and a half-breed.

So, the fat bishop and Father de Feren had thought that they could simply use her to seek out the half-breed son of Aillen Mac Fionnbharr, did they? Use her and then probably dispose of her, despite the promise that she would be allowed to go back and hide in the convent. As if! She smiled. The poor fools didn't realise just who they were dealing with.

The tale she had related in O'Leary's office had been partly true, but it was also a smokescreen. She had wanted them to underestimate her and her powers, and it seemed likely that she had succeeded. To them, she was nothing more than a pious convert to the cult of Christianity. As if she would ever have truly worshipped a weakling god like Jesus Christ! It would not be the Banshee Aoibheall who would perish when all of this was over; she would make sure of that. It was now her duty to keep the race of the Tuatha De Danaan alive on the face of the earth. Aoibheall, the last of the pure Tuatha De Danaan.

She had liked what she had seen of the modern world so far, and had decided that she wanted to be part of it. With her powers as a shape-shifting immortal she could live like a queen, especially if she could get her hands on the stones of Aillen Mac Fionnbharr.

Sister Bernadette's habit and wimple were carelessly cast on the simple bed of the small cell in the central Dublin convent. Aoibheall had felt grateful for the way the traditional nun's clothing had protected her from the obvious lust of Bishop O'Leary. He had particularly disgusted her, with his pallid, sweaty skin, beady, leering eyes and the rolls of fat that constituted his chins sitting in a pile on his dog collar. She had seen the way his eyes had almost stripped her naked, despite the protective shapelessness of her garb.

Even so, she was desperate to try on some of the modern clothes that she had seen the girls in the streets wearing. But no; that could wait. Being Sister Bernadette would be useful for the time being, but the Banshee Aoibheall knew that the devout and innocent nun was already the first victim of the Order's attempt to finally eliminate the Tuatha De Danaan.

Aoibheall would play along with the Order's game. She would use them to help her find the remnants of the stone of Falias. But once the shards were in her possession, she would wreak her vengeance.

There was a knock on the door of her cell and she heard de Feren call her name.

"Coming, Father!" she called, cheerfully.

Aoibheall took a long last glance into the mirror, and smiled again. She covered her head and reassumed the demure features of Sister Bernadette. Her green eyes flashed and the mirror shattered into a thousand pieces.

"Oops!" she grinned. "Seven years bad luck!"

Nineteen

James Malone's heart pounded in his chest, as he entered the office of Bishop O'Leary within the hallowed walls of St. Patrick's Cathedral. He remembered a summer day over five years earlier, when he had last entered the same building. He had felt nervous then at the prospect of being interviewed by Bishop Donleavy, but not nearly half as nervous as he did now. The Order would stop at nothing to find out the British kid's whereabouts.

He had considered just running for it as they had climbed out of the Bishop's official car, a sinister, long, black Mercedes-Benz. But where would he run to? The Order was so powerful; it was like some mythical sea beast with tentacles that stretched everywhere. They seemed to have a finger in every pie. James was quite sure that they had Ireland locked up like a cage. They'd certainly wasted no time in catching him after his details had been taken at passport control.

"Please take a seat, James." Bishop O'Leary motioned towards a leather chair before a large oak desk. "Wine?" he asked, pouring himself a large glass.

"No, thank you," James whispered.

Bishop O'Leary's office was richly decorated, but it was nowhere near as imposing as Donleavy's had been five years earlier. Even the Primate of all Ireland himself, up in Armagh, would have envied that office. O'Leary's office was very light and, despite the ornate artwork on the walls, looked comparatively businesslike.

Bishop O'Leary settled into a chair on the opposite side of the desk, and mopped his brow.

"So, James, you were going to tell me exactly what did happen at Finn's cottage on that accursed night."

James stroked his chin, and took a deep breath.

"Well, it's a long story," he began. The loud ring of an antiquated telephone interrupted him. The bishop picked up the receiver.

"Did I not say that I was not to be disturbed?" he barked before visibly blanching. "Oh yes, of course. I am sorry" he mumbled. His eyes grew wide, and his face took on the pallor of a corpse. "Five minutes? Why yes, of course."

Bishop O'Leary carefully replaced the heavy black receiver.

"You had better make it very, very quick, Father Malone. It would appear that the Bishop Donleavy himself is wanting to be seeing you, and I would prefer that I know what happened, and the whereabouts of this boy, before we go and see his Eminence."

Five minutes later, James Malone found himself once again standing outside Bishop Donleavy's office, staring at the same gargoyles he had stared at half a decade earlier.

"Are you sure that is all you remember?" Bishop O'Leary whispered in irritation, as he hopped uncomfortably from foot to foot and mopped his brow yet again.

"Yes," James whispered in reply. "Mickey Finn died, and then just disappeared. One minute he was lying on the ground - and then he was gone. Kaboom! Pizarro fell backwards into the burning cottage during the fight. Not a shred of him was left the next morning."

"And the stones?" the bishop hissed. "What happened to the stones?"

Malone did not have time to respond, however, as the door to Donleavy's office swung open and the tall figure of Father de Feren beckoned the two to enter. Bishop O'Leary's mouth dropped open at the sight of de Feren in the senior Bishop's office before him, and de Feren merely smirked.

The room was just as dark and sombre as James remembered, even with the candelabra full of lit candles. The priceless Old Masters on the walls and the fully drawn curtains looked just the same as they had five years earlier, when James had been a nervous young priest instead of an ageing hippy.

Almost lost in the shadows behind the huge oak desk sat the familiar figure of the ancient bishop. He looked even more gaunt and turtle-like now than he had the last time James had been summoned into his presence. His thin lips were drawn tight, and his tiny humourless eyes glinted with malice. His wrinkled leathery throat rolled constantly, as though he was desperately trying to swallow something.

Unlike Malone's previous audience with the head of the Order in Ireland, when he had been forced into a nervous gabble due to Donleavy's silence, this time it was the bishop who spoke first.

"So...the lost sheep, the prodigal son, our own elusive Father James Malone has finally returned to the fold," he croaked.

James grimaced and, from somewhere, he felt a surge of courage welling up inside him. Who did these people think they were? He wasn't a frightened little parochial parish priest anymore. They had killed a man he had regarded as a friend, and eliminated an entire race. These people were responsible for what was, effectively, genocide.

As his anger welled up, James noticed a nun sitting in the shadows off to the right of the desk, her head downcast.

"And the good Bishop," Donleavy continued.

"Excellent, excellent."

The old bishop stood and waved the two men towards two leather chairs in front of his desk. "Sit, sit," he ordered, while Father de Feren moved around his desk to stand alongside him.

"You have led us a merry dance, these last five years, Father. We had presumed you were dead. Yet, here you are; re-born, as it were."

Donleavy's voice sounded like sandpaper on glass.

"For over five years, we have waited patiently to hear the exact circumstances of the death of our dear Francisco Pizarro, and to find out who killed him. You will now relay to me the precise events of that night."

"I think I can answer..." Bishop O'Leary began to speak, his pomposity evident in the tone of his voice.

"I didn't ask you, Bishop," Donleavy growled ominously. O'Leary gulped, and went quiet.

James Malone pulled back the chair and sat down legs akimbo, like a defiant schoolboy before the headmaster's desk.

"And if I tell you, how many more people are going to die?" He suddenly sounded quite nonchalant.

From the corner of his eye he noticed O'Leary staring at him, horror-struck. No-one spoke to the head of the Order in Ireland like that. Donleavy glared at Malone.

"Impertinence! The work of the Order is sacred, Father Malone. We pave the way for the return of Our Lord. You may have lost your vestments, but I presume you still have your faith?"

"Not in a murdering bunch of gangsters!" Malone replied defiantly. "I'm not really sure who exactly you are paving the way for, but what I saw in Finaan did not seem to me like the work of people serving the Lord Jesus Christ that I used to believe in. This is 1979, Bishop. Your brand of religious fundamentalism belongs to the bloody middle ages. You are like the Spanish Inquisition and all those medieval fanatics who spent their worthless lives burning innocent people, because they held 'heretical' views!" he continued, his voice rising almost to a shout.

"Y...Y...Your Eminence, I..." Bishop O'Leary began to blurt out, but the raised hand of the older bishop stopped him immediately.

"Let young Father Malone continue," he croaked.

"Do you really think I am going to help you murder more innocent people?" Malone whispered.

There was long silence, punctuated only by the heavy breathing of O'Leary and the rolling throat of the old bishop. At last, Donleavy spoke.

"When you last sat before me, Father Malone, I had believed you to be intelligent but naive. Even so, I had high hopes that under the tutelage of Father Pizarro you might eventually become a valuable member of our Order. I was therefore somewhat dismayed when Pizarro reported that you had turned out to be a rather less than enthusiastic apprentice. I was even more disappointed when you disappeared. An apparent suicide."

He paused and took a sip of wine from an ornate goblet, swallowing noisily.

"However, it has been fully taken into consideration that, without your invaluable services, the demon Finn would still be alive."

Malone dropped his head. Donleavy's statement was true. Had he not told Bishop O'Leary about his original conversation with Mickey Finn, then events would not have led to Pizarro being in a position to strike the fatal blow.

Donleavy swallowed noisily, several times.

"I was of the belief that what you had seen had unhinged your mind, Father Malone. It would have been understandable, given the unnatural circumstance in which you found yourself in Finaan. Perhaps I underestimated the extent of that unhinging."

Malone looked Donleavy in the eye.

"I am not unhinged in any way, Your Grace." He almost spat the latter two words. Donleavy's thin lips curved in a hideous parody of a smile.

"Madness takes many forms, Father, and the devil's work is often the least apparent...yet it is the most insidious."

"What?" Malone gasped.

"I think you know what I mean, Father Malone." Donleavy continued to smile malevolently. "Your recent confession of murder to my colleague Bishop O'Leary here was a shock to all of us."

Malone laughed, and shook his head. "I thought you'd come up with something like that. A pathetic lie that you know you cannot prove."

"We do not need proof, Father." Donleavy sneered. "We are the Sacred Order of St. Gregory. Our word is law."

Malone began to stand, but felt the sudden weight of Father de Feren's hands on his shoulders. He hadn't noticed the tall, bald, bespectacled priest move and creep up behind him.

"Tell me where to find the boy. We know you know where he is," Donleavy growled.

"What boy?" Malone mocked the old bishop.

"We know all about Finn's bastard son," Donleavy gloated, and waved his hand in the direction of the nun. "Have you been introduced to Sister Bernadette yet, James?"

Malone coughed and shook his head, and Donleavy smiled, his Adam's apple bouncing excitedly.

"She is a real life banshee, so they tell me."

The old bishop sat back in his chair, allowing James time to contemplate what that might mean. Malone glanced over at the nun, whose head was still bowed demurely.

Bishop Donleavy leaned forward, and glowered at the young ex-Priest.

"Father de Feren tells me that she can read everything in a man's mind, just by laying the palm of her hand on his forehead."

He paused for effect, then he smiled again; a thin, malevolent grin.

"Unfortunately, there is often not a great deal of that mind left, when she has finished."

The colour drained from James Malone's face. "I have told you all I am going to," he whispered.

The old bishop looked at de Feren, and gave a curt nod. The nun looked up for the first time.

Malone gasped. He had been expecting an ancient crone as in the legends of the wailing banshees of old, but Sister Bernadette was not only young, but also stunningly beautiful. The tall thin priest smiled, and beckoned the nun over. She stood up, slowly.

Malone felt de Feren's hands pressing down on his shoulders even harder.

"Sister Bernadette - may I introduce, Father James Malone."

De Feren's heavily accented voice sounded incredibly loud after Donleavy's barely-audible tones.

Sister Bernadette glanced at de Feren, who raised his eyebrows and nodded. The nun began to walk slowly towards James, her startling green eyes sparkling in the candlelight. Malone was aware of O'Leary shifting uncomfortably next to him, and the gurgling sound of the old Bishop's undulating throat. De Feren's hands became even more pressing on his shoulders, as though he was expecting Malone to struggle and attempt to flee.

The banshee walked slowly, deliberately, like a model strutting along a catwalk. There was something incredibly feline about the way she walked, the way she stared at him. Malone was reminded of the stare of a cat concentrating on its unfortunate prey.

He thought back to that night at Mickey Finn's cottage. He remembered Pizarro, Finn and the boy, Michael - that was it, Michael -

but he had had another name - Wayne, Wayne Higgy-something. They'd hurled energy bolts at one another. He had not believed that such things were possible, but he had seen it with his very own eyes. The fairy folk did exist, and they did have powers way beyond imagination. He glanced at Donleavy whose mouth was open, his eyes widening in anticipation, then he looked up into the face of the banshee as she stopped in front of him. He looked right into those beautiful, huge, emerald-green eyes. He noticed that she looked sad, sorrowful even, as she reached out her hand towards his forehead.

Twenty

David Smith was a very busy man. He combined his profession as an auctioneer with an amount of Methodist laid preaching, and occasional lecturing in 'Business Studies' at the local adult education college. He also, somehow, found the time to run the Methodist Youth Club on Westmoreland Street, Shepton, every Thursday evening.

David Smith was also a very clever man. He had gained his degree in theology at Leeds University, in the days when getting a degree meant something. Now, he was of the opinion that almost anyone could get into university. Some fourteen percent of school leavers were now going on to university, or to polytechnics, he had read in the Yorkshire Post. Whatever next!

Tall and totally bald, David Smith was as opinionated a Yorkshire man as you were ever likely to meet, and he didn't suffer any nonsense with the teenagers who frequented his Youth Club. As far as he was concerned they were there to engage in good Christian dialogue, play some wholesome pop music, and maybe a little table tennis. The Youth Club was meant to keep them off the streets, stop them behaving like hooligans. Crisps, snacks and soft drinks were available, with the funds raised going towards the upkeep of the club. The whole point was to show these young people that the Church was not an old people's pastime, but that it could be fun; friendships could be made, and maybe a lifetime's commitment to the Methodist cause engendered.

What the Youth Club was not about was the playing of loud punk music, swearing, drinking alcohol, clandestine adolescent flirting, and the ensuing furtive snogging. All of which David Smith now seemed to spend every single Thursday evening battling against.

"What was it with kids nowadays?" he would moan.

David's latest problem was with a tall, good-looking American kid, who certainly looked older than the seventeen he claimed to be.

"Well, are you a member, lad?" Smith asked insistently, as the American kid stood at the Youth Club door with his hands in the pockets of his leather biker jacket.

"No, but my cousin Wayne, Wayne Higginbotham is - and as he couldn't make it tonight, he said that I should come, you know, in his place." The American kid drawled as he ran his hand through his long, dark hair.

"Well, Wayne Higginbotham doesn't run this club, you know." David Smith puffed up his chest. "I do, and I think you are older than seventeen. Do you have any proof of your age, son?"

The American kid shrugged, and smiled. "Sorry...Wayne forgot to tell me I'd need my goddamn passport to get in."

David Smith snorted derisively. Why do bloody yanks always have such perfect teeth? he thought to himself. The American continued.

"He said you'd probably let me have a temporary membership, like you did for your niece's French pen-friend last year."

David Smith's mouth opened and closed, but no sound at all came out. The American kid tilted his head to one side, and raised an eyebrow.

Cheeky young bugger! There's no way I'm letting you in, thought David Smith, as he puffed out his chest self-importantly; but a strange thing happened as he started to say it. He looked into the dark brown eyes of the youth, and instead of what he had intended he heard himself say, "Cheeky young devil! Ok, in you go. Fill in one of those forms later, please."

David Smith scratched his bald scalp, as the American walked coolly past him into the Youth Club. He knew he hadn't intended to say that, so why had he? He shook his head, and called out to the youth.

"What's your name, by the way?"

The kid turned and smiled.

"Finn," he said. "Short for Michael Finnegan; but back home, everybody just calls me Finn."

A very confused David Smith smiled weakly and nodded, then turned back towards the door to stop any other unwanted entries, his forehead creased in a deep frown.

As soon as he had walked into the main hall of the club, Wayne, in the guise of Mickey Finn, noticed Anne Ducket looking towards him. If she was here, then so was Stephanie, in all probability.

Must act cool! The words flooded his mind as he strolled over towards Paul Harland and Martin Taggart, who were standing by the record player.

"Hi!" Wayne said cheerily.

Martin and Paul looked at him with blank faces.

"Hi!" they said, in unison. Only then did it occur to Wayne that they didn't have a clue who he was. In his excitement, he hadn't planned how to explain his presence to his mates. He was just going to have to wing it.

"Hey guys, I'm Finn," he said, after what had seemed an eternity of silence. "Wayne's cousin...Wayne Higginbotham. He couldn't, er, make it tonight. So he asked me if I would come along in his place, you know?"

Wayne had even forgotten to use an American accent when he'd said "Hi", but he remembered as he began to speak.

"You must be Paul, right?" he said, holding out his hand. Paul Harland nodded, and held out his own hand. His shake was unenthusiastic.

"And if I'm right, you gotta be...Martin?"

Martin Taggart nodded and shook his hand, also quite limply.

"Are you American?" Paul asked, looking very confused. "It's just, well, you know, Wayne's never mentioned you."

"Yeah, I'm from Los Angeles, California," Wayne grinned. "Sure is a lot hotter than here."

Wayne's mates both looked distinctly unimpressed, and he began to feel a little uncomfortable. What was he doing wrong? Why didn't his mates like him?

"Can I buy you guys a soda?" he asked, with a shrug.

"Er, no thanks, er, Finn," Paul replied, having given Martin a cursory glance.

"Chips, maybe?" Wayne suggested. "Sorry - that's crisps to you guys, I guess."

"No, but thanks anyway." Martin smiled, and turned towards the box of seven-inch singles.

Wayne stepped back, shocked at the cool response his supposed friends had given him. He knew that most of the lads at school hated Yanks, mainly because their parents did. It was all something to do with the war. Yet he had not expected to receive such a cold shoulder from two of the guys he regarded as his best friends. He turned and headed off for the table where some fourth year girl was selling warm cola and stale crisps.

Anne Ducket had noticed Wayne's alter ego as soon as he had walked into the Youth Club. She hadn't been able to stop herself staring. She had never seen this stranger before, and couldn't quite believe her eyes. The stranger was tall, with long dark straight hair, tanned spotless skin, huge dark eyes and a smile that positively shone because of the whiteness of his teeth. He looked like a cross between John Travolta in Grease and that David Cassidy bloke that her big sister had been in love with, back in the early Seventies. Except that this stranger was cool, with his tight straight jeans and his black leather biker's jacket. She nudged Stephanie, who was stood talking to Caroline Ridings next to her.

"Who is he?" she whispered breathlessly. Stephanie turned and looked.

"Never seen him before," she said, looking at the strangers back.

"Nice bum!" Caroline giggled, and all three girls began to giggle like ten-year-olds.

"Nice everything!" Anne gasped. "Just wait 'till he turns round. He is just so fit!"

Stephanie glanced at the newcomer again.

"His hair's too long," she stated. "He looks like a biker."

Wayne bought himself a cola and wandered over to where his old friend from Gas Street school, Richard Hebden, was just finishing a game of pool.

"Excuse me?" Wayne asked. Richard looked up at him and his face hardened, almost as though Wayne had just told him that he was a spotty half-wit. "You must be Richard, right?"

"Yeah, and?" Richard responded unenthusiastically.

"I'm Mickey Finnegan, Finn...Wayne's cousin, you know, Wayne Higginbotham?"

"Oh!" Richard replied, looking embarrassed. "He's, er, he's never mentioned you."

"Oh, I, er, I just got in from L.A. Wayne couldn't make it tonight, so he said I oughta come. See what real life is like over here, check out the chicks and all that, you know?"

Richard smiled vacantly. "Oh yeah, right," he said with an understanding nod.

"Wayne said he's known you since first grade," Wayne continued, desperately trying to make conversation.

"Yeah," was Richard's cool response.

The uncomfortable silence was broken by Sarah Westwood, a fifth year at the Girl's High School in Shepton.

"Excuse me?" she addressed Wayne directly.

"Yeah?" he replied with a dazzling flash of white teeth, relieved to see a friendly face at last.

"My friend wants to know your name and where you're from."

Wayne grinned, and glanced over at where Sarah pointed. Adrienne Smith, another fifth year, smiled shyly in his direction, before turning to pretend to talk to someone else. Wayne's mood began to improve. Adrienne Smith was one of the prettier fifth years, blonde and busty with a nice smile. She had never even looked in his direction when he had been plain old Wayne Higginbotham.

"My name's Mickey Finnegan, but everyone calls me Finn, and I'm from the United States," he told Sarah, who flitted away, giggling girlishly.

Paul Harland approached him.

"Look, Finn." His voice was suddenly deeper than Wayne had ever known it, and his tone serious. "You took us by surprise before. I suppose we were just shocked that Wayne had sent his cousin along and hadn't even bothered telling us you were over here. Although he did say he had visitors."

Wayne shrugged. "You know what Wayne's like."

Paul smiled. "Yeah...he's probably still smarting over the other week."

"Other week?" Wayne queried, raising one eyebrow.

"Yeah," Paul laughed. "The last time he was here, he actually asked Stephanie Fleming out - but she knocked him back, big time. He was so embarrassed!"

"Stephanie Fleming?" Wayne asked, feigning surprise.

"The good-looking blonde-haired girl over there, in the really tight jeans and white top. The really fit one." Paul pointed towards a group of girls gossiping in a corner.

Wayne looked over, just in time to catch Stephanie's eye as she cast him a furtive glance. It seemed to him that their eyes locked for ages, and he could have sworn he saw her smile. He turned away, back towards Paul.

"Well, I can sure understand why he had to have a go."

Paul laughed. "Would you like to play pool?"

"Sure, buddy!" Wayne replied.

They were halfway through the game when Wayne managed to catch Stephanie's eye again. He had looked in her direction several times, but she had always been laughing and giggling with her gaggle of friends and facing away from him. That Anne Ducket kept staring at him instead, as well as Adrienne Smith.

This time, however, he turned and caught her staring at him. He flashed his widest grin and turned away again. When he looked back, she was still looking in his general direction, fiddling with her hair. He smiled again, just a smile, no teeth. She smiled back, and this time she was the first to break eye contact.

Wayne's heart leapt in his chest, and his breath suddenly began to come in short gasps. It felt like as though his stomach had just emptied. He fluffed his next shot so badly that Paul Harland laughed.

"I thought you Yanks were supposed to be able to play pool?" he said gleefully, slamming the next ball thunderously into a corner pocket.

"Some can," Wayne replied, his mind elsewhere.

Donna Summer's 'Love to Love You Baby' began to pound on the old stereo, and Wayne cast another glance in Stephanie's direction. She had disappeared. He gulped as he saw Anne Ducket walking straight towards him, a determined look on her face. She had removed her glasses.

"Hi," she beamed. "I'm Anne."

"Hi," Wayne replied, with a nervous smile. "I'm Mickey Finnegan. Friends call me Finn."

"So, you're American?" Anne asked, with a coy flick of her hair.

"Yeah," Wayne replied coolly. Anne Ducket was not his favourite girl, after her cruel mocking laughter when he had attempted to ask Stephanie out.

"Your shot," Paul sighed, as his ball stopped right on the edge of the pocket.

Wayne turned and played his shot, missing yet again. When he turned back towards Anne, he was taken aback to see Stephanie standing right next to her. Wayne smiled, and she smiled right back at him. Their eyes locked.

"Have you got a girlfriend, Finn...you know, at home?" he heard Anne Ducket ask.

"No," Wayne replied. "But I can sure think of a lady over here I'd like to be my girl."

"Really?" Anne gasped.

Stephanie's eyes dropped, and she bit her bottom lip coquettishly.

"Anyone in particular?" Anne asked eagerly, blind to his inattention.

"Oh yeah," Wayne whispered, "but I'm sworn to secrecy. Fifth Amendment."

"Your shot again," Paul snorted, his disappointment at not having cleared all the spots evident in his voice.

Wayne did his best to fluff his shot so he could get back to Stephanie, but he had to wait two more shots, as he made a hash of being useless and cleared three balls straight. Finally, his attempt to pot the black failed as it clattered the pocket and bounced out, the white ball disappearing instead. Paul Harland clenched his fist.

"Yes!" he exclaimed, as he lined up his winning shot.

Wayne turned back to Anne and Stephanie, who had now been joined by Caroline. He flashed his most endearing smile at Anne.

"Anne, I don't think you've introduced your friends."

Anne blushed. "Oh, sorry, Finn," she gushed. "This is Caroline."

Wayne shook her hand politely.

"Ma'am," he breathed, in his best movie-star voice.

"Good game, mate!" Paul called, having potted the final ball, punching the air in triumph while mouthing: "England One, USA nil!"

"Yeah, thanks buddy," Wayne called back over his shoulder.

"And this is Stephanie. We all just call her Steph, though. She's going out with a guy who's going to Oxford," Anne continued.

"It's not serious!" Stephanie snapped, and glared at her friend.

"Hey!" Wayne whispered, taking Stephanie's proffered hand. "He's a lucky guy."

"Hi," she responded, averting her eyes again. Anne sighed, and grimaced.

"Time for a drink," she sighed, finally noticing that Mickey only had eyes for Steph. Caroline and Anne wandered away, muttering darkly, leaving Stephanie and -unbeknown to them all, Wayne - standing face to face.

"So, how long have you been over here?" Stephanie asked, nervously.

"Not long," Wayne replied. "Wayne didn't exaggerate," he continued, after a moment's silence. In the background, the Stranglers' 'Peaches' reverberated around the room.

"What?" Stephanie glanced up at him, her face bemused.

"My cousin Wayne told me all about you. How stunning you were. He was sure not exaggerating."

Stephanie giggled shyly. "Wayne's sweet," she said. "Anne was really rotten to him. I felt so bad."

"No need," Wayne grinned. "For a limey, he's quite tough, you know."

Stephanie smiled at him, looking into his deep brown eyes.

"Steph, do you want a Diet Coke?" Anne Ducket bellowed across the room. Stephanie nodded an affirmative.

"I better get back to my friends," she sighed.

Wayne realised that it was now or never.

"Could you...I mean, would you like to...you know...come out with me tomorrow night?"

Stephanie looked horrified. "I can't - I've got a choir concert at the Parish church," she groaned.

"Oh..." Wayne's heart sank. Here we go again, he thought. "I'm sorry. I forgot you already have a boyfriend," he said, with a soppy grin.

Stephanie shook her head. "Oh no, it's not that. Martin's just a friend. I'm free Saturday night from about eight-ish?"

Wayne grinned again. "Cool!" he declared, "Eastwood's, eight o'clock, Saturday night?"

"Eastwood's?" Stephanie laughed. "But that's....yeah, sure, why not. I'll see you there." She smiled sweetly at him, and walked back over towards her friends.

David Smith marched across the floor as though marching across a parade ground. The raucous sound of the Sex Pistol's 'God Save the Queen' had just begun to emanate from the stereo.

"We'll have that rubbish straight off!" he bellowed at Martin Taggart. "That lot should have been shot for treason. I will not have that song played in here!"

He straightened his tie and cleared his throat, pleased at the way Martin Taggart had grumpily changed the single for something more respectable.

I wonder why that bloody Yank's looking so pleased with himself? he couldn't help thinking as he marched past the young American, who was grinning like an idiot.

Twenty-One

Elizabeth Ball, the headmistress of Gas Street Junior, Middle and Infant School, picked up the blue airmail letter off the doormat. She glanced and the address, and smiled. It was for Wayne. Ever since Elizabeth had played an instrumental role in finding Wayne, after he had run away to London and subsequently Ireland, five years earlier, she had been his point of contact with his birth mother, Terri.

In the early days letters had arrived quite frequently, but they had seemed to have tailed off over the last couple of years. Elizabeth had read in the gossip columns that the actress Terri Thorne had got engaged and had recently married her agent, Dean Vitalia. Elizabeth had wondered if that was why Terri wasn't writing quite so often, but this letter seemed to have arrived pretty close on the hells of the last one. Maybe Terri had just been busy with her career, a new husband, and the surrounding furore.

Elizabeth walked from the hall into the kitchen where her husband John was hidden behind his newspaper, as usual. This being a Friday it was the local paper, the Shepton Herald & Pioneer, that provided the shelter he seemed to enjoy hiding behind.

"There's another letter for Wayne, from America," Elizabeth declared brightly.

"Good!" John mumbled, in between mouthfuls of toast.

"That's two this month. I think that's as many as he's had this year altogether." Elizabeth poured herself a cup of tea.

"Mmm," John murmured.

Elizabeth sat down at the table and looked critically at the local advertising that appeared on the front page of the paper.

"I do hope things are going well there," she continued. "Terri seemed such a nice girl and Wayne was so pleased to meet her after all those years - well, so was she."

"Mmm," - the sound emanated from somewhere behind the local cinema listings.

"John, would you please have the good grace and manners to put down the paper when I'm talking to you?" Elizabeth almost shouted, in her shrillest Headmistressy tone.

"Sorry," John Ball muttered, as he carefully folded the newspaper. "I'll be passing the factory later. I'll drop it in for Frank," he continued, as he picked up a slice of toast and began to butter it. "How did Wayne do in his 'O' levels?"

Elizabeth smiled.

"As far as I know, pretty well. At this rate, I think there's a good chance he'll be able to go on to university after Wormysted's. I think that would a first for Gas Street."

The wide smile on her face betrayed Elizabeth's pride in that statement. Wayne had been something of a protégé of hers when she had been a third grade class teacher at Gas Street Primary School. He had been the only child in his year to pass the eleven-plus exam and go on to Wormysted's. Indeed, he had been the last child to pass the exam for three years, until she had taken over from the retiring Mr. Braithwaite as Head of the school.

As Cedric Houghton-Hughes had been the only other eleven-plus success in the three years before Wayne, Elizabeth had quite a lot of respect for sisters Doris and Margaret. She thought about the events of five years earlier that had brought her much closer to Wayne. She smiled, and realised that John must have been on a similar wavelength, as he suddenly said "Do you remember that night we drove all the way down to London looking for the little tyke?" He laughed, spluttering toast crumbs over the table.

"Yes!" Elizabeth grinned. "Then I had to drive over to the far west of Ireland to find him, the very next day. Eleven years old and getting from one end of these islands to the other."

"Fancy him having that film star as a mum," John shook his head. "I still can't get over it. I saw her in that Tornado movie. Lovely-looking young woman, by 'eck."

Elizabeth frowned playfully. "Did you get as far up as her face, John Ball?"

John blushed.

"I erm, I better get off to work," he stammered, and then gave an embarrassed little cough as he stood up. "I'll er, I'll drop that letter in to Frank on my way past."

Elizabeth handed him the blue envelope, and smiled wryly as he kissed her on the cheek.

"Have a good day at school, love," he said.

"I will." Elizabeth Ball grinned. "I will."

Twenty-Two

The Churchman rushed through the open door into the darkened room, his expensive and ornate Cardinal's robes flying behind him. In the darkness, he could just make out a woman nursing a crying child. She looked up and her eyes caught the reflection of a candle flame, making her look even more furious than she obviously was.

"Where have you been?" she hissed.

The Cardinal crossed himself, then fell to his knees, took the woman's hand and kissed it.

"I came as quickly as possible, my Lady," the Cardinal gushed.

"Well, it was not nearly quick enough," the woman berated him angrily. "My little Prince here has got himself into quite a state." The child wailed even louder.

"What is it? What ails the boy?" Cardinal D'Abruzzo asked, his voice strained, panicked even.

"Look over there!" The woman used her free hand to point into the darkness, to a table on which the priest could just make out a golden chalice.

"What?" he asked, confused.

"Look in the cup, you fool!" the woman yelled angrily. The child wailed even louder.

The Cardinal stood and walked briskly to where the chalice stood. Inside the cup a small stone glowed with a faint green light, as though a bulb had been inserted into its centre. The Priest crossed himself urgently.

The child clambered down from his mother's knee.

"Your Irishman, Donleavy, promised me the last time he saw me that he'd find whoever was doing the magic," the child whimpered. "You both said I'd be safe. That all the nasty, evil ones had been, or would soon be, dealt with. Yet the stone now glows almost all the time. Someone, somewhere, is using a lot of magic. Only one of the immortals could use it like that. You promised us they were all dead. Yet, 'God's Assassin' seems very much alive to me!"

The Priest fell to his knees.

"Please forgive us, My Lord. The Sacred Order is doing all it can to find out who has the stones. We will find him. I swear to you."

The child stopped sobbing, and stared indignantly at the Cardinal.

"You had better..." the child stated; the threat implicit, the voice no longer that of a child. "You have but one week!" the child whispered, then turned and walked slowly back to its mother.

The Churchman crossed himself a third time, his face a mask of horror. After a last worried glance at the mother and child he backed out of the room, his head bowed.

Twenty-Three

"Is he...is he dead?" Bishop O'Leary stammered, as he stared at the slumped body of James Malone in the neighbouring chair. Bishop Donleavy sipped some wine and rolled it indulgently in his throat, his eyes alive with malevolent excitement.

"No, he is alive, but he will not return to the mortal realm in this age of man. Unless I will it," Sister Bernadette stated sadly, as she stepped back away from the motionless figure.

"What did you find out, Sister?" Donleavy croaked eagerly, as loudly as he could manage. Sister Bernadette, the Banshee Aoibheall, bowed towards the senior bishop.

"His mind was quite clear, Your Grace. Pizarro and Finn did die in the way he has said. The boy, the son of Aillen Mac Fionbharr, was there and he wielded power that matched Pizarro's; however, it was the boy's mortal guardian who dealt the death blow to Francisco Pizarro. The death of Canon Burke was an accident as he fled the scene."

Bishop O'Leary grimaced, as he glanced nervously at the body of James Malone again. "I thought only the true Tuatha De Danaan could wield such magic."

Bishop Donleavy snorted. "Pizarro was a half-breed, and yet he could wield enormous power." He looked at the banshee, and curled his lip disdainfully.

"So, where do we find this son of the devil, Banshee?"

The nun sighed.

"Malone knows of two names: Michael and Wayne. Which is the boy's true name? I cannot tell. As far as Malone is aware, the boy lives in England, Your Grace. He lives in a place called Yorkshire. His mortal guardian, the one who killed Pizarro, calls himself the boy's father. He has been raised by mere mortals, so his powers will be untrained."

"Excellent!" Donleavy gushed. "Do we have the boy's surname?"

The nun shook her head.

"It begins with Higg, but Malone's memory is not clear. He does not remember."

Donleavy pursed his lips.

"A pity; it will take time to find the boy when we have little more than two Christian names and a few letters of a surname to go on. However, it is a start. There must be a way of sourcing the information we require. You have done well!"

The old bishop began to rise slowly and arthritically from his chair.

"Bishop O'Leary, would you please call my assistant, Father Logan, for me? Have him bring the car to the service door and have him dispose of our poor young friend's body. We will make it appear that, in a moment of insurmountable remorse and insanity, he really did decide to end it all this time. A sad tale indeed! You will tell the detective leading the Gardai team investigating the events at Finaan that Malone finally confessed to you the murders of both Father Pizarro and Canon Burke, after they had discovered that he and Father Callaghan had been embezzling church funds. His previous suicide had merely been his plan of escape." Bishop O'Leary nodded his assent, and rushed off immediately.

The old man struggled around his desk until he stood before the slumped figure of James Malone. He crossed himself before delivering a blessing to the former priest.

"Even those under Satan's spell deserve the blessing of our Lord," he sighed, as he concluded his prayer for the young man's soul. Donleavy then looked up at Father de Feren.

"Your task now becomes the most important work yet done in the history of Christendom. You will go to England; to Yorkshire. You will use all of the Order's resources to find this spawn of the devil and deal with it. Do not be fooled by its appearance, when you do succeed in finding it. It is not a boy. It is possessed. It is evil. As you can see..." The old bishop waved his hand over James' body, "...it has the ability to bewitch those who lack faith, and the weak of mind."

Father de Feren nodded. "We will succeed, Your Grace." He beckoned Sister Bernadette to follow him. The nun smiled.

Sister Bernadette knew much more about the contents of the mind of James Malone than she had said, but that was her business.

Twenty-Four

"Yes, two of the prawn cocktails please, and then..."

Wayne, in the guise of his 'cousin' Finn, looked expectantly at Stephanie Fleming as she peered at the menu in Eastwood's fish restaurant.

"Erm, fish and chips, I suppose," Stephanie shrugged. "I mean, this is a fish and chip shop, isn't it?"

Wayne gasped at the hint of criticism in her voice.

"Hey! This is an incredibly sophisticated restaurant...that just happens to be attached to a fish and chip shop, or so Wayne tells me. I mean a fish and chip shop would not serve anything as cosmopolitan as a prawn cocktail, would it?" Wayne, in his Finn disguise, drawled. "It even has Dover Sole on the menu, and wine. It has a choice of wines, see? Really good stuff...'Black Tower', 'Blue Nun,' 'Piat D'Or,' 'Mateus Rose.' They even do Californian wine in a carafe. You wouldn't have wine with fast food, would you? It would be like asking for a glass of Beaujolais to swig with your burger and fries in a MacDonalds back home."

He looked up at the ancient waitress.

"So, two haddock specials with chips and...?" He glanced at Stephanie and raised his eyebrows. "What the hell are mushy peas?"

Stephanie twisted her face. "Bleargh!" she mouthed, and stuck her fingers in her mouth in the vomit mime.

"I've gotta try 'em - they can't be as nasty as grits. Just the one portion of mushy peas, please, and hold the bread and butter," Wayne stated authoritatively.

The waitress peered myopically at her pad as she scratched out the order.

"Old bread and butter? We only do fresh in here, love."

Wayne sighed and glanced at Stephanie, who was giggling and trying to hide behind her menu. When Stephanie Fleming giggled, she screwed up her button nose in the cutest way imaginable.

"Er, I just meant no bread and butter, thank you. Ma'am. Oh yeah, and a bottle of ice cold Blue Nun.'"

The waitress gave Wayne a look that he knew meant Damn Yank! She'd probably been a jilted G.I. girlfriend during the war. Overpaid, oversexed and over here - and if that young lass didn't take care, over her!

"So two prawn cocktail, two Haddock special and chips and a bottle of Blue Nun, as cold as we can make it, two glasses. One mushy peas. No bread and butter."

The waitress repeated the order, whilst casting Stephanie a suspicious glance. "Are you eighteen, love?" she asked, pursing her lips disapprovingly.

"Yes, just." Stephanie smiled sweetly. "This is part of my birthday celebration."

The waitress pursed her lips even tighter as she cast Wayne a dirty look, then she turned and hobbled arthritically towards the kitchens. Wayne laughed, in what he imagined to be a manly, American, way.

"Hell in tarnation, we're the only people in here under sixty-five."

Stephanie glanced around.

"It's the pensioner's special: two pounds for fishcake and chips and a pot of tea. I don't think she believed I was eighteen, so I don't think I'd have got away with asking for the pensioner's discount." She giggled again, and Wayne Higginbotham knew that he was in love.

It must have been love for Wayne to decline bread and butter. There was nothing Wayne Higginbotham liked more than filling a thin slice of white bread with lashings of butter, and then hot chips. It was the way the heat melted the butter and the mixture of hot beef dripping and melted butter ran down the chin. Mmm. Not exactly attractive on a first date, though, and not very Californian.

"But I've never had wine in a proper restaurant before," Stephanie Fleming giggled, as Wayne splashed the clear, golden, Liebfraumilch into her glass.

"Shh," he cautioned her gently. "Don't forget, you're meant to be eighteen."

Stephanie made a mock serious face and deepened her voice in imitation of Mickey's sonorous, deep American drawl.

"Sorry Finn, just like, trying to have a little fun, you know!"

Wayne laughed, his whiter-than-white Californian teeth dazzling his companion as they sat by the canal side window. A candle on the table reflected romantically in the dark water outside, and in her dilated pupils. What beautiful bright blue eyes Stephanie Fleming had.

Wayne Higginbotham had never been happier, despite his apparent rejection by his real mom, which tonight seemed to be more than making up for. Here he was, sat in what he considered to be a reasonably posh restaurant, opposite the girl of his dreams. This almost matched the moment when he had initially met his birth mother, Terri, over five years earlier.

Wayne had managed to make the evening's arrangements without raising any suspicions in the Higginbotham household. As far as Doris and Frank were aware, Wayne was staying at a friend's house for the evening. He had promised faithfully to be home by ten-thirty. They were going to be out, anyway - Doris at a friend's house, and Frank at work. The evening was going to be paid for by Wayne's earnings from a Saturday job that he had started a couple of weeks earlier at the town's hardware store: Manly's. The job was hard work. It involved lifting gas canisters and moving heavy boxes around Manly's ancient warehouse, which was tucked down one of Shepton High Street's narrow alleys, but Fred Manly paid him the princely sum of over two pounds for every full Saturday worked. If he was going to have a steady girlfriend to take out, Wayne was going to need all the money he could lay his hands on.

"What are you thinking about?" Stephanie asked, in her lovely, melodic, softly-accented voice. "You look a million miles away."

Wayne took a large sip of his wine, and laughed.

"I was just reflecting on what a lucky buck I am, being here with someone as awesome as you."

Stephanie smiled coyly, and ran her fingers through her hair.

The waitress took the empty prawn cocktail glasses and placed two large plates of battered haddock and chips with small side salads in front of the couple. She cast the 'American' a filthy look.

"Enjoy your dinner, won't you, love?" she hissed sarcastically. Then she bustled away through the still-quiet restaurant.

"You don't have fish and chips in America, do you?" Stephanie asked, swiftly changing the subject.

Wayne shrugged. "Not where I'm from. It's all hamburgers, French fries, and hot dogs." He took another large sip of the German white wine.

Stephanie flashed him a dazzling smile. "It must be so exciting living in Los Angeles. Have you ever seen any movie stars?"

Wayne shrugged casually. "Yeah, sure. In fact, I've met Terri Thorne a couple of times."

"Who?" Stephanie asked, her forehead creasing in a puzzled frown.

Mickey refilled his glass. "You know, she's that beautiful, blonde actress. She's been on television an awful lot and in quite a few big movies. She was in that disaster movie Tornado, you know?"

Stephanie shrugged, and politely refused the offer of more wine by putting her hand over her glass.

"Oh, no thanks, I'm not used to it. I'll be getting tipsy. I never got to see Tornado. I don't like disaster movies anyway; they're far too scary.

Who else have you seen? You must see loads and loads of stars. Tell me about the city, the beaches, and Disneyland and Hollywood?"

Wayne held up a hand in mock protest.

"Whoa, slow down, girl! I'll be here all night boring the pants off you, telling you all about something we can talk about another time. I want to know all about you: the beautiful, bright, and bubbly Stephanie Fleming."

He took a large sip of wine; willing a very wicked thought that had just bounced into his head, regarding the subject of Stephanie's pants, to go away.

Stephanie grimaced, and rolled her eyes. "Oh no, my life is just not at all interesting. I'm so boring. I mean, this is my entire life story...okay. I was born here in Shepton and I've lived at number 59 Greenacres all my life. My dad's an English teacher at the Girl's High School and so was my mum - a teacher, that is - until me and my sister were born, and then she gave it up to look after us. We have a dog called Butch, and a cat called Kitty, and a goldfish called Jaws. I've never even been out of England. We go to Cornwall every year for our holidays and that's it - that's me. That's my life."

Wayne laughed. "Hey, that's not boring. Tell me about Shepton. It seems a kinda cute little ol' town. I mean it's got a real live castle that must be, like, hundreds of years old. Nothing in L.A. is over a hundred years old."

Stephanie sighed resignedly. "A lot of people like it. Believe it or not, folk from down South come up here for their holidays, you know? They hire cottages in the Dales and drive around going Isn't it quaint? and gawping at all the local peasants, saying how they'd like to get out of the rat race and spend their lives leaning on gates, chewing straw and uttering lines of wisdom like There's nowt so queer as folk, and 'Appen! But they never do. They go back to their exciting lives in London and laugh at the thick Yorkshire folk they saw. The castle isn't that special, it just happened to get rebuilt after the Civil War. It's only famous for surrendering. All I want to do is to get away from here. I mean, going to university like my boy...like my friend, should help. You just don't know how lucky you are, living somewhere hot and sunny and in such a big city where there is so much going on all the time. Nothing ever happens here, ever!"

Wayne ignored that she had almost alluded to having a boyfriend and, noticing that her glass was quite low, offered Stephanie a refill, which she politely refused. He eagerly recharged his own glass, and took a sip. The wine was so cool and clear and crisp. It slipped down very easily.

"Tell me about Hollywood?" Stephanie pleaded.

Wayne sat back in his chair and waxed lyrical about a place he had only ever seen on television. Stephanie sat transfixed, taking in every word and savouring every glamorous name that Finn dropped.

"Wow!" was all she could say when Wayne had finished. He reached out for the bottle of wine, but, to his horror, Wayne noticed that it was very nearly empty. This was the first time in his life that Wayne had drunk more than half a glass of wine. He had felt that Finn was going to have to be sophisticated if he was going to charm Stephanie, and that had meant ordering a bottle of wine with their fish and chips. But how had it gone so quickly?

"Are you okay?" he heard Stephanie ask.

"Sure!" he responded, realising as soon as he had said it that the word had been uttered in his ordinary Wayne voice as opposed to Mickey's. "Sure!" he repeated with more American gusto, continuing "So tell me about your friend, the Oxford scholar."

Stephanie coughed politely and shifted in her seat, her face flushed slightly. "Martin? Oh, it's nothing serious. We're just good friends. He'll probably dump me as soon as he gets to Oxford, anyway."

Stephanie looked away, out of the window over the darkened canal. Wayne knew he'd embarrassed her, but what she had said had delighted him. Even so, he thought he ought to give her a moment to compose herself.

"I guess I'd just better pop to the restroom for a second."

Wayne stood, and realised he could hear a faint buzzing in his head. He strolled, slightly unsteadily, to the toilet, splashed his face with water then, covered his face with his hands for a second. He felt slightly dizzy, but he would be okay. He dried his hands under the drier and stepped back out into the restaurant, returned to the table, and sat down.

Stephanie gasped.

"Wayne? What are you doing here?" She sounded horrified and in that moment Wayne realised that he'd stopped being Finn at some point in the toilet. He thought as fast as his befuddled mind would allow.

"Oh, hi Steph, I, er...I was just looking for my cousin, you know, Finn? The American?" Stephanie smiled at him, but looked more than a little perturbed.

"He went to the toilet," she stated, somewhat confused. "He didn't mention that you would be coming."

Wayne stood as quickly as he could manage.

"I'll, er, I'll just go and get him," he stammered, as he edged as quickly as he could away from the table.

"Well, why don't you just wait here until he comes out?" Stephanie asked, her face screwed up in bewilderment.

"No, no, it's okay," Wayne blustered. "I have an important message for him, from America, Los Angeles, America...you know, California...er...in America."

Stephanie giggled. "Yes, Wayne, I think I know where he's from."

"Yes, er, right...bye!"

Wayne swiftly disappeared off into the small toilets of the fish restaurant. Finn emerged almost immediately, and marched nonchalantly to the table.

"Sorry I took so long," he grinned sheepishly.

"Did you see Wayne?" Stephanie asked, glancing back towards the toilets. "Believe it or not, he just went into the loos to find you."

"Who? Wayne?" Finn asked, looking as baffled as he could manage.

"Wayne Higginbotham, your cousin? You can't possibly have missed him." Stephanie shook her head, and took a small sip of wine. "He just walked up and sat down at your place as though he'd been there all night. In fact, he was even dressed exactly like you."

"No way!" Wayne gasped, pretending to look totally shocked. "Man, he's always followed me round like a puppy dog, but to try and steal my girl, and dress like me? I'll kill him. No wonder he must have hidden from me in those restrooms."

Stephanie shook her head again, and shrugged. "I suppose he's okay, you know, for a bit of a geek. He actually asked me out the other week. Did he tell you?"

Wayne spluttered into his wine and feigned total amazement. "Wayne asked a chick like you out? You are kidding me?"

Stephanie laughed.

"No, really. It was at the Youth Club. Anne was so horrid to him. He was quite sweet really, I suppose. I felt quite sorry for him."

"Really?" Wayne asked with a raised eyebrow.

Stephanie shrugged. "Well, only a bit. I mean...can you imagine him taking me out? Nowhere would let him in. He only looks about fourteen," she laughed.

Wayne couldn't help but grimace a little as he drained the last dregs from his glass. The table seemed to move away from him as he tried to put his hand on it, and he inadvertently slapped his knee. He realised that he was having to concentrate extra hard on maintaining his Finn persona.

Stephanie began to tell him all about her dreams of visiting California, when Wayne coughed politely and made an excuse about having to go back to the bathroom.

"Are you sure you're okay?" Stephanie asked, with a degree of concern. "You've gone very pale."

"I think the fish might have disagreed with me," Wayne gasped, realising he had forgotten to take on Mickey's tan. "Anyway, I had better find out what happened to Wayne. He didn't come out of the toilet...I mean, restroom."

Once inside the safety of the toilet, Wayne let himself go back to his own shape. He gripped the edges of the sink to stop the whole place spinning. He felt sick, but knew that if he threw up, he would blow the whole date.

"How could you have been so stupid?" he demanded of his reflection in the mirror, just as an elderly man walked in. The man looked at him, shook his head, and locked himself in a cubicle.

Wayne took his level of concentration to a new level, took a deep breath, checked his reflection and walked boldly back into the restaurant, which was now filling up rapidly with its usual, slightly younger, Saturday night trade. The pensioners' discount ended at nine o'clock. He sat down and noticed immediately that Stephanie was staring at him with an open mouth.

"Are you okay, Stephanie?" he asked.

Stephanie sniggered, and then slowly leaned towards him. "That's so mean, Finn - taking the mickey out of your cousin!" She stifled a snorting giggle by putting her hand over her mouth. Wayne stared uncomprehendingly at her beautiful features, which were becoming increasingly blurred.

"Where'd you get the Wayne wig?" she asked and then began to giggle again.

Wayne grinned knowingly, reached up, and felt his head. Instead of Finn's long straight black hair, he could feel his own natural bushy curls. He gulped, and then laughed.

"Cool, eh? Close your eyes," he whispered to Stephanie.

She did as she was told, still giggling manically. Wayne's mop of curls morphed magically back into the long sleek shiny tresses of Michael Finnegan.

"Okay...you can open them now," he whispered.

Two tables behind Wayne and Stephanie, an old woman's mouth dropped open. She took off her glasses, and then sniffed her cup of tea.

"What's up, love?" the old woman's female companion asked. The old woman replaced her glasses, and took a long gulp of tea.

"Eeeh, I think I'm going daft, or else senile, Vera. Either that, or that young bloke over there has got some newfangled hairdo that changes wit' flick of a switch. I could've sworn I just watched his mop of curls go all straight and long."

Vera sniffed. "Aye, it'll be some new Japanese doodaa. They can do owt nowadays."

"Wow, how did you change that so quickly?" Stephanie asked, amazed at the swift transformation.

"Oh, a whole lotta practice," Wayne lied.

"Can I have it?" Stephanie asked.

"What?" Wayne asked.

"The wig, silly," Stephanie grinned.

"No, no...couldn't do that," Wayne gabbled.

"Oh go on...let me just try it on?" she pleaded.

"No!" Wayne snapped, just a little too sharply.

Stephanie pouted and placed her cutlery across her plate in a demonstration that she had finished. "Fine," she muttered, just loud enough for Wayne to hear.

Wayne thought quickly through the mists of his increasingly befuddled brain.

"I'm just very precious when it comes to wigs and stuff. You know, I once got headlice at junior high and I passed them on to a girl who I thought was real cute. She's hated me ever since."

Stephanie looked up at him from under hooded eyes. "Okay," she smiled. "I guess I'll let you off for being a spoilsport. Did you find Wayne, by the way?"

Wayne shook his head. "It's real weird, but there was no sign of him in the restroom. He must have slipped right by me and I didn't notice him. I guess my mind is just concentrating on you."

Stephanie giggled.

Wayne, now confident that he was fully back in Finn's form, decided that the best thing he could do to salvage the situation would be to bring the evening to an early close.

"Well, I guess I'd better get the bill and get you home, ma'am, before your pa sends out a posse as a search party," he joked, in an accent that was now far more rural Texas than streetwise L.A.

Stephanie laughed and tossed her hair over one shoulder, which caused Wayne's mouth to drop open for several seconds, until he realised how stupid he looked.

"It's okay. My dad said I had to be in by ten 'o' clock sharp, and it's still only just after nine."

Wayne took a deep breath.

129

"Oh, okay. Look Stephanie, I'm sorry, but the reason Wayne wanted me was to tell me that my mother's ill. I've gotta get home as soon as possible."

"Is your mother over here too?" Stephanie asked. "And I thought you said you hadn't seen him?"

Wayne nodded. "Er, well, no, no, I didn't...not exactly...but I think that would have been what he had wanted to tell me, had he found me, that is, because Mom wasn't real well yesterday."

"Are you sure that you're not just escaping? I haven't bored you, have I?" Stephanie asked, looking extremely worried. "I mean...compared to all those Californian girls, you must think us Yorkshire lasses are dead plain."

She leaned across the table again. Wayne moved in towards her.

"No, Stephanie Fleming you are, without a doubt, the most beautiful girl I have ever seen in my life." He sighed.

Instead of looking pleased, however, Stephanie looked confused.

"Finn, your eyes..." she said, sounding very concerned. "Your eyes are blue. I'm sure they were brown earlier."

Wayne took yet another deep breath. Now he felt really queasy.

"No, they're brown - always have been," he stated confidently.

Stephanie blinked, and looked into his eyes again. Finn's eyes were definitely brown, a deep chocolate brown. She sat back in her chair.

"Oh my God! That's so weird," she said, shaking her head. "I could have sworn your eyes were sort of blue, or green, a second ago. My God, that wine must have gone straight to my head."

"Really?" Wayne asked incredulously. "It must have been a trick of the light. You know, a reflection off the canal or something."

"It must definitely be the wine," Stephanie confided, shaking her head. "I've only ever drunk one glass before. I must be a bit drunk."

Wayne coughed. "Aye, me too."

"God, now you even sound like Wayne now!" Stephanie laughed. "Stop taking the mickey out of him - it's mean."

Wayne grinned, although the entire room was now spinning.

"I'm real mean like that," he laughed. "Er, Ma'am?" he shouted to the waitress who shuffled over, her face still capable of souring milk at twenty paces. "Could I have the check, please, and can I get a cab?"

The waitress scowled and cocked her head to one side. "You what, love?"

"The bill and a taxi, please," Wayne muttered.

Stephanie giggled. "Wow, that really did sound like proper Yorkshire."

Wayne grinned as the waitress bustled off again. "I took drama lessons in the ninth grade. Hollywood dreams, and all that."

He was aware that Stephanie had cupped her head in her hands and was leaning on her elbows on the table, gazing at him admiringly. No one had ever gazed at Wayne Higginbotham like that.

"I'm real sorry I've gotta go," Wayne sighed, as he took his change from the waitress, tossed a fifty pence piece on to the table as a tip, and began to help Stephanie on with her coat. "Have you enjoyed yourself?"

Stephanie nodded eagerly and, before he knew what was happening, planted a kiss right on his lips.

"Can we do it again, sometime soon?" she asked.

Wayne smiled and kissed her back, somewhat clumsily. Stephanie flinched slightly.

"No silly, not that," she breathed, as she pulled away. She glanced around at what looked like an ocean of old people glowering at them disapprovingly. "I meant go out again," she whispered, then giggled.

"I'd love to," Wayne whispered back, once again sounding much more like Wayne Higginbotham than Michael Finnegan.

Once they were out of the restaurant, standing in the September twilight, Stephanie turned towards him. She reached out, put her arms around his neck, pulled his head down and kissed him again. Wayne thought he had died and gone to heaven when he felt her tongue burst into his mouth. He'd heard of guys blowing their first kiss by being too aggressive, so, after his last amateurish effort, he let Stephanie take charge. The kiss seemed to last forever. She eventually pulled back, and looked into his eyes.

"I like you, Mickey Finn," she purred.

So, Wayne Higginbotham had kissed a girl properly for the first time in his life. It wasn't even slightly marred for him by the fact that she thought she was kissing someone else. Someone totally different, someone who didn't even actually exist. Wayne would remember that kiss until the day he died.

As the taxi carrying a waving Stephanie Fleming disappeared into the distance, Wayne blew out a huge sigh of relief that he hadn't thrown up everywhere. He looked around quickly to check that no one was watching, and then allowed Michael Finnegan to slowly morph back into the shape of a smug, grinning Wayne Higginbotham. He punched the air in delight and then set off on the short stagger home.

Thank goodness Doris was out and Frank wouldn't be home for a while. That gave him a chance to sober up a little and also to reflect on what had been a wonderful night, even if it had nearly been a disaster on more than one occasion. He was going to have to improve in the shape-shifting department. Even so, Wayne Higginbotham's bad times were finally over.

As Wayne had emerged from the shape of Michael Finnegan and staggered off, whistling down the street, a drunk who had just come out of Eastwood's neighbouring takeaway section caught sight of him mid-transformation. The drunk dropped his fish supper on the pavement where he stood, and vowed there and then that he would never ever touch another drop as long as he lived.

In a darkened room in the very heart of the Vatican City, a rock that had been suffused in a faint green glow slowly dimmed, and returned to its former status as a dull common pebble.

Twenty-Five

James Malone could hear the sound of water trickling nearby and the warmth of the sun gently kissing the skin of his cheek. He slowly opened his eyes and, blinking in the light, inhaled sharply. The smell of clean, fresh air filled his lungs.

He was no longer in a gloomy room, sitting opposite an ancient bishop, half-hidden in the shadows. He was lying on a soft carpet of long, lush, green meadow grass, which rippled in the soft, warm breeze like the waves of a tropical sea.

Even more surprising was the fact that he discovered himself to be as naked as the day he'd been born. He clambered up onto one elbow and looked around. A babbling, rock filled stream meandered leisurely past him, down the hill towards a small lake in what seemed to be the middle of a wide green valley.

The hillside meadow in which James was lying was filled with glorious yellow buttercups and hordes of daisies, all bending in the warm breeze. The top of the meadow was bordered by a forest of deciduous trees - oaks, ash, chestnuts - and behind the trees, mountains. A wall of grey rock shining in the sun that seemed familiar, and yet seemed somehow bizarrely out of context. Above the mountains a vivid blue sky was punctuated by a smattering of fluffy white clouds floating slowly by. The other side of the valley matched the side he was on; sloping meadows, then trees, then rock and then sky.

Despite his nakedness, James was warm. The sun was high in the sky and his first thought was that he had dreamed everything that had happened, and he was back in California. If so, what the hell was he doing lying on a hillside, buck naked, in broad daylight? His second thought, which sent a chill shivering down his spine, was that he was dead.

"Holy Jesus!" he gasped out loud, and sat bolt upright. A bird warbled loudly nearby and James jumped in alarm. He closed his eyes and then slowly opened them again, then put his hand on his forehead. His skin felt slightly clammy, but otherwise normal. He pinched his forearm, much harder than he had intended. "Ouch!" he exclaimed.

He looked around frantically, and then stood up. As far as the eye could see, the scene was one of bucolic idyll. No walls, no fences, no roads, no people. On a distant hillside, James could just make out what looked like a few white sheep, grazing lazily on the rich grass. James took a deep breath.

"So that's it then. Here I am, just over thirty and I've gone and got myself killed." A wasp buzzed nearby, and James clicked his tongue. "Typical, my own personal version of paradise and it's got bloody wasps in it."

"It's not your version of paradise...it's mine," a soft, feminine voice spoke, right next to him. James quickly covered himself and turned to see the nun, Sister Bernadette, standing there - shockingly, every bit as naked as he was. He couldn't help but run his eyes up and down her perfect body as his mouth dropped open and shut repeatedly, soundlessly. Her long, shining raven hair cascaded over her shoulders, and her emerald green eyes flashed wickedly.

"Well at least somebody's pleased to see me," she grinned coyly as she glanced at James' hurried attempt to adequately cover his nudity, and his inadvertently apparent, growing appreciation of her female form. Aoibheall pretended to gasp as she raised her hand to her mouth and averted her eyes in mock embarrassment. She turned and walked off down the field unhurriedly, and cast a fleeting glance to see if James was following.

He remembered now what had happened. He had been sat in an office in St. Patrick's Cathedral, attempting to explain what had transpired at Finaan without giving anything away about the English boy. The nun - in fact, the banshee, who was now strolling slowly down through the meadow, unashamedly naked - had touched his forehead, which Donleavy had said would scramble his mind. So that was it. He was probably not dead, hence the wasp and the lack of angels; just mad. Quite, quite mad.

He glanced down. Even if he was dead, he still had the lustful urges of the physical body and the bits and pieces that went with it.

"Are you going to stand there all day like a bashful schoolboy?" Aoibheall's voice teased him from a little way down the hill. "Or are you going to come and talk to me?"

Malone blushed even redder. If I'm mad, or dead, I suppose I've got nothing to be ashamed of, he thought as he started to amble down through the meadow, his hands strategically cupping his embarrassment.

"Do you like it here?" Aoibheall asked plaintively, as he drew up alongside her. Before he had time to respond, she took his hand and began to lead him further down the hill.

"It's how I imagined paradise should be," she continued. Her face was raised up as she looked up at the mountains and breathed in deeply, filling her lungs with fresh mountain air. "When I was trapped in my little cell in the convent, I would come here all the time and run naked through the fields. It felt so nice to be rid of that horrible coarse woollen habit." She laughed, her voice as melodious as the mountain stream. "Then I'd jump in the lake and swim all the way to the other side, and then lie down and dry slowly in the sun. It passed the time. One hundred and thirty five years is a very long time to pass."

She quickly glanced round at James and caught him staring at her naked form again. He looked away quickly, flushed with embarrassment, and she laughed again, sweetly. There was no scorn or derision in her voice, just a playful teasing tone that was probably even more embarrassing.

"Yes, I do like it here," James gushed, looking as far away from Aoibheall as he could. "It's like Mayo, sort of, crossed with a bit of Switzerland and some Southern California."

Aoibheall laughed again. It crossed James' mind that banshees seemed to laugh easily, contrary to their hag like wailing image.

"I've never seen Switzerland, or California," Aoibheall stated wistfully. "But if it is like this, I would love to go there one day. This is based on Connemara; but in a perfect summer, a summer in Erin's Isle, long before the Celts ever came, or the English."

She smiled sadly and shook her head. "It's a place that never really was, nor ever will be."

They both looked ahead, down to the lake.

"Am I mad? Or am I dead?" James asked.

Aoibheall laughed again. "Neither, you eejit," she gently chided him, then took his hand and set off down the hill again, glancing surreptitiously at his groin.

"I don't think dead men get that excited!" she laughed, as he pulled his hand away from hers to try and cover himself again. "You are in a special place in my mind and I am in yours. It's a fairy thing. We can talk here without those bloodsucking priests hanging on to our every word."

James grimaced. "Ah, so this is my interrogation, is it? Well, it's better than being tied to a chair and having my fingernails pulled out, I suppose."

Aoibheall laughed again. "That could be arranged," she grinned and moved around in front of him, taking both his hands and placing them around her waist. She wrapped her arms around him and pulled him close; he felt her soft warm flesh press against his, and gulped nervously as his body reacted naturally. She looked up into his eyes, her emerald pupils glinting mischievously in the sunlight.

"By the feel of it, you obviously find this type of torture slightly preferable," she laughed again, before releasing him and jauntily skipping away.

"Beats the rack, I suppose," James shrugged. A soft Scottish brogue from some far distant other world echoed in his mind:

"Do you expect me to talk?"

"No Mister Bond - I expect you to gambol through the countryside with a beautiful naked girl..."

The thought of Carrie crossed his mind and he felt a severe pang of guilt. Here he was, frolicking in an imaginary field with a naked nymph straight out of the pages of Irish mythology, and he would probably never see Carrie again. He sighed, and began to descend further down the hill.

Aoibheall had sat down, and was hugging her knees to her chest. James sat down beside her and followed her eyes on to the surface of the lake, where a pure white swan slipped gracefully through the gleaming, mirror-like water.

"There will be no need for interrogation, James Malone, for I know what happened that night at Aillen Mac Fionnbharr's cottage," she murmured.

James raised his eyebrows.

"I have seen everything that you saw," she continued. "I have seen it through your eyes. How Pizarro stabbed Mac Fionnbharr, how he broke your arm and how the boy fought him, blow for blow. I saw the Englishman jump over the wall, hit Pizarro, and then hurl the knife that killed him. I saw Pizarro fall back into the flaming cottage and I saw it collapse around him. It was what he deserved. I have seen it all; just as you saw it."

James took a deep breath. "Are you going to tell them?"

Aoibheall turned and looked at him. "Tell them about Wayne Higgins? Or is it Higginton? The son of Aillen Mac Fionnbharr? Tell them that he lives in the Dales of Yorkshire, so that they can kill the son of one of my people?"

James looked confused. "Your people?"

Aoibheall looked back towards the lake.

"The banshees were once a part of the Tuatha De Danaan. Faithful wives, daughters, mothers...now all gone, save me. I have no love for this Aillen Mac Fionbharr, James Malone, nor for any of his line. It was he who cast us from our homes and forced us into our long exile. It was he who was responsible for the long centuries that I have spent wandering this island, waiting for a chance to gain my retribution. The near century and a half I have spent locked in a dark convent cell, where I ne'er saw the sun's light, save through glass and bars."

"I take it that's a yes, then," James sighed.

Aoibheall laughed, but the sweet sound was tempered by a weary sadness.

"No, James Malone, I will not tell them all I know, for I love the Sacred Order of St. Gregory even less than the cursed Royal line of the Tuatha De Danaan. I know that I am the last of all the immortals. The boy is born of mortal womb, so he will only have the life span of mortal man. Do you think if they knew that, that they would suffer me to live?"

James snorted. "No chance!"

Aoibheall fell back onto the grass, and stared into the bright blue sky.

"That is my thought too. I will tell them a little, help them a little. I will do enough to avoid rousing their suspicions. I will cheat the Order. I will save the boy for myself and gain my retribution through him."

James frowned. "You intend to kill Wayne yourself?"

Aoibheall laughed again. This time the sound was joyful, albeit chiding.

"No, you eejit, I did not say I would kill him, but he has the stones, doesn't he? The stones that belonged to Aillen Mac Fionbharr and to Francisco Pizarro?"

James was confused. "What do you intend to do?"

Aoibheall turned on her side, facing Malone. "Do you find me comely, James Malone?"

"Of course," he mumbled, turning away from the banshee.

"As comely as your American girl?"

James turned back to face her, but kept his eyes firmly on hers.

"Yes, probably."

"Only probably?" she teased, sulkily.

James rubbed his hand over his face. "I don't even know your real name. I don't suppose it's really Sister Bernadette?"

Aoibheall grinned. "Sister Bernadette would die of shame rather than be seen in front of a man without ten pounds of coarse, itchy black wool covering her sinful body. My name is Aoibheall."

A wasp buzzed over James' head. He ducked.

"Well Aoibheall, would you be good enough to tell me why there are bloody wasps in your version of paradise?"

She laughed. "To make it as real as possible, of course."

James pondered her answer momentarily, then grinned a little sheepishly.

"And why are we totally buck naked, as pleasant as that is, looking from my direction? I mean...I didn't have to get rid of itchy clothing."

Aoibheall nodded, and smiled shyly for the first time. "Thank you. Your nakedness pleases me too. Nakedness symbolises no secrets. As soon as I laid my eyes on you I knew you had a good soul, and that you would reveal the truth to me."

She glanced down at his body, and her mouth curled in a wicked grin. "The truth often reveals itself of its own free will, if all the layers of vanity and ego are removed."

James coughed and sat up self-consciously, his face bright crimson again. Aoibheall laughed, and rolled onto her back.

"Ah, there is still a reticent priest lurking in you, James Malone."

James coughed. "So, you haven't answered my question. What will happen to the boy?"

Aoibheall, her eyes closed, smiled. "Trust me, he will be fine...as long as he renders to me that which is owed to me."

James bit his lip. "The stones?"

Aoibheall nodded. "As the last true immortal of the Tuatha De Danaan, the stones should be mine. It will be due payment for the suffering I have endured. A blood debt, finally paid in full for my sweet Culhainnein."

James Malone took a deep breath. "And if he won't give you the stones, willingly...?"

Aoibheall stretched her body out sensuously on the grass. "Could you resist me, James Malone?" James gulped and drew his knees tight up to his chest. The banshee laughed. "Of course not, nor shall he. He is a young boy, with a young boy's lust."

James looked away from the stunning body of the woman, and perused the view over the lake.

"Aoibheall, am I ever going to be allowed to return to normality?"

Aoibheall shaded her eyes from the sun. Her red lips parted and her mouth twisted in a half smile.

"You are truly an honourable man, James Malone. You whisper that you find me comely and your body proudly proclaims the extent of your desire. Yet you lie next to my naked form and all you do is ask questions. You will return to the mortal realm if..." - she twisted up nimbly, planted a firm kiss on his lips and playfully groped and tweaked his manhood - "...you can catch me."

Before James had time to react she had jumped up, and was racing down through the grass towards the lake. He pulled himself up and began to run after her. The grass got taller and taller. He could hear her giggling as she ran.

"Come on, James Malone, I'm at least a couple of thousand years older than you," she shouted over her shoulder, before plunging head-first into the shimmering waters of the lake with barely a splash. James was aware of the beating of wings on the water as the swan fled before him, as he dived into the lake after Aoibheall.

It was cold, much colder than he expected, freezing his every sinew, and it was much darker and deeper. He wondered why he hadn't broken the surface of the water when he had made such a shallow dive, yet the light of the surface seemed much farther above him than he had expected. He pushed with all his might and strained to reach the surface, yet it remained tantalisingly out of reach. He could feel bubbles pouring out of his nose as his lungs emptied and began to ache. More bubbles surrounded him, rushing angrily past his flailing form, and his ears felt as though they were about to explode. An express train seemed to be travelling through his head, as he made one last desperate push with his legs and arms.

James emerged into the light with a huge gasp, and gulped in desperate lungfuls of air in between spluttering coughs. Around him he could make out dark, dirty, warehouse buildings, as seagulls circled and cried above his head. He spun around in the water and noticed a black car disappearing along one of the wharves: The Bishop's limo. James recognised where he was from his schoolboy fishing trips. He'd been unceremoniously dumped in the River Liffey, just before it flows out into Dublin bay.

James Malone struck out for the nearest bank. It seemed that his brain hadn't been scrambled and that he wasn't dead, yet. If he could reach the bank he would be okay. If he could just reach the bank he could do something about stopping the Order. As he swam, he realised that he had been stripped of his clothes. He wondered how real his dream of being in Aoibheall's enchanted valley had been. He wondered exactly how much she had told them.

He raised his head to see what progress he had made, but the bank seemed to be no closer. As dirty, salty, Liffey water splashed into his face and filled his mouth, and as he felt his limbs freeze in the cold, he wondered if he would live long enough to find out.

Twenty-Six

Frank Higginbotham was tired; very, very tired. He had worked eight consecutive days on a twelve-hour shift pattern at the factory. Two of his co-workers, who also screwed thingummys onto widgets and put them into boxes, were off sick, and demand for the thingummied up widgets was absolutely unprecedented.

It was nearly half-past eight on the Saturday night, and Frank's shift was nearly over. He was not due to return to work until the following Monday morning, so Sunday promised to be a totally lazy day. He licked his lips in anticipation at the prospect of a glass of Mackeson stout in front of the edited soccer highlights on 'Match of the Day', later that evening. Half an hour more and he would be finished. Frank packed another widget into a box with a satisfied sigh, and patted his pocket.

John Ball had dropped a letter in to the factory earlier that afternoon; another letter from America addressed to Wayne. Frank knew it was from Wayne's birth mother, Terri, and although he knew that Wayne would be delighted to hear from her, he also had some mixed emotions about the whole thing.

Frank felt guilty for playing his little role as a secret courier, a go-between in the conspiracy that prevented Doris from finding out that Wayne and Terri wrote to each other. Doris would have been furious had she known. No, worse than that - she would have been apoplectic with rage! As far as she was concerned, she was Wayne's mum, and Terri had relinquished any claim to him from the very moment she had signed the adoption consent forms.

Doris had even conspired to keep Wayne's adoption a secret from him. Wayne had only found out that he wasn't the Higginbotham's natural son at the age of eleven, when he had overheard a doctor discussing his family history while he was in hospital. As far as Doris was concerned, Wayne would have been as guilty of infidelity as any philandering husband if he was to contact his real mother, and Frank would have been a traitor for helping him.

Frank was nowhere near as possessive as Doris, although it had crossed his mind several times that Wayne might just be seduced by the glamour of his real mother's fame and Hollywood lifestyle...that he might suddenly just jet off and leave the Higginbotham's modest little house in Yorkshire. But no. Frank and Doris had raised Wayne to be a proper little Yorkshire man, and his feet were too firmly planted on the ground. Frank had been surprised that Wayne had received another letter from his natural mother so soon after the last one, however. Terri's letters had become rather sparse over the last few months, so two in reasonably quick succession was somewhat unusual.

As usual, the letter had been addressed to Wayne care of Elizabeth Ball, his old teacher from Gas Street Primary School. She had been instrumental in finding Wayne when he had run away to find his roots, just before he had started at Wormysted's. Elizabeth had driven Frank all the way to the West of Ireland, the very day after her husband had driven them both down to London and back, hot on Wayne's trail. Elizabeth had met Terri on that occasion and had agreed that it would be better if Doris remained unaware of her adopted boy's continued correspondence with his birth mum, and therefore agreed to be the recipient of Terri's letters - passing them on to Frank, who subsequently handed them on to Wayne.

Frank blew an exasperated sigh. "What would our lass do if she ever found out, eh?" he whispered, to no-one in particular.

"Talking to thissen, Frank?" Albert Tatler, the foreman in the factory laughed as he approached Frank's workstation. "Tha's going nuts, old lad."

Frank squirmed. "Aye, mebbe, Albert. Another few thingummies and I think I'll be proper doolalley tap! Nay, I were just thinking out loud."

Albert gripped his shoulder jovially. "Get thissen home, Frankie lad, tha's done more than enough. I think the world'll survive wi'out one more widget."

Frank stretched his back. "Aye, mebbe. I'll just finish this one and then gerroff home. Our lass is out late tonight with friends. So it'll be a nice glass of stout, wi'me feet up in front o't'telly wi'our lad."

Albert nodded approvingly. "Aye, good night, Frank. Enjoy what's left o't'weekend. I'll see thee Monday morning."

He wandered off across the factory floor, as Frank screwed the last thingummy onto the last widget and placed it carefully into a box, which he put on to a conveyor belt to be whisked off to who knows where. He yawned, stretched again and rubbed his eyes, before pulling on his coat, clocking off, and walking out of the factory into the fresh evening air.

His small 50cc Honda motorcycle was parked in a shed at the back of the car park, specially designed for bikes, motorbikes and scooters, but at this late hour on a Saturday evening his was the only one there. It was starting to rain gently and by the time he had traversed the car park and got to the bike shed, it had become a full persistent Yorkshire drizzle. Frank was glad he'd parked the bike well under cover. He put on his helmet then yawned again, before pulling down the straps and fastening them. He reversed the bike out of the shed by pushing back with his feet, then he kick started the motorcycle, drove up to the factory gates, and pulled straight out.

There was a loud skidding squealing noise, and the lights were upon him before he even had time to realise it.

The thought I didn't look! flashed through his brain, and he was conscious of an enormous impact - and then of falling, falling, falling towards the hard black tarmac, which he never seemed to reach.

Oh heck, I'll be late, Frank thought as he fell. Wayne's letter...I've got to give him his letter...

Then, there was nothing but a strange buzzing noise and darkness.

Twenty-Seven

"So you think that this night's activity was truly clever, do you?"

Aillen Mac Fionnbharr's voice was as angry as Wayne had ever heard it. Indeed Wayne had never known his true father be angry before. It came as something of a surprise, as it had been Frank, his adopted dad, that he had expected trouble from.

Wayne had arrived home some minutes earlier, half-expecting to find Frank home from the widget factory. He had munched a couple of polo mints on the walk home, hoping vainly that they might disguise the strong smell of alcohol on his breath. The last thing Wayne had wanted was a long and heavy confrontation with Frank about underage drinking and irresponsible behaviour. He had been quite worried, but in his drunken state he had managed to convince himself that he would be able to bluff his way out of trouble, or use his powers to influence Frank. The fact that he couldn't even stand up straight without swaying hadn't occurred to him. It was with some relief, therefore, that when he got to the green, glass-panelled front door of 18 Cavendish Street, he found it still locked and the house in total darkness. Maybe Frank had gone to the pub.

Wayne shrugged, heaved a sigh of relief, unlocked the door and made his way in, out of the drizzle that had just started. He ran straight up to his bedroom, where he fell contentedly back on to the bed, dreaming of the gorgeous Stephanie Fleming and that kiss. He could still smell her hair, her perfume. He could still taste her lips.

He had been asleep for no more than half an hour when the roar of a passing car woke him. He looked at his watch and turned on the small black and white television in his room. The familiar strains of the theme tune to 'Match of the Day' burst out of the set. Where was Frank? Wayne wondered. He had promised to watch the football highlights with him. His mouth now tasted of stale wine and greasy fish and chips, instead of Steph's kiss.

The first match had just kicked off when a green mist had begun to envelop the area at the end of Wayne's bed and the familiar figure of a tall, plaited, Tuatha warrior appeared.

"Hi, Da!" Wayne slurred cheerily. It had been some time since Aillen had made an appearance in Wayne's room, and the boy had missed his real father.

"So, you think that this night's activity was truly clever do you?" Aillen had snapped furiously as soon as had materialised.

Wayne blinked in surprise. "What?" he exclaimed innocently.

Aillen had repeated his question, and added, "You know what I mean, boy!" He folded his arms and twisted his mouth in an expression of displeasure. "I await your explanation," he growled.

"I don't know what you mean!" Wayne threw his arms out in a submissive gesture, before standing and turning off the television.

Aillen grimaced. "If I had physical form I would box your pointed ears," he snarled.

Wayne's mouth dropped open in shock at his father's tone. He sounded like an Irish Dai Davies.

"Are you talking about the shape-shifting?" Wayne asked, hesitantly.

Aillen threw his hands up in exasperation. "Of course I am referring to that, you fool. Do you not realise that you are but a novice at the art of disguise yet? That even if you were proficient in the art of changing your appearance, such gifts are not to be used for the frivolous pleasures of a moon struck, love-sick youth's longings? I warned you the last time that the use of such magic is only for those times when you truly need it!"

"Well, I did truly need it if I was ever going to go out with Steph - and anyway, you did it," Wayne responded scornfully.

"What?" Aillen gasped.

"Well it's true, isn't it?" Wayne snapped back. "That was how you got my mom into bed, by pretending to be someone else?"

Aillen was momentarily lost for words. "Yes, but..."

Wayne, keen to press home his advantage, wagged his finger at the apparition standing before him. "She'd have run a mile from old Mickey Finn and probably even further from Aillen Mac Fionnbharr - but she was okay with Danny Finn, wasn't she?"

Aillen raised his pointed eyebrows and rubbed his forehead, as though he was developing a headache. "Oh my son, how little you yet understand the working of magic. This is all my fault," he moaned sadly. Wayne shrugged his shoulders.

"Well, I went and copied you. I thought if it had worked for you, it might work for me. So, to try and get to go out with Stephanie Fleming, I did exactly what you did and invented a cool American kid. I called mine Michael Finnegan - Mickey Finn for short. Sound familiar? Good eh? Mickey Finn? You were Danny Finn?"

The grin that broke out across his face betrayed his expectation of commendation from his mystical parent, but Aillen merely shook his head sadly.

"I expected better of you, Michael," he whispered forlornly. "When I shape-shifted to woo your mother, I was already nearly three thousand years old. I practiced night after night, and can even hold my disguised self in the realm of dreams. You are but yet a boy. I did not enter the liaison with your mother as lightly as you imagine. I knew the sands of my time were draining away and that I needed a son and heir, quickly."

He smiled sadly. "As lovely as your mother, Theresa is, and as much as she reminded me of my own poor dear Celebdhann, my need was as much political as romantic."

Wayne, sobering up rapidly in his anger, gasped, "Oh - so that's okay then, is it? You didn't really fancy my mom - you wanted to get her knickers off for political reasons. I suppose that means I'm just a political tool, am I?" Wayne shouted.

"That is not what I said!" Aillen angrily snapped back. "You are my son, and the last prince of the Tuatha De Danaan. Had I not lain with your mother there would now be no Tuatha De Danaan, and no hope left for the world."

Wayne shrugged, and fell back on to his bed. "Some use being a prince when I can't even go out with a girl without getting told off."

Aillen slumped onto the bed, and sat beside his son.

"When I wooed your mother, I was as accomplished a shape-shifter as any of the Tuatha before me, ever. You were never in full control of your abilities, once the first fruit of the vine had passed over your lips."

"I was so!" Wayne snorted derisively.

Aillen shook his head. "Michaeleen, Michaeleen. You are but learning the ways of the Tuatha. You have a long, long way to go before you can pass yourself off as anything you think of. You are..."

"I've been practising loads and I'm pretty good now...look!" Wayne interrupted, slurring his words slightly. He morphed into a likeness of Johnny Rotten, and snarled at Aillen, who raised one single eyebrow patiently.

"Your abilities are truly impressive, but you are still no more than an apprentice. It takes more than adopting strange forms to assume different personalities, as I believe you found this evening."

Johnny Rotten dissolved slowly back into the shape of Wayne Higginbotham.

"You lost concentration and lost your chosen form on several occasions, did you not?" Aillen quizzed his son. "You changed shape in the full view of a mortal, who will put it down to an excess of ale tomorrow, no doubt, but who could have been as sober as a judge. And yet you tell me you were truly in control?"

Wayne sighed, and shook his head sadly. "Sorry, Da."

Aillen stood, and walked over to the chest of drawers in Wayne's bedroom.

"I am sorry, my son, that I have not taught you better. I am not vexed by your childish failings this night, in front of the comely wench." He glanced approvingly at Wayne, who afforded a slight smile. "I am vexed because you have put yourself in great danger. You are a good shape-shifter, Michael, but you are not fully of the Tuatha De Danaan. You are a half mortal, and therefore you have to use more of the stones' energy."

Aillen pointed vaguely at the drawer in which Wayne kept his shards of the stone of Fal.

"I warned you that there are other stones out there, Michaeleen, and all of them glow when the magic is being used. Magic like you used this night is powerful magic indeed. If another shard is in the possession of the Order - and I would presume they have many - then they will know that there is still one who can wield such magic. I swear this; they will do everything they can to find whosoever wields that power."

Wayne pouted. "How come I could do magic before I ever even got the stones, then?"

Aillen put his ghostly hand on his son's shoulder.

"Michaeleen, you were born with power, great power, even without the stones. You are destined to be the Slanaitheoir Mor. Yes, you can become invisible to mortal eye, change your shape, emit bolts of pure energy, place thoughts in people's minds, or take memories from them; all without the stones. However, that natural power you possess is limited. You could not change your form for more than a few ticks of the clock without the additional power of the stones, believe me."

Wayne grimaced, and Aillen looked his son straight in the eye.

"Have your fun, my son, but be careful. For our enemies are many, and they are powerful. All there is of us now, is you."

Wayne shook his head. "Don't forget my sister."

Aillen scratched his head. "We have searched and searched for your sister. Yet, there is no sign of her. For whatever reason, it seems her Tuatha side is dormant, or she is lost." There was a long silence as the ghostly figure of Aillen Mac Fionnbharr and Wayne Higginbotham considered their missing family member.

Eventually, Wayne shrugged his shoulders.

"Have I passed my tests so far, by the way?"

Aillen looked puzzled. "Tests?" he repeated.

Wayne nodded eagerly. "Yes. The first time I saw you, you said I would have three tests to pass before I became the Slanethy-mor-thing.

Pizarro was the first...I assumed the next two of them were being disowned by my mom and knocked back by Steph. I mean...they were pretty big blows, you know, and I think I've coped well, haven't I?" Aillen looked even more confused.

"You speak in riddles my son; you say your mother has disowned you? Theresa?"

Wayne nodded. "Yeah. She's preggers by some American film bloke she married and doesn't want me being a fly in the ointment when it comes to her movie career."

"Preggers? Fly in the ointment? Knock backs? Is it English you are speaking, Michaeleen?"

Wayne was about to respond, when there was a loud pounding at the front door. Aillen grimaced, stood, and stepped back into the swirling cloud of green mist.

"The two tests you must still face have yet to start my son, and they will be much more severe than perhaps you have expected, I fear. We shall talk again soon. Take care, Michaeleen." With that, he was gone in a twirl of mist.

There was another sharp knock on the door. Wayne had sobered up a little during his audience with his father, and now he just felt a bit sick. He wondered who could possibly be knocking at that time of night. Maybe Frank had forgotten his key.

He ran as fast as he could down the stairs and opened the front door, to find a policeman and policewoman standing in front of him.

"Oh!" Wayne gasped, desperately trying to appear as sober as a judge.

The policeman, Sergeant Hartley, felt sure that he knew Wayne as soon as he saw him, but couldn't quite remember why. The serious nature of his mission took precedence over idle speculation, however.

"Mr Higginbotham?" he asked.

Wayne shook his head. "No, that's my dad. He's at work, although I've been expecting him back for a while now."

The policeman looked grim. "So your father is a Mister Frank Higginbotham?"

Wayne nodded. A knot suddenly and ominously began to tie itself in his stomach.

"I'm afraid there's been an incident, Sir. It seems there was a road traffic accident, earlier this evening." The policeman coughed nervously. "I'm afraid a Frank Higginbotham, of this address...your father...has, unfortunately, subsequently passed away."

Twenty-Eight

James Malone jumped into his brother's car as quickly as possible. Two old ladies stood gaping, open-mouthed at the sight of his pale, bare posterior passing in front of them, as he hurled himself across the pavement from the phone kiosk.

"What kept you?" James demanded furiously, as he slammed the car door and hunched down into the passenger seat. Dan Malone sat at the wheel of his hired Ford Cortina, and grinned mischievously.

"Well you could've taken the bus, if you thought I was taking too long."

James hunched lower in the seat, desperately trying to hide his nudity, while simultaneously drying himself with the towel Dan had brought. "Ha bloody ha!" he laughed sarcastically, and shivered.

"Anyway, what in the name of the Holy Mother were you after skinny dipping in the filthy bloody Liffey anyway?" Dan asked, as he pulled away from the pavement of the dockland side street. "When we rang the Gardai this morning they said you'd been released yesterday, and that as far as they were aware the Finaan case was now closed. Ma couldn't work out why you hadn't come straight home. She was worried again, Jimmy boy. So what the hell happened for you to end up stark-bollock-naked in the Liffey?"

James Malone frowned. "What time is it?" he asked scanning the dashboard for a clock. Dan glanced at his watch.

"Half eleven, and I'm supposed to be on a plane back to London in one hour and fifteen minutes - not riding around the back end of Dublin with my mad, bad, naked brother."

James appeared stricken. "What day is it, Dan?"

Dan turned and looked sceptically at his younger brother. "Jaysus! Talk about jet-lag. Are you meaning to be telling me now that you don't even know what day it is?"

James shivered. "For God's sake. What day is it?"

Dan cast his brother a curious look, his forehead creased in a scowl. "It's Saturday. We flew in yesterday morning and you, I presume, spent last night in the cells as a guest of the O'Connell Street Gardai. " He looked back through the windscreen again, and raised his eyebrows. "Or did you get so drunk celebrating your freedom that you lost an entire night?"

James shook his head, and closed his eyes.

"The Order tried to kill me, Dan. I wasn't swimming, or skinny-dipping in the bloody Liffey, you eejit. I was thrown in. As far as they were concerned, I was a corpse."

Dan Joyce took a deep breath, flicked the indicator stalk, and steered over to the side of the road. He stopped the car with a squeal of the tyres, and turned off the ignition. He took his hands off the wheel and turned angrily towards his younger brother.

"Right, James. I've kept my mouth shut, so far. I don't know what the hell happened back there in Mayo. The story you told me in L.A. and what you told Da in the hospital is the biggest load of baloney I've ever heard in my life; and trust me, I've heard some pretty unbelievable stuff. You may have that American girl, Carrie, and our Da, believing your stupid, bloody tales of elves and fairies and murdering phantom priests. But then - and I'm not saying she's not a lovely girl - but Californians are all away with the fairies anyway, and will believe anything. As for Da, he always did believe every word you ever said." James opened his mouth to protest, but Dan held up his hand.

"In my career, James, I've had to stand up in Court in front of Judges and Juries and tell tales that would seem totally incredible to any sane man, but I've never heard anything even half as wild as your story. Did you really think, even in your wildest dreams, that I'd believe this stuff? Now if it is drugs, like Ma says, we can get help. If it's the drink, we can get help...but for the sake of sweet, bleeding Jaysus, will you stop blarneying on about the Order and the Tuatha de bloody Danann. For God's sake James it's all in your mind, and it's Ma and Da who are suffering. Look, I know a good psychiatrist in London; he'll be able to help you, so he will."

The sound of the nearby Dublin traffic permeated the car, covering a long silence. James, his face set in a furious scowl, stared defiantly straight ahead, out of the windscreen, and shivered violently.

It was Dan who finally spoke again. "Let's go home."

Dan Joyce drove all the way to the Malone house near Howth in silence. James settled back and feigned sleep, but his shivering grew more intense as the journey progressed.

He thought about his struggle to reach the banks of the river as the tide seemed intent on pulling him out to sea. He had just managed to make a huge last effort to reach the bank, before exhaustion had finally overtaken him. James had then been able to manoeuvre himself along until he had reached a boating ladder. He had then sneaked around the derelict wharves and warehouses in his naked state, desperately looking for a phone box. He had seen one near an old pub, and had reversed the charges on a call home. It had been Dan who had answered and agreed to pick him up, although James' description of his location had been vague, to say the least. That was why Dan had taken so long to find him.

As the BMW pulled up outside the Malone house, the brothers' mother rushed out to greet them. Her eyes were red and her cheeks stained with mascara.

"Ah Jimmy, what have you been doing now?" she wailed as James clambered out of the car and tried to use the towel to preserve his modesty. "Your girl Carrie's been on the phone for you. I couldn't tell her where you were. Why didn't you ring? Ah - look at the state of you! You're as naked as the day you were born. Have you been off doing that streaking thing?"

James simply pulled the towel around him tighter, and shivered.

"Ah, will you be having a nice warm cup of tea?" Mrs Malone asked, taking her son around the shoulder and ushering him towards the front door. Dan slammed the driver's door.

"Thanks for coming to get me, Dan," he muttered sarcastically as he strolled around the front of the car, following his mother and younger brother into the house.

About an hour later, James had showered and dressed and was feeling much better, especially after one of his mother's cups of tea and a large slice of soda bread toast with lashings of fresh Irish butter.

"How's Da this morning?" James asked, contentedly putting his steaming mug down on the kitchen table. A roaring fire blazed in the grate, and he had finally stopped shivering. Mrs Malone shrugged.

"The same as yesterday, although he's been terribly worried about you. He's got his knickers in a right twist about all this Order business."

Dan walked into the kitchen at that moment, and scowled at the mention of the Order. He cast James a withering glance, displaying his annoyance.

"I'm staying until tomorrow now, Ma," Dan announced, and then under his breath, "if anybody actually cares."

"Oh, that's good, dear," Mrs Malone chirped.

"Yes." Dan stated flatly, "All the other flights today are full. My secretary is sorting things out for me."

Dan looked at James, and folded his arms.

"So, Jimmy...Jimmy boy. What are we going to do with you?"

James Malone looked straight into his brother's eyes.

"I don't give a damn whether you believe me, or not, Dan. I'm not sure I believe half of it myself. But, whether you like it or not, I am not mad, drunk, nor am I on drugs. I swear to you, on Da's life, that all of this stuff - everything I've told you - is really happening."

James stood, scratching the stool's feet along the wooden floor.

"I'm going for a lie down, Ma."

Mrs Malone smiled and nodded. "Of course dear, you must be shattered."

Dan pursed his lips and took a sip of tea. He replaced the mug carefully on the table. There was a bang as James slammed his old bedroom door.

"Ma?" Dan whispered, quietly.

"Yes, dear?" she answered.

"We have to have a chat about James."

Mrs Malone's face fell.

"I think he may be very, very sick," Dan said, slowly and painfully.

Twenty-Nine

The Banshee Aoibheall smiled contentedly. She had far more information on Wayne Higgy-whatever's whereabouts than she had told the Order. If she was going to get her hands on the shards of the Stone of Falias, however, then she was going to have to use de Feren so that she could get to England.

She had no money, no modern clothes, and a less than rudimentary understanding of the way the modern world worked. She had been worried that maybe de Feren would send her back to the convent and carry out the task of finding the boy on his own. It came as a pleasant surprise, therefore, when he had announced on the Saturday evening, following the disposal of Malone's body, that she would be travelling with him to London on the following Monday.

De Feren had spent the day poring over the Catholic adoption records in Dublin and had found no reference to a 'Wayne.' If the boy now lived in England, de Feren had reasoned, then it was likely that he had been adopted over there. Once in London, he informed her, they would travel to the offices of the 'Crusade of Rescue', in Ladbroke Grove. The Crusade of Rescue was a charitable Catholic Society, set up in 1928 by a Cardinal Vaughn, to arrange the adoptions of destitute Catholic children into good Catholic families. The records there were fantastic, and if the boy had been adopted in England then it was likely to have been through that agency, as his poor mother would probably have been a good, Irish Catholic girl. All they had to do was find the names Wayne and Michael in the files, and a surname with Higg in it. Hopefully by the simple process of elimination, and a lot of hard work, they would eventually find him.

Father de Feren informed Aoibheall that she could take Sunday off, as a day of rest. He advised her to spend the day praying for the success of their mission. Aoibheall had other ideas, however. She wanted to see more of the modern world, so in the guise of Sister Bernadette she spent most of her Sunday just watching people around St Stephen's Green in Dublin, enjoying a pleasant warm September afternoon. It felt good to her to be out in the sun again, after being locked in the dark Limerick convent for so long.

As she returned to her room that evening, however, bitterness had crept into her heart. Bitterness at how unfair it was that she was effectively so alone in the world. She hoped that James Malone might survive his being thrown into the Liffey. Aoibheall had liked James. He would make a good slave. She had deliberately left his mind intact, to give him some chance of survival, and had ensured that he could wake from his magical coma as soon as he hit the water. The rest was up to him. Why were mortals so weak?

All of the mortals she had used over the years had been pathetic. The story she had told the priests of her last lover being a widower with children, who had starved to death, had been almost too delicious. He had actually been a Lord, Lord Weston - and yes, she had married him and helped bring up his brats, but she had ruined him. Lady Weston's cruelty had become the talk of Connemara in the years leading up to the great famine. Lord Weston gained the reputation of being one of the cruellest landlords in Ireland, all because of his domineering wife.

When she had bullied her husband into shooting two starving peasants for stealing apples, it had all became too much for the hungry locals, who had stormed and burned down the house. Her husband had shot two more of the unfortunates, but had finally succumbed to a well-aimed pitchfork. Aoibheall had barely escaped with her life. and in the guise she now favoured, had seduced the lecherous old village priest, Father Lydon. Through his Order contacts, he had given her help and subsequent sanctuary in the distant Limerick Convent.

James Malone had reminded her of Culhainnein, her long-dead Celtic lover. He had been a mighty warrior, but too weak to fight the mighty Fionnbharr, all those years ago. The tale she had told Bishop O'Leary and Father de Feren about her Tuatha past did have some truth in it. She had been betrothed to a Tuatha prince. She had, in fact, been betrothed to the young Aillen Mac Fionnbharr, but he had discovered that she was a cruel, spoilt and spiteful girl, and had fallen instead for King Dagda's daughter, Celebdhann.

Aillen and Celebdhann had, in due course, married and had been exceedingly happy. In her jealousy and rage Aoibheall had cursed the happy couple and betrayed them to the war band of the mortal that she regarded as little more than a plaything: Culhainnein. Although Aillen and his bride survived the Celtic war band's attack, many good Tuatha warriors had died, including two of Aillen's brothers. For her treachery, Aoibheall had been cast out of the Tuatha De Danaan, along with her mother and grandmother, to wander the earth as a banshee - Ban derived from the word for 'woman', Shee from sidhe, 'fairy'.

Aillen and his other brothers, under the leadership of King Fionnbharr, had wrought vengeance on Culhainnein and his warriors and killed them all. It was just so ironic that the boy they were now seeking was Aillen's bastard son. It was said that revenge is a dish best served cold, and now she had the perfect opportunity for her ultimate revenge on the prince, who had spurned her, so long, long ago.

De Feren planned to kill the boy; but no, she would not allow that. It was as she had promised James Malone. She would allow no harm to come to the son of Aillen Mac Fionnbharr, for death was too easy. As long as she could get her hands on the stones of Falias that the boy must have, then she could make him her plaything. She would keep him alive long enough to extract every joyous ounce of revenge. Oh, what fun she would have!

She kissed the small stone in the ring on her finger, and it glowed softly. If she could perform the magic she had performed over the centuries, using such a small scraping of the stone of Falias, then imagine what she could do with much more of it.

The Banshee Aoibheall looked at her reflection in the mirror. She caressed her perfect milky white cheeks, pursed her ruby red lips, ran her fingers through her shining raven black hair and admired the brilliant emerald green of her eyes. Then she took a deep breath, and relaxed. For a mere moment, the stunningly beautiful girl was replaced by a hideous, wrinkled, corpse-like crone. The tiny stone in her ring stopped glowing.

Thirty

Carrie Horden was worried. She had not heard from James since she had waved him and Dan off at the door of her house in Box Canyon the previous morning, Thursday. She had expected him to ring as soon as he got to the family home in Dublin, yet he hadn't. She had waited several hours and had then rung the number that Dan had given her. It had been James' mother who had answered, and Carrie had been appalled to hear that James had been arrested at the hospital, almost as soon as he had arrived. His mother had said that Dan, who was a lawyer after all, had stated that they had no sound reason to hold James for any length of time, and he expected him to be released after a brief questioning session.

The hours passed and there was still no word. Carrie watched darkness descend on the valley. The distant mountains glowed red and then disappeared, as the long straight amber lines of the L.A. streets and boulevards began to glow and glimmer, like a neon patchwork. Eventually - exhausted, and feeling so worried that she was almost nauseous - Carrie took herself off to bed. Her dreams were tormented by visions of James in prison, or being tortured by evil cloaked figures, and she had woken in the middle of the night in a cold sweat.

The nearby yip of a coyote set a neighbour's dog barking, then another. Carrie tossed and turned but couldn't get back to sleep. She looked at the glowing neon display of her alarm clock: four-thirty am.

Half past twelve, Saturday, in Ireland. She just had to try again. This time, it was Dan who answered.

"Jaysus, Carrie, it must be the middle of the night over there! What are you doing ringing at this hour?"

Carrie explained her concern, and Dan had sighed heavily.

"Oh, he's here. He's okay, Carrie. He's just upstairs - probably sleeping off the jet-lag and a hangover."

"Hangover?" Carrie repeated, incredulously. Dan had laughed.

"It seems he got so drunk last night that he lost all his clothes and fell in the Liffey."

"What?" Carrie asked crossly. "What the hell is the Liffey, for Christ's sake?"

Dan had explained about the Dublin's River Liffey, which only seemed to make Carrie even more upset and angry.

"And he was, like, buck-naked you say?"

Carrie could not believe what she was hearing. She had been worried out of her skin, while that no-good Irishman had been getting so drunk in some Irish pub that he had decided it would be a good idea to take a skinny-dip in a city river!

"I'll get him for you," Dan had offered.

"No, it's okay," Carrie hissed. "Tell him to get his beauty sleep. He's gonna need it if he's going to explain his way out of this one! I'll speak to him later."

She had thanked Dan, slammed down the phone, and then gone back to bed. This time she was too angry to sleep.

By the time the phone rang at eight am, she had worked herself into such a fury that she decided she wasn't going to answer it. She heard a message being recorded and the familiar sound of James' Irish brogue as she walked into the shower.

"I'm going to wash that man right out of my hair," she sang, as she aggressively lathered her hair with shampoo.

By the time she was dressed and ready to set off to go to the office for a busy Saturday's real estate selling, she had calmed down enough to listen to the message. She put her steaming mug of coffee down on the table, and pressed play.

"Hi babe, it's me, Jimmy." Carrie snorted derisively. "Sorry I didn't ring last night." Jimmy's voice sounded suitably contrite. Carrie made a face.

"Dan told me that he'd told you that I'd gotten drunk. Well, he's an eejit. I didn't."

Carrie raised her eyebrows and mouthed "Yeah, right!"

"It was the Order, babe. The Gardai - that's the cops here - passed me on to them. It was a set up. They tried to kill me..."

Suddenly Carrie stopped making faces, and sat bolt upright in the chair.

"They threw me into the river unconscious. I'd been interrogated by them and then knocked out. I guess I was supposed to drown; I almost did. Now, listen to me, babe. Dan doesn't believe a word I've told him about any of this stuff: about the Order, the immortals, or what happened at Finaan. I think he thinks I'm an alcoholic, or doing heroin, or something. I hope you believe me, because if anything does happen to me then it's gonna have to be you who lets the world know about the Order. The head of the Order in Ireland is one Bishop Donleavy. His number two is another bishop, a fat creep called Desmond O'Leary. If I die, you've got to get someone to nail 'em, Carrie."

There was a pause as James took a deep breath.

"I hope you're not so pissed with me that you don't listen to this message, babe. I love you and you're what made me pull myself out of that river. Without you I would have been after just floating away."

Carrie's eyes filled with tears, as James paused again.

"I've gotta stop them, Carrie. They're going to try and kill the kid I told you about. The English kid who was in Finaan. I've gotta go to England to try and find him. Hopefully I'll get to him before they do. If I don't make it, I want you to know that I love you and I've got to let people know about the Sacred Order of St. Gregory. Someone has to stop them. I love you. Goodbye, babe." The answering machine fell silent.

Carrie sat numb for what seemed to her an eternity, then she grabbed the phone and dialled urgently. In a house in Dublin, the phone rang and rang, unanswered.

Thirty-One

"Which hospital is he in?" Doris asked, her voice strained.

Wayne stared into the darkness, through the back window of the police car. Rows of illuminated windows passed by; people in their little houses having normal Saturday nights, watching their tellies, doing whatever they did on their normal little Saturday nights.

"Arnedale," he whispered, quietly.

"I hope he's going to be alright," Doris said, choking on the last word.

Wayne turned to her. "Alright?" he repeated, incredulously. He turned, and looked desperately at the Officers in the front of the car. The policeman, Sergeant Hartley, and his female companion, stared obliviously out of the windscreen of the car as they sped through the dark Yorkshire countryside. Wayne almost choked.

"I'm sorry, Mum, did they not tell you?" he gasped, putting his arm around his adoptive mother's shoulder. His mouth dried up. He took a deep breath, and though his voice cracked, managed to say "He's gone. They said he'd passed away. I'm sorry. Dad's dead, Mum."

Doris turned and glared at him. She pulled his arm off her shoulder and glowered into his eyes.

"Don't be daft. They didn't say that," she blurted out. "They didn't tell me he were dead. They just said that there'd been an accident."

Wayne's head dropped, and he stared at the floor of the car.

"I don't suppose they thought the pub was the right place to tell you. They told me, Mum. They told me he'd passed away."

As soon as Sergeant Hartley had told Wayne about the accident, whilst standing on the Higginbotham's doorstep, he had asked where Mrs Higginbotham might be found. When informed that she was at a friend's house, but just might be at 'The Junction Inn' nearby, the policewoman had been despatched in the car to get her, while Wayne had found a jacket and locked up the house.

It was all so unreal as far as Wayne was concerned. There just had to have been some mistake. That 'Candid Camera' man from the telly was going to pop out any second and tell him that it was all just a sick joke, or he would wake up and find that it had all been a horrid dream. Frank Higginbotham could not possibly be dead. He was only fifty-nine years old, for God's sake! No one died at fifty-nine - not in Wayne's experience, anyway. You didn't die until you were seventy, or even older.

It was as the police car, complete with Doris in the back, pulled up at the kerbside outside the Higginbotham's front door that Wayne had expressed his misgivings about what he had heard the sergeant say.

"You did say he was dead, didn't you? There's no possibility of a mistake?" Wayne asked the policeman timorously. The sergeant grimaced.

"Aye, I did...I'm sorry, son. If it's any consolation, they said he didn't suffer. It were a quick do, like."

No, thought Wayne silently. It was no consolation.

Frank Higginbotham had saved his life when Father Francisco Pizarro had had Wayne at his mercy. He had appeared from out of nowhere, as if by magic, vaulting over an impossibly huge wall and landing a punch on the deadly immortal assassin who had knocked him virtually senseless. The priest had dropped his dagger and had staggered backwards in shock. In the blink of an eye, Frank Higginbotham had picked the dagger up and hurled it at him with deadly accuracy, straight into the chest of the stunned assassin. The last Wayne had seen of the evil priest, he had been staggering back into the burning cottage that had been Mickey Finn's, just before the whole thing collapsed around him.

Frank had done it. Not him, Wayne Higginbotham, with all his phenomenal magic powers. Not the ancient and immortal Aillen Mac Fionnbharr. No; it had been the plain, boring old soldier, Frank Higginbotham, who had despatched the Order's deadliest assassin.

The policeman put his hand on Wayne's back to usher him into the car as the policewoman held open the rear door.

"I remember now. You were the lad who ran away that time, weren't you?" Sergeant Hartley asked, as Wayne had clambered onto the back seat of the car next to his mother. Wayne nodded and tried a small smile that just curled the corner of his mouth.

"Aye, I knew it. Never forget a face, me!" Sergeant Hartley had announced pompously to his companion. "Aye, led us a right merry dance this one did when he were a nipper. Ha! Got all the way to London and then Ireland to cap it all. Aye, a right merry dance." Sergeant Hartley sat down in the front passenger seat, chuckling to himself. The policewoman glowered at him reproachfully and, taking the hint, he had coughed and gone quiet.

The rest of the journey took place in virtual silence until Doris had asked about the hospital, and Wayne had been forced to inform her of her husband's passing. Then silence reigned again, apart from the occasional heavy sob from Doris. Eventually, the car pulled up outside Arnedale Hospital's Accident and Emergency unit.

Doris jumped out of the police car almost before the policewoman had time to open the door, Wayne following closely behind. Sergeant Hartley walked after them, rubbing his chin ponderously, desperately trying to remember what it was that had been funny about that lad; but, for the life of him, he couldn't remember what it was.

This being a Saturday night, people were milling around in the entrance to the hospital and in the waiting room in various states of inebriation; an array of fight victims, or those who had fallen over in a drunken stupor and injured themselves in some way. Wayne glowered at the pathetic collection of motley individuals, all waiting to be patched up because they couldn't hold their drink. Then there were those more sober types, waiting to collect the motley crew once they had been stitched or bandaged. Then they would go back home and forget all about this particular night. He fought back the tears, and clenched his teeth.

The policewoman whispered to someone at the reception desk, and then beckoned for Doris and Wayne to follow her. A doctor appeared by a cubicle door, his face gaunt and pale. He nodded at the policewoman and then grimaced as he acknowledged Doris and Wayne. He opened a door. The policewoman sighed, and turned away.

"We'll wait out here. You take your time," she whispered, sympathetically.

Frank Higginbotham was lying on a bed surrounded by a curtain in a room little larger than a cubicle at the back of the busy A & E department, his entire body covered by a stark white sheet. Wayne was amazed how quiet it seemed in the curtained cubicle where his adoptive father's body was laid out, however. The aura of death seemed to stifle normal everyday sounds. The noise from outside seemed strangely muted.

The doctor mumbled his condolences and carefully lifted the sheet off the head of the body, exposing Frank's face. The doctor asked Doris if she could identify the deceased as her husband, Frank Higginbotham. Doris couldn't; her eyes were too full of tears. Wayne looked at his adoptive father, and nodded.

"Yes, that's my dad," he stated despondently. "That's Frank Higginbotham."

Doris let out a howl that chilled the blood, as she put her arm over the body and let her head sink on to Frank's chest.

Wayne's heart sank. So it really was real. Frank Higginbotham was really, really dead. Yet, to Wayne, he just looked as though he was asleep.

Wayne had expected him to be a mess, all scratched and bloody, but he wasn't. He was very, very pale, true, but apart from that, Wayne would not have been too surprised to hear him snore. He was desperate for his dad to snore, and then they could all laugh about the mistake and carry on as if nothing had happened. But Frank didn't snore. Frank didn't do anything. He just led there, totally silent, totally still.

Wayne felt anger surging in his body. He felt his power grow, as if a switch had been flicked and a huge nuclear reactor had started to energise inside him.

Blink! Wayne commanded in his head. For God's sake, Dad, you defeated Hitler, you destroyed Pizarro - just defeat this, will you? Blink!

Frank's face remained unnaturally pallid and still. Wayne concentrated all his mental energy.

"Wake up, Dad!" he whispered as he gritted his teeth and raised his hand. He tried desperately to push life-giving, magical power into his father's body. He didn't give a damn how much the stones might glow.

He heard Doris wail again, gritted his teeth even more, and put his hand on his adoptive father's forehead.

"Dad!" He screamed in his mind. Nothing happened. Frank just led there, his eyes stubbornly closed. Cold. Still. Dead.

Wayne took a deep breath and in one final surge, summoned all his powers and screamed in his mind, WAKE UP, DAD! I COMMAND YOU!

The doctor shuffled his feet and cleared his throat.

"Er, maybe, it...er..."

Wayne gasped, bit his lip, then pulled away from the man he had considered his true father for eleven years. The doctor covered Frank's face, and nodded to Wayne.

"Your dad's personal possessions are over there. We'll take him to the mortuary until the undertakers come." He waved vaguely at a table next to the bed, where Frank's watch, his wallet and some other bits and pieces had been carefully placed in a transparent plastic wallet. With a leap of the heart, which was followed by a searing pang of guilt, Wayne noticed a slightly crumpled blue airmail envelope amongst the other bits and pieces. Wayne picked up the wallet.

So that was it, then. All that magic, when it came down to it, it was as much use as a chocolate fireguard. He bit his lip again, forcing back the tears.

Doris had sat down on a chair outside the cubicle, weeping into a tissue. The doctor mumbled some more words of comfort to her, and then left.

"We'd better get you home," the policewoman whispered, taking Doris gently by the arm, after confirming once again that the body in the cubicle was indeed that of Frank Higginbotham, just to be sure. Doris snivelled her agreement and stood, letting the policewoman take her weight. Sergeant Hartley, head downcast, followed the women as they walked slowly past the motley Saturday night casualties and their friends. Wayne noticed all the eyes following the weeping woman; all the eyes thinking that at least someone was in a worse state than them.

Wayne felt the anger growing in his head again. He could blow all of these people into outer space, just by raising his hand. But what good would that do? He could kill, but he couldn't give life back to the people he loved. What was the point of it all? He turned back towards the cubicle containing the body of the man who he had thought of as his only father for eleven years, and had called Dad for sixteen. Frank Higginbotham, soldier, hero and Wayne's saviour. He was the Slanaitheoir Mor, not Michael Sean O'Brien. Not Wayne Higginbotham. A tear crept into Wayne's eye, and he realised that he hadn't really had time to cry yet.

He turned and began to leave the waiting room, hastening past the eyes, after the slow moving figures of the policewoman, the sergeant and Doris who were some way down the bright white corridor, near the exit. Although he was conscious that his eyes were now full of tears, still he could not break down and cry like he would have expected. He turned for one last time, and looked back towards his Dad's cubicle.

"Bye, Dad," Wayne whispered. "Thanks for everything. I'm sorry...I didn't really think you were embarrassing. Not really!" He bit his lip. "I loved you, Dad! I really did!"

Thirty-Two

Father Pierre de Feren stood before the window, staring out at the evenly-spaced trees on the other side of the street and the line of cars parked under them. Rain battered the window, and streaks of water ran down the panes of glass. It was his second day in the Crusade of Rescue's records office, and so far he had not managed to find any reference to a Wayne, or a Michael, or anything even close in the years that would have seemed appropriate. He had leafed through index card after index card, file after file, all dating back to the early sixties, and had not seen anything relevant. It was hard to imagine that so many children had been born out of wedlock, all by young Catholic girls, and mostly from Ireland.

De Feren sighed. It would not be like this for much longer. When the Messiah returned, things would be very different. People's morals would be much improved by the threat of the impending judgment day. Oh, how he longed to see people grovel at his feet begging for his mercy, as a key servant of the master - especially those morons in Brunarbre, the small village near Bruges where he had served as a priest for a number of years. Oh yes, they would all be quick to understand now! They would all understand and rend their hair and clothes in guilt, and squirm in wretched supplication. All he had been guilty of was love. A forbidden love maybe, but love was God's greatest gift. How dirty they had made it sound. He had been rescued from the shame by the Order, and he would be forever grateful. But the rest; oh yes, they would all be sorry.

"Father de Feren?" A timid voice interrupted the Priests meditation. De Feren turned and noticed a young priest standing before him, holding a parcel.

"Yes?" he replied.

"It's a diplomatic parcel, Father - it was couriered over from the Vatican Embassy. It must be really important."

De Feren raised an eyebrow. "Ah, yes, it is," he whispered, taking the parcel from the younger man, who stood, waiting expectantly. De Feren appraised him for a second.

"Is there anything else?" he whispered.

The young priest, who had expected at least a word of appreciation, as well as holding the forlorn hope that he might be party to finding out what was so important that it had had to be couriered by motorbike from the Vatican Embassy, shook his head.

"No, Father."

De Feren turned dismissively and placed the parcel on his desk next to a pile of cards that awaited his inspection. He made no move to open the parcel. The young priest shrugged, and left the room in something of a sulk.

De Feren picked up the card on the top of the pile. He had worked his way methodically through the alphabet to 'O', and as most of the names of the girls giving birth in the Crusade Mother's homes had been Irish, that list was quite extensive. He resumed his work with a grunt of impatience. He examined card after card, but saw nothing of any interest. A card in his hand was turned over, then another, but he saw nothing of note - until, suddenly, something made him turn back two cards - something he had seen that had not registered in his brain immediately, but now called him back. The name Michael Sean O'Brien, born March 1963, adopted May 1963; Mr and Mrs Higginbotham, 12, Frederick St. Barlickwick, West Yorkshire.

"This is it! Higginbotham!" De Feren shouted triumphantly.

Aoibheall, who had been sitting patiently in the office, rose from her chair and walked over to the desk where de Feren was working. There was no reference on the card to the name Wayne, but Higginbotham was too close to Higg-something to be a coincidence, especially linked to Michael. She took a deep breath, and feigned nonchalance. De Feren was so excited that spittle had gathered in the corners of his mouth.

"See, he is in Yorkshire!" he exclaimed.

Aoibheall found the tall Belgian disgusting; not least because he had not shown any interest in her, since his evident pleasure upon not being presented with a horrendous harridan when he had first encountered her. Aoibheall knew his preferences were far less orthodox than beautiful young girls. She also knew why he was so dedicated to the Order.

"I believe I have found our elusive demon spawn. We shall investigate, and see if this is definitely the boy." De Feren declared smugly. He peered up at the Nun through his thick-wire rimmed spectacles, and smiled.

"Our hour is at hand, Sister. We must now prepare for a journey to the North - and if he is the one we seek, then we shall take the appropriate action." He stood, and his lips twisted in a gross parody of a smile.

Aoibheall curtsied. "I will prepare, Father," she said, with only a small hint of sarcasm.

She felt a surge of excitement. This was definitely the son of Aillen Mac Fionnbharr; she could feel it. Soon, thousands of years of resentment, anger and hatred would be avenged. She would take the stones, and all the power of the Tuatha De Danaan would be hers.

Aoibheall began to plan her next steps very carefully.

Thirty-Three

Dan Malone was furious.

"What do you mean, you're going to England? You've only just got here and most of that time you've either been with the Gardai, in the pub, I suppose, or floating stark naked down the Liffey!"

The brothers had just left the hospital, where their Father had seemed to be recovering well, especially after seeing his younger son again. James shrugged.

"The Sacred Order of St. Gregory is after going to kill this kid, Dan," he stated adamantly, as the pair walked through the car park towards the hired Cortina. "You may not believe anything I've told you - for Christ's sake, I find it hard enough to believe it myself - but, I'll be telling you this...it is as real and horrible as Leeds United not being great anymore."

Dan stopped walking, put his hands on his hips, and blew his cheeks out in exasperation.

"I don't know you any more, Jimmy. I just don't know who you are. What you've become. You were a parish priest, someone respectable. I know I struggled to recognise you in L.A, but it's not just the hair, the tan and the pearly teeth...it's much more than that. Now you seem like you're just some drink or drug-addled bum, who seems intent on causing Ma and Da as much pain and grief as possible. I really, really think you should see a professional."

James Malone stopped walking and turned slowly to face his brother.

"You pompous, bloody eejit!" he shouted, furiously. "You absolute feckin' ass! How dare you? I am not mad. I do not do drugs and I do not drink and I sure as hell would not hurt Ma and Da - not for anything. Whether you believe it or not, Dan Malone, everything I have told you is the absolute bloody truth. The Tuatha De Danaan and the Sacred Order of St. Gregory are every bit as real as you and I are. You can mock me and scoff and accuse me of what the hell you like, before you run off back to your safe, middle class, little London penthouse - but what happened to me five years ago was real. Real enough for me to fake my own death and to give up everything. Everything that is happening now is real. What I am after going to do now, is to set out to save someone's life. To me, Dan, that is a damn sight more important than getting some crook off the hook, just because he's been able to pay you your exorbitant fees. I have as much of a moral mission now as I ever had as a respectable village priest - much more of a mission. in fact. Go back to your courtrooms in London, Dan Malone, and save your feckin' opinions for the jury."

James walked straight past his brother, back towards the hospital. Dan rubbed his forehead and grimaced.

"Oh Jaysus, alright - I'm sorry!" he bellowed, in the direction of the rapidly-disappearing figure of his younger sibling.

James stopped, and chewed his lip. Dan shook his head and approached him.

"I'm sorry," he repeated. "I suppose, I just....well, you know...California, happy hippy land. The girl Carrie seems a bit sort-of New Age. I just added two and two and came up with five. You just disappeared on us, James. What were we supposed to think? Five years, all of us believing you were dead, then all these weird, unbelievable stories and, frankly, bizarre behaviour. Would you believe it all, if you were me?"

James snorted. "Do you not think things must have been serious for me to just up sticks and disappear for five years, Dan? Think about it! No word, no contact. Nothing! Everything that I ever loved, ever valued, all abandoned in a single moment. My job, my vocation, my ma, my da, my brother? Did you not listen to a single feckin' word that I said in L.A?"

Dan sighed, and held up his hands in capitulation.

"Okay. We knew, as I said in L.A, that something serious had happened, but there were so many rumours about what had actually happened in Finaan. I mean...of the three other priests in the village, one committed suicide, another died in a car crash within hours, and the third mysteriously disappeared. Then you supposedly went and did yourself in. The stories - the possibilities - were rife. The press had a field day."

An ambulance rapidly pulled past the brothers, its siren squawking horribly. James assessed the man standing in front of him.

"You may not know me now, Dan, so you say, but you knew me then. I would not have gotten mixed up in anything weird, for all the tea in China. You know that!"

"Gotten?" Dan repeated, with a grin. "You even talk like a Yank now!"

"Five years is a long time," James whispered. "Five years without a word to Ma and Da - or even you, you fat slug!" His mouth curled in a wicked smile, as he used a long-forgotten childhood insult on his older sibling.

"Five years is time enough for a man to change a lot, and not only in the way he talks," James continued. Dan nodded.

"For five years, I was on the run, running away from powers far greater than me. Things I didn't even understand. Running away from what I'd seen and from everything that I'd ever believed in. All because of what happened that night. It wasn't just three men that died in Finaan, Dan. It wasn't just three priests. The Spanish priest wasn't even human. I saw him hurl fireballs straight from the outstretched palms of his hands. I saw the last survivor of a great race die and disappear into thin air. I saw a kid do the sort of things that only happen in comic books. I saw it all. Me! The most serious, level-headed kid in Howth. Remember? I saw it, Dan. I really, really did. As I said at home, I swear it on Da's life!"

Dan sighed. "So, where are you after going now, fella?" he asked, a degree of resignation in his voice.

"Yorkshire," James replied.

"And I suppose you'll be needing a lift and money?"

James took a deep breath, and nodded. Dan Malone put his hand on James' shoulder.

"I'll give Sarah, my secretary, a ring. She'll get us on a flight if there's any room left."

"Thanks, Dan," James nodded his gratitude.

"I'm not due in Court now until Thursday." Dan muttered. "Actually, there's only one way you're going to get me to believe any of this nonsense, I suppose, and that's to get me to see it for myself. I suppose I could handle a couple of days in Yorkshire. We'd better make a good job of explaining it all to Ma."

James grinned, and hugged his big brother. "You always did look out for me, Dan. You're not bad for a big fat bourgeois slug!"

Dan tousled his younger brother's long hair. "I'm still not sure I believe a word of it, though!"

Thirty-Four

Carrie could not remember spending a worse day at work. What was the point of playing around with the values of real estate when, somewhere far away, people's lives were at stake? Even so, she had bills to pay and a boss to please and she did not want to lose her job, even if she did feel inordinately distracted. She had spent the first hour of another beautiful, hot and long September day visiting properties in the Simi Valley area. By the time she got back to the office it was too late to ring Dublin because of the time difference, and anyway, her boss would not have been too pleased at the prospect of long transatlantic calls being made on the office phone. Carrie did her best to live up to her image of the beautiful, smiling, friendly California girl, but her mind was in turmoil and her guts writhed around inside her, as though they wanted to break free.

"You okay, honey?" her colleague and friend Kelly asked over a quickly-grabbed 'salad to go' light lunch. "You look like the weight of the world is pressing down on your shoulders, girl."

Carrie had told her about her boyfriend not ringing her when he had got to Ireland, about Dan's tale of him being found in the river, and James' story about the Order. Kelly had just laughed.

"Sweetpea, you are like so naïve. As soon as that boy hit that little island he would have done his duty, seen his father - and then he would have hit the bar. He's a man, honey...an Irish man, at that. You heard the one about why God invented alcohol?" Carrie shook her head. Kelly laughed.

"It was to stop the Irish ruling the world. Go buy yourself a pet snake, honey -they're far more reliable."

"He's not like that," Carrie whispered, her eyes downcast beneath her fashionable shades. Kelly rolled her eyes.

"None of 'em are, honey. Not until you get to know them. I know; I've got that t-shirt." Carrie feigned a snorted agreement.

The clock turned incredibly slowly. Every time Carrie glanced at it, she was convinced it had stopped. Outside the office's large plate glass window, Californians went about their normal business, lived their weekend lives; headed for the mall, or the beach, or just cruised. The sun shone, and the temperature outside Carrie's air-conditioned cocoon hit 95 degrees. Yet Carrie couldn't stop thinking about that dark little island, halfway round the world. An Ireland she had never seen, but a place that James had described so well that she felt like a regular visitor.

Then, finally, the working day came to a close. Carrie raced home so quickly that she did not even notice the flashing blue and red lights in her rear-view mirror as she hurtled along the Valley Circle Boulevard. Not until she heard the ominous wail of the police cruiser's siren did she snap back into reality.

Carrie slammed the ticket down on her kitchen table as soon as she entered her house at six o' clock, and ran over to the phone. The message light was flashing. She eagerly pressed the button, and waited.

"Hi Carrie, it's Mom, why haven't you pho-" Carrie squealed with annoyance, and clicked on to the next message.

"Hi Carrie, it's Annette - look, when are we -" Carrie pressed the button again.

"Is that Miss Caroline Horden? This is -" Carrie didn't wait to see what the telephone sales message was about; she was hoping for a far more important call.

"Hi, Carrie!" James' familiar, friendly brogue emerged from the answering machine. Carrie breathed a huge sigh of relief, and slumped into the chair by the phone.

"Look, babe, it's Saturday night here. I guess you're at work today and that old goat won't let you ring from the office. That is, if you got my last message and you are still speaking to me. If you didn't get it, that message was my big apology for not ringing you and my explanation of what happened. I've sort of got Dan on my side now, babe. I don't think he really believes anything I've told him, but he's going to take me over to Yorkshire, in England. We're going to try and get the kid out of there, and maybe I'll bring him home, over to the U.S. He'd be safe in the Canyon...well, as safe as anywhere. Would you mind that, babe? I know it's a cheek, but I don't know how else we're going to get him away from the Order. We're flying to London tomorrow, Sunday. I'll try and ring you as soon as I can. The flight is at three pm our time and we'll get to Dan's apartment in Hampstead around five, he reckons. I'll try and ring you from there. I love you, babe. Oh, by the way, the Order have gotten themselves a real, live, banshee; can you believe that? Love you, bye."

The message ended. Carrie let her head fall back against the soft back of the chair. At least it sounded like James had Dan on his side now. Dan was built like a quarterback, so Carrie felt some relief at that. She looked at her watch. Well, it would be at least fourteen hours until she would hear from him again.

She pressed the button on the answering machine.

"Hi Carrie, it's Mom…"

Thirty-Five

Margaret Houghton-Hughes put her arms around her older sister and gave her a long, heartfelt, hug. Despite the frequent bouts of animosity between the sisters, which was down to Doris' acute jealousy and Margaret's awareness of it, they had been quite close as children. Suddenly, all the bad feelings of recent years were washed away by the enormity of the tragedy.

Wayne had telephoned his aunt from the hospital call box before the police had taken them home; Doris had been in no state to make a phone call. Wayne had felt strangely calm once they had left the hospital. So calm, in fact, it had worried him. What had happened to all that anger he had felt? What had happened to all his sorrow?

By the time the police car had deposited Wayne and his mother back on Cavendish Street, Margaret and Stanley, along with Wayne's cousin Cedric, had arrived. Stanley's huge, shiny new Rover Hatchback was parked right outside number eighteen.

As soon as they had emerged from the cars both sisters had immediately rushed into each other's arms, burst into tears, and held each other tight.

"Eh, Doris, I'm so sorry, love!" Margaret had wailed.

With a last mumbled condolence, Sergeant Hartley and his companion began to leave, saying that Doris and Wayne should contact them if they needed anything. Sergeant Hartley acknowledged Stanley Houghton-Hughes with a nod.

"They'll be alright with us," Stanley assured the policeman. "Aye, they'll be alright with us."

Sergeant Hartley took a last quizzical look at Wayne Higginbotham and wondered what it was that disturbed him so much about that boy, before driving off into the darkness of the early hours of the morning.

Stanley Houghton-Hughes had recently attended a training course at the Yorkshire Ridings Savings Bank's Halifax headquarters on how to counsel bereaved staff, so the rotund, bluff, bank manager approached his nephew and slapped his hand firmly on his shoulder.

"Now then, Wayne lad, is there owt you need to talk about?" he asked, as sympathetically as he could manage. Wayne grimaced and shook his head. Uncle Stanley nodded sagely. Empathy not sympathy; that's what the lad needs, he thought, remembering a part of his course.

"You're the head of the house now, lad," Stanley stated bluntly. "When my dad died, during the war, I became the head of the house and I wasn't much older than you. I viewed it as an opportunity. It was time for me to prove myself and step out from under the old man's shadow, and it'll be the same for you. Although you're going to have to look after your mother now, you know!"

Wayne took a deep breath, and nodded. "How did he die?" he asked.

Stanley raised his eyebrows: "Didn't the police tell you?" he blurted in astonishment.

Wayne grimaced. "I meant your dad, Uncle Stanley, not mine."

Stanley Houghton-Hughes coughed. "Oh aye, sorry. He died in action."

Wayne nodded eagerly. "Was he a hero, like my dad?" Uncle Stanley flinched, and bowed his head.

"Well, no, not exactly. Not so to speak. He, er, was in the Home Guard and he, er...well, he...he fell off his bike." The last few words were muttered quietly. Wayne nodded.

"A motorbike? Like my dad's?"

Stanley coughed. "No lad, it was a pushbike. He just happened to fall off it right under an American Army lorry. Bloody Yanks!"

"Oh!" Wayne gasped, wishing the conversation had never started. Stanley quickly changed the subject.

"I told Frank to get rid of that bloody stupid old motorbike a thousand times," he harrumphed, shaking his head. "I said to him, I said, Frank, get thissen a Rover, or a Triumph, or sommat decent. Not one of them Japanese rust boxes, but sommat solid, sommat British! Even a Ford! I used to like my Fords, I did. Get some steel around thissen, Frank, I said...but no, he wouldn't listen."

Wayne shook his head sadly, and whispered, "He couldn't afford it, Uncle Stanley. We just couldn't afford a car. Not even a Japanese rust box."

Uncle Stanley pursed his lips."Aye, well...bad do, though. Bad do."

He ushered his wife and sister-in-law towards the Higginbotham's front door.

"Any road up, you're both coming to stay with us for a while, so let's just get some stuff and get you both off to bed. There's nowt to be gained from these two standing in the middle of the street wailing like a couple of banshees at this time of the morning." He put his hands on Doris and Margaret's shoulders, and propelled them towards the door.

Cedric glanced at Wayne. "You alright?"

Wayne glumly nodded back. "Yeah, I suppose so."

Cedric shook his head, and sighed. "I don't suppose the poor bugger stood a chance on that moped."

Wayne grimaced. "No! No, I don't suppose he did."

Wayne wandered upstairs and disconsolately opened his bedroom door, in a daze. He tossed the plastic wallet containing his father's meagre possessions on to his bed. He wasn't interested in reading the airmail letter at that moment. His mom had abandoned him for a slimy sleazeball, while the man who had loved him and raised him as a son was lying dead in a hospital morgue. He would read it later, sometime. He took some pyjamas from a drawer, and a few items of clothing. He picked up his washbag and turned to leave the room.

He didn't see the cloud of green mist begin to appear by his dressing table mirror, and he didn't see the face of his real father, Aillen Mac Fionnbharr, staring out at him.

Wayne turned out his bedroom light, gently closed the door and trudged sadly downstairs. Through the mist, a voice behind Aillen sounded concerned.

"This is indeed a bad turn of fortune."

Aillen raised his head, and sighed.

"The timing could have been better, but from such woe is strength derived. The Northman was a fine man, a great warrior and a good father to my son. His passing at this time is a cruel blow for the boy, but he will rise up all the stronger."

The voice behind Aillen was joined by a second. "Will he succeed in the test, that even now draws near, after such ill tidings?" Aillen sighed again.

"The Northman would have helped him. He had good counsel and knew well the ways of war. The boy is alone now, on that side of the veil. His sister remains lost in the darkness. I know not how he will fare, but know this! My blood runs in his veins, your blood runs in his veins. On the side of his mother, the blood of the great Boru runs in his veins. He is born of the royal line of the Tuatha De Danaan and of the mighty, mortal kings of the age of heroes. He will be strong, when he needs to be."

As the luminous mist began to fade and Wayne's room slowly returned to darkness, three shapes might have been discerned in the dissolving vapour: Aillen, the last Prince of the Tuatha De Danaan, mighty Fionnbharr, the last High King of the Tuatha and Nuada Airgetlam, known as 'Silver Hand', the first High King.

With one last glance back, Aillen gritted his teeth.

"He has to succeed, or it is all as dust. Everything that ever was, everything that is, all that ever shall be, is as dust!"

Thirty-Six

Aoibheall found the train journey North fascinating. She had heard of railways, even before she had entered the convent, but the enormous bullet-headed monster that she climbed aboard with Father de Feren was nothing like what she had imagined.

Indeed, little was as she had imagined. The world had changed a great deal in the years that she had been hidden away. It was the transport infrastructure that impressed her the most. Where had all the horses gone? Cars, vans and enormous lorries seemed to be everywhere; and, most frighteningly, men were flying overhead in the sky, in metal contraptions! She had crossed the Irish Sea in a huge iron ship, which had seemed to dwarf any ship afloat in her day. De Feren had laughed at her childlike amazement.

People spoke to each other, even though they were far apart, on things called telephones. They spent hours watching flickering picture shows on something called a television. The world was so much noisier than she remembered, and it wasn't just the machines. Music seemed to emanate from almost every doorway. Weird rhythms abounded, drum beats that she had not heard since her youth, in the wildest Tuatha gatherings. Fashion too had changed, much more than she ever could have imagined. Women were now totally shameless and exposed more flesh than she had ever seen before; and men no longer wore top hats, caps, or indeed anything on their heads.

Of course, she had heard about some of the marvels, while shut away deep in the bowels of the convent. She remembered seeing her first aeroplane from her cell window many years earlier and being told by a fellow nun that men now flew like birds all over the world, but it wasn't until she got to Dublin and then London, by car and ferry, that she realised just how different the world really was.

So far, de Feren and Aoibheall had lost two full days in the search for Wayne Higginbotham. Now it was Wednesday morning, and they were on their way to find the boy, at last. It would soon be over.

Sitting next to de Feren on the Inter-City 125, Aoibheall, in the guise of Sister Bernadette, looked every bit the fresh, innocent young Irish novice, out in the world for the first time. Underneath her sombre garb of plain black habit and black and white wimple, however, the Banshee Aoibheall was getting more and more excited about getting her hands on the stones of Falias.

She watched the other passengers: businessmen, businesswomen, shoppers, families, old people and youths. All would soon bow before her dark and terrible persona. She would be the queen of them all. She smiled faintly. Father Pierre de Feren was still under the impression that she could be used to find the boy, and then be conveniently discarded.

Aoibheall knew his mind. She knew that there was no way she would be allowed back into the convent. De Feren would kill her as soon as he had despatched the son of Mac Fionnbharr. That would tie up all the loose ends and signal the final demise of every last one of the immortal Tuatha De Danaan. He must have thought her really stupid.

Aoibheall's smile grew wider. She turned and looked at her travelling companion, who was staring out of the train window, watching the English countryside flash quickly by. Soon, she thought. Soon.

The train hummed smoothly along, passing rapidly through towns and cities, fields and meadows. Eventually, Father de Feren's head drooped onto his chin, as he nodded off into the uncomfortable doze of the traveller. His mouth hung open and a slight snore emerged at the same time as a thin line of dribble.

Aoibheall's smile grew wider still. She looked around the carriage at the nodding, sleepy heads, at the readers and those already dreaming. She gently lifted put her hand and placed it firmly on his forehead.

Father de Feren woke with a start. "Comment? Qu'est-ce qui se passe?" he demanded.

Instead of sitting on a fast-moving express train, he found himself lying in a wide valley, under a vivid blue sky. He scrambled to his feet and, much to his embarrassment, realised that he was absolutely stark naked. He looked around urgently to see if there was anyone who might see his shame. There was no one at all around. He was totally alone, in a deserted valley that he had never seen before.

The valley was wide with green hills on both sides and a placid, silver lake at the bottom. Mountains glowered from behind the hills, while he seemed to be standing in a wide meadow, full of long grass and wildflowers. The sun warmed his back, a hot sun, not unlike the heat of Rome in late summer. Clouds skittered across the sky in a pleasant warm breeze.

"Welcome to my world, Father." The soft female voice came from behind him, and caused the priest to yelp in surprise. His arms flew to cover his embarrassment.

"What witchcraft is this, Banshee?" he spat, as soon as he had recovered a degree of composure and had turned to see the equally-naked figure of Aoibheall, standing shamelessly before him, her hands on her hips. The beautiful banshee smiled, coquettishly.

"Witchcraft, Father? Mmm, I suppose you could call it that. I prefer to think of it as a shared, mutual, imaginary experience."

"I care not what you call it. You will cease this...this immoral nonsense, immediately!" the priest shouted; his eyes wild, yet carefully averted from the perfect female form before him."I knew I should have been more careful! All the sidhe are untrustworthy, even those who proclaim themselves to be followers of Christ."

Aoibheall smiled wickedly."Followers of Christ? Ha! Hiding in that miserable hole of a convent, was, for me, as hell would be for you, Father. Yet, being in that hole saved my life. All the others of my kind have fallen into the netherworld that is the doom of the sidhe. I, Aoibheall, alone have survived. I am now the last of all the true 'fairy folk'. I am the very last of the pure-blooded Tuatha De Danaan."

The priest stepped back.

"Whatever it is you plan, Banshee, I command thee now: return me to the real world, to the train, and I shall attempt to forgive this, this, witchery!" He raised one hand, and pointed at the banshee."If thou dost not, I shall commit thee to eternal damnation."

Aoibheall laughed and looked pointedly at the Priests' naked body.

"My, my, Father. You really don't like me at all, do you?"

De Feren crouched and crossed his hands over his groin to hide his shame. "Take me back now, you foul hag -, I command thee!" he bellowed.

"Hag?" Aoibheall repeated, reeling back in mock horror, her hand over her mouth. "Hag, is it?" She began to laugh, a laugh that broke into a monstrous cackling noise. "I'll show you a hag, priest!"

The beautiful black-haired, green-eyed banshee turned suddenly into a hideous misshapen form that might once have been human, but was now bent, wrinkled and wizened. The form lifted its head, as de Feren recoiled in horror.

"Get back!" he screamed, as he turned to run, then "Ouch!" as a large wasp stung his bare backside. The hideous form cackled.

"Just one of my little pets, Father."

De Feren's eyes now betrayed his fear. Aoibheall smiled, triumphantly.

"Look at me now...see me as I truly am, God man. See me now and be grateful for your squib of mortality, that it saves you from this." The banshee approached the priest, who fell to his knees and clasped his hands in prayer.

"Let me go, please, I beg you," he squealed, his eyes wide and bulging in terror.

Aoibheall cackled again. "See me now, Pierre de Feren. See that which knew of your designs on my destruction. See that which will achieve what you will not. Then, see nought more...forever!"

Aoibheall raised her bony arms, off which brown flesh hung like rotting meat on a skewer. She screamed - a long, agonising, piercing wail - and rushed towards the Priest, who gasped and promptly collapsed into a dead faint on the sweet, green, meadow grass.

The Inter-City 125 rattled and rumbled slowly to a stop at Leeds City station. Doors crashed open and banged noisily, and people shouted over the roar of numerous clattering diesel engines.

Sister Bernadette alighted from the train with a spring in her step and walked briskly out onto the station concourse. Once out of the station, she opened the black wallet in her hand and counted the notes.

"Bless me, Father, for I have sinned," she grinned as she stuffed the notes into a small bag that she carried, tossing the wallet carelessly into a waste bin. "Thank you, Jesus! Thank you, Lord."

As the train pulled out of Leeds City station, a woman placed her bag in the overhead luggage rack and peered down at the sleeping priest.

"Excuse me, love? Do you mind if I sit here?" she asked. The priest did not respond, and she touched him lightly on the shoulder. He rolled forward in his chair, his mouth open, and his head crashed on to the table before him.

The woman screamed.

Thirty-Seven

Cardinal D'Abruzzo sat at his desk, with his hands clasped in prayer. His heart pounded wildly in his chest as he mumbled obscure verses in ancient, formal Latin.

"At last!" he had declared, when Bishop Donleavy had telephoned him earlier that afternoon to inform him that Father de Feren had finally discovered that the wielder of the magic was, in fact, the half-human son of the demon named Finn. He had been exultant that the boy's identity had been discovered. Even at that moment, de Feren was on his way to deal with what was, hopefully, the very last of the immortals and their offspring. D'Abruzzo was very much aware that his time was running out. The boy had given him one week, and the days had passed quickly.

"Be certain that this time there are no mistakes," D'Abruzzo had demanded menacingly. He had heard the Irish Bishop's throat rolling at the other end of the line.

"There will be no mistakes this time. I swear," Bishop Donleavy had insisted.

"And this deserter, Mahone...he is dealt with?" D'Abruzzo had continued.

"I am afraid that Father Malone has met with an unfortunate accident, Your Eminence. It appears that - even after five years in absentia - the events that took place in The West of Ireland weighed heavily upon his soul. He deemed it better to take his own life." The old bishop chuckled. "As they say in the Hollywood movies: He who swims with the fishes..."

Cardinal D'Abruzzo allowed himself an indulgent smile. "Excellent. And are we quite, quite certain, Bishop Donleavy, that this boy is definitely the very last of the Tuatha De Danaan demons? They are like lice; they seem to have a nasty habit of continuing to crawl out of the woodwork every time we believe that we have killed the very last one."

"Yes, yes, he is definitely the last," Donleavy had continued to insist. "Along with our tame banshee - and she too will be dealt with, when she has fulfilled her destiny. I swear my life on that."

Cardinal D'Abruzzo pursed his lips, nodded, and closed his eyes in anticipation.

"So...the ultimate victory is now close at hand, my friend Donleavy? Good! You have done well, this time! Let me know as soon as the boy and the banshee have been dealt with." He replaced the receiver, and heaved a deep sigh.

A young priest knocked on the door and hearing the Cardinal's command, entered the room. "Your Eminence?" he bowed.

"Assure the child's mother that it will all be over, very, very soon," Cardinal D'Abruzzo announced. "Tell her that all will be well. 'God's Assassin' himself will be assassinated. Thanks be to God!"

"Yes, your Eminence." The young priest bowed, and left. The Cardinal smiled, and poured himself a large glass of wine.

"Your work is nearly done, Your Holiness, Pope Gregory. I am sorry it has taken us so long."

Thirty-Eight

"Carrie?" James was terrified that his girlfriend had not listened to either of his messages and was going to slam the phone down at the other end, as he nervously whispered into Dan's trendy beige trimphone.

"James, is that you?" came the eager response. "Where are you? What's happening? Are you okay?"

Carrie's torrent of questions poured out of the phone's tinny speaker.

"Yeah, I'm fine, babe," Malone laughed. "I'm at Dan's place in London. We're going up to Yorkshire tomorrow. I sort of remembered where this kid said he lived, so we're going to try and find him."

There was a sharp intake of breath from Carrie.

"And what about the Order guys that tried to kill you? Are they not, like, going to be trying to stop you?"

James stroked his chin. "I just hope they don't know where he is yet. I don't think I gave anything away under my 'interrogation.'" He gulped guiltily at the memory "If I didn't, we have a head start on them."

"And you're still going to bring him here?" Carrie asked, slightly uncomfortably.

"If that's okay with you, babe?" James answered. "We've gotta hide him somewhere out of the reach of the Order."

"Sure," Carrie answered, while being anything but.

"How are you, babe?" James asked tenderly.

"Missing you," Carrie pouted.

"I'm missing you too," James cooed. "It shouldn't be much longer, babe; then I'll be home like a flash."

"How's your da?" Carrie asked, remembering the whole original purpose of James' European trip.

"He's fine," James answered, although he did feel a touch guilty. The whole Order issue and Wayne's safety had distracted him, and his father's well-being had not been his first priority.

The couple exchanged more lovers' pleasantries, before James put down the phone with a contented sigh.

"Everything okay?" Dan asked, as James entered the kitchen.

"Yeah, everything's cool." James smiled. "Thanks for all this, Dan. It is important, you know...I mean, really important. I think it's about a whole lot more than just one kid's life."

Dan put the plate he'd been drying down on the kitchen table. "In what way?" he asked, scowling inquisitively. James pulled out a chair, and sat down by the table.

"The Order believe that once all the demons, as they call the 'fairy folk', are gone from the face of the Earth, then Jesus Christ himself will be free to return."

Dan slumped into a chair.

"Jaysus Christ...you're talking the second coming here, fella?"

James screwed up his face. "So they say."

Dan shook his head. "So.....are you quite, one hundred percent sure, we're fighting on the right side here?" he asked, with more than a hint of sarcasm in his voice."I mean, aren't we all supposed to be waiting for the second coming with great anticipation? The Rapture, and all that stuff?"

James grinned.

"I know people, Dan. I know whether they are good or bad, noble or dishonest. I guess it's just a defence mechanism I've built up over the years. I am totally confident, to this day, that there wasn't a bad bone in Mickey Finn's body. The kid Michael, Wayne, or whatever, was a nice, modest kid; very polite, maybe a bit shy, but definitely smart. These people are not demons, Dan. Not like in the horror movies."

Dan laughed, shaking his head.

"No, they're just your regular shape-shifting immortals who can blast fireballs out of the palms of their hands, just like most of us can cast dirty looks." His face suddenly took on a serious aspect. "What happens if you are wrong James? What happens if this kid you're trying to protect is the Anti-Christ? Not that I believe in such things...but just what if?"

James Malone grimaced. "This kid isn't like that Damien in the Omen movies, Dan. I know that. I also know that the Order is an evil organisation. The people, the way it operates...it's just so totally ruthless."

Dan shrugged. "Do you think the SAS are a bunch of nice guys? MI6? The CIA? Do you think they stop every five minutes to help old ladies across the road? Yet they're supposed to be the good guys, aren't they?"

James Malone raised his eyebrow. "If I'm wrong, Dan - and maybe I am - then I'm a fool, but I don't think that good guys throw innocent people into rivers to drown, hang Priests, or burn women and children alive. That's just what I've actually seen so far, with my own eyes."

Dan shrugged again, as he yanked the ring-pull off a beer can and passed one to his brother. "There are always innocent casualties in war."

James grinned ruefully. "Well let's try and make sure we do something to limit the number of potential innocent casualties...and one of them is this kid in Yorkshire."

Dan smiled. "Years of good Catholicism and a thousand confessions wasted. I've got some calls to make in the morning. We'll set off early tomorrow afternoon and start looking first thing Tuesday...okay?"

He raised his can. James nodded his agreement.

"Slainte!" He used the Irish word for 'cheers', then took a sip of the cold beer.

What if he was wrong? What if the Order was a well-intentioned organisation and it was just that some of its members were a bit too ruthless in trying to achieve their aims? After all, Dan was right. If the intelligence services hadn't sacrificed innocent people from time to time, then they would have lost the Cold War years ago. Bond always left a trail of beautiful corpses on his way towards stopping the bad guy from ruling the world. The Order seemed incredibly powerful within the Catholic Church, with its tentacles stretching almost to the top, if not to the very top.

No, the Order was evil. James could feel it. He could feel it in the very marrow of his bones. He was definitely right.

At least, he hoped he was.

Thirty-Nine

Funerals should always be in the rain, Wayne Higginbotham thought to himself, as he watched the line of sombre, dark-coated mourners enter St Stephen's Catholic Church.

The weather was unseasonably miserable for September, with a blustery North wind that would have been exceptional, even if had it been January. The wind cut through layers of clothing, chilling people to the bone, sending them scurrying in search of any source of shelter and warmth. Frequent heavy rain showers had already been dumped on the town by the heavily-laden clouds that rolled ominously over the nearby moors. Now another enormous black cloud was emerging from behind Castle Hill, rolling and churning like an agonised beast, like some meteorological harbinger of doom, threatening to burst over the small market town and wash everything away.

"Neat!" Wayne sighed under his breath. "Come on, bring it on! Let's have a huge, bloody thunderstorm. Let's send Dad out with a real bang."

He clambered out of the undertaker's black funeral car, which pulled up outside the church doors right behind the coffin-bearing hearse, and adjusted the plain, thin black tie that Doris had bought him especially for the funeral. It had probably been the only normal thing she'd done since Saturday evening. Her every waking moment had seemed to Wayne to be filled with incessant tears, or violent curses, in equal measure. The tears he had expected - after all, Frank had been her rock and had shouldered just about every burden in the Higginbotham household - but the curses surprised Wayne. Doris didn't just seem upset; she seemed extremely angry and bitter. The misfortune that had befallen her was so unfair. Why Frank? Why her husband?

Wayne could almost understand that response. He felt the same. Life was unfair; there was no doubt about it. What Wayne found hard to tolerate, however, were comments like "Why not Stanley?" and "Why wasn't it Margaret's husband?"

How could Doris be so mean about her own sister and brother-in-law? Especially as Doris and Margaret had seemed so close when Margaret had arrived to help on Saturday night. Aunty Margaret and Uncle Stanley had been so kind to them. Sometimes, Wayne just didn't understand Doris Higginbotham.

Crows cawed noisily in the trees; laughing, mocking the earthbound mourners, as Frank's simple coffin was borne into the sombre darkness of the Church.

Despite the inclement weather, the turnout for Frank's funeral was surprisingly good. It seemed, to Wayne, that Frank must have been more popular than Wayne could have imagined. Strange faces muttered hushed words of condolence to Doris and the boy as they passed, rushing from the car to get to the shelter of the church.

With some embarrassment, Wayne noticed a very pretty blonde girl, of about his age, giving him a shy, sympathetic smile, as he strolled down the aisle towards the front row. He should not have been fancying someone at his own father's funeral. It just wasn't right.

Wayne looked down at his shoes, and found his way to his place in the pew. Doris slumped beside him - arm in arm with the sister upon whom she had wished so much misfortune - and Jesus stared mournfully down at him from a huge golden crucifix on top of the ornate altar, which was littered with golden candlesticks and steaming gold vessels.

Wayne's mind was far away during the service. The reflections of myriad candle flames flickered in the huge stained-glass window behind the altar. Colourful scenes from the bible were depicted, and yet Wayne could not help but feel cross that the Romans were dressed as Medieval knights and Jerusalem looked like a Norman castle. Why couldn't they have at least made the scenes historically appropriate?

Should he have been thinking such things while his dad's coffin was standing right there in front of him? Waves of guilt kept flooding over him. Why had he not been able to save him? He was meant to the Slanaitheoir Mor!

He half-noticed the Priest waving the incense burner over his father's coffin like a Witch Doctor, rattling the bones and chanting incomprehensible incantations in some clearing in the deepest, darkest African jungle. He mechanically mouthed the words of the prayers and hymns, but his mind began to focus on his own mortality.

Would he end up in a box in this Church, with somebody in fancy dress waving an incense burner ceremoniously over his corpse? Was he actually an immortal like his real father? Did immortality come with the whole Tuatha De Danaan package? Or were shape-shifting, fire-bolt firing, invisibility and directing the thoughts of other mere mortals the only benefits of being a half-breed Tuatha Prince? What was the point of having the bloody powers anyway, when he hadn't been able to even save his own dad? Wayne shook his head and closed his eyes.

"Amen," the congregation collectively intoned at the appropriate points. Church was even more ritualistic than football. Now there was a weird thought. Wayne imagined half of the congregation as 'away' supporters, and instead of rhythmically chanting the Lord's Prayer, they were chanting "You're not singing anymore!" at Frank's mourners, who responded with "You're going home in an effing ambulance!" Even Wayne couldn't use the swearword, even in his head, on such an occasion. Wayne half-smiled, and then guiltily cleared his throat. He turned and appraised the stunning blonde again. Was she an unknown cousin?

He turned back to the front, and kneeled as the Priest invited the congregation to pray. He could hear the Priest and all the mourners droning on in the background, but suddenly he was aware of something else that made the hairs on the back of his neck stand on end. A sudden chill made his entire body shiver; he could hear someone calling his name.

"Michael!"

Wayne opened his eyes, and looked round. Row after row of mourners kneeled, with their heads bowed. He noticed the pretty blonde again. She glanced up and caught his eye. He quickly looked away as his face flushed.

"Michael, hear me..."

He heard the voice again. It was a girl's voice, sweet and melodic. Wayne turned and looked back towards the girl. Was it her? She would get told off by the priest, if it was her. Fancy shouting out a name while the priest was in full mumbo-jumbo mode!

Everyone sat back on the pews. The organ began to rattle out the first bars of a familiar hymn. Someone coughed, noisily. Everyone stood, again. The pretty blonde was looking down at her hymn sheet, seemingly oblivious. Wayne turned back towards the altar, where the priest was still droning on and on over Frank's coffin.

"Michael!"

Wayne realised that the voice wasn't shouting his name out loud. The sound was actually emerging deep in his own head. He was the only one who could hear it.

"Michael. I have come for you."

Wayne glanced around quickly again, just to make sure. Everyone was singing, or pretending to, and no-one looked as though anything out of the ordinary was happening.

Something else was weird. Whoever was calling him was using his birth name. No one knew his real name was Michael, except his real mom and his Irish relations. He didn't even think Aunty Margaret knew his name had been Michael.

Wayne closed his eyes, and concentrated. Could it be his long-lost sister trying to contact him telepathically? He was about to try and respond, when some sixth sense told him not to.

There was something wrong about the voice. Something almost too friendly. It reminded him of beautiful, tempting, scantily-clad vampire women, crawling slowly and seductively over their victim's bed, all deep cleavage, big bosoms - and then, suddenly, even bigger teeth. He'd seen them in late-night Dracula movies.

"Michael, where are you? I know you are close. I can feel you." The way she said feel made Wayne shudder. A baby began to wail somewhere towards the back of the church.

"Amen," the congregation chanted, as one.

Wayne was suddenly aware that the Priest was moving slowly down the aisle, still waving his incense burner; left then right, left then right. Once the last choirboy had passed, Cedric Houghton-Hughes led the way out of the front pew of chief mourners. Wayne shuffled slowly, mechanically, out after Doris. He glanced at the blonde again. Her eyes were fixed forward, and she didn't even seem to notice him. Could the voice have been hers?

Wayne steeled himself for the cold that he would feel standing by the graveside. He walked out of the Church doors and shivered, but it was not yet the cold that sent the shivers up and down his spine, again.

A nun stood by the steep drive to Saint Stephen's church, watching the mass of sombre people walking out of the church. She seemed to carefully examine each and every mourner in turn. Even from a distance, Wayne could see that her eyes were an unusually vivid shade of green. It looked to him like she was looking for someone in particular.

"Michael, I know you are there." The voice was as clear in his mind as if the girl speaking was stood right next to him. Wayne felt strange; a little nauseous. It was as if he could smell something sweet. Something rotting. Something dead.

There was definitely something funny about that nun. Some sixth sense had gone into overdrive as soon as he had seen her.

Wayne had been stuck behind his Uncle Stanley as the mourners had exited the church, so the nun didn't seem to have seen him. He was now sure that the voice was hers. No...he'd imagined it. The grief surrounding the occasion was sending him mad.

"Get a grip, Wayne," he silently whispered. But his imagination had gone wild. What if she was his sister? No - his sister would be too young to be a nun.

From over his Uncle Stanley's shoulder, he watched the nun sniff the damp Yorkshire air.

"Michael! You cannot hide from me!"

The voice emanated right in the centre of his head again, causing him to wince painfully. When he opened his eyes the nun had turned, and was slowly walking away. Wayne was sure he'd seen her mouth twist into a smile as she'd turned.

As Frank Higginbotham made his last journey, from the church to the grave, borne by six undertakers as pallbearers, Wayne found himself staring back towards the convent. He only snapped to attention when he felt Doris sag against him, as the coffin was lowered slowly into the grave and the priest began mumbling about ashes and dust.

Suddenly, Wayne Higginbotham felt very alone, very vulnerable, and - for the first time in many years - just a little bit frightened.

Forty

Aoibheall had felt a surge of excitement as the little train stopped at the small country station. She read the sign on the platform - Shepton - and exhaled a long, satisfied sigh.

"Soon now, so soon..." she muttered to herself as she stood up, ready to alight from the train. She had seen "Shepton" in the mind of the handsome, renegade priest, James Malone. A fact she had been careful not to relay to the fools in the Order. This was the town where the boy had been living five years earlier. The boy had mentioned it to the priest in mindless conversation. Now, here she was.

A vicious-looking youth, with spiky hair and chains decorating his black leather jacket, opened the door for the pretty young nun and smiled shyly as she thanked him with a grin. She stepped down on to the platform and took a deep breath of clear Yorkshire air. She felt her spine tingle as the cold wind hit her; but the tingle was not a reaction to the freezing conditions, but to the feeling that suddenly pervaded her very being, a feeling generated by her proximity to remnants of the stone of Fal.

Aoibheall asked a porter on the platform where she might find the local Catholic Church. The porter gave her long and precise directions, and the nun set off to walk into the town. With every step she took, the energy of the stones seemed to grow within her. By the time she passed the end of a street called Cavendish, she felt she could almost reach out and touch them. The feeling gave her a sense of pure exhilaration, despite the driving wind and rain. It was a feeling such as she had not had for centuries. Yes, she had been near the stones of other immortals during her long years in exile, but never had she experienced a sensation of the stones so powerfully.

Aoibheall also felt truly free, for the first time in as long as she could remember. Father de Feren would be well on his way to Scotland by now, and would never come out of his coma. By the time the Order had found out what had happened she would be long gone, along with the stones. She would use the stones to make a fortune, and would begin a new life that would lead to her being worshipped as a goddess. Mortals would prostrate themselves at her feet, or face her terrible wrath. She would have a slave for every menial task. Malone, if he still lived, and the boy, would be the first two. It was all so close now; nothing could stop her. The Banshee Aoibheall began to laugh.

A boy passing by on a 'Chopper' pushbike turned to stare at the laughing nun carrying the small, ancient, battered case, and was so bemused by such an innocuous sight that he steered into the kerb and fell off in a heap. Aoibheall laughed even louder.

Soon she reached the long tree-lined drive of Shepton's Catholic Church, St. Stephen's. She needed to find out where the Higginbotham boy lived. She felt sure that the local clergy would know of his whereabouts, because the boy was bound to have been adopted by a good Catholic family.

Suddenly, Aoibheall began to feel something strange. Something she had not felt in a long, long time. She could feel that somewhere nearby, there was another like her. It could only be him. She knew that he was very close to where she walked. She could sense his presence. The fat bishop had been told she could 'sniff out' those of her kind...and here was the proof.

Aoibheall closed her eyes as she walked up the steep drive, stooping in the wind. St. Stephen's was at the top of a small, but steep, hill. Somehow, she knew that the son of Aillen Mac Fionnbharr was very, very close. She could feel him. She really could almost smell him.

"Michael..." she whispered, as she slowly climbed the hill. There was no response. "Michael, hear me," she whispered again.

She noticed a line of black cars parked outside the Church. A funeral. Aoibheall stopped and stared. The boy was in the Church. She knew it.

"Michael..." she whispered. "Michael...I have come for you." Her body tingled with excitement, as she felt a sense of fear. The boy had heard her, and was terrified.

Moments later, the Church doors opened and a coffin was carried out on the shoulders of six grim-faced pallbearers, followed by a large crowd of mourners. Aoibheall carefully scanned each and every face, staring intently. He was there. He had to be there.

A woman wept as she walked behind the coffin, and a big man had his hand on her shoulder. She must be the widow, or the mother of some dead child, Aoibheall thought, although the notion of pity did not cross her mind. There were a few boys amongst the mourners who looked the right sort of age, but she couldn't tell if any of them was her quarry. None of them seemed to notice her.

Yet, someone had. She could feel someone gazing at her, but could not see who it was that had noticed her presence.

The coffin was borne towards an open grave. Death - mortals were so pathetic about it! They should have been grateful!

The banshee stared as mourners continued to pour from the church doors and walked to surround the grave, either clutching tightly at their coats or putting up umbrellas, facing them into the wind to avoid them being blown inside out. Her sense that the boy was close was almost palpable, yet she could not stand staring at a funeral party for long without seeming conspicuous, and there was nothing she could do here anyway.

"Michael, I know you are there," she whispered, before smiling ruefully and turning to walk towards the small convent building that was attached to the Church.

She knew he had heard her, and she knew he had seen her. She knew he was frightened, now. He would be found soon enough; and the stones would be hers.

Forty-One

It was some time before Father Pierre de Feren awoke, and even longer before he dared to raise his head. When he did he found that he was no longer in the pleasant, bucolic valley, but lost in a featureless thick grey fog. He could see no farther than a couple of feet in front of his nose, even though it seemed to be daytime.

There was no sign of the rotting, demonic hag. He was grateful for that, at least. De Feren was also grateful to realise that he was now back to being fully clothed in his black cassock and cloak.

The priest waited a while for the fog to disperse. When it did not, he stood up and started to walk, aimlessly. After several minutes, de Feren realised that he didn't have a clue where he was - let alone where he was going. The fog remained stubbornly thick, and swirled around him like cloying smoke.

The priest walked on again for what seemed like hours. There was no discernable change in the density of the fog, the light, or the ground upon which he walked. "Banshee!" he shouted. "Banshee!" he repeated, even louder and more desperately. "Get me out of this, or you will rue the very day you were born!" he bellowed furiously.

The fog swirled around him, ominously and silently.

"Banshee!" De Feren bellowed again. "We can make a deal. What do you want from me?"

There was still no response. There was no sound at all.

Father de Feren began to walk forward again, but there was still no change in the thickness of the fog, or what he could make of the terrain. By now, surely he should have found some sort of physical obstruction; an incline, perhaps, a hill, a stream, a lake, a wall...anything?

The unnerved priest stopped, knelt down, and began to crawl through the thickest mist, which seemed to hover just above the ground. "Banshee!" he yelled, although he knew now there would be no answer. The fog continued to swirl menacingly around him, and Father Pierre de Feren began to feel afraid.

Was he dead? Had the accursed fairy murdered him? He should never have trusted a sidhe; he cursed at his own stupidity, under his breath. "Banshee!" he wailed despondently, and slumped on to his bottom. How could he have been so stupid?

Father Pierre de Feren sighed, and fell on to his back. He would sleep and meditate for a while, and see what happened in the passage of time. Inside, however, he already knew.

It was some hours later that Father de Feren awoke, stiff, cold and uncomfortable. The light and the fog were exactly as before. He knew now what he had to do.

Father Pierre de Feren, chief assassin of the Sacred Order of St. Gregory, knelt and began to pray.

It wasn't long before a child appeared through the fog. The child was small, probably about four years old, with a mass of blonde curly locks, and cherubic features. Father de Feren fell flat on his face before the infant.

"So, Pierre, have you failed me already?" the child hissed, his voice deep way beyond his years. He glowered disparagingly at the prostrate priest.

"Please forgive me, my Lord. I have been betrayed!" De Feren wailed. The child looked around.

"Mmm...it looks like it. How did you arrive in such a miserable predicament, Pierre?"

De Feren hesitated momentarily. "Trust, my Lord. I am guilty of having trusted another."

The child sighed his annoyance. "Never trust anyone, Pierre, especially a fairy woman. I thought you of all people should know that by now."

The priest raised his head slightly. "I implore you, My Lord...help me, and I will not let you down. I am so close to achieving our final victory..."

The child shrugged. He bent down and picked up two pebbles.

"Eeney, meeney, miney, mo!" he chirped tossing each stone into the air in turn. "Where's the demon? Do we know?"

"Yes - yes, my Lord! I know who and where the demon is!" The priest wailed.

"Is he here?" The child tossed a pebble into the fog. "Or is he there?" The other pebble was tossed away. "Where, oh where, is the demon's lair?"

"I know where he is, my Lord! I was on my way to destroy the demon, when the Banshee tricked me. I know exactly where he is. There will be no mistakes, I swear. We are but hours from achieving the Orders' aims."

De Feren kept his eyes averted from the child, who grinned.

Oh banshee, banshee, fairy girl,
Leaves mortal hearts in such a whirl,
So fair of face and thin of waist,
Womanly charms, seeming so chaste,

193

You did your best to woo this man,
Using all the tricks a woman can,
Yet though you tried your very best,
You found this male unlike the rest,
For with Pierre it's all such a waste,
For girls are not to this priest's taste...

The child giggled manically, as de Feren squirmed in the mist. Suddenly, the giggling stopped.

"If you are the best I have, then I am surely doomed," the boy spat. "So be it! Rise, Pierre de Feren. Finish your work and do not dare to ever fail me again...or you will think that such a place as this is Paradise lost."

De Feren raised his head to grovel and thank the child, but he had already disappeared.

A breeze began to blow through the mist as de Feren clambered to his feet. The breeze quickly grew stronger, twirling the mist into strange patterns, yet leaving the Priest untouched.

The fog began to swirl, faster and faster, until de Feren began to feel like he was standing in the very heart of a tornado. His mind began to swirl like the fog, and he started to feel sick and faint. The noise became tremendous. It filled his head; it was like being in front of an express train in a tunnel. He found he couldn't catch his breath - and then, gasping desperately, he felt himself falling backwards...down, down, down into a bottomless abyss.

Then it all stopped. Nothing but darkness, darkness everywhere.

He tried to take a huge gulp of air.

"Doctor, I think he's coming round," he heard a female voice say, somewhere far away in the distance.

Forty-Two

James Malone had felt a total eejit - wandering up and down the High Street of the small Yorkshire town, asking strange people if they knew of a Wayne, or maybe a Michael, Higgins? Higginton? The good people of Shepton were typically blunt Yorkshire folk, and they were not afraid to give someone that particular look that conveyed their opinion that they thought the questioner was well and truly bloody stupid.

Dan and James had driven up to Shepton on the Monday evening, booked into the first hotel they could find, and had then spent a fruitless Tuesday asking everyone they met on the town's wide High Street about Wayne - or was it Michael? The problem was that James couldn't remember the boy's address, or even his proper surname. All he could remember was the Wayne, or the Michael bit, and something like Higgybottom, maybe. Tuesday was half-day closing, so by lunchtime the streets were emptying. Dan had taken the right hand side of the High Street, and James the left.

At the top of the High Street, a Parish Church loomed over a large roundabout with a tall cenotaph in its small, grassy island. Trees filled the churchyard, and trees lined both sides of the High Street. There was a cobbled area, about five yards wide, behind the trees on both sides of the street, and then the pavement and shops. The Irishmen would have found the location picturesque on a reasonably pleasant September day, but the urgency of their mission didn't allow for such sentimentality. By five 'o' clock, Dan had had more than enough.

"Jaysus, James, this is worse than looking for a needle in a haystack! I asked one fella how many people live in this town, and he told me it was around fourteen thousand. Fourteen thousand people is an awful lot of bloody people, you know. What chance have we got? He told me there'd be a lot more people about tomorrow. Wednesday's a market day. He said all those cobbles will be covered with market stalls, and that folk come from all around the Dales. We'll have another go then. Come on...I'll buy you a pint."

James shrugged his shoulders somewhat despondently. "You'd think someone would know someone with a name like Wayne, or Michael, Higg-something," he moaned. "I mean...if the boy was John Smith, we'd be in real trouble! Ah well...come on, then. I'll hold you to that pint."

The brothers had settled on the old station hotel, 'The Midland', as their base, and both were more than somewhat tired by the time they hit the bar.

"At least we've got another day, and the town will be busier tomorrow. Although the weather forecast is lousy," James stated, as he stared into the thick creamy white head of his pint of Yorkshire best bitter, later that evening. Dan nodded.

"We've got most of it," he agreed, "but I'll have to be leaving at about three tomorrow afternoon. I'm sorry, Jimmy. I'm in court first thing Thursday, and I still have briefs to read. Will you be coming?"

James shrugged. "I can't leave until I've found him, Dan. I've got to try and get him somewhere safe."

Dan snorted. "L.A. safer than the Yorkshire Dales. What is the world coming to?"

James laughed. "Look...would you tell Ma that I'm sorry I couldn't stay longer.? When all of this is over I'll bring Carrie home to visit and play the dutiful son, I promise."

Dan grimaced. "If you're right about all this, let's hope there's still an Ireland to come home to."

Wednesday lunchtime found Elizabeth Ball in a rush, and not just to get out of the foul weather. She needed some new pens, and the only place to get them was Waterfalls, on Sheep St. Sheep Street was adjacent to Shepton's High Street and acted as a sort of tributary. For a miserable squally Wednesday, the town was quite busy with people thronging the popular market stalls. The voices of hawkers and traders bellowed out noisily, proclaiming the quality of their wares

Elizabeth had been at Frank Higginbotham's funeral that morning and had passed on her condolences to Wayne and to Doris. It was such a shame; Frank had been such a decent man. She couldn't think of many men who she could have driven all the way to the West of Ireland with, and back, and not have felt in the slightest bit threatened. Elizabeth knew that she was still a very attractive woman and that some of the older boys in her school - let alone teachers and fathers - found her large bosom extremely distracting.

She decided to call on Waterfalls on her way back to school from the funeral; it would save her a journey later. Her thoughts had been elsewhere as she had clutched her coat tightly around her neck to ward off the unseasonably freezing wind, when the tall, long-haired man had approached her. She had been quite taken aback when he had addressed her directly:

"Excuse me, Ma'am," he had asked, quite cordially. "I'm looking for a boy who I believe lives in this town. He's called Wayne, or maybe Michael...and his surname is, I think, Higgyton, or Bottom, or something like that."

Elizabeth gasped, and her mouth dropped open stupidly."What?"

"I know, I know, it's completely mad," the man, whose accent was a strange mixture of Irish brogue and laconic American replied, throwing his hands up in a despairing gesture. "But I am desperate to find the lad. It's a matter of life and death. If you do know someone with a name like that, please tell me. I think he's in very great danger."

Women shoppers bustled past, staring at the dishevelled long-haired man and the woman he'd accosted, all grateful that it hadn't been them whose time he was wasting. Folk begging in the street...what was Shepton coming to? Elizabeth Ball cocked her head to one side, and raised a sceptical eyebrow.

James Malone gulped, and continued, "I mean...really great danger."

Instead of shaking her head and making a prompt escape as most people had, James Malone was more than a little surprised when the woman in the dark overcoat in front of him scowled, and asked, "Exactly what sort of danger is this Wayne, in?"

James Malone rolled his eyes. "You probably wouldn't believe me if I told you," he said.

"Try me." Elizabeth Ball demanded.

"Look...there's someone looking for him...they could even be in this town right now. They believe he's got some sort of religious significance and they...er..."

"What's your name?" the woman asked, brusquely.

"Er, Malone. James Malone." James answered, hesitantly.

Elizabeth Ball scowled pensively. "Are you a reporter?"

James Malone laughed. "No, I'm just an old friend of Michael's. I was there when, when..." Elizabeth Ball tapped her foot impatiently, and James shrugged."Let's just say we went through a lot together, in Ireland, five years ago."

Elizabeth gasped; her hand flew to her mouth. "You were with Wayne? In Ireland? Five years ago?"

Now it was James turn to gasp, incredulously. "You do know him, don't you? Thank God. At last! Holy Mother!" He turned and punched the air victoriously. James Malone felt an enormous weight rise from his shoulders.

"Yes, I do know a Wayne Higginbotham. I know him very well indeed," Elizabeth stated: "Just wait there a second. I'll be right back," she ordered, as she turned and marched briskly into the 'Waterfalls' stationery store.

"Dan!" James shouted to his brother, who was just in the process of accosting someone further up the street. "I've found someone who knows him!" James shouted and punched the air triumphantly again.

Dan apologised to the stranger and then marched down the crowded street, smiling indulgently. He slapped his brother on the shoulder.

"Well done, Jimmy. Look, I'm going to have to leave you to it, then. I've got to get back to the smoke. If you've found someone that knows him, then you're more than halfway there. Pity...I was hoping to be seeing him do some magic, so I was."

James grinned, nodded, and hugged his big brother.

"Thanks for everything Dan," he said, slapping his brother's back. Dan pulled away, and took out his wallet.

"You might need this." He proffered James four £50 notes. "If you need me, ring me. Unless I'm in court, I'm available." He punched James gently on the shoulder. "Go on, Jimmy. Save this boy and then the world, little brother. Take care of yourself."

With that, he walked away up Sheep Street, towards the car park.

"Right then, young man," Elizabeth Ball's voice barked from behind James. She dodged an old woman pulling a wheeled shopping basket, while clutching a plastic rain hood at her throat.

"I have to get back to my school. Before I tell you where Wayne can be found, I'm going to need a full explanation of exactly who you are and why you think Wayne Higginbotham is in danger. I was there, in Ireland, five years ago. I took his father Frank over there. We both brought Wayne home. Just for your information - and this may be no more than coincidence - but I've just left Frank's funeral. So your story had better be good!"

James Malone raised his eyes to the cloudy heavens. "Frank dead? Oh my God. Is Wayne okay?" he gasped, grasping Elizabeth's shoulders.

Elizabeth frowned. "He's as well as can be expected, for a sixteen-year-old boy who has just lost his father. Yes, he's fine. Look, I'm late as it is...I really must go. I'll have to see you after school."

James nodded. "How did Frank die, though?"

Elizabeth shrugged. "The poor man was knocked off his motorbike. The woman driver who hit him is totally traumatised, so they say, although they also say she was over the limit. Saturday night, you know."

"It wasn't a nun, by any chance, was it?" James asked, his face aghast. Elizabeth looked at him as though he was mad.

"A nun? No it wasn't a nun, unless nuns have taken to pub-crawling around Barlickwick on Saturday nights. Now, I really must go. Where can I meet you?"

"I'm staying at the Midland Hotel near the station. Meet me at six o'clock, if that's okay?" James stated, hurriedly.

Elizabeth turned, and then called over her shoulder, as James also turned to walk away, "Eight would be better - I have a husband to feed!"

James Malone walked along a bustling, crowded street, in a strange Northern English town, with a strange mix of emotions flooding his mind. He was elated. He had found someone who could lead him to Wayne. He was also frustrated, as he would have to wait nearly seven hours before he would actually find out where the boy was.

He was lonely. Dan would be hurtling towards Leeds now in his BMW, and Carrie was five thousand miles away. And he was terrified. Was it pure coincidence that good old Frank had been killed in an 'accident' just a few days earlier?

Had the Order got to Shepton ahead of him? He was probably going to have to face them again, and he'd only just survived one encounter, by the skin of his teeth. Had the banshee got more information from him than he had thought possible? Had she meant him to drown? She hadn't seemed that mean. In fact, James Malone felt a guilty surge of lust at the very thought of the raven-haired, naked, green-eyed beauty in that bucolic valley.

An old woman barged past him, almost knocking him over: "Bloody hippy, gerrout o't'road!" he heard her mutter.

James Malone rubbed his forehead as he began to walk up the High Street, past the street market and the cacophony of noise.

"Come on, Ladies. The best meat you'll ever eat and all produced on the farm right here in Yorkshire!" someone shouted.

"Let's just hope that nothing happens to Wayne in the next few hours!" James muttered out loud, as he dodged through the jostling crowd.

Forty-Three

Terri Thorne was disappointed. She had not heard from Michael, even though she had asked him in her last letter to ring her, so that she could apologise for the content of the preceding letter. She knew the second letter would have gotten to England days ago. So - why hadn't he contacted her? Could it be that Doris had found out about their relationship, and had forbidden him to ever contact his real mother ever again? That was a possibility!

Had Frank decided to stop the contact? No, she doubted that. Frank was a decent man; plain, very plain, but decent. Maybe it was Michael himself? Maybe that last letter had really upset him, and anything that she now sent to him was going to find its way straight into the trash-can even before it had been opened. Terri bit her lip. That was highly possible; probable, even. How could she have been so goddamn foolish?

She had thought about her first-born son every single day, ever since the nuns had ripped him and his sister from her arms, all those years ago. She had finally found him after eleven years of praying, wishing, and just wondering what had become of him - and now she had possibly gone and lost him again. How stupid was that? How stupid was she?

She wiped a tear from her eye. The traffic on the Interstate was jammed solid. As she sat and clutched the steering wheel of her car, she looked up at the moon beginning to climb high over the Malibu hills. Terri wondered what Michael would be doing, as that same moon waned and the sun began to rise in England.

Terri couldn't help but think of Wayne as Michael. That was the name she had given him when she had been a naïve sixteen year old called Theresa O'Brien. A sixteen-year-old girl then living in London, but from the most remote part of Ireland. A sixteen-year-old obsessed with the impossible dream of being a movie star one day. Despite the fact that his adoptive parents had changed his name, he would always be Michael to her.

She looked at her watch' nearly eleven. Dean wouldn't be home for a while yet. Even if the traffic didn't clear for ages, Terri knew that she'd be home before him.

Had she done the right thing, marrying Dean? It didn't seem right that he wanted her to cut off relations with her own son. Was that because he felt his own child would be less loved? Sometimes men were so pathetic.

Whatever; she wasn't about to lose Michael all over again. Terri decided that, as soon as she got home, she would write yet another letter and that she would carry on writing until Michael finally did respond. And if he didn't, she would be on the first goddamn flight to England she could get, once the baby had been born.

Terri Thorne would not lose her son again, ever! And if Dean didn't like it? Well, that was just tough! Michael Sean O'Brien was her son, and that was that.

The traffic started to move again. Terri felt a small kick inside. She smiled.

"Michael will teach you to play rugby and soccer when you're older, yes he will." she cooed; then, with more than a hint of regret in her voice, "I hope."

Forty-Four

The voice incident in the church had freaked out Wayne. How could someone have got words to materialise right in the middle of his head? And who, apart from his birth family, knew that his original name had been Michael? Had it been the strange, green-eyed nun he'd seen...could she possibly have been his sister?

The very word sister seemed incongruous. He had tried to imagine what she would be like, but he just couldn't get a clear picture of her in his mind. Would she look like him? Poor girl! The nun hadn't looked like him, as far as he could tell, but it had been difficult to judge from that distance, in her wimple and nun stuff...no. Terri had said that they hadn't been identical twins, anyway.

Would she have been raised in the North, or would she be all posh and Southern? Could she have been taken abroad? Could it really have been her putting that name in his head? Had she developed her own Tuatha skills? Who the hell else could it have been?

Wayne sat forlornly on the side of his bed, fiddling with the slightly crumpled blue airmail envelope in his hand, turning it over and over. He had waited until after the funeral to open it - mainly as a sign of respect for Frank, but also maybe even out of respect for his mum. Doris wasn't the nicest, sweetest mum in the world, by any stretch of the imagination, but he had thought of her as 'Mum' until he'd reached the age of eleven; and she would never have let him down to put someone else, or her 'career', first.

For the first time in his life, Wayne had actually felt sorry for Doris at the funeral. So many people had said how nice Frank had been and how sorry they were to hear of his accident, yet so many had so obviously been thinking, "Poor devil, imagine being married to that old bat!"

Doris was definitely not a popular woman. She had a very Yorkshire habit of saying exactly what she thought, when she thought it - and if it upset people, well, bad luck! "I say what I mean and I mean what I say," she would often declare, as well as "I say what I think...and if they don't like it, they can lump it!" She had duly managed to upset just about everyone she knew over the years - Doris Higginbotham would never have made a career as a diplomat!

She had alienated Frank's family very early in their relationship by refusing to convert to Catholicism, despite having promised to do so. The Higginbothams were a renowned strict Catholic family in Shepton, and Frank had been a very devout church-goer, until he'd met Doris. Doris had been confirmed in the Church of England and was proud of it. She had, however, made a solemn promise to convert to Catholicism after the wedding; but had changed her mind even before the reception had finished.

The final straw for Frank's family had been the fact that the Higginbotham family influence had been instrumental in the adoption of the boy that Frank and Doris had named Trevor, and then subsequently the second attempt with Wayne. Without them, 'The Crusade of Rescue' would never have considered a mixed marriage as a suitable environment to raise a good little Catholic child. Doris had repeated her conversion promise to 'The Crusade of Rescue' when they had initially been offered a Catholic baby to adopt. But, once again, as soon as the adoption process had been legally sanctioned, Doris reneged on her promise, citing a simple change of mind.

Frank had merely accepted her volt-faces, as it was easier than getting into long, interminable rows. The Higginbothams, however, were horrified by her behaviour, and eventually they gave up on Doris and Frank. They even stopped visiting them, after a particularly nasty row between Frank's sister and Doris on the latter's doorstep, in which Doris had threatened to do the poor woman some serious physical harm if she continued trying to convert her.

Wayne had grown up not knowing his father's side of the family at all. He had been amazed to see so many people he did not recognise at the funeral, people who had turned out to be uncles, aunts, or cousins. Well, it was all over now. Frank was in his grave, and Wayne and Doris were back in Cavendish Street for the first time since that fateful Saturday night.

The post-funeral 'tea' at the big Raven Hotel near Gas Street School had seemed interminable. Frank's family had whispered in conspiratorial groups, while Margaret and Stanley had done their best to console Doris. Wayne and Cedric had passed the time talking about cars, football and girls, all the usual sort of stuff. The pretty blonde girl who'd been at the church hadn't turned up at the funeral tea, much to Wayne's disappointment. Wayne had asked Cedric if he had known who she was. Cedric didn't have a clue, but did admit to having also noticed her.

The boys' conversation was interrupted when Elizabeth Ball, who had taught both of the cousins at Gas Street Primary School, grabbed Wayne's hand and expressed her sympathy with tears in her eyes.

"I'm so sorry, Wayne," she had said. "Frank was such a good man. I'll never forget him, nor our trip to Ireland. I'd like to stay longer, but

I've got some stuff to get from Waterfalls and then I've got to get back to school. I'm afraid the next generation of Cedrics and Waynes are waiting. No rest for the wicked. Good luck, love." She patted Wayne's cheek, and blew her nose on a clean white tissue.

Wayne had thanked her, whilst wondering how she was going to get his mom's letters to him now that his dad was dead.

Once Elizabeth had gone, Cedric had nudged him and whispered.

"I know I shouldn't say this - but do you think your dad and her...you know...in Ireland..."

Wayne had snorted. "Don't be daft. Me dad, well...he wouldn't have."

Cedric shrugged. "I would've. Best pair of knockers in Shepton. I used to fall and skin me knees just so she'd give a cuddle. My head was just the right height." He mimed his head getting buried, as he popped his eyes and sucked in his cheeks.

Wayne actually laughed out loud, and then quickly silenced himself, as sad-faced mourners glowered at his inappropriate behaviour.

Occasionally, someone interrupted Wayne and Cedric's conversation to pass on their sincere condolences, but mostly people just munched their ham and cucumber sandwiches and supped their tea, or ale.

Once the funeral tea was over, Margaret had pleaded with Doris to stay longer at her house, but Doris had insisted that they must return home. Living with the Houghton-Hughes was like having "her nose rubbed in it," she had declared to Wayne, later. Doris could not abide the Houghton-Hughes' middle class pretensions and had been driven to distraction by the opulence of their home.

Wayne had been more reluctant to leave. He was going to miss having a bathroom on the same floor as his bedroom, instead of two levels below. Going to the loo in Cavendish Street meant going down two flights of stairs, one of which was an uncovered stone staircase and was absolutely freezing in winter. In fact, it was absolutely freezing in the summer too.

Back in his bedroom, Wayne stared at the return address on the back of the envelope, and sighed. "I don't suppose I'll ever get to Los Angeles now," he whispered.

He was about to open the envelope, when he heard the sound of gentle sobbing seeping through his closed bedroom door. Doris was crying again. Wayne put the envelope down and climbed off his bed. He would read Terri's letter later. Right now, his mum needed him!

It was about half an hour later, after Wayne had given Doris a long hug and reassured her that everything was going to be alright, just after he had put his head down on his pillow and begun to drift into what he hoped was going to be a good night's sleep, that he heard the voice again.

"Michael." The voice awoke him immediately. "Tomorrow, at last we shall meet, Michael. Tomorrow..."

Wayne jumped out of bed, and turned on the light. He was alone in his room. He walked over to his window, and looked out. There was no one in the back street behind the house. The cattle market beyond was in total darkness. He felt the skin on his scalp crawling. This was definitely not his sister. There was an implied threat in the voice; or certainly something very unpleasant.

Wayne opened his drawer and checked his pieces of the stone of Fal. They had been securely hidden in an old pencil case ever since Doris had tried to throw them out. They were there, safe and sound. Wayne took them out and laid them on his bed. How could such innocuous-looking stones contain so much power?

Wayne put the stones back into the tin pencil case and looked around his room. There was a model of the Starship Enterprise on top of his wardrobe. Wayne climbed onto his bed, and put the stones under the ship's stand.

"Are the dilithium crystals in place, Scotty?" Wayne said out loud.

"Aye, Captain. We have full warp capability." Wayne imitated the Scottish accent of the television show Star Trek's chief engineer. "Prepare phaser banks and photon torpedoes, Mister Scott. Shields up!"

"Aye, aye, Captain."

Wayne climbed down from his bed and grimaced. Maybe this was going to be one of the tests that Aillen had talked about. He walked over to his dressing table and picked up the small action figure of Luke Skywalker from the movie Star Wars.

"You must use the power of the force, Luke."

Wayne shivered and climbed back into bed, leaving his light blazing. Somehow, Wayne didn't feel like sleeping in the dark.

Somehow, he didn't feel like sleeping at all.

Forty-Five

It seemed like hundreds of years since Aoibheall had had so much freedom. The freedom to walk alone, unhindered, through the streets. The freedom to do exactly what she wanted, when she wanted.

After so many years hidden away in the convent, mostly locked up in her tiny cell, Aoibheall had quite forgotten the simple pleasure of feeling the kiss of the wind and the rain on her cheeks. She had forgotten how nice it was to watch the leaves fall and see clouds scudding through a wide blue sky.

She had to admit, however, that she found freedom a little bit daunting. Without Father de Feren to guide her through the streets she found herself wandering aimlessly, staring like a simpleton at the strange items in shop windows, marvelling at the vehicles on the roads and gaping open-mouthed at the people, with their weird haircuts and clothes. Before long she was quite lost and had to ask a stranger directions back towards the sanctuary of the Shepton convent. She had called into a shop to buy a bar of chocolate, her first taste of such a delicacy, and had been acutely embarrassed when the shopkeeper had laughed at the fifty-pound note she had tendered.

"Have you nowt smaller, love? Nuns must be made of money, these days. I'll bet you're not one of the poor sisters, are you?"

Aoibheall had hurried out of the shop as fast as her legs could carry her, as the laughter seemed to follow her out into the street. Well, she thought silently, I will have plenty of time to find out how the world works, once I have those stones in my hands.

The chocolate was worth the embarrassment. It was the most delicious thing Aoibheall had ever tasted. By the time she got back to the convent, she had eaten the lot.

The few nuns in the convent had provided "Sister Bernadette" with a very comfortable room, available for the duration of her short stay. It even had a small black and white television in a corner. It was totally wasted on Aoibheall, because she didn't have a clue how to work it.

Aoibheall had told the nuns that she had been sent to Shepton by the 'Crusade of Rescue', to check up on young Michael - or Wayne, as he was now called - to see how his Catholic education was coming along. They, in turn had informed her of Frank Higginbotham's untimely demise. One of the nuns, a very good friend of Frank's sister, even knew Wayne's address, which the banshee claimed to have lost.

Aoibheall was ever so grateful to the nuns for their hospitality and information.

As she settled down to sleep after a long hot bath, she reached out again, trying to reach Wayne's mind.

"Tomorrow, at last we shall meet, Michael. Tomorrow." As she drifted into slumber, her lips were curled in a smile. Chocolate and power...what could be better?

Forty-Six

Father Pierre de Feren opened his eyes.

"Ah you're back with us in the land of the living, at last!" a young nurse in a blue uniform said, as she wrote notes by his bedside.

The bewildered priest glanced nervously around. He was in a hospital bed. The only one occupied in a ward, a group of four. He breathed a long, deep sigh of relief.

"Where am I?" he asked, his Belgian accent clearly discernable.

"St. James' Hospital, Leeds, Father." The nurse smiled amicably.

"How long have I been here?" the priest asked, frantically clutching the girl by the arm.

"Only a few hours," the nurse responded curtly, firmly removing the priest's hand from her arm. "They found you on a train. Out cold you were, Father. It is Father de Feren, isn't it?" she asked.

"Yes!" The priest replied, impatiently. "So, today is?"

"Wednesday, love," the nurse answered, twisting her lip at the stupidity of the question.

"Good...what time is it?" De Feren demanded.

"Just after eleven at night," the nurse replied, now sounding impatient herself. "Look, don't get your cassock in a knot, love!" she added. "You're here for a while, so you might as well relax."

"What do you mean, a while? What's wrong with me? How soon can I leave?" De Feren asked, his voice betraying his stress. The nurse went back to her notes.

"As soon as the Doctor says, love. We have loads of tests to do. You've been in quite a nasty little coma, you know. You need to rest. We don't know what caused it; there's no sign of a head injury or anything."

The Belgian priest glowered at the young nurse. "I have some very important business in a place called Barlickwick. It is a matter of life and death."

"It'll be my death, if I let you out before Doctor Mainwairing sees you. He'll kill me." The nurse laughed. "With a bit of luck they might let you out tomorrow evening, or maybe Friday."

"Tomorrow?" De Feren coughed; his tone one of outrage. "But you don't understand. I must leave this hospital now!"

The nurse laughed. "And where are you going to go, at eleven o' clock at night, love? I'd rest if I were you. You need, and we need, to find out why you were in a coma. It might be very serious." The nurse shrugged, and walked off towards the next bed.

The priest gritted his teeth, fell back onto his pillow, and sighed. He closed his eyes. The banshee had at least a day's start on him. How would he catch her, now? For a moment de Feren felt panic-stricken, but then he remembered his training.

What did it matter what sort of start she had on him? If she killed the boy and took the stones, then he would find her, and simply kill her. If the boy was more powerful than they had expected and killed her, then it was only the boy he would have to kill. If she had left the boy alive, then he would just have to kill them both. It was all just numbers.

"Ah, Father de Feren." A man's voice disturbed the Priest's thought process. "I'm Doctor Mainwairing. I'm a little bit concerned to hear that you want to leave us already."

The doctor, along with the nurse that de Feren had complained to, was strolling purposefully towards the priest's bed.

Father de Feren nodded. "I have some urgent business that I need to attend to, doctor."

"Good God, man! At this time of the night?" the Doctor snorted. He stroked his chin and picked up the file from the bottom of de Feren's bed.

"Hmm...coma, no signs of head trauma, but concussion possible..." He stuck out his bottom lip, and gave the nurse a reassuring nod. "No, Father, I'm afraid I'm going to have to insist that you stay with us - at least until we've had a chance to carry out some X-rays and a few tests, tomorrow. We need to keep you under strict observation. That coma was nasty, and we need to know what caused it." The doctor replaced the file, and grinned at the fuming priest. "I would think you'll be out by Saturday, at the absolute latest."

Father de Feren smiled sarcastically. "And by then the treacherous snake of a banshee will be hundreds of miles away!" he grumbled, under his breath. The doctor ambled off towards patient in the next bed area, while the nurse gave de Feren the sort of look that said "Told you so, didn't I?"

Father de Feren took a deep breath, and settled back on his pillow. He was a patient man. It was pointless arguing with authority. He would wait, and take the first chance he got to escape. The doctor was right. There was little he could do at this time of night, but he would be leaving the hospital first thing tomorrow, whatever the Doctor might say. He knew exactly what had caused his coma, and didn't need X-rays to prove it.

Once the doctor and nurse had disappeared from sight, de Feren leaned over the side of his bed and lifted his jacket from a chair. He felt for his wallet. It wasn't there. He frantically patted every pocket, and then threw the jacket back on to the chair. He yanked open the drawer on the table unit by his bed. His passport was there, but his wallet was not. With his heart pounding wildly in his chest, de Feren fell back onto his pillow again.

"Aoibheall!" He spat the name in disgust. Father de Feren would need money to continue his search for the boy; that was another problem he would have to face the next morning. He closed his eyes and began to daydream, and when the nurse returned, Father de Feren had fallen asleep.

A beatific smile creased his lips. Father de Feren was planning his revenge.

Forty-Seven

James Malone ran his hand through his long, dark hair.

"So...Jaysus...where do I start?" he sighed.

"I always find that if you start at the very beginning, then you may find that the story makes a lot more sense. Don't forget - I did hear snippets of the tale in the car on the way back from Oughterard, five years ago. If you convince me that you are who you say you are, and that your intentions are honest, I will take you to Wayne," Elizabeth Ball replied, with a smile. She had already convinced the Irishman that the boy should be left alone, so soon after his father's funeral.

The bar of the Midland hotel was almost deserted. Wednesday evenings were not generally busy in the slightly run-down hotel that had long past its hey-day. A plump, balding, middle-aged travelling salesman was propping up the corner of the bar, staring morosely into a half-empty beer glass, desperately trying to convince himself that it was half-full. A young barmaid diligently polished unused glasses while chewing furiously on pink gum, which occasionally emerged from her mouth as a lurid bubble.

Elizabeth had fixed John's dinner and then gone straight out to meet James in the hotel bar. She had told John about having met a stranger who was looking for Wayne in the town that afternoon.

"It seems he met Frank and Wayne when we were in Ireland," she had explained. "He says that he was there when Wayne met his real dad."

John had merely shrugged his shoulders. "Why was he looking for Wayne?" he had asked, after a long silence.

"That's what I want to find out. Let's just say I'm curious," Elizabeth had replied, raising a single eyebrow. She had kissed John on the cheek, grabbed her handbag, and left. "I won't be late," she had shouted.

"Be careful," John had muttered. "You know what curiosity did for the cat!"

Now, here she was; sat in the Midland Hotel bar, waiting for James to tell her why he had come all the way to Shepton to look for Wayne, after five long years had passed.

"So...what really did happen that night in Ireland?" Elizabeth asked.

"If only I had a thousand pounds for every time I've been asked that question," James laughed. "Did Wayne, or his da, not tell you what happened?"

Elizabeth shook her head. "They both said that what they'd seen, they couldn't quite believe. So if they didn't believe it, having been there and seen it, they said I'd have no chance in believing it. I didn't push it at the time, as Wayne had a lot on his mind, what with his real mum and all that. So...what happened? I've always wanted to know the full story, but Wayne left Gas Street, and time passed, as it does. It was just never the right time to ask, I suppose." Elizabeth shrugged. "So, go on, tell all. What happened? What was your role in the events?"

"Apart from me being the eejit who helped to get Wayne's real father killed?" James bemoaned sadly, while running his forefinger around the rim of his pint glass. Elizabeth took a sharp intake of breath.

"Do you...do you know who Wayne really is?" James asked hesitantly.

Elizabeth nodded. "As far as I am aware, Wayne Higginbotham was born Michael O'Brien. He's the adopted son of the Higginbothams, but I did meet his real mother while we were still in Ireland. She's Theresa O'Brien, better known as the Hollywood star 'Terri Thorne.'"

She sat back, looking pleased with herself, and took a sip of her lemonade. James Malone smiled sadly.

"All of that is true, but now I'm going to make a real eejit of myself. Do you know who his real father was? Or, more to the point, what he was?"

Elizabeth grimaced. "He said he'd met his father at the cottage, you know, that night. That he'd been a great man, but that he was gone. I couldn't get them to elaborate on it. Frank wouldn't say any more, either. You...you just said he was killed, and that you feel partly responsible?"

James frowned. "It's a long story." He took a very deep breath. "You see, Wayne's Da, wasn't...well, he wasn't like us."

Elizabeth narrowed her eyes suspiciously. "What do you mean?"

James took a sip of his beer. "Okay - I'll take your advice, and start right at the beginning. Some six years ago I was cycling over the Partry Mountains in the west of Ireland. There's a road that runs over from the Westport road to the village of Tourmakeady. I was a young parish priest working in Finaan at the time, and I would often be up that way. I used to love cycling in those hills. So, on this particular day I just happened to bump into an old fella who lived in a very remote cottage, right out in the wilds. We had a bit of the craigh, the way you do, and he told me - jokingly, I thought - that he was one of the 'little people'."

Elizabeth grinned. "The 'little people'?"

"Yeah, right!" James grinned back. "That's what I thought, until I happened to mention it to my bishop, in Knock, a few days later. The whole world went mad, and suddenly people were coming all the way from Rome to do the old fella in."

"What?" Elizabeth asked incredulously.

James shrugged, and leaned closer to Elizabeth. His voice became little more than a whisper, despite the fact that the bar was nearly empty.

"There's a secret society in the Vatican, called the Sacred Order of St. Gregory. They exist to destroy evil forces, like vampires and so on. You know...unnatural stuff."

Elizabeth shuffled uncomfortably. "Like Ghost Busters?" she asked, sounding incredibly sceptical.

"Exactly!" James nodded his agreement, and took another sip of his pint. "The Order sent an assassin over to kill this old man, because they believed he was a demon. It seems they've been killing the Irish 'fairy folk' for hundreds of years."

Elizabeth now looked confused, as well as downright sceptical. "So where does Wayne fit into all this?"

James sighed. "Hold your horses, lady, I'm coming to that. The old man turned out to really have been one of the little people - no less than the last Prince of the Tuatha De Danaan."

"The what?" Elizabeth blurted, barely able to stifle a giggle. "They sound like a pop group!"

James smiled patiently. "The Tuatha De Danaan was a magical, immortal race, who supposedly lived in Ireland before the Celts."

Elizabeth grimaced. "Like, a mythological people?" James nodded eagerly.

"It's all a part of Irish folklore. Anyway, they - the Tuatha, that is - got pushed out by the Celts, but instead of leaving Ireland they went underground. But not like a resistance movement...I mean literally underground, into the caves, barrows and burrows that pepper the Irish countryside. You know, Newgrange and all that. They are the leprechauns of legend, the 'fairy folk' - you know - the 'little people'."

Elizabeth grinned. "Right, I'm with you now. This is turning into one hell of a story, and I still really don't see where Wayne fits in."

James shrugged. "The old fella's real name was Aillen Mac Fionnbharr, an immortal warrior Prince. A shape-shifter. The 'little people' really do exist, and he was one of them."

Elizabeth twisted her mouth, sceptically. "How can he be a 'was', if he is immortal? As for shape-shifters...well, come on!"

James wiped his forehead. "Immortality is just about not dying naturally, you know - of old age, disease, that sort of stuff. If someone blows your head off with a shotgun then it's pretty hard to survive, even if you're immortal. And I didn't believe in all this stuff, either."

Elizabeth looked confused. "So, you still haven't said how Wayne fits into all this leprechaun business?"

James took a deep breath and nodded patiently. "I'm about to. Has Wayne ever done anything strange? You know, sort of weird? Anything remotely magical that you know of?"

Elizabeth laughed. "No, of course not. Don't be ridiculous! How silly! Wayne's just..." She stopped in mid-sentence. Evidently a thought had just exploded in her mind, and she coughed and turned back towards James.

"There was something funny...something really strange that happened, now you come to mention it. When he was still at Gas Street, not long before he went and ran away to Ireland, he was involved in a fight with a much older boy. A local hooligan called Baz."

James leaned in conspiratorially, and Elizabeth looked acutely embarrassed.

"I'm only telling you what I heard, of course, but it appears that Wayne knocked him out, somehow. I mean, this Baz character was all of sixteen - a huge brute of a youth - and Wayne was a very skinny little eleven year old. Indeed, they do say that Baz hasn't been quite the same since."

James smiled. "Had you seen him in action that night back in Mayo, maybe you'd understand a bit more. Did you ever notice anything funny about his ears, by the way?"

Elizabeth smiled. "Yes they were cute and very... well... pointed... no..." Her voice trailed off, and her mouth dropped open. James nodded.

"Michael O'Brien is the son of the aforementioned Aillen Mac Fionnbharr and Theresa O'Brien. Your young, adopted, Yorkshire boy, Wayne Higginbotham, is the last of the Royal line of the immortal Tuatha De Danaan."

Elizabeth's mouth hung open, as James continued, "And the Sacred Order of St Gregory want to make sure that the line terminates there. Just like they did five years ago, when their hit squad took out Aillen Mac Fionnbharr and would have killed Wayne himself - if his adopted dad, Frank, hadn't burst in like Bruce Lee and knocked down the chief Order assassin, before lobbing a knife right into his chest."

Elizabeth reached down mechanically and took a large gulp of lemonade. "No wonder Frank didn't want to talk about it..." Elizabeth whispered, her face as white as a ghost.

214

"Would you be liking something maybe a bit stronger?" James asked her, having downed the dregs of his pint. Elizabeth nodded, dumbly.

On his return from the bar, James delivered the most shocking news.

"You say you were at Frank's funeral today," he shrugged. "It could be a coincidence, but as I said, Frank was responsible for the death of the Order's chief assassin, five years ago. I only escaped their attentions by faking my own suicide and getting away to California. As soon as I got back to Ireland last week, for the first time in five years, to see my sick father, the Order was on me like a flash. I was interrogated, and when they'd finished with me I was dumped in the River Liffey and left for dead. I don't think I told them anything useful, but they used a mind-reading trick on me, so I can't be one hundred percent sure. That's why I asked you about the nun, earlier. They have a real live banshee working for them, disguised as a nun. She can read minds. It is possible that they now know where Wayne is. If the Order isn't already here in Shepton, then they're probably on their way. We've got to get Wayne out of here, before all hell breaks loose."

Elizabeth Ball shook her head. "And to think I was suspicious of you and your questions, because I thought you were a reporter looking to dig up dirt and scandal on Terri Thorne. Now, I wish you were. Like I said to you, Frank told me they'd seen some unbelievable things at Wayne's real father's house, but they swore they couldn't tell me what had really happened."

James nodded understandingly. "That night, five years ago. Wayne saw his father brutally murdered by the Order. Frank arrived just in time to save Wayne's life. Another priest who had helped the Order crashed his car, and was killed trying to escape."

Elizabeth wiped her face with both hands, took a deep breath, then downed the cognac James had placed in front of her in one gulp. "I remember the press was full of the tragedy at the time. Several clergymen and an old farmer died in one small, rural Irish community. Because it was so near to where we'd been, I asked Frank if they had been involved in any of that, and Frank told me not to be silly. That it was all just coincidence." Elizabeth closed her eyes. "Why didn't they tell me?"

James shrugged. "Would you have believed them at the time?"

Elizabeth looked into the Irishman's eyes. "Probably not, probably not. But I do think I'm beginning to believe you, now. I better give you Wayne's address."

Forty-Eight

Wayne had almost forgotten about the voice when he awoke the next morning, his bedroom light still blazing. He was amazed that he had actually fallen asleep, eventually. Strange how things always seem much better in the daylight, he thought. There was no way he going to go to school. He would have the rest of the week off as a period of mourning, and would go back the following Monday.

Doris was sitting in a chair, smoking and looking at photographs, when he got downstairs. "Are you staying off today?" she asked, distractedly.

"Yeah," Wayne sighed.

Doris continued to look at the photos.

"I'll get my own breakfast, then," Wayne suggested, sarcastically. Doris didn't seem to notice that he'd actually said anything, and Wayne shrugged and went off to get his breakfast.

He was just finishing his bowl of Corn Flakes at the kitchen table when he heard a knock at the door. He heard Doris clamber up to answer it and he heard a few mumbles at the door, which he ignored. Wayne swilled the bowl and put it in the sink, ready to wash up later. He looked out of the kitchen window, over the auction-mart and the railway station beyond. At least it wasn't raining today.

For some reason, the same cold feeling hit Wayne's stomach as had happened during the funeral. He felt the hairs on the back of his neck rise, and his flesh began to crawl, as though it was trying to creep off his bones

Wayne turned away from the kitchen sink - and looked straight into the large emerald green eyes of a beautiful young nun. The same nun he had seen in the churchyard at the funeral.

"This lady's come all the way up from London, to see you, Wayne," he heard Doris almost sob from somewhere behind the nun. "She's come from that Catholic agency doodaa that we got you from."

The nun turned towards Doris. "May I speak with your son in private, please?" she whispered, in a voice so melodic that it sounded to Wayne as though she had sung the words.

Doris' bottom lip quivered. "Aye, but don't take him back, love. He's all I've got, now."

"Don't worry, Mrs Higginbotham," the nun whispered, looking deep into her eyes. "Wayne's not going anywhere." She smiled sympathetically at Doris, who smiled back, turned and shuffled back into the living room.

The nun turned towards Wayne. "Would you, er, like a, er,, drink?" Wayne asked, as normally as he could manage.

"No, thank you, Wayne - or should I call you Michael?" the nun replied, bearing a slightly enigmatic smile. Wayne knew there and then that this was definitely the nun he'd seen yesterday at the funeral. This was the person who'd been putting words in his mind.

"Is there anywhere where we can talk privately, Michael?" the nun asked, sweetly. Wayne nodded, and indicated the narrow staircase between the kitchen and living room.

"My room. It's on the left."

The nun smiled, turned, and ascended the stairs. Wayne followed close behind her. Normally, Wayne would have been delighted to have a green-eyed beauty alone in his bedroom, but a nun? And a creepy one at that?

Once they were both in the bedroom, Wayne closed the door behind him.

"I'll come straight to the point, Michael," the nun whispered, as she stared at the posters of Debbie Harry that adorned his bedroom walls. She sat down on his bed, her green eyes flashing.

"Wayne!" Wayne interrupted her. "My name's Wayne."

The nun smiled patiently. "As you wish, Wayne. I'm Sister Bernadette."

She slowly and deliberately pulled the wimple off her head and shook her long, shining, black hair, which tumbled over her shoulders just like the advertisements for shampoo on the telly. "I see you like girls, Wayne," she whispered, nodding towards a poster of a half-naked model. Wayne felt his cheeks blush. The nun smiled, licking her lips seductively.

"You haven't been with a woman yet, have you, Wayne?" She slowly began to unbutton the shapeless nun's habit, exposing a generous amount of cleavage.

The youth gulped. He'd fantasised about stuff like this, but there was a warning signal going off in his head which stopped him getting carried away.

She looked up at him from under her long dark eyelashes. "Does what you see, please you...Wayne?" She left a long pause between her question and his name, as she opened another button.

Wayne's mouth felt very dry and his breath came in short sharp gasps. Aoibheall slowly shifted on the bed, then reached down and pulled her habit up to her thighs, revealing long shapely legs. Wayne could feel his heart pounding against his chest; yet despite his extreme state of arousal, he could still hear that alarm bell ringing at the back of his mind.

The nun smiled, and patted the bed again. Her green eyes flashed, her ruby-red lips parted, her white teeth gleamed, and her black hair shone in a shaft of September sunlight that crept through Wayne's bedroom window. He tried to say something mature and sexy, but his voice, usually deep and sonorous, just emitted a croak. "Wow," was all that he could manage.

The nun ran her tongue over her top lip and leaned forward so that her breasts fell pendulously, as more of her cleavage fell open. Wayne gulped again as he admired her porcelain white skin, her milk-white breasts, her legs. He took an involuntary step forward, his eyes wide, like a rabbit stuck in the glare of oncoming headlights. Those green eyes...

The alarm bell rang, still louder.

The nun slipped a little more forward, exposing more leg.

"Er, no - er, look, are you really a nun? You're not one of them Strip-O-Gram girls, are you?" Wayne asked as he blinked his eyes, just to make sure that what he was seeing was real. Sister Bernadette laughed, a tinkling melodious laugh, and patted the bed, indicating that Wayne should sit down by her.

"I know not of such things, Wayne. Do not be shy, young man." The girl's voice was like honey dripping onto silk.

Wayne took another step forward, as she raised her hand towards him. He reached out to take her hand in his own.

"Wayne, I can teach you so much..."

The words did not pass the nun's lips but entered Wayne's head straight into the centre of his mind, and the memory of the image that he had envisioned the previous day flashed into his brain. Beautiful, tempting, scantily clad vampire women, that crawled slowly and seductively over the victim's bed, all deep cleavage, big bosoms and then suddenly, even bigger teeth...

The spell was broken like a dropped crystal glass, shattering on the ground. Wayne remembered the voice in the Church. The implicit threat, in that same seductive voice, that had invaded his mind. The fear he had felt.

He stepped back, and his expression hardened.

"Who the hell are you? What are you? What do you want?" Wayne demanded angrily. "I already have a girlfriend - well, sort of - and there's something about you that I just don't trust. You're definitely not a real nun, are you?"

Sister Bernadette giggled girlishly. "Spoilsport!" she laughed."It is so long since I had a man that even a naïve, virginal boy would have done." She laughed again, but the sound was harsher, mocking in tone. She stared deliberately at Wayne's still-bulging groin. "Even such meagre fare would have been satisfying. Very well, Michael - we shall do this the hard way." The nun sat upright and pulled her habit back over her legs and then began to button it up, covering her cleavage.

"I am named Aoibheall and once - long, long ago - I was betrothed to an Aillen Mac Fionnbharr. I think you may know him?" She laughed at Wayne's open-mouthed reaction. "Oh yes, I know who you really are, Michael Mac Aillen, Mac Fionnbharr. I am now the last of the pure blooded Tuatha De Danaan, and the only one with any right to the shards of the stone of Falias. All I want is that which is rightfully mine."

Wayne swallowed the small amount of moisture left in his mouth. "My Father said that he was the last of the Tuatha De Danaan."

The nun raised her hands, almost as if she was about to bestow a blessing.

"Your Father placed me and my entire family in exile. His bitterness was all-consuming. He did not regard us as a part of the family of De Danaan. We, my mother, my sisters and I, became the women fairies, the Bann Sidhe. The modern word may be more familiar to you: banshee?" Wayne nodded dumbly, and the nun continued.

"If you value your life, Michael Mac Aillen, you will give me the stones and I will consider that an adequate recompense. Stand in my way, and my revenge will be more savage and much more satisfying and complete. You are but a half-breed: half Tuatha, and half mortal. You have no right to the stones."

Wayne had edged past the banshee and was now standing by his wardrobe. Aoibheall stood and approached him, slowly and threateningly.

"I can feel the power of the stones running through my blood, they are so close," she laughed. "They are in this very room, aren't they?"

Wayne shrugged. "Dunno what you're talking about," he muttered, as nonchalantly as he could manage. Aoibheall's expression hardened, and her green eyes flashed in anger.

"Do not trifle with me, boy. The stones make me powerful. You know not with what you deal. I will ask you one last time, boy. Where are the stones? I want them - NOW!" The beautiful young nun suddenly seemed to decompose before Wayne's eyes, and within seconds her beauty had given way to what was little more than a living corpse.

The horrific features of the banshee froze Wayne to the spot. His stomach heaved and his mind was paralysed with fear. It wasn't that the face was just old; it seemed to be rotting before his eyes, crawling with white wrinkled maggots. Must get a grip, must get a grip...he repeated to himself, as the creature advanced slowly towards him.

"The stones!" it hissed.

Must respond in kind, thought Wayne, as his bowels demanded to be emptied and his breath caught in his throat. The banshee held out a rotting limb that had once been an arm, and reached towards his throat.

"I tell you what...you don't look quite so fit now!" he blustered. "I'm glad I didn't get your knickers off!" The banshee stopped, momentarily confused.

Wayne closed his eyes, and concentrated. He concentrated like he had never concentrated before.

Aoibheall the Banshee gasped, as the slight figure of the sixteen-year-old youth began to grow and grow before her. Within seconds she was confronted by a seven, maybe eight-foot-tall, black apparition. It seemed to be breathing deeply through some sort of machine, and little red lights blinked on a black box on its chest. More lights flashed and blinked on other boxes that hung on its broad black belt. The apparition's head was covered by a vast, shining black helmet that completely covered its face, totally obscuring any features. It wore a long black voluminous cloak that ran to the ground, while the rest of its apparel seemed to be made of thick black leather.

Aoibheall took an involuntary step back. She knew in her heart that this was only the boy, but she had never before encountered, nor beheld, such a frightening vision. The banshee flinched at the fearful rasping sound of the creature's laboured breathing.

The black apparition took a menacing step forward. It leaned down towards the startled Aoibheall and raised its left arm, pointing a long black leather gloved finger at the corpse-like fairy. In a voice deeper than any voice she had ever heard, the apparition addressed her.

"You don't know the power of the dark side of the Force!" it rumbled menacingly, edging another step forward. Its right hand took what looked like a bladeless weapon from the dressing table behind it.

The banshee retreated until she had reversed into Wayne's bed. She could now feel the enormity of the power that emanated from the son of Aillen Mac Fionnbharr. She had seriously underestimated the boy.

The huge black apparition took another step forward, and lifted its black-gloved hand slowly towards the ceiling. The Banshee felt herself being physically lifted from the ground by the throat, even though the hand was a foot away from her. She began to choke; she couldn't catch her breath. She had seen many monsters in her time, but never anything as dark and terrifying as the figure that now stood before her.

She could not see the eyes, the windows to the soul. It was always the eyes that Aoibheall worked on, it was the eyes that had always given her victory. Yet with this demonic figure there was only her own hideous reflection, her own terror, shining back at her in the black orbs that covered the creature's eyes. Aoibheall felt her lungs begin to strain.

A streak of burning red light, about four feet long, burst out of the apparition's weapon; buzzing hideously, like an army of crazed bees. The black apparition continued to breathe, as though underwater. As the blade of light waved in front of the banshee, it buzzed even louder.

"Some people don't seem to believe in the power of the Force!" the figure rumbled again, still towering over the terrified banshee even though her feet were off the ground. It leaned in towards her; it breathed in, then out, then in.

"It is your misfortune..." it continued, "...that I..."

It breathed out, and stepped forward again, until the nose portion of its hideous mask was right in front of Aoibheall's nose.

It breathed in. "...am not..." - breathed out - "...one of those..."

Aoibheall's lungs felt as if they were ready to explode. She somehow managed to scream, despite not being able to breathe. Somehow, that broke the grip of the demon.

She turned and scrambled as quickly as she could over Wayne Higginbotham's bed and fled out of his bedroom door and down the steep narrow stairwell, changing back into the form of the beautiful girl nun as she ran.

"...people!" The apparition finished its sentence, before slowly morphing back into young Wayne Higginbotham.

Wayne sat on the bed, his heart pounding in his chest. He put his head in his hands and took a very long deep breath. It was a full two minutes before Doris knocked on his bedroom door.

"What did you say that upset her so much?" Doris asked, bemused. "She just ran straight out o' t'front door - never even said goodbye. She was running like her backside was on fire."

Wayne grinned. His heart was still pounding, but he was beginning to recover.

"She demanded to know why I didn't go to Mass every Sunday," Wayne lied. "When I told her it was none of her business, she got all uppity. So I told her to get out before I kicked her up the backside."

Doris couldn't help but look pleased. "Well, that told her then, didn't it?" she laughed.

221

"Aye!" Wayne laughed. "That told her." Doris left Wayne's room, looking the happiest Wayne had seen her for days.

Once she'd gone, however, he sat back down on his bed and tried to calm himself. His right hand still tightly gripped the toy light sabre that he'd used in his "Darth Vader" impression. He stood and put the toy next to the tiny action figure that had inspired him, just in time. "Looks like I passed the first test!" he said out-loud.

It was just before lunch that the same disembodied voice that he'd heard at the funeral, and just before bed, appeared in his mind. At least now he knew who it was.

"I will be back, Michael Mac Aillen, Mac Fionnbharr. This is not over. Today luck was with you, and I was not well enough prepared. I will not underestimate you again. I WILL have those stones."

Wayne concentrated, and suddenly he could feel Aoibheall's presence. His response was a chant that he'd heard the hooligans at Leeds United's football ground bait the opposition supporters with: "Come and have a go, if you think you're hard enough!"

Strangely, he knew that she'd heard his response, just as clearly as he had heard her challenge. Somehow, that thought made him feel a whole lot better.

Forty-Nine

No one thought to ask the middle-aged priest what he was doing, walking through the corridors of St. James' Hospital in the early hours of the morning. Perhaps some thought that he'd been administering comfort, or performing the last rites for some unfortunate soul. The duty sister on the ward had been kept busy by a sudden rush of admissions late into the evening, following a Leeds United midweek match. She didn't notice until much later that the purse that she had left in her handbag, behind the ward reception desk, had been emptied.

It was about half an hour after de Feren had left the ward that she noticed his empty bed. She had presumed that he was in the bathroom; after all, why would anyone who had only just come out of a coma, risk leaving the hospital?

By seven am on Thursday, Pierre de Feren was on the early train to Shepton, nursing his old black briefcase on his knee and an enormous grudge in his heart.

Father Pierre de Feren was embarrassed. Embarrassed at having allowed himself to be duped by the banshee, embarrassed at having to call upon the 'Holy child' to get him out of the banshee's enchanted coma, and embarrassed at having to call on the Order to report on what had happened.

He had made the call to Dublin from a phone box in Leeds City Station. earlier that morning. Bishop Donleavy had been less than pleased to be woken by his number one field operative confessing to having lost the banshee, his wallet, and to having failed to complete the task. Rome had been expecting the last immortal to have been found and eliminated by Tuesday at the latest, working on de Feren's previous reports. Now here he was on the Thursday morning, and the sidhe was still alive, as far as he knew. Donleavy had told him, in no uncertain terms, to get on with the job - and quickly.

De Feren opened his briefcase and checked the address, which was the last known dwelling of the Higginbothams, according to the Crusade of Rescue's central records: 12, Frederick St. Barlickwick. He pursed his lips and stared out of the commuter train's rain-streaked window, at the passing grey Yorkshire scenery. Lines of bleak moorland, criss-crossed by dark, grey, stone walls. Knots of dark trees and dark stone buildings. It had been sixteen years since the Higginbothams had adopted the child, Michael. Would they still be at that address?

De Feren shrugged. He would deal with the boy as a matter of course, but his new priority was finding the banshee. He would have his revenge and deal with the last of the 'fairy folk' in the process. It would be a perfect case of killing two birds with one stone.

If the Banshee Aoibheall was still in Barlickwick, then she had very little time left. De Feren smiled at the prospect of killing the woman who had mocked him in his naked vulnerability. As far as she was concerned, he was dead. She would be more than a little surprised by his miraculous resurrection, and his revenge would be sweet. He would deal with her, and then the boy. He opened the briefcase and replaced the file with the Higginbotham's details.

The diplomatic parcel that De Feren had received at the 'Crusade's' office was carefully secreted away in a hidden compartment in the case. De Feren reached into the case, and stroked the parcel. He closed his eyes. If all went well, he would back on the train later the same day, and the Earth would have been cleansed of the Irish demons forever. Father Pierre De Feren would be made a Canon, or maybe even a Bishop. He licked his lips at the prospect of promotion.

Two hours later, however - following an eight mile taxi ride from Shepton station to the small town of Barlickwick, which had used up the last of his stolen money - Father de Feren was beyond furious. He had so far had to knock on almost every single door in Frederick Street and no one had heard of the Higginbothams, nor had they seen a beautiful young nun; indeed they had not been questioned by a woman of any description.

De Feren couldn't understand what was going on. Why had the banshee not been making the same enquiries that he had? Unless, of course, she had not disclosed all that she knew following her search of James Malone's mind...

With that slow-dawning, sickening, realisation in his mind, Father de Feren knocked on the only door that he had not yet tried. The door of the very last house on the street.

A little old lady, almost bent double with arthritis, answered the door, and peered myopically up at the priest. "Oh, a vicar. It's no use you bothering with me, love," the woman mumbled through toothless gums. Father de Feren took a step back.

"I haven't bothered wi't'church since me husband died, and that were during t'war. God's done nowt for me, so I'll be jiggered if I'll be doing owt for him. So you needn't bother coming round trying to convert me, just because I'll be kicking the bucket soon!" She was already turning back into her house, and beginning to close the door.

"Wait!" De Feren almost shouted. "I am not looking to convert anybody. I am looking for a family called Higginbotham. Do you know of them?"

The old lady looked startled. "Eeeh, Higginbotham? Aye, Doris and Frank Higginbotham. I haven't seen owt of 'em since they moved back to Shepton, years ago, love."

"Shepton?" the priest repeated, incredulously.

"Aye, Doris wanted to be nearer her sister, what wi't'adopted babby and all..."

De Feren interrupted the old woman in mid-sentence.

"Do you have their address?" he barked impatiently. The old woman shook her head.

"No, love, I used to. I used to send them a Christmas card every year, but they stopped sending me one, so I thought I wouldn't bother either and then I went and lost their address. You forget where you put your stuff when you get to my age, and..."

The old woman frowned. The priest who had disturbed Women's Hour on the radio had already disappeared around the corner of the Street.

"Rude man!" the old lady sighed, as she slammed her front door.

Fifty

The Silver Ford Orion screeched to a halt at the kerb outside 18 Cavendish Street, just as the nun hurriedly disappeared through the alleyway opposite. Elizabeth Ball clambered out of the driver's seat, and James Malone the passenger side.

"So, this is where Wayne lives?" James asked rhetorically. "Let's hope he's still okay."

Elizabeth smiled reassuringly, but the smile disguised an incredibly nervous feeling that was growing by the second. Until she saw Wayne safe and sound she would feel extremely guilty, having asked James to calm his impetuosity of the previous evening. She fully understood, by the end of their conversation at the Midland Hotel, why he had stressed the need to act immediately.

"We've already wasted so much time. We've got to get to him tonight!" he had pleaded, but Elizabeth had been adamantly opposed.

"Doris Higginbotham has only just buried her husband, and Wayne his father. How do you think they'll react if you barge in at this time of the night, telling them that a squad of assassins are on their way? At least wait until tomorrow. I'm sure one night won't make any difference. Anyway, he knows me well; it'll reassure him if I'm with you, rather than you going to see him alone. After all, I imagine you've probably changed an awful lot in the last five years." She raised an eyebrow. The last time Wayne had seen him, he had been a clean-cut young Irish priest. Now James was a long-haired, unshaven, Californian beach bum.

James had eventually, reluctantly, acquiesced.

"I'll pick you up just after ten." Elizabeth had insisted. "I've got to go to school first, to cover my absence."

When James had spoken to Carrie that night, he had been more on edge than he could ever remember. The prospect of coming into contact with the Order again terrified him, especially after his recent lucky escape, but he was also excited at the prospect of frustrating their aims. Carrie had told him to stay cool and that was what both he and Elizabeth were trying to do, as Elizabeth knocked on the lime-green, glass-panelled door of number eighteen.

James and Elizabeth glanced nervously at one another, as the initial knock went unanswered. Elizabeth knocked again; harder, this time. Eventually, she saw a shadowy shape moving towards the door through the glass panel, and then the sound of a safety chain being unfastened. Doris Higginbotham opened the door.

"Hello Doris...is Wayne alright?" Elizabeth blurted.

"Hello, Mrs Ball," replied a rather shell-shocked looking Doris. "He's as well as can be expected, given the circumstances."

"Circumstances?" Elizabeth snapped. Doris recoiled slightly.

"Aye, with his dad only just being buried, and whatnot. You'd better come in, love." Elizabeth breathed a huge sigh of relief, as Doris cast a cursory glance at her companion.

"Oh, I'm sorry, Doris - this is James Malone."

"Would you like cup of tea?" Doris asked, as she indicated that the couple take a seat on the Higginbotham's black and orange, imitation-leather sofa. Both nodded.

"I've just had the kettle on for that young nun that was here, but she just upped and bolted. It were a right funny do."

James stood, his face a mask of anguish. "Young nun?" he asked, "Very pretty, big green eyes?"

"Aye that's her." Doris replied. "Our Wayne sent her off with a flea in her ear, I think. She fair flew out of that front door."

James grabbed Doris' arms. "Have you seen Wayne since the nun left?"

Doris frowned. "Aye, course I have!" she scowled.

"Is he alright?" James insisted.

"Aye. Why wouldn't he be?" Doris answered, looking uncomfortable.

"Where is he, Doris?" Elizabeth also stood up, concern now etched on her features.

"Well he's up in his room, upstairs," Doris replied, screwing up her face incredulously. "Why? Is there sommat up?"

James Malone had already leapt through the living room door and was bounding up the staircase three steps at a time. Elizabeth walked up to a shaken-looking Doris, and gave her a hug.

"Let's have that tea, Doris. There's a lot we've got to talk about."

Fifty-One

Wayne Higginbotham found himself once again sitting on his bed, staring at the crumpled airmail envelope. Should he open it now? Or should he not? Was he ready to have his heart ripped out again and his hopes and dreams dashed against the wall...or was he going to be pleasantly surprised, this time?

"Oh well, there's only one way to find out," Wayne whispered, to no-one in particular. He inserted his thumb into a gap in the seal of the envelope, and started to rip it open.

Suddenly, he heard the almighty pounding of feet up the stairs, and the sharp report of a single knock at his bedroom door. He had heard the knock at the front door moments earlier and had heard Doris talking to someone downstairs, but he hadn't expected anyone to come charging up the stairs.

"Next test?" he murmured quietly. "Come in."

Wayne was certainly not prepared for the sight that confronted him when the door opened. He screwed up his eyes as he appraised the well-tanned, long-haired, unshaven man in front of him; he certainly looked somewhat familiar.

"Are you alright, Wayne?" The Irish brogue was familiar, even if the face was not. Wayne twisted his mouth in disbelief, and with more than a hint of hesitation uttered, "Father Malone?"

James Malone laughed; his relief was almost palpable. "Jaysus, Michael, you had me worried!" He hugged Wayne like a best friend that he hadn't seen for years. "Well, you've certainly grown a bit since the last time I saw you," Malone grinned as he stood back, hands on hips, and appraised the bemused youth standing by the side of his bed.

"So has your hair," Wayne replied, with a smile. James Malone suddenly looked much more serious.

"The nun who was just here...did she do anything to you?"

Wayne shook his head, and laughed. "She tried. She seemed to want the stones, you know, my dad's - the ones we found that night in Ireland." Malone nodded eagerly.

"She was quite insistent, said that she was a banshee, and that she'd once been my Dad's girlfriend. Then she did a shape-shifting trick to try and scare me." Wayne related the events as though that sort of thing happened every day in Shepton.

"What did you do?" Malone asked, aghast.

Wayne shrugged. "I turned myself into 'Darth Wayner' and scared the bloody living daylights out of her. She scarpered as fast as her legs could carry her."

"Darth Wayner?" Malone repeated, in amused disbelief.

Wayne laughed. "It was the only thing I could think of at the time, Father."

James Malone hung his head and smiled, sadly.

"I'm not a priest now, Wayne. I gave it up as soon as we left your father's cottage in Mayo. I'd seen too much in the days preceding the events at Mickey Finn's place. By the way...I'm sorry to hear about your dad, Frank. He was a fine man."

Wayne stood, and walked over to his window. He stared out at the rainswept auction market, and at the grey clouds passing over the grey green moors in the distance. There was a brief uncomfortable silence, as James struggled to find the appropriate words.

"So, you've just been living the life of a normal schoolboy, then?"

Wayne turned, and shrugged. "What else would I do? That's what I am - a normal schoolboy. A bog-standard Wormysted's Grammar School Sixth Former."

James Malone put his tongue in his cheek and raised a sceptical eyebrow.

"Oh, alright...not quite totally, one hundred percent, normal," Wayne smirked. "So, what have you been up to since the morning we left Mickey Finn's?" he asked the long-haired ex-priest. "You sound more American now than Irish."

Malone rubbed his chin thoughtfully. "Ah, this and that," he replied. "I'll tell you when we've got more time."

Wayne scowled. "What's going on, Father? I'm sorry - I mean, James. It's not just the banshee, is it?"

James put his hand on the boy's shoulder.

"There's something we need to discuss, Wayne. The Order is back, and this time it's you they're after. The banshee was working with them, but it sounds like she's gone freelance, if it's just the stones she was after. I think you've just had a very, lucky escape, young man. I don't know if the Order had anything to do with Frank's death, but I wouldn't put it past them. We've got to get you and your mother away from here - and quickly. Is there anywhere safe that she could stay?"

Wayne thought for a moment. "Only with Aunty Margaret, really. She's my mum's sister."

"Is that a long way away?" Malone queried.

Wayne shook his head. "No, just the other side of town...but what about me?"

James Malone patted Wayne's shoulder. "Grab some stuff, and let's go. Doris can stay with her sister, and we'll get you to L.A. for a few weeks. The Order will never find you there."

Wayne gasped. "I've always wanted to go to L.A. That's where my real mom lives now!" he gushed excitedly, before a grim realisation hit him. "But I can't go."

James, already halfway out of the door, turned back.

"What? Why?" he exclaimed, in a voice that expressed his bewilderment. Wayne threw his hands in the air in frustration.

"Let's see...one, school; two, Stephanie; and three, because I haven't got a passport." James Malone sat down on the stair with a despondent thump.

"What an eejit. I never thought of that," he muttered, before brightening. He stepped back into Wayne's room. "We'll order you a passport, and stay with my brother in London until it comes."

"But what about school?" Wayne insisted. "What about Steph?"

James Malone frowned. "We'll worry about that stuff later, Wayne." He paused for a moment. "Steph?"

Wayne blushed. "My girlfriend...or, rather, the girl I'm trying to cop off with."

James Malone nodded knowingly.

"Ah, I see. We'll have to deal with that later, too. Just grab those things and let's get out of here - pronto. If the banshee's already been here then the Order's assassin, de Feren, can't be far behind - and I really can't believe that Aoibheall will have given up so easily, if it's your stones she's after. Let's just get you out of danger."

"Aoibheall?" Wayne repeated. "Yeah, that was her. Is she really dangerous?"

James pondered Wayne's question, and memories of his brief time in Aoibheall's world flooded into his mind.

"I don't know," he said honestly. "Had she wanted me dead, I think I would now be dead...so I'm not sure."

"How are we going to explain all this to my mum?" Wayne asked, as he grabbed a sports holdall from his wardrobe, and began to empty his underwear drawer into the bag. "She's not going to be best pleased about me disappearing off to London or to the States - or anywhere else, for that matter - especially not the day after we buried my dad."

James Malone winked. "I think I've got that one covered. Now, come on...let's go!"

Fifty-Two

Aoibheall sat on a bench in the dingy Churchyard of Shepton's Christ Church, licking her psychological wounds. How could she have been overcome by a mere boy; a virgin boy? A boy barely out of puberty?

Aoibheall the Banshee - scourge of Connaught, the harridan, the harbinger of doom, the deadly damsel of death, the one who had terrorised mortals for centuries - had been scared witless by a spotty teenager. Nothing like this had ever happened to her before; not since her exile from the Tuatha De Danaan.

Why had she fled so readily? Why had she not been able to tap into the power of the stones? And how come a half-breed mortal had possessed so much power?

Aoibheall had expected that taking the stones would have been easier than taking candy from a baby. She certainly hadn't expected the boy to be able to shape-shift and manipulate matter at the same time. He had stopped her from breathing and had physically lifted her off the ground, just by moving his hand.

The boy had shown fear at first, but then he'd recovered. When he'd used his powers, he had become more potent than any being she had come across in hundreds of years. Many of the greatest of the Tuatha De Danaan had not had such abilities.

"Come and have a go, if you think you're hard enough!" he had said, using telepathy every bit as well as she did. "Come and have a go, if you think you're hard enough." Taunting the most frightening of the 'fairy folk' in all of Erin's Isle! The more she thought about it, the more depressed Aoibheall became.

Wayne Higginbotham seemed to be more than just a lucky mortal. The current possessor of several of the shards of the stone of Fal seemed to be a real Tuatha. A young Tuatha warrior, who already seemed to possess a masterly degree of expertise in the skills of his forefathers. Yet, he was a half-breed...it was all so confusing.

So, how was she going to get past him, and get her hands on those stones?

A shaft of sunlight illuminated the churchyard, as the last of the morning rain clouds scurried off over the grey-green Yorkshire moors. Lines of cars and lorries hurtled past on the nearby road, making that infernal roaring noise and leaving clouds of noxious vapours that spread over everything, rendering the mouth dry and the nose offended. People rushed along the footpath by the churchyard walls, all intent on doing whatever it was that they had to do as quickly as possible. That was the trouble with this modern world; everything was done at such a frenetic pace, and so noisily.

Aoibheall was already tiring of it. The novelty of the technological marvels was already wearing off. The modern world was just as mortal as the starving Ireland of the 1840s. Men and women were still trying to fit everything that they had to do into their meagre three score years and ten, or less. Mortals were like ants, rushing around aimlessly in their brief flicker of life, desperately trying to achieve something meaningful, anything, and then - poof! - they were gone.

Aoibheall smiled ruefully, and looked around the graveyard. Gravestones were propped up against the black stone wall, each one bearing witness to someone who was now long gone and who had achieved absolutely nothing that would change the world. That was what it was like to be a mortal. She glanced at the dirty black Victorian Church. "No wonder they cling to their pathetic, merciful, God," she muttered.

Aoibheall closed her eyes. She was back in her vale, a part of Connaught long past. She felt the warmth of the sun on her flesh, and the singing of birds by the lake shore. The kiss of the soft grass on her bare feet felt almost as good as the kiss of a man on her lips.

She could have been happy with Culhainnein, the only man she had ever really loved, but all of that was long gone. Even without the intervention of Aillen Mac Fionnbharr, Culhainnein would have now been dead for over two millennia. He had been just another weak mortal.

Aoibheall's thoughts strayed to James Malone. She had liked him. He had been handsome and amusing. Aoibheall hoped that he had survived his little swim in the river. She had given him a chance by not locking him permanently into her world, unlike what she had done to de Feren. The Priest would now be sat dribbling in the corner of some cell, in whatever they used as a Bedlam in this day and age. That thought pleased her.

The thought crossed Aoibheall's mind that, if Malone had been strong enough to survive, then maybe she should give up trying to get the stones and live as a mortal woman for a while. She could easily steal Malone from the American girl that she had seen in his thoughts, and she could spend a few seasons enjoying this modern world. She could retire.

Aoibheall laughed. Retire? There was no retirement for a banshee. No long rest, leading to eventual oblivion. And James Malone was just another mortal - just like Culhainnein. Just like all the other mortals that she had lain with over the long centuries.

Aoibheall the Banshee was the last of the immortal Tuatha De Danaan, and the Earth was hers to take and to rule. The half-breed son of Aillen Mac Fionnbharr would not stand in her way, powerful or not. She looked around the sweet, fragrant Irish valley, and gritted her teeth.

"This will soon be your home forever, son of Aillen Mac Fionnbharr. You shall taste the wrath of the banshee!"

"Turned out nice now, hasn't it?" a male voice spoke, somewhere in the distance. Aoibheall was rudely yanked out of her dream world and dumped unceremoniously back in the stinking, polluted mess that was the latter part of the Twentieth Century.

"I beg your pardon?" she said to the tall, balding priest standing in front of her.

The man smiled. "I said, it's turned out nice again." Aoibheall smiled politely.

"It looks like the Lord may bless us with something of an Indian summer, after all," the priest stated, looking quite satisfied with himself. "I hope you are enjoying the day, sister," he continued. "It's not often that your side come into my domain!" The priest chortled.

Aoibheall smiled weakly. "Your side?" She repeated.

The priest coughed nervously.

"I'm sorry, I meant no offence...it's just that you Roman Catholics do tend to stay in your own Holy places, usually, I mean, normally...I mean...I mean...well, do enjoy yourself, Sister."

The priest coughed again and blundered off up the path towards his church, whistling a hymn. Mortals could be such half-wits, Aoibheall reflected.

She knew now what she had to do. It was pointless hiding amongst these mortals and pretending to be like them. She had a birthright as an immortal to rule these ants - and if she could lay her hands on those stones, that is what she would do.

This time, however, her approach would be a little subtler. Wayne Higginbotham would not have the time to change into some frightening monster. He would be rendered no more than a shamed, naked, little boy, hiding his little manhood, grovelling for his life. She might even take his virginity, just for the fun of it.

The only thing she had to do was to bide her time and wait for the right opportunity to get to the boy, and time was something that Aoibheall the banshee had in abundance. Aoibheall had more time than anyone else in the entire world.

Suddenly, a new sensation hit her senses. From across the busy main road that bordered the churchyard, an aroma of delicious intensity crept through the air and invaded her nostrils. Aoibheall looked up, and saw a bright red glowing neon sign: Eastwood's. Suddenly, Aoibheall the Banshee realised she was absolutely starving. She stood and marched off purposefully towards the glowing light.

Ten minutes later, the most frightening fairy in Irish folklore, Aoibheall the Banshee - who planned to be a goddess, who would enslave the entire world - could be seen sat in the corner of the churchyard of Christ Church, Shepton, greedily munching a large portion of haddock and chips with lashings of salt and vinegar, straight from the newspaper.

Fifty-Three

Father Pierre de Feren noisily slurped his tea from the plain white mug, his face like thunder. Hitchhiking had not been a dignified way for a man of the cloth to travel, especially one as important in the hierarchy of the Sacred Order of St. Gregory. Even so, he had eventually arrived at St. Stephen's Catholic Church in Shepton, having accepted a lift from a virtually incoherent Irish builder in an old, dirty white Transit van. The builder had, no doubt, taken his good deed as an excuse to miss confession for the next six months.

It had been little consolation to de Feren that the nuns in the tiny Convent, next to St. Stephen's, had made a huge fuss of him and insisted that he sit down to rest and enjoy a nice cup of tea before discussing anything.

"Two visitors from the 'Crusade of Rescue' we have after visiting us now," an Irish nun, who had introduced herself as Sister Brigid, had declared, when de Feren had finally managed to announce that he had come from the 'Crusade's' office in Ladbroke Grove. "How wonderful! Unfortunately, your Sister Bernadette has taken our only guest room."

"Ah, Sister Bernadette? Is she still here?" De Feren asked hopefully.

"Oh yes," the nun replied: "She went out early this morning to see poor young Wayne." De Feren spluttered in his tea, and spilt almost half a cup into his saucer.

"Wayne Higg...?" he asked, desperately attempting to sound calm and collected.

"Higginbotham - why, yes." the nun chirped. "The poor boy lost his father over the weekend, in a road accident. They buried him yesterday, just next door." Father de Feren nodded, and made a sympathetic noise.

"It is a strange coincidence that I too am here to see young Wayne," De Feren whispered. "Someone in the 'Crusade' must have got their wires crossed. Even so, now that I am here, I would like to see the boy. You don't happen to have his...?"

"Address? Of course I do," the nun interrupted the priest, while jumping up and grabbing a piece of paper from her desk. "I'll write it down for you."

De Feren stood.

"But will you not be resting a bit more, Father? You must be shattered," the nun fussed, as she passed the piece of paper to the priest.

De Feren looked at his watch. "Three in the afternoon already," he sighed. "No...I really must go and see the boy before it gets too late. I really was hoping to get back to London tonight."

"I've got a little car - it would be a pleasure to drive you down to the boy's house," the nun smiled, hopefully.

De Feren shook his head. "After my journey, a walk in the sunshine would be a blessing, and it is quite pleasant out there now."

The nun pursed her lips. "Suit yourself, Father. I'll be giving you directions that'll be getting you there in a jiffy."

De Feren pulled his coat back on. "Thank you," he said, and the coldness of his smile made the nun shiver.

As the tall priest swiftly disappeared down the drive, Sister Brigid shook her head.

"What's the matter?" Sister Maria asked the older nun.

"I don't know." Sister Brigid whispered. "But, dear Lord - please forgive me for saying this about a Reverend Father - but that fella, bless me on all that is holy, gives me the creeps."

Fifty-Four

Wayne Higginbotham would have been delighted had he known that two beautiful women in Los Angeles, California, were both thinking about him at that moment in time.

Carrie Horden stood in the yard by her white fence, and watched the moon sail elegantly over the San Gabriel Mountains.

"Come back soon, Jimmy," she sighed. "I hope this kid is gonna be okay. Sixteen-year-olds tend to be a nightmare - all bad moods, bad attitudes, and rampant hormones. Do I really want a smelly youth hanging around?"She sighed again, and turned and walked back into the house.

"But this kid is not totally human, so I guess he could be different," she shrugged. "Hey, wait until I tell Amber that I'm gonna have a real life fairy in my house!"

Amber was a hippy friend of hers who was totally into all things supernatural and the occult. She had been raised in the Haight Ashbury district of San Francisco during the Sixties, and had joined in the whole summer of love thing at the age of seventeen. She lived down in the valley and now made a living out of making and selling herbal candles. Carrie imagined her friend's reaction.

"He's bringing a fairy home, oh man! But Carrie...I thought James was just so, like, straight!" she said, imitating Amber's slow drawl. Carrie acted out her own response. "Not that kind of fairy, babe, I mean...fairy!"

Carrie could see Amber's face as her mouth dropped open. "Oh wow, man. Like you've gotten a tiny, gossamer-winged, bona fide Tinkerbell?"

"No - more like a smelly five foot eleven punk rocker, wearing a biker's leather jacket."

Carrie laughed out loud, and then fell back on her couch. "Oh my God, Jimmy, what have you gone and gotten us into?"

Not far away, Terri Thorne was also staring at the moon from her yard. She couldn't sleep. Dean still wasn't home and the baby was kicking hell out of her insides. The pool hadn't been covered for the night, and the moonlight shimmered on the smooth water. The warm breeze caressed her face, and she could still smell the heat of the day just past. In the distance, the never-ending rumble of the freeway was punctuated by the intermittent wails of police sirens.

Terri waddled over to the fence at the end of the yard and stared at the mesmerising lights of Beverley Hills. People were having normal lives down there. Normal little people, with normal little lives. Eating, sleeping, making love, arguing, fighting; worrying about their jobs, about money. All those little American soap operas, acted out in the darkness. How many of them had problems like hers?

"What happens if you never got that letter, Michael?" Terri whispered at the moon. "You'll still be believing all that rubbish I wrote in the last letter. Oh God, please don't be cutting me out of your life now. I am so sorry!"

Tears filled Terri's eyes. She turned to walk back into the house, but through her smeared vision she was suddenly convinced that she could see someone in her pool. She wiped her eyes. There, in the water, she could see a man's reflection. She wanted to scream, but couldn't.

The man was tall, clean-shaven, but with long hair in plaits. He was wearing a long tunic, a broad belt and high boots, as though dressed for a part in some medieval movie, and - most striking of all - he bore a shining band around his forehead. The figure was colourless in the moonlight.

Terri looked around frantically to see where the reflection's owner was stood, but she was alone in the yard. She blinked her eyes rapidly. She had to be dreaming. She hadn't been drinking or anything. She pinched herself.

"Ouch!" she yelled, then glanced back at the pool. The reflection was still there, and now the figure was smiling at her.

Every sinew of her body was straining to run, to scream - to do anything but stay rooted to the spot, looking at what she now believed to be a ghost. Then, she heard a voice. It seemed to be coming from inside her head.

"All will be well, my love." The reflection was still there, still smiling at her.

She threw her head around, looking for a beam of light, a projector, something, anything. This was it. Terri Thorne had gone totally and utterly gaga! She was having another breakdown.

Terri closed her eyes, and slowly counted to ten. "Get a grip, girl!" she said, out loud. "Come on...get a grip!"

The sound of the voice invaded her head again.

"Our son loves thee, Theresa O'Brien. All will be well. This much I swear to thee."

Terri knew that voice. She had heard it somewhere else; somewhere far away, long, long ago. Suddenly, the panic began to subside and an overpowering feeling of peace and serenity came over her.

Terri opened her eyes, and gazed at the shape in the water. The image was fading, but the face was still smiling. Instead of being dressed in weird ancient clothes, the figure now seemed to be wearing a tee shirt and jeans, with slicked-back hair. Now, she remembered. Every goose-bump on her body seemed to rise at once.

"Danny?" she gasped.

"This was how you knew me, once, not that long ago, my sweet Theresa." She could hear the laugh in the voice. "Yet this was how you last saw me, when I told you who I really was, Aillen Mac Fionnbharr. That was the day you ran away from me. Remember?"

The reflection had almost totally faded, yet now it was back in the tunic.

"Yes," Terri cried. "When you told me you were one of the fairy folk...one of the Tuatha De Danaan."

"Yes, my love. Remember...our son loves you. He will always love you, as will I. Never, ever doubt that!"

The voice slowly faded, as did the reflection, and then suddenly both were gone. Terri Thorne collapsed in a heap.

Fifty-Five

"You see, it's all because Wayne - or Michael, to give him his real name - is the son of an informer," James Malone explained to a dumbfounded Doris and Margaret Houghton-Hughes, as they sat in Margaret's opulent drawing room. Elizabeth Ball bit her lip, as the four of them sat at the dining table.

"I don't understand," Doris Higginbotham said morosely, as she took another tissue from the box and wiped her red eyes. Her sister Margaret held Doris' hand on top of the table. James Malone sighed patiently.

"It all goes back to an IRA feud in the 1950s. You see Michael - I'm sorry, Wayne's - father, Mickey Finn, was an IRA man in Belfast. It seems he was captured by the RUC and did a deal with them, which meant that he would be let off scot-free if he operated as a mole within the organisation."

"It's like that James Mason picture, isn't it?" Margaret asked knowingly.

"James Mason picture?" James Malone repeated, confused.

"You know that one where he's an IRA man and he gets shot. You know, Doris. We saw it at the Plaza, years ago." Doris looked uncomprehendingly at her sister, and shook her head.

"You don't think the IRA did for Frank, do you?" Margaret asked conspiratorially.

James shook his head, while Doris began to wail noisily. Elizabeth smiled at him, and passed Doris another tissue.

"But what's that got to do with our Wayne?" Doris cried. "He's got nowt to do wi'Ireland!"

James shrugged. "These fellas have long memories, Mrs. Higginbotham. You see, Mickey Finn got a lot of top IRA men arrested, and when the troubles started up again in 1969, some were killed. It seems, though, that the IRA caught up with him a few years ago, and tortured him before executing him. Now, you see, in Ireland - like in parts of the Balkans, or Turkey, or wherever - these feuds transcend generations. Even though the argument might have been between somebody's grandfathers, the whole thing passes on down the line."

"That's stupid, that is!" Margaret chipped in.

"Aye, you're right there, Mrs Houghton-Hughes, but that's how it is. Anyhow, the hitmen must have found out that Mickey went and had a son with a woman called O'Brien. So, eventually, they found out who adopted him and they have come over to wipe him out, to gain revenge for his da's crimes, as it were."

"But it's nowt to do wi'him!" Doris wailed again. "I've only just buried me husband, I can't lose our Wayne as well. Can't you tell 'em he's a good lad?"

"Why don't you just get the police?" Margaret sniffed. "You see, this is the trouble when you adopt...you just don't know what you're getting!"

Doris stopped wailing long enough to glare viciously at her sister.

"We're not all as lucky as you, our Margaret. I couldn't have one of me own."

Margaret Houghton-Hughes shrugged, and raised her eyebrows. "I'm not saying there's owt wrong with Wayne. It's just that you never know what went on before you got him."

James intervened before the sisters came to blows. "Ladies, ladies, please. Look, Mrs. Houghton-Hughes..."

"Margaret," Margaret interrupted the young ex-Priest, flirtatiously.

"Er, yeah...Margaret," James continued. "Getting the police is pointless. Can you imagine your local bobby coming up against a team of professional IRA killers?" The sisters shook their heads, as Doris blew her nose loudly.

"These men are professional assassins. They wouldn't know mercy if it got up and slapped them round the face. The only answer is to get Wayne away for a while."

"How long for?" Doris whimpered.

"I'd say just a few weeks," James replied.

"What about his schooling?" Margaret asked.

"We'll get them to give him some work to take away," James bluffed, not having considered Wayne's schoolwork.

"So...where would you take him?" Doris asked, her voice still choked with emotion.

"I've got a place in California," James responded. "He'll be safe there."

"As long as there's not one of them there earthquakes," Margaret sniffed disapprovingly.

"Won't these IRA hit makers just go over there to try and do us in?" Doris sniffed.

James shook his head. "No. It's just Wayne they're after."

"So he'd have to go off without me?" Doris exclaimed, incredulously. Elizabeth Ball took Doris' hand across the table.

"I know this is just the worst possible timing, Doris, but it is for the best. You can stay here with Margaret, and Wayne will be safely out of range of this hit squad."

James noticed Margaret raise her eyebrows when Mrs. Ball had mentioned Doris staying there.

"But I've only just lost me husband. Our Wayne is all I've got." Doris wailed.

"All the more reason to keep him safe," James weighed in, despite a 'back-off' glare from Elizabeth.

Doris pondered the situation for a few minutes, while everyone sat in an uncomfortable silence. "I wish our Frank was here," she moaned, eventually. She dissolved into tears once more.

Margaret Houghton-Hughes stood. "You say Wayne packed a bag?" she asked.

James nodded. "He's ready to go, as soon as you agree."

Doris glanced miserably at her sister and, in a whisper that was barely audible, gave her grudging assent.

"Aye, you might as well take him now, I suppose. I'd rather he got away before these hit men, doodaas, arrive."

"I'm not going anywhere right now."

The four adults turned, to see Wayne standing in the drawing room doorway.

"I thought you were watching telly upstairs, love?" Margaret asked timidly.

"I was," Wayne shrugged, "but I'm not now. I've got to go to the Youth Club tonight." There was an audible gasp from all four adults.

"The Youth Club?" James almost choked.

"Youth Club?" Margaret Houghton-Hughes repeated disbelievingly.

"Youth Club?" Doris almost shouted. "We buried your father just yesterday, and you want to go to the bloody Youth Club?"

Wayne nodded. "If I'm going to be away for a while, I've got people to say goodbye to."

"Don't tell them where you're going," James Malone stated flatly.

"I'm not stupid," Wayne sniffed.

"What time does this Youth Club finish?" James asked. Wayne shrugged.

"Half-nine-ish," he said waving his hand in a gesture of approximation.

"Can you leave a bit early? It's only a matter of life and death, you know...like, your death!" James asked, his voice edged with sarcasm. Wayne shrugged again.

"Suppose so!" He turned and walked back out of the room.

James Malone's head sank into hands. "Has he not heard anything I've said?"

Doris shook her head. "I can't believe he's going away for weeks on end, and he'd prefer to go to the Youth Club than be with me!"

Margaret Houghton-Hughes pursed her lips knowingly.

"It's probably a girl," Elizabeth opined, as she and James left the Houghton Hughes' house. James nodded ruefully.

"Somebody called Steph, I believe. Let's just hope he doesn't get himself killed chasing a girl."

Elizabeth grimaced. "Wasn't that a bit unbelievable?" she asked.

"What?" James scowled.

"You know, the whole IRA hitman story."

James ran his hand through his hair. "You mean less believable than fairy-folk, banshees and secret Vatican societies full of rabid, psychopathic priests bearing meat-cleavers?"

Elizabeth smiled sorrowfully, and shrugged.

"Hmm...I take your point. I just wish the timing could have been better."

She climbed into her car, leaned over, and unlocked the passenger door. James climbed in.

"I've told him to be at the Midland Hotel by nine pm. His uncle can bring him down. We'll catch the night train to London and stay at Dan's until his passport is sorted."

Elizabeth nodded.

"What a mess," she whispered, under her breath.

Some hours later, Doris and Wayne were standing in Margaret's kitchen, arguing.

"Look - I have to go to the Youth Club. It's non-negotiable!" Wayne barked.

"Oh no, you're not, young man!" Doris bellowed. "And don't you think you can talk to me like that and get away with it. You're not too big for a thick ear!"

Wayne blew out a huge, exasperated sigh.

"Look, Mum...I've got to go. I'll be back here by half-past eight, I promise."

Doris puffed out her chest. "I've said no, and I mean no. You could go and get yourself killed by these IRA men - and if you do, don't bother coming home to me. You're no good to me dead!"

Wayne was getting increasingly frustrated. "Mum, I'm sixteen years old and I am going to the Youth Club tonight. There's someone there I love, and I intend to tell her that. I don't care about the IRA."

Doris' mouth dropped open again. "Oh!" she whispered. Wayne walked over to give his mother a hug, but she stepped back, avoiding his touch. "Aye, I knew it. I've only just lost me husband and you'll be off getting wed before long."

Wayne laughed. "Married? Mum, I'm only talking about going to the Youth Club for an hour or so. I've got to tell this girl how I feel before I go and disappear. I think talk of marriage is a little premature, don't you?"

Doris shrugged. "Aye well...if she means more to you than I do, or your dad, then I suppose you'll just have to go, won't you."

Wayne grimaced. "How can you say that? You know I love you. Dad knew, too."

"Oh aye!" Doris blustered, "You're disappearing off for God knows how long, and you don't even want to spend the last few hours with me!"

Stanley Houghton-Hughes walked into the kitchen.

"Now then, I do hope we're not having a domestic argument, not under my roof! Wayne, be good for your mother. Our Margaret has told me what's going on - and Wayne, you cannot go to the Youth Club. These Irish fanatics are all ten pence t'bob."

Wayne glowered at his Uncle. "But, Uncle Stanley..."

Uncle Stanley held up his hand, "I've said all I'm going to say, and I say you are not going. That's what I say," he blustered.

"Yes, Uncle Stanley," Wayne groaned. His glower had now descended into a furious glare. He turned and stomped off miserably to the spare room.

Doris shook her head.

"I don't know, Stanley...these kids today! Thank you, anyway."

Fifty-Six

Father Pierre de Feren opened the diplomatic parcel very carefully, and removed what looked like a small toy gun.

"Bonjour, ma petite," he whispered, as he caressed the black metal barrel. La petite was de Feren's favourite weapon. An adapted starter pistol, it fired one tiny pellet into its intended victim. That was always enough.

"So much more subtle than a normal gun, and so much less messy," De Feren had often said, when questioned about his methodology. The tiny pellet, which de Feren personally manufactured, was filled with a potent poison that had been used by the Order for centuries, having originally been brought back from South America by the Conquistadors for the Spanish Inquisition. De Feren tucked the pistol into the pocket of his black coat and re-packed the parcel in his old briefcase, before unlocking the public toilet door and stepping out into the daylight.

Shepton bus station was typically busy for the time of day. Schoolchildren and shoppers thronged the bus shelters as they made their way home. No-one paid any attention to the tall Catholic priest as he strolled nonchalantly past, heading for the metal footbridge over the canal.

Once he had crossed the canal, Father de Feren found himself in a much quieter part of the town. The dirty black hulk of Christ Church loomed to his left, while to his right a small manufacturing works glowed with sparks and the glint of welding tools. A swift right turn past a small auto parts shop, populated by greasy overall-wearing mechanics, and he was stood directly in front of 18 Cavendish Street.

Father de Feren crossed the road before him and knocked purposefully on the green, glass-panelled door. There was no answer.

If Aoibheall had already been here, then the boy might already be dead. The prospect chilled de Feren, but there was nothing he could do if that was the case - La Petite would just not be used today. He would find the banshee; nothing was more certain.

De Feren knocked again, then stood back and stared up at the bedroom windows. They were closed. He tried to peer through the front window, but Doris' net curtain prevented him from seeing inside.

"There must be a back entrance," De Feren muttered as he set off down the street, but he had not gone far before he realised that the only way to the back of Cavendish Street, in that direction, was a private passageway through a dentist's surgery. A quick walk in the opposite direction proved more satisfactory. At the end of Cavendish Street a peculiar house stood, shaped like the bow of a ship.

De Feren walked around the house and found himself walking down an un-metalled road that served as a back street. The road dropped quickly, allowing the houses that were only two storeys at the front to become three storeys at the back. The houses overlooked a roofing contractor's storeyard and then a large open area, with animal pens that de Feren presumed must be some sort of agricultural market. Several of the houses shared a communal back yard and, by his calculations, number eighteen was the one right in the middle. The black-coated priest deftly lifted the latch and stepped into the back yard, furtively glancing around to see if anyone was watching. All was quiet.

De Feren put down his bag and removed a small black lever-like instrument, with a flattened curved end. He inserted the flattened end into the side of number eighteen's shabby blue back door, by the Yale lock, and pulled back sharply. The door creaked, groaned, and sprung open.

The priest looked around again, just to make sure that no one had heard, and then swiftly disappeared into the dark cellar of the house. He took a torch out his briefcase and crept silently along a dark stone-floored corridor. He opened a door to his left and noticed that someone had combined a laundry room with a bathroom. "At least they must wash, occasionally," the priest muttered.

Ahead of him in the darkest part of the cellar, it looked like someone had been storing a motorbike. There was a large oil stain on the floor, and tracks where someone had pushed tyres through the oil. There were more oil cans and sundry equipment left untidily around the basement.

With a sneer, de Feren began to climb the stone staircase to the ground floor. He quietly opened the door, which led directly into the living room of the tiny house. It was deserted, and the television stood like a silent sentinel in the corner. He turned off his torch; there was enough light now that he was out of the basement. The priest appraised the surroundings. Everything looked cheap, especially the appalling print of Constable's The Hay-Wain, which held pride of place on the wall above the gas fire.

De Feren walked silently into the kitchen, with its ubiquitous tall cupboard with the drop down front, a standard Fifties kitchen appliance. A table, a sink unit, a small refrigerator and a dirty white gas cooker filled the rest of the meagre surroundings. Coats hung in the alcoves on either side of the central fireplace, where another gas fire provided the sole source of heat in the room.

The priest curled his lip derisively and then turned and began to stealthily ascend the narrow central staircase. He pushed open the bedroom to his right. Evidently, this was where the boy's adoptive parents slept: a large double bed, wardrobes, and a dressing table. The only relief from cheap chain store furniture was a small brass log box. Two cross-framed sash windows looked out over the Street to the old foundry opposite, from where sparks were still illuminating the grimy workshop windows.

De Feren turned and crossed into the other bedroom. A model Saturn V rocket stood proudly on the single window ledge, and other various toys were scattered around the room. Posters of barely-clad females adorned the walls, and the priest pursed his lips in distaste. He opened various drawers and peeked in the wardrobe. There was no obvious sign of the stones. Maybe the banshee already had them?

De Feren grimaced. Having ascertained that the house was empty, he clumped down the staircase and returned to the living room. He sat down in an armchair and patted the pocket of his coat that contained La Petite. As an extra weapon, he placed the small jemmy that he had used to break into the house in his other pocket.

Sooner or later someone would come, and then he would know what had happened. He would know whether the banshee had got here first, killed the boy and taken the stones - or whether he had won, and the kill was to be his.

The lack of a body, or comatose youth, in the house had given him a much greater faith in the latter option. He knew the answer would walk through the front door of the tiny terraced house before too long.

"And now we wait," he whispered, and closed his eyes.

Fifty-Seven

Finn strode into the Youth Club as though he owned the place. For a boy who had only just lost his Father, Wayne Higginbotham was feeling remarkably pleased with himself. His escape from the Houghton-Hughes' house, despite Uncle Stanley's ban, had been a masterpiece of the shape-shifter's art.

Cedric Houghton-Hughes, Wayne's cousin, had declared at tea-time that he was going to pop round to his friend Peter's.

"Fine, son," Uncle Stanley had responded.

"Don't go talking to any strange Irish men. Especially any wearing berets and dark glasses," Margaret had nervously advised her son, who had raised his eyebrows sarcastically at Wayne.

"I think they'd be in disguise, Mum - they only wear that stuff at IRA funerals." He rolled his eyes dismissively.

Wayne stood and followed his cousin upstairs, put on his jeans, his tee shirt and his leather jacket, and emerged downstairs, looking exactly like Cedric.

"I'm off!" he had shouted.

"Fine," Uncle Stanley had replied with a wave, his eyes glued to the television news.

"Be careful!" Aunty Margaret had shouted back.

"I will," the false Cedric had shouted back.

"I didn't know our Cedric had a leather jacket," Margaret had pondered, after a few seconds of reflection.

"No, neither did I," Stanley had muttered.

"Maybe he's borrowed our Wayne's," Doris had suggested.

"Aye, mebbe," Margaret had muttered bemusedly, "but it's not really his style."

Both Stanley and Margaret had been a little taken aback, therefore, when Cedric stuck his head into the drawing room less than two minutes later, wearing a bright red cardigan and brown cords.

"I'm off!" the real Cedric had shouted.

"Fine, again," Uncle Stanley had replied with a wave and a dismissive shake of his head, his eyes soon re-glued to the television screen.

Margaret had frowned. "But you've got changed!"

Cedric had screwed up his face. "Course I have - I wasn't going to go to Pete's in me school uniform."

"My uniform," Margaret had corrected her son, "but what about that leather jacket you had on?"

248

"What leather jacket?" Cedric had asked incredulously.

"I thought you'd borrowed Wayne's jacket," Margaret had insisted.

Cedric made a 'my mother's losing her marbles' sort of face and waved, replying "Yeah, okay - bye, Mum," before quickly rushing out of the front door.

"Well, that's a funny business!" Margaret had shrugged.

"What's that, love?" Doris had asked, as she brought her sister and brother in law cups of tea.

"Our Cedric has just gone and got changed again."

"Aye that's kids, today." Doris had mumbled, and disappeared back into the kitchen, shaking her head.

It wasn't just the way he'd escaped that had lifted Wayne's spirits, however. When he had stomped off to his room after Uncle Stanley had forbidden his visit to the Youth Club, he had finally found the time and courage to read Terri's letter. He had been expecting an even stronger brush off, so he was more than delighted to read:

Terri Thorne
2145 Coldwater Canyon Drive,
Beverley Hills,
Ca, 91241,
USA.

My Dear son Michael,

Will you ever forgive me for that last letter? I am so, so sorry. I'm blaming alcohol - too much tequila in my Margheritas, I think. I will never ever let you go again. I know I haven't written you as much as I promised, but what with...oh God, here I go making excuses. There is no good excuse for my behaviour, and I am so sorry. Dean can go take a long hike if he doesn't like our relationship. I am your Mom and always will be.

I've enclosed a check for $2000. Hopefully you and your lovely dad, Frank, can tell a little white lie and say you're taking a fishing trip and come and stay a short while.

Please ring me and let me know if you can make it.

Gotta go.

All my love,

Terri.

Wayne had had to wipe away a tear at the reference to Frank, but overall he was absolutely delighted that his mom had reconsidered her decision to abandon him again. She was the best! Wayne had kissed the letter and the cheque. His escape to L.A. with James Malone now took on a whole new significance.

So that was why the figure of Michael Finnegan had virtually strutted into the Youth Club. Wayne had morphed into his American alter-ego in a side street near the Youth Club on Westmoreland Street, after a brief glance around to ensure that no one was watching.

He hadn't noticed the pretty dark-haired girl that had followed him at a discreet distance, and who was now crouching behind a parked car. The girl had been on his tail almost since he had left the Houghton-Hughes' house; however, Wayne's contentment had dulled his senses. All he could think of was meeting Stephanie, maybe getting a passionate kiss, and then flying off to Los Angeles to see his mom.

The tinny music from the little stereo was turned up full blast as he entered the club. A few familiar faces nodded, and then Wayne saw Stephanie Fleming leave Anne Ducket's side and come running over to him. To Wayne's delight and surprise, she planted a kiss firmly on his lips.

"Hi, Finn," she grinned.

"Hey!" was all that Wayne could think of as a response. Stephanie took him by the hand.

"How's poor Wayne?" she asked, her face full of concern.

"Great," Wayne replied; then, when he saw Stephanie's face cloud, he remembered why she would be asking. "Well, as great as can be expected, given the unfortunate circumstances...you know."

Stephanie frowned. "I feel so sorry for him...poor kid, losing his father at his age. He's such a sweetie."

"Yeah!" Wayne agreed. "Tough little cookie too, you know. He's been so brave about it all."

Stephanie smiled sadly. "Tell him I'm thinking about him, won't you?"

"Sure." Wayne grinned, "I'll tell him tonight."

"How's your mum, by the way?" Stephanie asked concernedly.

"Great," Wayne replied, then remembered that his mom being ill had been the excuse for his early termination of his drunken date with Stephanie. "Well...better, anyway. You know." He coughed. "Wanna grab a Coke or something?"

Stephanie laughed. "Okay."

Wayne bought two bottles of Coke and then sat down next to Stephanie on one of the plastic chairs that surrounded the large open hall of the Youth Club.

"Hi Finn, how's Wayne?" Paul Harland, Wayne's best friend, greeted 'Finn' with a wave. "Is he alright?"

Wayne nodded. "He's doing fine, thanks."

Martin Taggart, another friend of Wayne's, breezed over. "Hi Finn, how's Wayne?" Martin asked.

"He's okay...bearing up, you know?"

Martin nodded sagely, and wandered off.

Richard Hebden, Lance Boyle, Brian Bamforth, Liam Riley, Alan York, Mick Blackburn, Sarah Westwood and finally Anne Ducket all made their way over to 'Finn' and asked about Wayne's welfare. Anne had seemed the most concerned of all.

"Are you sure he's okay?" she had asked, looking all worried and concerned. Wayne noticed that she wasn't wearing her usual black-rimmed glasses and was wearing her hair in a ponytail. As a matter of fact, she looked quite attractive.

"Wayne's quite popular, isn't he?" Stephanie stated whimsically.

"Yeah, more than he'd think. I thought Anne Ducket hated him," Wayne mumbled.

"God, no!" Stephanie exclaimed and put her hand over her mouth. "She's got the total hots for him. That's why she was so nasty about him asking me out."

"She fancies Wayne?" Wayne gasped in disbelief. Stephanie nodded eagerly.

"Yeah - that's why she's gone and got contacts. She was hoping you'd bring him along tonight - to cheer him up, you know? I think she had her own plans on how to cheer him up." She laughed.

Wayne frowned. "Women!" he whispered, almost silently. He heard Stephanie start to say something, but a familiar prickling sensation started to raise the hairs on the back of his neck. He felt his scalp begin to crawl.

He rapidly turned in his seat and looked round the hall. There was nothing untoward that he could see.

"Finn?" Stephanie pouted. "Were you listening?"

Wayne shook his head. "Look, Stephanie, honey." His voice had taken on a particularly serious tone, and he saw Stephanie's face fall. "I can't stay long tonight..."

"You're going home, aren't you?" Stephanie interrupted him, her eyes welling up with tears.

"Yeah, I have to. I'm sorry." Wayne mumbled sadly.

251

"I knew it was all too good to be true. How long have you got?" Stephanie asked, with a sniff.

"About an hour, I guess." Wayne replied.

A chill ran down his spine, and he turned again. There seemed to be nothing out of the ordinary, but he knew that feeling. He'd had it at the church, and in his own house; in the presence of the banshee.

Stephanie nodded. "I knew you'd have to go back, sooner or later. Look I've just got to go to the toil...bathroom." She leaned over, put her arms round Wayne's neck, and kissed him. He felt her tongue burst into his mouth, and responded as well as he could. She pulled away, leaving him gasping for air.

"Won't be long," she breathed, as her eyes misted over. "Don't you dare go anywhere."

David Smith was just about to run over and stop any inappropriate intimacy, when Stephanie ran tearfully to the toilets. "Humph!" he muttered.

The chills that were running up and down Wayne's spine had quite unnerved him. One thing was for sure; if it was that banshee again, then this time she'd have to face someone much deadlier than 'Darth Wayner.'

Wayne sat back in the plastic chair and narrowed his eyes.

"Go ahead, Banshee - make my day!"

Fifty-Eight

David Smith hadn't seen the young Irish girl before, but there was something very appealing about those beautiful, big green eyes.

"Have you been here before?" he asked pleasantly.

"No," the girl replied. "I'm new in town and I thought that this would be a good way to be making friends." David Smith nodded approvingly.

"Ah yes, and much safer and nicer than one of those awful new disco places. If you'd just take one of those forms and fill it in for me, I'd be very grateful. There's no need to do it now - bring it back next week, if you like." He pointed to a pile of papers just inside the entrance, and the Irish girl nodded her agreement.

As she passed him David Smith asked, almost as an afterthought, "And your name is...?"

The Irish girl turned and smiled. "Aoibheall - Aoibheall Flaherty."

Aoibheall had followed her fish and chip lunch with a slow walk around the town. She had called into the Rackham's store on the High Street and used some more of the money that she had stolen from de Feren to buy a pair of jeans and a tee shirt. She had discarded the nun's habit in the department store changing room. An assistant had found the habit and wimple while Aoibheall was paying at the cash register.

"Excuse me, Sister, you've forgotten these." Aoibheall had flashed her a wide, satisfied smile.

"Throw them away. I won't be needing them again," she had told the astonished girl. "I've finished with Jesus...and, as far as I'm aware, he's finished with me."

Aoibheall followed those purchases by buying a denim jacket from a market stall and a pair of high-heeled shoes from the Freeman, Hardy, Willis store. Soon, she looked more like all the other young people around the town. When she had caught her reflection in a shop window, she hadn't been able to help but marvel.

"Not bad for just over two thousand," she had mused. "But these tight trousers do make my bum look a bit big."

Aoibheall had sniffed the air like a dog trying to pick up a scent. She knew that Wayne was no longer in the stone house, where she had made her first attempt to frighten him, and so she had decided to wait in the bus station until she could sense him again.

She had been sat on a bench when she thought she saw the back of a familiar tall, bald figure, striding purposefully towards the canal bridge.

"No, that's impossible!" she had mumbled to herself, as the black-cloaked figure disappeared into the distance. She convinced herself it must have been that protestant priest who had tried to engage her in conversation in the Churchyard.

Time had passed slowly. The crowds in the bus station had thinned, and still Aoibheall waited. Then, all of a sudden, she could feel the boy's presence somewhere nearby.

She had stood sharply and had marched hurriedly towards where she felt the boy was going to be. Then she had caught sight of him, way ahead in the distance.

"I will follow him," she had thought gleefully. "I will follow him and see what opportunities come my way. The stones will soon be mine."

Eventually, Wayne had cut up a side street. Aoibheall had rushed to catch him, but had suddenly noticed that the boy had stopped and was looking around, as if to check that he was alone. The banshee swiftly ducked behind a parked car, just avoiding the boy's gaze. When she had peered out again, another, seemingly older youth, was standing exactly where Wayne had been stood seconds earlier. Aoibheall had smiled knowingly. Good try, boy, she thought, but you can't fool one of your own so easily!

The youth had entered a large brick building on a street called Westmoreland Street, according to a white sign on the side of a wall. Aoibheall had stopped a passing teenager and asked what went on in the building that the youth had entered. The teenager had told her that it was a Youth Club, and that he was going in.

"My name's Paul Harland, by the way. Why don't you come on in and give it a go?" he had said, with a smile Aoibheall had smiled back.

"Sure," she had said. "Why not?"

Once inside the club, Aoibheall was careful not to go near the youth that she knew was Wayne in disguise. She stuck to walls and dark corners, moving quickly to hide behind people every time he looked around. One thing was obvious to the banshee. The boy had changed his shape to impress the pretty girl who was fawning after him like a lovesick puppy. That gave Aoibheall an idea, but executing it might prove difficult.

She edged as near to the couple as she dared, and listened. She saw Wayne turn suspiciously a couple of times, almost as though he was aware of her presence. Aoibheall had thousands of years of practice at not being seen, however. The boy did not notice her.

Suddenly the girl had stood abruptly, kissed the boy, and then almost ran towards the toilets, wiping her eyes. Aoibheall, sensing an opportunity, followed her, quietly, surreptitiously. As she entered the toilets she noticed one other girl, applying makeup in a mirror. The girl she had followed must have stepped into a cubicle. The banshee waited.

The other girl closed her compact and left the toilets, shooting a 'what are you staring at?' kind of glare at Aoibheall, who grinned. "Careful, sweetheart!"

The sound of a toilet flushing snapped the banshee to attention and as soon as the cubicle door opened she moved straight in towards the unsuspecting Stephanie Fleming.

Stephanie had no time to scream as she felt herself being pushed back into the cubicle; the other girl's hand had gone straight over her mouth. Stephanie had tried to push the dark-haired girl with the vivid green eyes off, but the girl had brought a hand up and placed it over her forehead. Stephanie's attempt at a scream died in her throat.

The nest thing Stephanie Fleming knew, she was lying stark naked in a warm meadow, full of long grass and wild flowers. She could see mountains and a lake. It was all just too beautiful to be real.

Stephanie Fleming realised immediately that she was dead.

Aoibheall pulled up the zip on the short, tight skirt that she had removed from the girl. She knew from the girl's stolen thoughts that she was called Stephanie and that the boy was calling himself Finn. This was all turning out to be so easy.

She pulled the jumper over her head and rolled up the jeans and tee shirt that she had bought that afternoon. It was a shame to lose them so quickly, but she had plenty of money, and once she had got her hands on the stones she would have all the clothes she could ever wish for. She had been surprised by the girl's underwear. It was all so skimpy, and she had never worn a bra before in her life. It was the knickers that had really shocked her, though. Why bother? she had thought to herself as she had removed them from the girl's prone body. They were certainly a lot less substantial than the standard convent issue.

She had then lifted and sat the naked girl on the toilet, with her feet tucked up under her bottom so that no one could see them if they looked under the cubicle door. Aoibheall then made quite sure that the cubicle door was locked and, with amazing agility, easily climbed out over the top.

Wayne was a bit concerned that Stephanie had taken so long, but he relaxed as soon as he saw her walking towards him. She looked different, somehow. More seductive, more hungry, more…

Stephanie's arms went straight back round his neck, and she kissed him just like before. However, Wayne felt really weird; something wasn't quite right. Despite a feeling of near-ecstasy in experiencing Stephanie's kiss, he felt a chill in his spine and an empty feeling in the pit of his stomach. The alarm bell that he had heard when the banshee had tried to seduce him was ringing in the back of his head again. With everything else that was going on in his body at that moment, it was little wonder that he was confused.

"Let's go somewhere where we can be alone," he heard the girl of his dreams whisper into his ear. "Let's go and..." Wayne heard her whisper a shocking word that he had never thought Stephanie Fleming would use, then he felt her breathe into and lick his ear. David Smith marched over towards the couple, who were obviously getting quite out of hand.

"It's okay, man, we're leaving," Wayne managed to gasp, as Stephanie almost frogmarched him by the arm towards the Youth Club door. He saw envious glances coming from his mates - or should he say, Wayne's mates. But he couldn't understand why he felt so weird and mixed up. After all...wasn't this what he'd spent most of the last few months fantasising about?

"Where can we go?" Stephanie panted, staring straight into Wayne's eyes, who was breathing like he'd just run the school cross-country course in a new record time.

"I've g-got the k-key to my - I mean, W-Wayne's - h-h-house," he stammered.

"Will anyone else be there?" Stephanie breathed, her eyes widening seductively. Her lips parted, and she licked them provocatively.

"N-n-no," Wayne managed to say, before Stephanie grinned wickedly and marched him off down Sackville Street. Maybe the alarm bells were going to ring every time he got lucky!

It only seemed like seconds until Wayne was sticking his key in the door of 18 Cavendish Street. He was having real trouble maintaining his concentration and keeping his shape as Finn. What was he going to do when it all got really exciting? He'd been useless at holding his shape when drunk...what about when he was ecstatic? Why was he so damn nervous? He would later describe the feeling that he had at the moment as sheer dread.

Wayne opened the door. Stephanie pushed past him, then pulled him roughly inside by the lapels of his leather jacket.

"Tonight's the night, lover boy." She almost growled the words, through lips that were barely parted. This was not like the Stephanie Fleming, he'd imagined; this was even better.

The front door slammed behind him as Stephanie pushed Wayne up against it, whilst she grabbed the top button of his jeans and yanked it open. Wayne just couldn't believe that Stephanie Fleming would act like this. Strangely, the voice didn't sound like Steph's. It sounded more like...

Suddenly, there was a loud crack. Stephanie's face froze. She stopped laughing and after a momentary look of surprise, and a gasp, her eyes glazed over.

Stephanie Fleming fell forward, straight into Wayne's arms, and it took no more than a split-second for a horrified Wayne to realise that Stephanie Fleming was dead.

"STEPHANIE!" Wayne screamed.

Then his head exploded, in a shower of stars.

Fifty-Nine

James Malone was worried. Wayne had promised to show up at the Midland Hotel before nine pm. It was now nine-thirty pm, and there was still no sign of the boy. He had said his uncle Stanley would drive him down, so where could such a simple plan have gone wrong? Reluctantly, James rang the Houghton-Hughes' telephone number.

"Hello?" a fraught female voice answered.

"Is that Mrs Houghton-Hughes?" James asked, trying to sound as calm as possible.

"What have you done with him, you murdering, bloody terrorists?" the voice shouted frantically.

"Mrs Houghton-Hughes, Margaret - it's me, James Malone. I was wondering why Wayne isn't here?"

"Oh God...I'm sorry, James," Margaret sighed. "But, you see...Wayne's disappeared."

James closed his eyes, and sighed. "Disappeared? How? What happened?" he asked.

"It seems he sneaked out to go to the Youth Club while our backs were turned. Stanley and Cedric went down to look for him, half an hour ago. They should be back by now." James could hear wailing in the background.

"That's our Doris," Margaret said. "She's only just lost her husband and now she thinks her son's been done in. If he does turn out to be okay, she's going to kill him herself!"

James Malone rubbed his forehead. "Look, Margaret...please keep in touch. Ring me if you hear anything." He put the phone down as soon as Margaret had taken his room number and agreed to keep him informed, and started to pace around his hotel room, feeling totally useless.

"How could he be so stupid?" James wondered aloud. "We could have been well on our way out of here."

Doris wailed even louder once the phone had been put down.

"I thought that might be him," she moaned.

"I know, I know," Margaret tried to reassure her sister. "It's just like when he ran away that time."

"Aye, but he didn't have the IRA chasing him that time, did he?" Doris cried. "What am I going to do if they've killed him, Margaret? He's all I've got now."

"He'll be back, just like the last time." Margaret tried to sound cheerful. "Our Stanley'll pull up outside and he'll jump out of the car, just like nowt's happened."

Unfortunately, even Margaret knew that she didn't sound particularly convincing.

"But he'd said he was coming here," Stanley Houghton-Hughes insisted. "He said he had a girl to meet, but I told him he wasn't coming. I told him it would be over my dead body. I said to him: it'll be over my dead body. That's what I said!"

David Smith shrugged. "Wayne Higginbotham didn't show up here at all tonight. That cousin of his came - you know, that flashy American kid. Typical Yank, in my opinion. One flash of his shiny white teeth, and that pretty Fleming girl was all over him like a bitch on heat."

Stanley Houghton-Hughes looked at Cedric, and frowned. "Cousin?" he repeated. "American cousin?"

Cedric shrugged, and raised his eyebrows. Stanley Houghton-Hughes looked back at David Smith.

"Wayne doesn't have an American cousin - not to my knowledge, any road."

"Well, that's what he said he was, when he first came, last week," David Smith sniffed. The last thing he wanted to do was upset his bank manager. "You can go in and ask his friends if they've seen him?" he offered. "Most of them have gone, but there are one or two stragglers, and the few that help to tidy up. I generally lock up at nine-thirty."

Stanley Houghton-Hughes pondered the option for a moment, and then addressed Cedric. "You'll know his friends, son. Pop in for me and ask around. See if any of 'em know owt."

Cedric blew out a huge sigh. "Okay..." he mumbled, "but I bet the Yank was an IRA man."

"IRA?" David Smith repeated, his face suddenly adopting a strange pallor. "A terrorist? Here? In Shepton?" Stanley Houghton-Hughes glowered at his son.

"No, no, no, just our Cedric's stupid idea of a joke - ha, ha! I'll wait in my car."

David Smith shook his head. "I'll be locking up in five minutes."

Five minutes later, Cedric Houghton-Hughes emerged with Paul Harland and Anne Ducket. Stanley had got out of his car and was standing at the Youth Club door.

"Is it true that Wayne's disappeared and might have been murdered?" Anne asked tremulously, her voice breaking. She burst into tears.

Stanley shook his head. "No, no...let's not jump to conclusions."

"That Finn seemed such a nice guy," Paul stated nonchalantly.

"See?" Cedric piped up. "What could be more suspicious and obviously made up than Finn?"

Anne wailed even louder, and Stanley Houghton-Hughes grimaced.

"Oh, do shut up, Cedric!"

The last of the kids left the Youth Club, and David Smith shrugged again. He turned off the lights.

"I'm sorry, Mr Houghton-Hughes, but there's nothing more we can do - apart from going to the police."

"Aye, mebbe you're right," Stanley Houghton-Hughes agreed, as he rubbed the back of his neck. "There's nowt else for it!" David put the key in the lock of the front door of the Youth Club.

Cedric suddenly looked puzzled. "Did you hear that?" he asked, looking at the side of the building, where the toilet windows were located.

"Dad, can you hear someone screaming?"

Sixty

"STEPHANIE!" Wayne screamed, as the girl that he had fallen in love with sagged at the knees and fell straight towards him; her mouth open, her eyes glassy, green, and looking straight through him. The blow came out of the darkness. He felt a sharp pain on the top of his head, and everything exploded in a shower of sparks and stars. Everything went totally black.

Wayne didn't know what first woke him: the smell of the petrol, the splashing sound, or the shuffling feet. Or was it the singing? He opened his eyes and tried to move but he was bound tightly - his arms behind his back, his feet and legs bound together. His head throbbed like the worst toothache he had ever experienced. From what he could see, he was in the basement bathroom of his house, 18 Cavendish Street. He tried to speak, but his mouth was covered by something sticky. Wayne could tell that he was back in the form of Wayne Higginbotham. He must have morphed back into his natural shape while unconscious.

"Ah, so you are awake!" The voice was accented...European? French? "In one way, that is good. In another way, it is bad."

The voice made a noise halfway between a cough and a laugh.

"Bad for you, anyway. I am very sorry that you will have to suffer - the mortal half of you, that is. I am sure the Lord will look after you. As for that part of you which is demon...I hope you burn in hell for all eternity."

Wayne managed to twist his body enough to see a tall, black-clad figure, pouring what looked like petrol on the cellar floor. The figure turned, and in the little light available, Wayne saw a bald, bespectacled priest looking at him. At first glance he reminded Wayne of the archetypal Gestapo characters in popular Second World War dramas on television.

"I believe you were there when my predecessor, Francisco Pizarro, died," the priest said sadly. "He was a good friend of mine. He taught me a great many things."

The priest now carelessly emptied a bottle of meths onto the floor. Wayne tried to shout, but only managed a muffled yelp.

"You see; I have taken no chances," the priest continued. "You and the girl were both obviously overcome by the sins of lust and gluttony." The priest picked up an old vodka bottle, which Frank had used to store spare petrol. "It seems you were both so drunk that you were incapable of rational thought. In your carelessness, you set fire to the house. The police will suspect nothing, from what bits and pieces they retrieve."

The priest grinned maliciously. Wayne twisted and, from the corner of his eye, noticed a naked female back.

"In any case, I think she would have been a bit too experienced for you, boy. I do not think she was quite the girl you thought she was." The priest chuckled. "She would have taken you to places you would not have wanted to go...believe me."

Wayne desperately tried to shout "Stephanie!" but just a muffled roar emerged. He closed his eyes. If he could just change his shape into something small, he could escape the bonds. He concentrated as hard as he could, but nothing happened, and he twisted and turned, roaring with frustration.

"Ah, yes," the priest announced. "One thing Pizarro taught me, is that if a demon is bound tightly enough, then it cannot shift its shape. I can see your muscles trying to alter, but they are too restricted. Sorry! I am afraid you must face your inevitable fate; your doom. It is, of course, all in a good cause. Your demise enables my God to live, so to speak. So...look at it this way. You have done someone a - now, how do you English say it? Ah, yes - a good turn."

The priest emptied the final bottle of flammable liquid on to the floor of the basement.

"I would like to stay and chat for a little while longer, but I have a train to catch. Goodbye, and may Our Lord preserve your half-mortal soul."

The priest turned, and walked away. Wayne, his eyes wide with terror, heard him clumping heavily up the stone staircase. Then he heard the sickening sound of a match being struck, and a sudden crackle of flames; then, the distant sound of the front door of 18 Cavendish Street slamming shut.

Now, this one was going to be a real test!

Sixty-One

The girl had just turned off her bedside light and turned over to go to sleep. She could hear the whispering of some of her dormitory companions nearby, but she was absolutely shattered, and sleep overcame her in seconds. Her dreams were the usual round of weird situations, based either at school, or at home, where everything was mixed up and often quite embarrassing.

The voice just seemed to be a part of the complexity of the dream, at first. It was a boy's voice; quite deep and resonant, and annoyingly insistent. It began to irritate her, because it was disturbing a particularly nice part of her dream, a part where Henry St. John Brocklehurst was asking her over for supper. The girl opened her eyes and Henry disappeared along with the rest of the dream, but the voice remained firmly locked in her head.

"Sister, I know you are out there. Can you hear me, sister? Please help me...you are my only hope. I am tied up, in a cellar at 18 Cavendish Street, in the town of Shepton. Please remember that! My sister, please remember, 18 Cavendish Street, Shepton, Yorkshire. I am your twin brother, Michael, but I'm now called Wayne - I was adopted, too. Please help me. Ring the police, the fire brigade...but first ring a mister James Malone at the Midland Hotel, Shepton. Please, my sister, help me. I am dying. I am desperate. Help me!"

The girl climbed out of bed as if in a trance. She picked up some coins from her bedside drawer and marched mechanically along the dorm, until she came to the door. She opened it and, despite it being long past lights out, walked along to the payphone on the wall. She picked up the receiver and rang directory enquiries.

"Midland Hotel, Shepton, Yorkshire, please."

Her coins dropped as she was put through. She spoke for a minute, and then replaced the receiver. She picked it up again and asked for the fire service in Shepton, Yorkshire. She had just put the phone down after ringing the Shepton Police Station, when Miss Bettany, the house-mistress, came running down the corridor.

"I say, Lucy, what are doing out of bed, dear? Who are you ringing at this hour?"

Lucy seemed to snap awake and looked at Mrs Bettany, her eyes wide in shock.

"I don't know, Miss. I dreamt that my brother asked me to make an urgent call," the girl gasped, incredulously.

"Are you trying to be funny, Lucy Hetherington?" Miss Bettany whispered angrily.

"No Miss; I'm sorry. I must have been dreaming...but it all seemed so real."

Miss Bettany took a deep breath, put her fists on her ample hips, and sighed. "I almost believe you, young Lady, although thousands wouldn't. Back to bed, please. Your brother, indeed! We'll talk more about this tomorrow."

Miss Bettany walked off, leaving Lucy to reflect on what had happened as she walked back to bed.

Lucy Hetherington, a boarder in the lower Sixth form at Roedean, the celebrated school for girls in Sussex, was the only child of Rupert and Melinda Hetherington, one of the richest couples on the Channel island of Jersey. She was now, also, very, very confused, not to say embarrassed. She would probably be in real trouble the next day for wasting police time. A twin brother? Adopted? What nonsense - what an absolutely ridiculous dream!

It took Lucy ages to fall asleep. As if I'd have a brother called Michael...or, even worse, Wayne, she snorted, as sleep finally overtook her.

This time nothing disturbed her dream, which was unfortunate, as Henry St. John Brocklehurst turned out to be quite a cad.

Sixty-Two

Cardinal D'Abruzzo scurried along the long corridor as fast as his short legs could carry him. His heavy footfalls echoed eerily off the wooden panels and ornate works of art that filled the walls, despite the thick carpeting.

He knocked urgently on the door of the room at the end of the corridor. There was no answer. The Cardinal knocked again, even more frantically. A woman opened the door a small way and peered through the gap, suspiciously.

"What do you want at this time of the night?" she whispered, her voice at once sleepy and angry."If you wake him, there will be all hell to pay!"

"I have news...great news." The Cardinal was dancing on the spot like a small boy who needed the bathroom.

"Well?" the woman asked sharply.

"It is done!" the Cardinal stated happily. "The last of the demons is dead. I have just heard it from Bishop Donleavy, in Ireland."

The woman snorted. "It was supposed to have been done five years ago, but your people still managed to find more demons that continued to threaten his life. However, I will inform him in the morning when he wakes."

"Thank you, thank you," the exuberant churchman breathed, as the door was closed in his face.

The abrupt and apparently impolite behaviour of the child's mother was understandable. Unless The Sacred Order of St. Gregory delivered on their promises and eliminated all of the immortals who had once wandered the Earth in huge numbers, then the child was very much at risk. The ancient prophecy had warned that the only being who could kill the Messiah on his second coming, and so prevent the dawning of the Day of Judgment, would be the offspring of an immortal.

Cardinal D'Abruzzo, like all the senior members of the Order knew the translation of the prophecy by heart:

A child no mortal man shall sire,
By mother's blood, royal line acquire,
Shall suckle he no milk white breast
Shall rise in exile, unbidden guest
Shall learn to change his form at will
His shape, his face, his ways to kill

Unseen, unheard, his telling blow,
His doom to lay blessed Messiah low
Then all shall wail and Kings shall fall
And darkness shall take us, one and all!

The prophecy had been discovered in Jerusalem by a Byzantine scholar in the year 590, the year that the founder of the Order, St. Gregory the Great, became Pope.

The interpretations had been many over the centuries. For nearly a thousand years the Order had worked almost exclusively in the Middle East, believing the Royal Line acquired line, and later the exile, unwelcome guest phrase, meant that the child would definitely be Jewish; a descendant of King David. The Crusaders had members of the Order in their ranks. Some of the Knights Templar had also been members of the Order. Even to this day, Cardinal D'Abruzzo found that many voices in the Order still held to the maxim that 'God's Assassin', as the subject of the prophecy had become known, would be a Jew.

Even so, from about 1500, the Order had decided to cover all angles by taking the first line of the prophecy as the one that defined the majority of their actions and that had led to extensive campaigns in Ireland, where the Church had discovered plenty of "immortals" to eliminate.

As far as the Order was aware, the immortal known as Mickey Finn had been the last of the true immortals, and it was believed that he had been dealt with five years earlier. Now, it seemed that his newly discovered progeny had been dealt with too. If indeed that was the case, then it looked like 'God's Assassin' had, at long last, been dealt with. The Messiah was finally safe.

Cardinal D'Abruzzo hoped that the child would be pleased, and would now start acting more like he had expected.

Sixty-Three

Dean Vitalia gently lifted his wife's head. Terri Thorne groaned.

"Hey baby, you   okay?" Dean asked sympathetically. "Jeez, I wondered where you were when you weren't in bed. I looked right round the house and began to panic. Man, I thought you was dead when you I saw you lying out here by the pool. What happened?" Terri Thorne groaned again.

"I don't know," she uttered, in an agonised whisper. "Vertigo, I guess. You know my blood pressure has been a bit low."

Dean lifted her and placed her carefully on a lounge chair by the pool.

"We better get you a doctor. What were you doing out here in the yard at this time of the night anyways?" Dean asked as he stroked his wife's face.

"What time is it?" Terri asked.

"Three am." Dean answered. Terri sighed.

"I couldn't sleep. This little sucker was kicking the hell out of me." She patted her swollen belly. "And I was wondering where you were..."

Dean raised his hands in an apologetic gesture. "Hey, I'm sorry, baby...you know how it is when you're entertaining clients. I guess I just lost all track of time." He grinned. "So my boy's going to be a quarterback, huh?"

Terri snorted. "Forget the doctor. I'll be fine."

She tried to lift herself into a sitting position but fell back slightly, and had to steady herself on the lounger.

"Look honey, I don't care what you say - I'm ringing the doc, and I'm ringing him right now," Dean insisted, as he stood upright and marched off towards the house.

Terri Thorne took a long deep breath, and looked at the surface of the pool. The water merely cast the reflections of the bright yard lights and the dark shapes of the palm trees that bordered the yard."My God, am I really losing my mind?" Terri whispered.

The replying voice sounded as if it was borne on the warm California breeze.

"No Theresa. You are fine. Hear me; all shall be well."

Terri looked around frantically. "Who is this? Who's doing this?" she shouted.

"Who's doing what?" Dean asked, looking confused, as he emerged from the French windows and walked back towards Terri, along the side of the pool. Terri started to cry.

"No-one, honey, no-one. I guess I was just having a nightmare."

"Gee, you look in a bad way," Dean sympathised with his wife. He put her arm over his shoulder. "Come on - let's get you into bed." He carried Terri towards the house and into the bedroom through the French windows.

When the doctor came, he advised that Terri should rest for a few days. She didn't tell the doctor about seeing the figure in the pool, or about hearing the voice borne on the wind; and she certainly didn't tell dare to tell Dean.

Sixty-Four

Sergeant Hartley picked up the ancient black telephone receiver, as it violently rattled and rang to announce yet another call. The noise was made even more annoying by the presence of a large round bell on the reception area wall, which almost deafened anyone within earshot.

Sergeant Hartley hated doing nights; it was the time when all of the crackpots crawled out of the woodwork. The drunks, the pranksters, the time-wasters - and, all too frequently, old widow Heckinthorpe, who telephoned almost every night to announce that those dreadful hooligans were vandalising things outside her house again. To the ancient Mrs Heckinthorpe, a youth walking along the pavement in anything less than a military quickstep was guilty of an offence worthy of a jolly good birching.

Sergeant Hartley took a deep breath. "Shepton Police Station, may I help you?" he asked, in his most cordial voice.

The voice on the other end of the line was that of a young girl. Her clean, crisp vowels, perfect pronunciation and obvious erudition, immediately alerted Sergeant Hartley's suspicions. The monotone in which she delivered her message was a sure sign that she was reading a script.

"I have been asked to tell you that there are people tied up in the basement of 18 Cavendish Street, Shepton. The house is on fire and they only have a few minutes left to live. I have already alerted the fire brigade. Please hurry, I..."

"Whoah, now - just hold on just a minute there, love, just hold your horses," Sergeant Hartley interrupted the girl. "I will need to take a few details from you, if you don't mind. Now, who did you say you were, and how do you know about this fire?"

There was nothing but a continuous buzz on the other end of the line. "Hello...hello?" Sergeant Hartley shouted, before slamming the receiver back into its cradle.

"Bloody students," he growled. "They must think us Northerners just got in off the banana boat. They think we've got nowt better to do than provide them with cheap entertainment." He imitated the girl's voice. "Oh, Officer, do come quickly, old chap, 18 Cavendish Street is burning down and la-di-bloody-dah - and please excuse me, I have a college ball to attend, so I can't give you any details." He shook his head.

269

"I didn't get to where I am today by not recognising time-wasters. It'll be Mrs Heckinthorpe next, I suppose."

Sergeant Hartley glanced at the old, large clock in the reception area, noted the time, took a large gulp of tea from his mug, and stroked his chin. It was as though someone had just turned a switch on inside his head.

"18 Cavendish Street...that's where we were last Saturday night! That's where that chap lived, the one who was knocked off his motorbike. It's where that weird kid lives. They must have seen it in the papers. My God, how sick can these people be?"

His pondering was disturbed by Inspector Harrison bursting through the reception door from the main part of the station.

"Sergeant!" she barked. "We've just had an emergency call centre alert. There's been a fire reported on Cavendish Street. The fire brigade have just let us know they are on their way. We've sent a panda car round to see what's going on. Isn't 18 Cavendish Street where that poor chap lived, the one who got knocked off his motorbike last weekend?"

"Yes, Ma'am, it is," Sergeant Hartley mumbled. Inspector Harrison bit her lip.

"If there's anything funny going on, I want you there. You know these people, if I remember correctly."

Sergeant Hartley nodded. "Yes, Ma'am."

Inspector Harrison knew the family too. She had been PC Hartley's partner, as he had been then, when Wayne Higginbotham had run away five years ago. Now she was the senior police officer at the Shepton station. She turned and disappeared back into the bowels of the police station.

Sergeant Hartley screwed up his face, and imitated Inspector Harrison. "If there's anything funny going on..." He shook his head. "If only we could see where calls are coming from, then we could come down like a ton of bricks on these time-wasters. The only funny thing going on here is that some posh Southern ghoul thinks it's a jolly good wheeze to send fire engines and the police out on false alarms, to an address she saw in daddy's 'Times.' Pah!"

Sixty-Five

James Malone snatched the receiver off its cradle before it had the chance to ring more than once.

"Malone!" he almost shouted.

"Call for you, Mr. Malone," the hotel receptionist informed him. There was a click.

"Is that James Malone?" the soft, almost timid, female voice on the other end of the line asked.

"Yes, speaking," James barked, surprised that it wasn't Wayne, or one of Wayne's immediate family.

"I have been asked to pass on a message," the girl announced. Her voice was disconcertingly flat, almost a monotone, but it was the accent that took James aback; it was just so frighteningly perfect. The girl sounded like a BBC radio announcer from the 1950s.

"There is someone called Michael, or Wayne, trapped in the basement of 18 Cavendish Street, Shepton, Yorkshire. He is tied up and the house is on fire. He believes that he has only minutes to live." The phone went dead.

"Hello, hello! Who is this? How do you know this?" James shouted. He pressed the button on top of the phone a couple of times, but the only sound coming from the receiver was an annoying electronic buzz.

James pulled back the curtain and looked out of his window at the twilight sky; it was almost totally dark now. He could almost see the back of Cavendish Street from his high vantage point in the Midland Hotel, but nothing amiss was apparent.

"Jaysus Christ!" he shouted, realising that he was standing staring out of his window while young Wayne Higginbotham could be choking - or even worse, burning - to death. He raced out of his room, leaving the door ajar in his wake, and almost flew down the stairs, knocking a couple of German tourists out of the way as he ran past the great arched window on the Hotel's landing. He ran out of the front door as though a horde of demons were on his tail. It was only then that he realised he should sensibly have rung the fire brigade. Too late now, he thought, as he charged across the Brougham Road and into the auction mart opposite the Hotel.

James Malone had no idea whether there was a way through the auction mart to the rear of Cavendish Street from this direction, but it certainly looked to be a short cut. He crossed a small stream by running over a concrete bridge. There was a yard in front of him full of roofing stones, and next to that a wall and a small terrace of houses. He jumped and scrambled over the wall. A small alleyway led straight through, past the terrace, on to the back of Cavendish Street. He could now clearly see number eighteen and, sickeningly, the reflection of flames dancing in the middle storey window.

"Holy Mother of Jaysus!" Malone exclaimed, gulping for air and trying to breathe like the athlete he had once been. He set off to run again, despite a serious stitch that felt like he'd been shot. He vaulted over the high wall, straight into the communal back yard that served several houses on Cavendish Street. The tatty back door of number eighteen was right in front of him. James could hear distant sirens in the background - first one set, and then another, hordes of sirens wailing in the night air - but he couldn't wait for them. Wayne's life was at stake. James kicked at the back door, which opened all too easily. Flames leapt out at him and he was beaten back, his eyebrows singed and the skin on his face flushed.

"Oh no!" he cried. despairingly.

He was aware of people from the neighbouring houses suddenly appearing in the yard. "I don't think there's anybody in there, love," he heard an old lady shout, but James knew better. The phone tip-off just had to be accurate. In whatever way the girl had got the information - and James had absolutely no idea - she had been spot on right so far. He turned, and saw a large aluminium dustbin standing by the wall behind him.

"Stand back!" he bellowed, as he picked up the bin and hurled it with all his might at the frosted basement window, which shattered. Smoke poured out of the gaping shattered glass, but the flames had not yet broken into the bathroom.

Malone climbed gingerly through the window, trying to avoid the shards of broken glass. He landed in a huge, white, enamelled laundry sink. He tossed the dustbin, which had also come to rest in the sink, into a bath to his left. Through the smoke he could make out two pink shapes on the floor; one was writhing.

James coughed and, straining, picked up the nearest shape. It was Wayne, butt-naked and tightly bound and gagged with thick black tape. His eyes were wide and bulging with terror. James' eyes were also stinging now, and he could hardly breathe.

The sound of sirens was everywhere. He could see loads of blue lights flashing at the back of the house and the sound of tyres screeching to a halt, shouting, and doors slamming. He passed Wayne out through the window, trying desperately hard to avoid the lethal tooth-like shards of broken windowpane. Unseen hands grabbed the boy and pulled him carefully through. Flames suddenly rushed into the bathroom, as a trail of paraffin and methylated spirit finally caught fire.

In the flickering light, James covered his face as best he could and reached down for the second body. It was a naked girl with long black hair. He turned the body as he tried to get his hands under her to lift her up. He could hardly think in the searing heat, with the smoke filling every orifice. Yet, in the light of the flames James saw the girls eyes flash open momentarily; vivid, emerald-green eyes. James Malone knew those eyes, and he knew that face. Right before him, in the light of the flames, it collapsed into a horrible, rotting, skull-like shape. A scream burst out of the remains of a mouth in front of him.

James instantly recoiled, dropped the body, and threw his hands over his ears. His head felt as though it would explode any second. He scrambled for the window as fast as he could manage, as a river of flaming liquid engulfed the room and what had been the girl.

"Come on mate, we've got you. I heard a scream - is there someone else in there?" a male voice shouted, as powerful hands grabbed him and pulled him unceremoniously through what was left of the window.

"What the hell?" the same voice then shouted, as a second high-pitched screaming wail began, increasing rapidly in intensity, forcing everyone to cover up their ears. Windows all along the street exploded, shattering glass everywhere. James Malone, his hands still covering his ears, fell to his knees on the cold stone paving of the yard, and promptly threw up.

A second group of firemen had just arrived and had been unfurling their hoses. Now they dropped the hoses and stood writhing in agony, their hands over their ears, as James, still coughing, climbed slowly to his feet.

Then, suddenly, the wailing stopped. James uncovered his ears. All he could hear was strange buzzing sound.

"Was there anybody else in there, mate?" he thought he heard the fireman who had pulled him out ask.

"What?" James asked. He coughed again, and gagged.

"Was anyone else in there?" the fireman mimed, slowly and deliberately. James shook his head.

"I don't know. I didn't see anyone else. I couldn't see anything. The smoke was too thick." An ambulance man began to pull him away. He shook his head resignedly. "No, there was no one else...just the boy. I don't think there was anyone else at all."

"What the hell was that noise?" another fireman enquired, as he rubbed his ears. "I've never heard owt like it! My ears'll be buzzing for a month."

"Eh?" the first fireman grunted.

Policemen, fireman, ambulance personnel and Wayne's neighbours alike all rubbed their ears, trying to stop the buzzing that followed the incredible wailing noise.

"It must have been some sort of alarm that had gone wrong," a policeman opined, but no one heard him.

"Where's Wayne? The boy?" James asked the ambulance man.

"What?" The ambulance man screwed up his face.

"The boy?" James mouthed.

The man pointed to another ambulance, which was pulling away, its blue lights flashing in the dark.

James nodded and climbed in to the next vehicle, taking a quick look back at Wayne's old home, which - despite several hoses pouring copious amounts of water in - was blazing furiously.

"Well, that was close," he muttered to himself. "Goodbye, Aoibheall. You deserved better."

Sixty-Six

"Bloody hell... she's got nowt on!" Stanley Houghton-Hughes shouted, his face blushing redder and redder. He fled from the ladies lavatory that he had only just entered to find out where the screaming was coming from. He grabbed Cedric's collar as his son, who had been just behind him, held the toilet door open, his mouth agape. David Smith uttered a silent oath and rushed off to find a tea towel or tablecloth - anything to cover the girl and preserve her modesty.

"Get here, you!" Stanley pulled Cedric back into the main hall of the Youth Club. "Go and wait in the car," he ordered.

"But Dad..." Cedric moaned, to no avail.

"Not here, please no... not a scandal here!" David Smith muttered, as he re-emerged from the Youth Club kitchen with a table-cloth. "She'll have to wrap herself in this," he stated as he approached Stanley, handing him the table-cloth.

"You'll have to give it to her - I can't go back in there. She'll think I'm an old pervert!" Stanley Houghton–Hughes held up his hand in protest. "It's your Youth Club. You'll have to do it."

"I'll do it," Cedric happily volunteered, as he stopped his reluctant march towards the Youth Club door.

"Oh no, you bloody won't! Out, you!" Stanley barked, grabbing the cloth from David Smith. "If you want sommat doing, do it yerself," he grumbled, before walking backwards into the ladies with his eyes tightly closed and a hand clasped over them.

"Here you are, love, wrap yourself up in this," he shouted, waving the cloth, vaguely in the direction he thought the girl might be standing. The girl took the cloth, and Stanley darted back out into the hall.

"Should I ring the police?" David Smith almost whimpered.

"You better wait and see what she has to say. Sounds like they might be busy with all them sirens going off, anyway," Stanley blustered, wiping his forehead with a large white handkerchief.

The girl emerged from the toilets a few seconds later.

"Are you alright, love?" David Smith asked timorously. The girl nodded, although her wide traumatised eyes and gasped breathing said otherwise.

"What happened, lass?" Stanley asked. "Did someone, well...you know...do sommat? Do you want us to get the bobbies?"

The girl shook her head.

"Was it that American lad?" David Smith asked. "I could have absolutely sworn I saw you leave with him."

The girl shook her head again. She looked shaken, but not harmed in any way. Stanley shook his head.

"Well, someone must have taken your clothes off, love?" His question hung in the air as he marched officiously past the shaking teenager to peer into the ladies lavatories.

"There was a girl, with green eyes..." the girl started to say, and then seemed to stop to think. "And then I was near a lake, surrounded by beautiful hills and mountains and flowers. I thought I was dead."

David Smith paled even more as he turned back into the hall. "Oh no - not drugs as well!" he whispered to himself. He could see the headlines in his mind's eye: SEX AND DRUGS SCANDAL IN TOWN'S YOUTH CLUB!

Stanley emerged from the ladies with a pair of jeans, a tee shirt, and a jacket. "Are these yours, love?" he asked the girl. "Can't find any smalls, though."

The girl shook her head hesitantly, her cheeks reddening at the mention of her underwear. "No...I was wearing a skirt, I think."

"Well these must be somebody's," Stanley stated, with all the authority his years of management had engendered.

The girl grimaced. "She was Irish, I think. Black hair, and those eyes...green eyes...huge, bright green eyes."

"Who was?" Stanley demanded. The girl shivered as she answered.

"The girl in the toilets. She put her hand over my mouth and pushed me, then..."

David Smith put his hand to his mouth. "I let an Irish girl in earlier tonight - a young, pretty thing, very vivid green eyes. I'd never seen her before."

Stanley stroked his chin, and frowned.

"Did she, er, do owt...you know? Owt she shouldn't have?" he asked the girl again, with a nod towards her groin.

She shook her head. "I don't know. I just seemed to pass out when she touched me. I don't remember anything else. All of a sudden, I was in this beautiful valley. It was like paradise...it was all so weird. Then, I heard a really horrible, long, wailing scream, like someone was dying, so I started screaming too, and then...then, there I was, locked in the loo." She shivered violently."Look, could you ring my dad, please? I just want to go home. Is Finn not still here?"

Stanley nodded. "Aye, give us the number, love, and we'll ring your dad. As for this Finn, well...that's a right funny do." He looked at David Smith. "I think you had better ring the police as well."

David Smith grimaced. He looked at the girl.

"Look, he's right. The police should know about this. Please tell me, though...you haven't been taking any of them hallucinogenic drugs, have you? I mean, I hadn't seen this Yank lad of yours until last week, and Mr. Houghton-Hughes here says he's no cousin of Wayne's. He's not a drug dealer or anything, is he?"

The girl's mouth dropped open and she stared at Stanley Houghton-Hughes. "Finn isn't Wayne's cousin? But that's impossible."

Stanley shrugged his shoulders. "Wayne's my nephew, love. I think I know his family pretty well."

The girl looked totally crestfallen. "They both told me they were cousins. I've seen them together. What's going on?" she asked, as a tear rolled down her face. "I'm so confused."

Stanley Houghton-Hughes nodded his agreement. "No...I have to admit that I just don't get any of this at all. I wonder what's going on with all them sirens? It must be every fire engine and police car in Shepton!"

Stephanie Fleming was too busy shivering to hear what Stanley had said.

David Smith emerged from his office. "Your Dad's on his way, Stephanie. So are the police, although they might be a while. Seems there's a right fuss going on, on Cavendish Street."

In the background, another cacophony of wailing sirens could be heard.

Stanley Houghton-Hughes' mouth dropped open.

"Cavendish Street?" he gasped. "Oh - bloody hell!"

277

Sixty-Seven

Wayne realised he was still alive when everything began to hurt. His mouth and throat felt like someone had sandpapered them, while there was a taste in his mouth like he'd been drinking petrol. As for his head...the throbbing was unbearable. He tried to open his eyes but they were still stinging, and he could tell they had been bandaged. His ears were buzzing like colonies of wasps had burrowed into his brain. A single thought rushed into his head.

"Stephanie!" he moaned and tried to speak, but all he could manage was a peculiar groaning noise.

He felt attentive hands feeling his forehead, lifting the back of his head and plumping his pillow. He tried to speak again. "Ste...pha...nie." A woman's voice made a gentle, hushing sound, and he tried again. "Ste..."

The woman's voice was more insistent this time. "Shh..."

The feelings of guilt and remorse were totally overwhelming. Wayne could see Stephanie laughing and smiling and flashing those gorgeous blue eyes, just last Saturday evening. Then he saw her falling towards him, her eyes glazed. Then he could see her naked back, in the spartan basement bathroom.

"Stephanie," he whimpered, and drifted back into welcome unconsciousness.

"I ought to box your bloody ears!" were the first words Wayne Higginbotham heard, as he woke up in Arnedale hospital. Doris Higginbotham was only half-joking.

Wayne turned and peered at his mother through blurry, bloodstained eyes. His bandages had been removed, so his eyes couldn't have been too badly damaged, he realised, somewhat relieved.

"Hi, Mum. How's Stephanie?" he murmured. His throat and mouth were still sore, his head still ached, and he could still taste petrol fumes.

"Stephanie? Stephanie who? I'll give you bloody Stephanie!" Doris snapped. "What the hell do you think you were doing, putting us through all that? You're lucky to be here, my lad! I've lost me husband, me house, everything I've got - and I almost lost me son, too - all within a single week. I mean...what did I do to deserve all this?" Doris began to sob. Wayne rolled his sore eyes.

"It's all right for you," Doris moaned on. "Everything I had was in that house...all the photos of your dad...everything."

A nurse approached Wayne's bed. "How are we today then?" she asked, cheerfully.

Doris blew her nose loudly. "You swallowed quite a bit of smoke, Wayne. We had to put you on a ventilator for a while. If that handsome Irishman hadn't got to you when he did, you'd have been a goner, young man." Wayne tried to smile.

The nurse pulled curtains around his bed and measured his pulse by holding his wrist, whilst checking her watch.

"Good! The doctor will be along in a minute to check you over. Alright, love?" Wayne managed a weak nod of acknowledgement.

He heard Doris starting to drone on again, so he closed his eyes and tried to block out the overbearing feeling of grief, concentrating on remembering exactly what had happened.

As soon as the crazy priest had left and Wayne had heard the crackling of flames, he had tried to move. The only way he had been able to move was by imitating a worm or a maggot. He had managed to turn on his side and roll a couple of times, until he had been almost up to Stephanie's naked back. Her hair had looked strangely black in the twilight of the cellar, but it was pretty dark in there.

He had tried to shout through the tape that covered his mouth, but the girl had remained motionless. Wayne had then noticed rapidly advancing rivers of flame in the corridor outside. He had rolled again, until his feet were just by the bathroom door. He had then managed to bend his legs, just enough to kick the door shut. Then he had shuffled away from the door as quickly as possible.

He had wondered how was he going to get out of this one. He still hadn't been able to morph, nor had he been able to rouse Stephanie. He wondered momentarily why the priest hadn't bothered to tie her up, before remembering the glassy look in her eyes as she had fallen towards him.

She was dead, wasn't she? Stephanie Fleming was dead.

The thought had made Wayne feel sick. To make matters worse, he had then noticed thin wisps of smoke beginning to filter under the bathroom door.

Oh bum! he had thought to himself. I must be able to do something!

Wayne had closed his eyes, and concentrated. He had first thought of calling Aillen Mac Fionnbharr, but ghosts weren't much use in this sort of emergency.

The wisps of smoke were getting thicker.

He concentrated harder; he could see faces. There were people in his mind's eye. He shouted in his imagination, but no-one could hear him. Wayne searched and searched his mind; and then he saw the girl.

She looked sort of familiar, but he was quite sure he didn't know her. Her hair was brown and slightly wavy. She looked really pretty, with a cute little nose and full red lips. She was asleep in a pristine white bed, her mouth slightly open and one hand thrown back on to her pillow.

This is no time to be a peeping dirty! Wayne had thought to himself, but in the same instant he had sort of recognised who it must be that he was looking at. That must be my sister, he had thought, somewhere deep in the recesses of his brain.

The smoke had begun to fill his nose and he could hear the paint on the bathroom door beginning to blister and crack. Wayne concentrated like he had never concentrated before, his forehead creased into a thousand folds.

"Sister, please, help me...you are my only hope. I am tied up in a cellar at 18 Cavendish Street in Shepton. Please remember that! My sister, remember 18 Cavendish Street, Shepton Yorkshire. I am your twin brother, Michael, but I'm now called Wayne. Please help me. Ring the police, the fire brigade, but first ring James Malone at the Midland Hotel, Shepton. Please, my sister, help me. I am dying. I am desperate. Help me!"

Wayne saw the girl twitch and then stir; then the image had disappeared. Smoke had fully filled his nose, and he had begun to really strain to breathe. He had been able to hear the crackling of flames outside and the crashes and bangs as things exploded, or collapsed, upstairs.

He'd been too late and the girl would probably think she'd just been dreaming - if she even really existed. What a fool he'd been...and all because he'd wanted to kiss Stephanie Fleming, just one more time!

The smoke had grown thicker and thicker; it had swirled and danced as it had poured under the door. Wayne had begun to slip into unconsciousness. He had known that he had been about to die, as his lungs began to feel as if they were ready to explode. Seconds ticked by like hours. If that was what drowning was like, then you really did have time to review your entire life. The bathroom door had begun to disintegrate, and he had seen bright orange and yellow flames.

He had closed his stinging eyes. He hadn't been able to breathe at all. So much for Wayne Higginbotham, the slaneymore-whatever it was, the superhero.

He had heard what sounded like shattering glass nearby, and had felt his eyeballs bulging crazily inside his closed eyelids as he had tried to find air...any air.

There had been another explosion - this time, it sounded like the bath breaking -and Wayne had suddenly been aware of being picked up and the sudden sublime feeling of cool night air on his skin. He had then known no more; not until he had woken up here in the hospital.

Why him? Why had he survived? How had he survived?

Poor Stephanie. He couldn't get the picture of her pretty face out of his head. Her beautiful, clear, bright blue eyes. Her beautiful, vivid, emerald-green eyes...?

Wayne's eyes snapped wide open. When Stephanie had fallen towards him, he had been sure her eyes had been a vivid shade of green. Yet... Steph's eyes were definitely blue....

A strange little sliver of hope began to filter into his mind, or was it just wishful thinking? No; he must have dreamed the green eyes.

Doris had finally stopped ranting and raving and weeping and sat silently by his bed, waiting for the Doctor to come along. Wayne didn't want to open his eyes. He knew if he did, she would only start off again. Then, through the buzzing in his ears, he heard his Aunt Margaret's voice.

"Are you in there, Doris?" Wayne heard the rustling of the curtains surrounding his bed, as Margaret had obviously slipped into his curtained-off sanctuary."Well, what a night it was last night!"

"You can say that again," Doris sniffed loudly, but Margaret continued, managing to sound quite jolly despite the overwhelming air of tragedy.

"You know our Stanley went to that there Youth Club last night, to find your Wayne? Well, you didn't get the full story, did you? What with all the panic with the police and the fire and Wayne and what-not. Well, he told me what had happened, later on. It turns out that this chap was locking up the Youth Club, when our Cedric had heard screaming inside. It was coming from the ladies loos. Our Stanley had rushed straight in. Well, you know our Stanley, he just doesn't care, does he? He's not afraid of anything, our Stanley. Anyway, he'd burst straight into the ladies loos and the first thing he clapped his eyes on was a teenage girl, standing there as large as life - absolutely, totally and utterly stark naked! Aye...not a single stitch on. Our Stanley got quite an eyeful, he says! Anyway, when they'd calmed her down and got the full story out of her, it seems that she'd been attacked - by some girl with long dark hair, and really unusual green eyes. The chap who runs the place said he'd let this dark-haired girl in, even though he'd never seen her before. Now, this is where it gets really fishy; she was Irish! Aye, Irish!"

"What's that got to do with our Wayne?" Doris sniffed.

"Well!" Margaret exclaimed with undisguised glee, and a massive degree of satisfaction at her own cleverness. "The chap who runs the Youth Club reckons this girl, who they'd found in the nude, had been seen snogging and canoodling with an American lad - now, listen to this - an American lad who'd been pretending to be your Wayne's cousin for the past two weeks. A cousin your Wayne doesn't even have! It all fits now, doesn't it?"

"What fits?" Doris asked, now totally confused.

"Well, they must have been the IRA gang, you know, who tried to do in your Wayne. One of them there hit squads. I've seen stuff like it on the telly."

Despite the buzzing, Wayne had heard most of the conversation. He couldn't pretend to be asleep any longer.

"Who was the girl, Aunty Margaret?" he croaked.

Margaret turned around in surprise. "Ooh I'm sorry, I didn't mean to wake you Wayne, love. Don't you worry yourself about it."

"Who was the girl they found?" Wayne repeated, insistently. "Please tell me."

Aunty Margaret shrugged. "Our Cedric said she's at the Girl's High School - Stephanie Fletcher, or sommat like that, I think he said."

"Fleming?" Wayne gasped painfully, hope flooding through his mind.

"Aye, that's her." Margaret chirped. She turned back to Doris, and screwed up her nose. "Fancy - they even pinched her knickers!"

Wayne closed his eyes and, despite all the pain and the incessant buzzing in his head, he smiled. Stephanie was alive and well. But how had she got from being shot, lying seemingly dead in a burning basement, full of flames, to being back in the Youth Club loos?

Wayne then remembered his strange feeling of dread and Stephanie's sudden wantonness. He remembered the change in her voice, just as they'd entered the house.

So he hadn't dreamed those vivid, green eyes, after all, nor had he imagined the strangely black hair in the cellar bathroom. Wayne's stomach turned.

He remembered where he had heard that voice before. He remembered the bald priest's words: I think she would have been a bit too experienced for you, boy. I do not think she was quite the girl you thought she was.

282

It hadn't been Stephanie Fleming that he'd taken home; Stephanie Fleming was alive and well.

It had been Aoibheall the Banshee who had perished in the cellar of 18 Cavendish Street. It had been Aoibheall the Banshee's scream that had caused the buzzing in his head.

Wayne Higginbotham had heard the cry of the banshee, and he had survived to tell the tale.

Sixty-Eight

"You have done well, Pierre." Bishop Donleavy's smile was almost warm. Father Pierre de Feren acknowledged the praise with a curt nod, and a thin smile.

"Thank you, Your Grace."

The bishop stood painfully, and edged around his ornate desk to pick up a crystal decanter, filled with a blood-red liquid.

"A little celebration is in order, I think," the old bishop chuckled under his breath, forcing his throat to undulate even more violently than usual. "You are absolutely certain, Pierre, that this time our celebrations are not...how shall I put it...premature?"

Father de Feren pouted and shrugged in the same gesture, in the way that only French-speakers seem to be able to manage.

"The boy was tightly bound and gagged with tape; he could not change shape, nor could he summon aid. When I left, the house was already ablaze. There was no way he could have escaped. It would have been impossible."

The bishop passed the tall Belgian priest a glass of wine.

"Might it not have been opportune to stay in the town and appraise the results of your operation, maybe, in the local media?"

Father de Feren shrugged again. "Only an amateur stays around to ensure that his work has been properly done. Have you not heard the old police saying, Your Grace, that a criminal always returns to the scene of his crime? I am a professional. I do not need to wait and see if I have achieved my goal. I know when I have succeeded."

The bishop nodded approvingly. "And what of the police?"

De Feren smiled. "I think they will suspect nothing. The alcohol-fuelled wickedness of youth will be blamed for the tragic fire in the house. That, and the fact that the boy's father was foolish enough to store fuel in the basement." De Feren smiled triumphantly. "It is said that bids of a feather flock together. The boy was with the banshee, although both were in different body shapes."

The bishop raised his eyebrows in surprise. "The banshee? Is she now dead?"

De Feren grinned. "Yes. It was a case of - how do you say it? 'Two birds with one stone.' I knew it was the banshee with the boy as soon as she opened her mouth, despite the fact that she had assumed the form of another girl. She forgot to disguise her voice in her eagerness to get her prey into her lair. The boy, I had to take a risk on. I was not sure whom the banshee was bringing into the house. Fortunately, the youth with her was the Higginbotham boy. I do not think the boy had any idea that he was with the banshee."

The bishop took a sip of wine, and chuckled. "So, he was doomed even had you not been there...how amusing. Did you get the stones?"

De Feren snorted derisively. "They will be no more than lumps of charcoal now. Why should I have risked all to recover such trivialities? The immortals are no more and we cannot use the stones...so why take risks?" He shrugged yet again, and took a small sip of wine. "Your Grace; the last banshee, and the offspring of the demon Finn, are both now dead. Our Lord is safe to return, at last. The work of The Sacred Order of St. Gregory is finished."

The bishop sat back down behind his desk. There was a long silence, broken only by the ticking of an old Grandfather clock in the corner of the room.

"So...fourteen hundred years of history finally comes to a close," Bishop Donleavy murmured. "Even so, my dear Pierre - in the absence of any proof confirming your claims regarding these demons, I shall not yet be recommending demobilisation of the Order." Father de Feren nodded.

"Five years ago, similar claims were made about our inevitable victory over the forces of darkness. No bodies were ever found, except for two of our priests who had died, away from the battle site. No stones were found that time, either. Eventually, of course, we found out that we had not achieved that final victory, when we discovered that the stones were still being used."

The bishop appraised the tall, bald, Belgian priest.

"I am to travel to Rome tomorrow, Father. I have an audience with the Cardinal. I informed him of your success immediately, of course, as soon as you rang to tell me about it; but tomorrow I shall face the same questions that I have just asked you. For my sake, I hope that the Cardinal is as trusting as I am...and for all our sakes, I hope you are justified in your own self-confidence. Let us now pray, Father, that it is so."

Sixty-Nine

James Malone limped painfully along the Hospital corridor, yet he felt like a man who had just won the Irish lottery. Despite his night in the hospital - his racking cough, his aching lungs, stinging eyes, the buzzing in his ears and various burns, cuts and bruises - he felt good. The girl had been who had phoned him, whoever she was, had saved Wayne's life just as surely as James himself had.

James had spent much of his time in the hospital wondering who the girl could be and how she had known about Wayne, about the fire, and the fact that he was tied up in the basement. He was hoping that Wayne might be able to tell him, and put him out of the misery of his frenzied speculation. He arrived at Wayne's bedside just after Doris and Margaret had left.

"Hey, Wayne!" he exclaimed with a grin as he saw the boy sitting up in his bed, before dissolving into a coughing fit.

"You make me sound like that picture above our fireplace...well, the one we used to have," Wayne replied, with a sad smile. James looked blankly at him. "The Hay-Wain - Constable, you know? Constable's Hay-Wain."

James nodded, and gave a wry grin to acknowledge the weak joke.

"How are you feeling?" he asked, as he pulled a chair up to the side of Wayne's bed. The boy nodded.

"A bit frazzled, a bit overdone. There's a ringing in my ears like a million alarm bells going off in my head and I think my skull was nearly smashed, but I feel like I'm alive - thanks to you." Wayne coughed, then held out a hand, which James shook with a grimace.

"Ouch! I forgot! I cut that hand," James laughed, despite the pain.

Wayne perused his rescuer. "You look worse than I do."

James shrugged his shoulders. "Thanks buddy. Pah - it's only a few flesh wounds. I'll be playing for the first fifteen again come Saturday."

Both laughed, and both began to cough.

"And to think I'd given up smoking because they said it was bad for me," James declared. "I might as well not have bothered!" He stole a grape from a bowl by Wayne's bed. "So...who did it?"

Wayne shook his head, and twisted his mouth to one side.

"I don't know, some priest...he sounded French, or something."

James nodded knowingly. "That would have been de Feren," he stated coldly, "the Order's new chief assassin."

Wayne acknowledged the name with a grimace.

286

"And the girl in the cellar, that I thought was Stephanie, was actually the banshee?"

James sighed and nodded his head, sadly.

"I guess so. She wasn't dead, you know, not when I got you out. I went to lift her up. She opened her eyes. Those fabulous green eyes...but the rest of her, oh God! It will haunt me for the rest of my days. That unbelievable screaming noise was her cry. The fabled cry of the banshee. They say it's a harbinger of death. I suppose this time it was -but her own. I do feel a bit sad about that. I don't actually think she was all that bad."

Wayne shook his head. "Well, I don't think she was all that good, either. To think that I kissed a woman who was probably older than a great, great, great granny. Yuk! Worse than that, I was ready to do more!"

James laughed. "Ah, believe me, lad, you'll go on and kiss and wake up with much worse, I assure you."

Both laughed and coughed again, which caused even more laughter and coughing.

James stretched lazily. "So, who was the girl?" he asked, with a sly grin. Wayne looked confused.

"What girl? I thought we just agreed that it was the banshee?"

James raised his eyebrows. "No, not her...the other one."

Wayne shrugged. "Oh, what - at the Youth Club, you mean? That was Stephanie Fleming. God, I hope she's okay. The banshee must have knocked her out in the loos and nicked her clothes, before locking her in."

Now it was James' turn to look confused. "But how did she get to the phone, if she was locked in the toilets? How did she know you were tied up in the basement?"

Wayne frowned. "She didn't..." he answered slowly and thoughtfully, while looking very, very confused. James stroked his chin, thoughtfully.

"So who was the incredibly posh girl who rang me at the hotel, telling me that you were all trussed up like a Christmas turkey and about to become just as crisp and well-done?"

Wayne looked totally bemused; and then remembered his efforts to contact his sister, before he had lost consciousness.

"Did she not give a name, or anything?" he asked, still unable to believe that he might have actually communicated telepathically with his closest blood relative.

James shook his head. "No. She just rang my room at the hotel out of the blue, said that you were in the basement at the house in

Cavendish Street, all tied up, and that the house had been set alight. She gave me the address, and then just rang off. No names, no pleasantries, nothing. I've got to say she was the poshest sounding girl I think I've ever heard. Real la-di-dah, you know? She made the Queen herself sound common. She must have rung the fire brigade and the police as well, because they were after arriving almost as quick as me."

Wayne rubbed his forehead. "I tried to make contact with someone. Someone close, sort of, by using my mind...telepathically, you know, like The Tomorrow People on the telly? But I didn't think it would work." He scratched his head, and grinned. "It sounds like it did!"

James laughed. "I should say it did. And you say she was close, but yet you really don't know who she was?"

Wayne grimaced. "No. I've really got no idea at all," he lied.

Why did he not want to tell James about his sister? he wondered, as the affable Irishman speculated about how long the two of them were going to have to stay in the hospital.

Did he not trust him? Why not? The man had just saved his life, for God's sake. James Malone had risked his own life to save him. So why did he harbour this strange reluctance to divulge his most important secret?

Somehow, Wayne knew he wanted to keep the secret of his twin sister from absolutely everyone. If the Order did succeed in one day killing him, then at least she would have a chance. She alone would carry the genetic heritage of the Tuatha De Danaan.

"So - what happens now?" Wayne asked, his mood suddenly turning sullen and downcast.

James scratched his head. "Once they let us out, you mean?" Wayne nodded, and James blew out a huge sigh.

"We get away from here. We get away before de Feren finds out that you're not dead and comes back to finish what he started."

Wayne closed his eyes. "So, I am always going to be on the run, then? You know, like a bank robber, or one of those witnesses that the police re-house and give new names and so on?"

James shrugged again. "I dunno. Once we get to L.A. the trail should be cold, so you should be in the clear."

Wayne grimaced. His headache was still pounding like a bass drum. "All my life I've wanted to go to L.A. Even before I knew that my mom lived there, I wanted to go."

James grinned, empathetically. "Yeah, it's a cool place, I can tell you. You'll love it."

Wayne sighed and looked out of the window next to his bed. Raindrops streaked down the glass, and the sky outside was dark and

288

grey, even though it was still only the early part of the evening. The lovely weather had changed again.

"I know I'd love it...but I can't go," Wayne mumbled.

"What?" James asked. He couldn't believe his buzzing ears. "You don't want to escape to L.A?"

Wayne smiled sadly. "I couldn't live on the run, James. Always wondering if the next assassin is lurking just round the corner, ready to pounce. When I do go to L.A. I want to enjoy it, not spend every waking hour looking over my shoulder, waiting for the next mad priest to come looking for me. It would be like one of those old Western films that Dad liked. The ones where the old gunfighter is always waiting for the kid to turn up, the one who'll eventually and inevitably turn out to be faster than him."

James looked shell-shocked. "You can't mean that!" he uttered incredulously. "So you're just going to stay here and wait for them to come back and finish the job?"

Wayne half-smiled, and stared intently at his friend. "I didn't say that, did I? I just said that I'm not going to run away to America...not yet, anyway."

James looked hurt. "Okay, whatever!" he sighed, shaking his head.

Wayne shrugged. "Anyway, I can't be on compassionate leave from school forever. I'm in the middle of my 'A' Levels now, and Dai Davies is a damn site scarier than any loony Priest."

"Dai Davies?" James repeated, incredulously.

"Deputy Headmaster at Wormysted's," Wayne explained. A nurse busied herself by Wayne's bed. There was a long silence until the nurse had gone.

James was about to speak, when Wayne cut him off.

"Do you know where the Order is based?" he asked. James looked surprised at the question.

"Yes. They have an office, if you can call it that, in the main Church in Dublin: St. Patrick's Cathedral. I've been dragged there twice, now."

Wayne nodded sagely, and a look of steely determination came over his face. He turned and looked into James Malone's eyes.

"James, I've been thinking..."

"Dangerous!" James chipped in with a grin. Wayne smirked sarcastically, before continuing.

"I was so upset when I first came round. You know, thinking that I'd been responsible for Stephanie getting killed, and all that. As soon as I realised that Steph was okay, though, I started to get angry; really angry. You know? I mean, who are these guys who think they can just go around killing people just because they think they can get away with it? They killed my real dad. They may have even killed my adopted dad...I don't know. They tried to kill me and they'd have killed Steph, if it had been her. I mean, what has she ever done to them?"

James breathed a long deep sigh. "That's the way the Order works, I guess. That's the world we live in."

Wayne Higginbotham sat bolt upright in bed, his fists clenched.

"Not my world. They've picked on the wrong guy this time, James. I might be just an average, poor, provincial schoolboy, but I've got one or two things going for me that most average schoolboys don't have."

James Malone frowned. "What are you saying, Wayne?"

Wayne smiled, but it was a humourless, bitter smile.

"Trust me, James. Just trust me. When we get out of here, the sacred bloody Order of Saint whatsisname - or whatever they call themselves - have got a few surprises coming their way."

Seventy

Terri sat up in bed. She felt much better. The bright sunlight flooded into her bedroom and the rumbling sound of traffic on the distant freeway reminded her of the real world. The everyday world, where normal people lived and worked and went about their everyday lives, and weird disembodied voices didn't plague them in the middle of the night.

Terri wondered if she was having another nervous breakdown. The doctor, who Dean had called out when he'd got home, had certainly seemed concerned when she said that she thought she'd heard voices. He hadn't really bought her rapid retraction when she attributed it to having possibly been the neighbours arguing, either.

Terri sighed. It certainly wasn't the best time to go loopy, with a baby due, a career to try and resurrect once the baby was born, and a husband who wasn't proving quite as reliable as she had hoped. Maybe that was why she was so stressed?

There was a gentle knock at Terri's bedroom door.

"Come in!" she shouted.

Conchita, the old Mexican lady who helped the Vitalias, entered the room carrying a tray of hot tea with sliced lemon.

"Buenos dias, Señora Vitalia," the woman smiled kind-heartedly. "The señor is asking me to look after you today. He say he has important meeting in Burbank."

Terri smiled back. "Thank you, Conchita."

She took the hot tea and sipped it gratefully, before resting the cup on her bedside table and turning on the television. Conchita soon disappeared to busy herself with the housework.

Terri's mind began to wander as the television droned on. She clicked the remote to turn the television off and settled back down on the bed. She began to think about that voice and the events of the previous night. Where had she heard that voice before?

As her memory began to focus, she remembered seeing the reflection of a man in the water of the swimming pool. A man dressed in an ancient costume. Suddenly, she sat bolt upright in bed as she remembered the figure changing into Danny Finn, the American boy she had fallen in love with some seventeen years earlier, back in Ireland.

The boy who had scared her and given her the first nervous breakdown when he had gone and changed his shape right in front of her in broad daylight, just as the figure in the pool had done last night. The boy she had fled from, whose children she had carried in her womb and been forced to give away for adoption.

The memories that had been locked away in the deepest recesses of her consciousness,, by endless therapy sessions, began to flood back into her mind. The experts had convinced her that such things as shape-shifters were mere figments of her imagination and that the whole thing had been no more than a hysterical emotional response to finding out that she was going to be an unmarried mother at the age of sixteen. Well, either she was as mad as a March hare, or Danny Finn had really been a shape-shifter after all; and was now capable of visiting her in Los Angeles.

Maybe she had better not tell Dean about this stuff, but what about Michael? Did he know his father had been something less, or maybe something more, than human? How could she ever tell him? Son, sit down. Listen, I've something important to tell you. It's about your Father. Your dad...he was...he was a leprechaun!

Terri began to laugh. The whole thing was so absurd. "Your father was a leprechaun!"

Conchita, who had been about to knock on the bedroom door to collect the tea things, hesitated. The Senor had asked her to watch for any strange behaviour and here was Señora Vitalia, laughing like drain. Maybe she had seen something on the television?

Conchita knocked and entered and immediately noticed that the television had been switched off. She collected the cup with a smile, and scurried away. How was she going to tell Señor Vitalia that his wife was loco?

A few miles further up the San Fernando Valley, in the Canyons, Carrie Horden was in a state of shock.

"Hospital? Smoke inhalation? Burns? Lacerations? Jesus Christ, Dan, is James okay?"

Dan Joyce's voice at the other end of the line reassured her that her boyfriend was fine and would soon be flying back to Los Angeles with the boy. Even so, Carrie remained unconvinced, until James himself telephoned her from the Arnedale Hospital later that morning.

"Yeah, I'm fine," he repeated, for perhaps the twentieth time. "The major problem I've had is covering our tracks and stopping the press getting hold of the story. Somebody must have told the local newspaper that I'd saved some kids life by diving into a burning building, and now they want to run a story about it."

Carrie gasped. "But hey, you could get a medal or something for what you did!"

James winced. "Yeah honey. I could be on the early evening news on television, and the Order would know straight away that the kid had survived."

Carrie slapped her forehead. "Oh man, of course...how could I be so stupid? But are you sure you're okay?"

James Malone once again assured her that he was in good health and fine spirits, and worried her again by relating that he was due to be interviewed by the police the next morning. However, by the time she replaced the receiver on the cradle, even Carrie had been convinced that James was as well as could be expected and that the police interview would be a formality. She also felt extremely proud.

Carrie had known immediately that she was picking up somebody special when she had stopped the car to pick up that lonely-looking hitchhiker, all those weeks earlier. Little had she realised that she was picking up a sensitive and caring lover, and a bona fide hero at the same time.

She walked out of her door and stood by a small lemon tree in the corner of her yard. The sun was already quite high in the sky and the valley below shimmered in the haze of the day.

"Well, Jimmy boy..." Carrie whispered, in what she hoped was the general direction of Great Britain, "let's hope that's all the excitement you're going to get this trip."

Seventy-One

"So, right...just run this by me again?" Sergeant Hartley insisted, his forehead tightly creased in a disapproving frown.

"Firstly, there's this Irish girl, masquerading as a nun, who goes around stripping innocent young women and stealing all their clothes. The particular innocent young woman in question - one Stephanie Fleming of 59 Greenacres, Shepton - states categorically that she was with your cousin, one Michael Finnegan, or 'Finn', up until the said incident took place in the ladies lavatory at the Westmoreland Street Youth Club, at around nine pm on Thursday last, 14th September."

Wayne rubbed his chin, thoughtfully. "Yeah, that's what I heard!"

Sergeant Hartley rubbed his forehead and then scratched his head as he stared at the notes he had taken.

"The same said American youth, one Michael Finnegan, claimed to be your cousin, but your mother says that she has never heard of him."

Wayne nodded sagely. "She wouldn't have."

Sergeant Hartley raised his eyebrows. "Hmm. Then we have - according to Mister James Malone, an Irish citizen, currently resident in the United States of America - a Belgian Catholic priest, who is linked to the IRA and who is out to do you in, because your real father was a British informer?"

Wayne nodded eagerly. "Spot on," he stated authoritatively.

"This same said Belgian priest was responsible for an attempted murder and also an act of arson on Thursday last. Indeed, according to the said Mr. Malone, he also attempted to kill a girl, although no body was found in the aforementioned burned building," continued Sergeant Hartley.

Wayne nodded. "Mmm," he murmured.

"You, Wayne Higginbotham, were rescued from the same said burning building - in the nude, tied, gagged and bound."

Wayne nodded again. Sergeant Hartley grunted and scribbled down some more notes, before turning to the constable sitting next to him.

"In the course of a single week, I have had one fatal road accident, one possible sexual assault, an attempted murder and an act of arson. I don't suppose an act of bondage will tip the scales." The constable nodded, and Sergeant Hartley raised his hands in frustration. "More work than I've had all year...and all of it is linked to just one individual!" He turned back to Wayne.

"Of course, I've asked C.I.D. to deal with the attempted murders, and I suppose the Special Branch will have to get involved with the IRA thing. As for young Miss Fleming; she hasn't pressed charges yet, although no one seems to have any idea who this Irish girl was or where she has disappeared off to. The only link to all of this seems to be you, young man. It was Ireland you ran off to, all those years ago, wasn't it?"

Wayne smiled, and nodded his head in agreement. Sergeant Hartley scratched his head again.

"So, Mr Higginbotham...would you mind telling me where you were, last Thursday night?"

Wayne nodded. "I was at home."

The sergeant scribbled on the pad. "Home being the Houghton-Hughes' house? Or 18 Cavendish Street?"

Wayne sighed. "18 Cavendish Street."

The sergeant sniffed. "Yet your mother says she never saw you leave your aunt's house. Indeed, you had been forbidden to do so, because of the aforementioned, supposed, IRA threat that Mister Malone had referred to."

Wayne smiled sheepishly. "I snuck out. I missed my own stuff. You have to take all this IRA stuff with a pinch of salt, you know. My mother is very gullible, and as for Mister Malone...well, you do know he used to be a priest, don't you?"

The sergeant looked offended. "Of course I do!"

Wayne winked. "Do you know why he's no longer a priest?"

Sergeant Hartley's eyes opened wide in anticipation as he leaned in towards Wayne. "Well, yes...er, well...no," he blustered.

Wayne raised his hand to his mouth in a drinking motion.

"He's not quite all there anymore," he whispered. "He lives in a bit of a fantasy world." He beckoned the sergeant in closer. "He believes in leprechauns and banshees and all that sort of stuff...says he's seen them!"

Sergeant Hartley snorted in amused disbelief. "No!" he gasped. "Never!"

"You ask him," Wayne shrugged, dismissively. "So it was him that told my mother about the IRA, and she is a bit gullible, especially in the light of recent events."

Sergeant Hartley coughed. "Aye, I see what you mean...but what happened at the house? How did the fire start? How did you get all tied up?"

Wayne sighed. "I really don't know. One minute I was clearing up, you know, my dad's stuff. I must have lit a match to see what I was doing - and the next thing there's a huge bang and the cellar is ablaze. My dad kept spare fuel for his motorbike in the cellar, so I can only presume I accidentally set some of it alight. I must have fallen and banged my head when it exploded. Mr Malone was passing, and heard me shouting."

The sergeant looked confused. "But he said you were all naked and tied up, like."

Wayne imitated drinking again. "Was any other body found?"

Sergeant Hartley shook his head.

"So, who would have tied me up?"

Sergeant Hartley shook his head. "I do believe there were other witnesses, but I'll get to them in due course. I don't know; naked and tied up, as well. Now your private life is your business, young man, but we're hearing all sorts of stories. This is a very serious matter. So who was the posh bird on the phone?"

Wayne shrugged. "Posh bird? What posh bird?"

Sergeant Hartley leafed through his notebook.

"I myself took a phone call on Thursday night at about twenty-past nine. It was from some posh girl with a very la-di-dah accent saying that somebody was tied up in the basement of 18 Cavendish Street. I took it as a prank. Can you explain that? I have a full statement from Fred Collier from Shepton fire brigade who states that at eighteen minutes past nine on the evening of the 14th, he took a call from someone with a distinct Home Counties accent, informing him of a fire at 18 Cavendish Street."

The sergeant flicked his notebook back a few pages and examined the statement that James had given him earlier:

"Aye...it also definitely says here, that a girl with a distinct Home Counties accent, rang Mr James Malone at the Midland Hotel, Shepton, on the night of the 14th and told him your precise condition and whereabouts. Just like the posh bird who rang me."

Wayne shrugged. "I can't explain that."

The sergeant pursed his lips. "And what about this supposed cousin of yours...the said, ahem, Michael Finnegan?"

Wayne nodded. "He's from my birth family. Seems him and Stephanie had a bit of a thing for each other. He's gone back to the States, now."

Sergeant Hartley frowned again. "The Immigration services have absolutely no record of a Mister Finnegan leaving the country for the United States, either last Thursday, or Friday. Any road, where was he staying while he was over here, if your mother didn't know owt about him?"

Wayne shrugged. "He was staying in a bed and breakfast place. He didn't say where. He'll have gone via Ireland, you know, from Shannon or Dublin. He didn't tell me which airport he was flying from, either. To be honest, we fell out before he left. I fancied Stephanie too, you see."

The sergeant wiped his forehead.

"So, what do you know about this Irish girl?"

Wayne grimaced. "The one who took Steph's clothes?"

Sergeant Hartley nodded curtly. "Correct!"

Wayne shrugged. "Nothing...nothing at all!" he lied.

Sergeant Hartley sat back in the plastic hospital chair.

"There's sommat funny about you, young Mister Higginbotham. I felt it in my bones that time you ran away. I can't explain it, but I get a funny tingling feeling in my stomach whenever your name is mentioned." He turned to the constable. "Got to the west of Ireland, he did - and no more than eleven at the time! A right funny do, it were."

Wayne looked concerned. "Are you saying that I've done something wrong, officer, because I don't remember committing any crime?"

Sergeant Hartley peered at the boy suspiciously.

"There's nowt I can rightly put my finger on, not yet...but you seem to be right at the core of all the strange stuff that's happened around here recently. I mean, this is all a right funny business...and you are the lynch-pin, as it were. I have to say I think there's sommat very fishy about you, young man, and not just that you probably do get up to all that kinky bondage stuff. Just call it a copper's intuition." The sergeant's eyes locked on Wayne's big green-blue pupils.

"But believe me lad, I'll find out, if it's..."

Sergeant Hartley couldn't explain what happened next. How everything seemed to come to him in a blinding flash. It could only have been one of those eureka moments that all good cops have, when the clues fit together like a child's simple jigsaw puzzle. Suddenly, he understood everything.

Doris Higginbotham was batty, James Malone was an Irish drunk, and Stephanie Fleming had made up some story about being assaulted after some teenage prank went wrong. There had been an awful accident at 18 Cavendish Street, the Yank had gone home via Ireland, and the mysterious Irish girl had simply moved on. The tingling feeling in his stomach was wind. It was all so obvious and clear. It had all been a series of unrelated and unfortunate events and unusual coincidences. The Higginbotham kid was alright, if a bit kinky. It was all just as simple as that. He sat back, and snapped his notebook shut.

"Well, thanks for your time, lad. You should be out of here soon. I hope you get things sorted out at the house. It's a bit of a mess, I'm afraid. Good morning."

Wayne watched the sergeant leave the ward, closely followed by the constable, who looked incredibly confused. He felt very guilty, having made Stephanie sound a bit of a floozy and James, the man who'd saved his life, a drunk. But these were desperate times and desperate times called for desperate measures, as one of his friends had said, weeks earlier. The last thing him and James needed right now was the police crawling all over them.

Wayne climbed out of bed and marched painfully off to find James, and let him know that he'd ridiculed James' earlier statement to the police. James Malone wouldn't be pleased, but then he wasn't going to be pleased by anything that Wayne was going to tell him. At this particular point in time, Wayne Higginbotham was much too angry to give other people's feelings much thought.

Seventy-Two

Doris Higginbotham blew her nose for possibly the fiftieth time since she had sat down at Margaret Houghton-Hughes' breakfast table half an hour earlier.

"What am I going to do?" she sobbed.

Stanley Houghton-Hughes pursed his lips, raised his eyebrows at his wife, Margaret, and announced that he was "off". He pecked Margaret on the cheek, and smiled weakly at Doris.

"It'll sort itself out, love, don't you worry," he blustered, before noisily clearing his throat, throwing his raincoat over his arm, and slamming the front door behind him.

Margaret patted her sister's arm. "At least you're both still in one piece, love," she whispered sympathetically. "Your stuff can be replaced, but you and Wayne couldn't have been."

Doris sniffed. "And Frank can't be replaced either. I do wish he were here."

She broke into heavy sobs again. Margaret stood up, and sighed. "I'll make us another cup of tea, love." She paused for a moment, and turned towards her sister.

"I'm afraid Frank's gone, Doris, love. There's nothing that can be done about that, but after what happened on Thursday night you should be grateful you've still got your Wayne."

"He should never have gone out!" Doris spat, taking Margaret aback at the amount of venom in her voice. "He was told to stay in, but oh no...the clever dick had to go out, gallivanting, didn't he? Clever dick knows better than me and everybody else who warned him, doesn't he? Trevor wouldn't have done owt like this."

Margaret rolled her eyes as she filled the kettle. "Wayne's just a normal teenage lad, Doris. He was just fed up being cooped up in here."

Doris Higginbotham snorted her derision.

"He's been a clever bloody so and so ever since he went to that Grammar School, I'll tell you. Well, he hasn't been that clever this time has he? Nearly going and getting himself killed. Burning down our house at the same time, to boot! It's a good job I brought a suitcase of clothes here, or I wouldn't even have a change of underwear. Everything is ruined, and all because of him!"

Margaret stirred the tea in the teapot, and poured two cups.

"I wish I'd never clapped eyes on him," Doris grumbled as she took a cup of hot steaming tea from Margaret. "Our Trevor was a much nicer

299

looking baby. He was always smiling, our Trevor, and he didn't have them stupid big ears. He wouldn't have done owt like this," she repeated pathetically.

Margaret was sick of hearing about Trevor, Doris' first adopted baby whose mother had taken him back before the adoption had been legally ratified, because he had contracted meningitis.

"I don't think you can really say that," she stated quietly and firmly. "Your Wayne has been a good son until all this happened, apart from that time when he ran away to find out who he really was and...well...I suppose we can understand that. It could all have been avoided, if he'd been told about his proper background in the first place. As for all this that's going on now, he can't help being the son of an informer, or whatever he is. The only thing Wayne did wrong was to sneak out. I think nearly dying is punishment enough for that!"

Doris Higginbotham stared, open-mouthed, at her younger sibling. Margaret rarely disagreed with Doris, and it was even rarer for her to vocalise that disagreement. Since they had been little girls in the nearby village of Carelton, Doris had been the dominant sister. Although Margaret had married a man with more prospects and had moved effortlessly up the social scale, Doris still considered herself to be the senior sister, and therefore the boss. Her mouth opened and closed like a fish gasping for air, but no sound came out.

"You were fully insured, our Doris. I know Frank took care of all that, and our Stanley's checked up at the bank. Everything is in order, so all your stuff and your property can be replaced and repaired. Wayne couldn't have been. Now you both have a place to stay here until your house has been rebuilt, so let's have a bit less moaning and a bit more gratitude. You should count your blessings."

Doris Higginbotham scowled, but for once her sister had beaten her into submission. She knew that she should have been grateful for Wayne's survival, but once again jealousy had overcome her. Jealousy that Margaret still had her husband, her nice posh house and her clothes intact. Jealousy that Margaret's son, Cedric, hadn't been involved in any incidents that had involved the police, and that Cedric was Margaret's natural son, not the unwanted offspring of some Irish tart she had never met.

Doris Higginbotham had always been jealous of her younger sister. Not just envious, but soul-twistingly jealous. The events of the last week had thrown that jealousy into overload, and even Doris realised that she had gone too far; not that she would have admitted it to her little sister.

There was a long, uncomfortable, silence, that was eventually broken by the electronic chirping of Margaret's trim-phone.

"Hello, Margaret Houghton-Hughes speaking?" Margaret answered the call. "Yes, of course," she breathed concernedly, after a moment. "This morning would be fine." She put the phone down.

"That was the police. Some men from London want to speak to you. They're coming here, later this morning."

Doris looked even more crestfallen. "What do they want? I've already spoken to that bobby!" she asked, as her voice rose from speech to a wail.

Margaret shrugged. "Whatever it is, it must be important for them to come all the way up from London..."

Seventy-Three

The two burly men seemed cramped, behind the plain wooden desk in Inspector Harrison's small office.

"The Inspector will be along in a second." The young WPC smiled nervously as she carefully placed two steaming mugs of tea on the desk in front of the men. "One with sugar, one without. Have you gentlemen ever been to Shepton before?"

The nearer of the two to her, a large, bald, bullet-headed man, with a nose that had obviously been broken on more than one occasion, shook his head.

"Nah, never even been to Yorkshire before. What abaht you, Nick?"

The second, equally large man, who had hair but had it shaved so short that he looked almost as bald as his colleague, sniffed contemptuously.

"Came up here once, to Leeds. Pulled in two members of an active service unit." He grinned, menacingly. "Well...the two that was left, anyway."

The two men chuckled at some private joke, as the young policewoman gave a nervous grin and turned away in a hurry.

"Sorry to keep you gentlemen waiting." Inspector Harrison announced breezily as she entered her office. The two men stood and shook her hand in turn.

"This is Sergeant Hartley." She indicated a short, rotund policeman who had followed her into the office, and the two men held out their hands to him.

"Detective Sergeant Dean, Detective Inspector Thomas," they announced in turn.

"As you know, Sergeant, these gentlemen are with the Special Branch, and are here because of the reports of what could be potential terrorist activity in recent events in the town." She glanced at the detectives. "Sergeant Hartley, here, has been dealing with the case so far, and has all the relevant information."

Her tone wasn't particularly friendly and she positively glared at the sergeant as he attempted to jauntily sit astride a reversed chair, which slipped from under him. He swiftly arrested his fall, turned the chair the right way round, and promptly sat down, somewhat red-faced.

"Aye...it's been an eventful few days!" he grinned, sheepishly. The men remained totally impassive, as they turned to face the sergeant, and he coughed nervously.

"It all started on Saturday the ninth of September, when one Frank Higginbotham of 18 Cavendish Street, Shepton, was killed in a motor vehicle accident. He was knocked off his moped by one Mrs. Elsie Hargreaves, of 14 Arneview Terrace, Shepton, who turned out to be slightly above the drink-drive limit."

Sergeant Hartley looked up nervously as one of the Special Branch Detectives stirred restlessly, and coughed. He took refuge in his notebook.

"This does appear to have been a bona fide road traffic accident, although the timing is a tad suspicious, considering subsequent developments. My own enquiries have not led me to any belief that the vehicle in which Mrs Hargreaves was travelling, or indeed Mr. Higginbotham's moped, had been in any way tampered with."

"Had that checked out, did you?" the bullet-headed Detective Sergeant asked, somewhat aggressively.

"Well, er, no...not exactly fully checked out, but..." Sergeant Hartley stammered, before he was interrupted by Inspector Harrison.

"At the time it was presumed to be a straightforward road traffic accident, and full forensic tests were deemed to be unnecessary, although our own traffic people did give the vehicles a good going over."

She raised a challenging eyebrow. The Special Branch men glanced at each other and nodded, knowingly.

"Please continue, Sergeant," Inspector Harrison ordered.

"At precisely 21:20 hours on the Thursday fourteenth, I personally took a call in the station here from an unknown young woman, claiming that a boy had been tied up in a basement and that the same basement had been subsequently set alight. The said basement being that of..." He paused for effect. "...18 Cavendish Street, Shepton." Sergeant Hartley looked up at his Inspector, and gulped nervously.

"I personally decided that the call was a hoax, a student jape. At 21:31, I was called by the Shepton fire brigade to attend an incident at the said 18 Cavendish Street, home of the recently deceased Frank Higginbotham. One Wayne Higginbotham, the son of the deceased, had been rescued from the basement, some minutes earlier, by one James Malone; an Irish citizen, currently a resident of the United States. Statements taken from Mister Malone, a fire officer, an independent witness and the ambulance man attending the scene, all state that the boy was pulled out of the house naked and tightly bound. In a subsequent interview which took place at the Arnedale hospital, Mister Malone stated that the aforementioned boy, Wayne Higginbotham, was the son of an IRA informer and that an active service unit had been despatched to Shepton to murder the boy."

"How does this Malone bloke know this?" the shaven headed Detective Inspector interrupted Sergeant Hartley.

"I'll, er, come on to that, sir." Sergeant Hartley continued. "At precisely 21:33 on the same evening, the fourteenth, one David Smith, organiser of a youth centre on Westmoreland Street, reported finding a distressed and naked teenage girl in the toilets of his Youth Club."

"Is there always a lot of bondage and nubile nudity going on in this town, then?" the bullet-headed detective sergeant growled, with a smirk. His senior colleague grunted an amused agreement. "Not quite as grim up North as they reckon, is it?"

Sergeant Hartley continued, after another nervous glance at his Inspector. "According to his statement, the girl stated that she had been stripped of her clothing by an Irish girl, unknown in the town. The Irish girl has not been seen since, but the stolen clothes were later found in the dustbin of the said property, 18 Cavendish Street. The strange thing is, we have several witnesses who've sworn blind that they saw this Stephanie kid leave the Youth Club with a Yank, who had been claiming to be the younger Higginbotham's cousin. There is no trace of him, either." He closed his notebook. "In my opinion, the..."

"Thank you, Sergeant," The Detective Inspector interrupted Hartley, and glanced at Inspector Harrison. "So, Ma'am, you think this Irish girl was the hit-man?"

Inspector Harrison pondered the question for a moment.

"The good sergeant is of the opinion that the IRA aspect of these events has been cooked up by this Malone fellow, who we are told is a rather unreliable and possibly alcoholic ex-priest. I'm not so sure. The boy's adoptive mother and his old headmistress were convinced enough to try and hide the boy. It seems he had sneaked home to mourn his adoptive father in the place where they shared many good times."

"When can we see these people?" The Special Branch Detective Inspector asked.

"We'll arrange that now." Inspector Harrison looked up at Sergeant Hartley. "Sergeant, please arrange meetings with Mrs Higginbotham and Mrs Elizabeth Ball, but firstly with Wayne and this James Malone chap. As soon as prudently possible, please."

"Yes Ma'am," Sergeant Hartley agreed, scurrying out of the office as fast as his legs could carry him. That damn kid had caused him serious embarrassment. "IRA, my foot!" he muttered, his face as red as a beetroot, as he picked up the phone.

Back in Inspector Harrison's office, Detective Sergeant Dean looked at his colleague, his face screwed up in concentration.

"You don't fink this Malone bloke could be any relation to that toad of a lawyer, Malone, do you? We had a cast iron case on that maggot Seamus O'Halloran last year, but his weasel words got the swine let off. We were stitched up like a kipper, good and proper."

Detective Inspector Thomas screwed up his small eyes. "Nah, that would be a bit too much of a coincidence, wouldn't it?"

Inspector Harrison addressed both men. "Does this sound like an IRA operation to you chaps? I do hope we haven't wasted your time bringing you all the way up here for nothing."

Detective Inspector Thomas nodded. "Nah! Sounds too amateur to me. The provos, or INLA, or any of them groups just put a bullet in the back of the head, if they want to get rid of someone."

"Yeah, and then make sure the evidence just disappears." Detective Sergeant Dean chipped in. "Now we're here, though, we may as well look into it. You never know what we might turn up. Sounds like there might be some good juicy stuff for the tabloids," D.I. Thomas opined. D.S. Dean suddenly grinned.

"Dan Malone, that's his name, innit? Bloody maggot!"

Seventy-Four

Cardinal D'Abruzzo embraced Bishop Donleavy, and kissed him expansively on both cheeks.

"Ahh, my dear, dear friend!" he grinned. "So, ultimate victory is finally ours. After all these long and painful centuries, the Order has finally triumphed."

He put his hand up as the old bishop bent to kiss his ring. "No, today I salute you, my friend." The Cardinal bent and kissed Donleavy's ring.

The two men walked slowly down the long ornate Vatican corridor, unselfconsciously arm in arm. Streams of strong September sunlight cut the through gloomy interior like searchlight beams.

"Is the child pleased?" Donleavy asked. The Cardinal raised his hands.

"When I gave him the news, he said he was pleased, but he watched the stones for three whole days and three whole nights. Eventually he was so exhausted that he fell asleep on the spot. When he awoke he sent for me, thanked me, and asked me to get rid of the stones. I will not need them again, for the Order has carried out its Holy task. That is what he said."

The Cardinal took four ordinary-looking pebbles from his pocket.

"See, my friend, the cursed stones that have given the demons their power; Hell stones."

He passed one to the bishop, who held it away from his body as though it would infect him with evil germs. Donleavy perused it, carefully.

"It seems such a small and ordinary thing," he muttered. "Yet I can feel the power of the evil that slithers and swirls within." D'Abruzzo raised an eyebrow, but said nothing.

"What will you do with them?" Donleavy asked, handing the stone back towards the Cardinal. The Cardinal shrugged.

"They will go into a box and be stored in the deepest darkest basement in the Vatican, where their evil can do no harm." He held up his hand, and refused to take the stone that Donleavy had examined. "Keep that one as a memento, my friend. Let it be a trophy, recognising our triumph, Bishop Donleavy, and a salutary reminder of all of the evil that has come from it."

The ancient Irish bishop hesitated for a moment, then nodded and thanked the Cardinal, before carefully placing the stone in his own pocket.

"Keep it safe!" The Cardinal urged.

The two men continued to walk along the corridor, through the streams of sunlight. Bishop Donleavy coughed nervously and looked around to make sure that no one would overhear him.

"And does His Holiness himself know yet of these astounding and momentous events?"

Cardinal D'Abruzzo stopped walking abruptly. His well-tanned face visibly blanched, and he too looked around nervously, before leaning his head almost to the Bishop's ear.

"The Order took a...strategic decision not to tell the new Holy Father. The time is not yet right. Not after what happened to the last one, last year."

Bishop Donleavy frowned uncomprehendingly. The Cardinal sighed deeply, and swiftly looked around again.

"The last Holy Father, God rest his soul, was shown the child almost as soon as he had ascended to the Holy Seat. The child was not in a good mood. He decided he had not been shown enough respect by his number one servant on earth."

The Cardinal drew his finger across his throat, and Bishop Donleavy gasped.

"It was the child? But they said..."

D'Abruzzo nodded, then took the Bishop's arm.

"Come, my friend, we must not dwell on such issues. A decision will be made when it is the right time to tell His Holiness. In the meantime, the order has been given to close down the operational network of The Sacred Order of St. Gregory."

Donleavy stopped walking. "With all due respect, Your Eminence, is that step not a little premature?"

The Cardinal shrugged nonchalantly. "That is the wish of the Child himself; and, let us not forget, the Order was established in his name." The Cardinal smiled patronisingly, and resumed his slow walk along the corridor.

Bishop Donleavy stood, motionless. For the second time in his long life, he felt unsure about the Order and its motives. The Child's behaviour had been less than holy so far...and if what the Cardinal had just alluded to was true, then Donleavy's life's work had been in vain.

Since he had entered the Church during the dark days of the Irish Civil War, he had been in the service of the Order. He had carried out its work without question for more than half a century, before he had been appointed its head in Ireland. He had killed for the Order many times; and yet now, his faith was being very severely tested.

The Child had caused Donleavy concern when he had first been introduced to him. What he had just heard caused him far greater concern.

Cardinal D'Abruzzo held open the door at the end of the corridor for Bishop Donleavy to pass through. The old churchman ambled up to the door as fast as he could. He caught the Cardinal's eye as he passed through. At over eighty years of age, Bishop Donleavy had learned to read a man's eyes. Cardinal D'Abruzzo was every bit as terrified as he was.

Seventy-Five

Wayne had been right. James Malone was not pleased. He was not pleased at all. In fact, he was absolutely, blazingly furious.

"I came over to England to save your sorry ass, I pulled you out of a burning building - and what gratitude do I get? You go and tell the police that I'm a raving loony and alcoholic to boot. Wow, Wayne...with friends like you, who needs enemies?"

Wayne sighed. "James, listen to me, I..."

James Malone turned towards the teenager and prodded a pointed finger firmly into his chest.

"No, Wayne, you listen to me. You were the one who disobeyed every goddamn piece of advice you'd been given about staying in. Just because you had the damned hots for some stupid girl, you let the Order get to you. Because of your own damned arrogance, you nearly lost your own life, you could have cost me mine - and because of your pathetic teenage lust, the banshee died."

Wayne went white and dropped his head to his chest. He hadn't considered that his actions had been arrogant and stupid. He hadn't seen past his desire to see Steph again. Wayne had believed that his shape-shifting to Mickey Finn would have rendered him invulnerable to the Order, or anyone else for that matter. He certainly hadn't considered that he'd put James' life in danger and he had actually considered the death of the banshee to be a good thing.

James turned from the boy and strolled over to the window area of the small ward, staring out over the open green fields which stretched away down to the River Arne. An old man was listening to the radio on headphones in a nearby bed. He smiled at Wayne, who just about managed to bend his lips enough to smile back.

Wayne shuffled up to where James was stood. He could see that the ex-priest's eyes were filling up.

"I am so sorry, James. You are right. I was arrogant and unthinking. I could have killed you and Steph. I lost my mother her house and all our stuff, and we've probably lost just about everything we ever had of Dad's. I can't say I'm sorry about the banshee, though. I think she was out to kill me, just as much as de Feren was."

James continued to stare out of the window.

"I just thought that if we told anything remotely like the truth, they'd either cart us away to the loony bin, or start an investigation that would stop you ever getting back to the States and would ruin my plan to get back at the Order."

James twisted his mouth. "Yeah, right! I suppose you did what you thought was best."

Wayne shifted uncomfortably as James continued to stare out of the window. "I better go then," he muttered, turning away.

He'd walked no more than five yards when James called him back. He'd turned away from the window and was walking towards Wayne, his face set in a grimace. He put his hands on the boy's shoulders.

"Do me a favour, would you, Wayne?" he asked. Wayne nodded sheepishly.

"Try and take good advice, when it's given."

Wayne nodded again, and grinned. "Mates again?"

James grinned, and playfully pretended to slap the boy's face.

"Now, what's this cunning plan of yours, then?"

Wayne took a deep breath. "The Order thinks that I'm dead. One day they'll find out that I'm not, whether I run off to L.A, stay here, or whatever. One day they'll come after me again. In the meantime, I have a life to live. I've got 'A' levels coming up and then maybe, hopefully, university. I've got a love life to lead. You never know...Steph might go for me on the rebound from Finn. I've got to help my mum re-build her life. You were right. The house burning down was my fault, and I owe her big time. This is no time to go abandoning her after she raised me. Her and my dad."

Wayne heaved a huge sigh. "I read an article in the paper about Liverpool, once."

James Malone frowned. "The city?"

Wayne shook his head. "No - the football team. They used to have manager called Bill Shankley, and he always said that the best form of defence was attack. Look how successful they've been. The only answer I can think of, following Shankley's advice, is to go on the offensive. I need you to help me do that, James."

James looked pained.

"What?" he asked uncomprehendingly. "I don't know who you think you are, Wayne, but even Clint Eastwood wouldn't be stupid enough to take on the Order. You are talking about an institution that has survived for one and a half millennia. Not some little bunch of boy-scouts. I mean...look what happened to you on Cavendish Street!"

Wayne shook his head.

"I wasn't ready last Thursday, I was sort of distracted. I think you know why." He shuffled uncomfortably. "I can assure you, I am more than ready, now."

James blew out an exasperated gasp, and slapped his hand to his forehead.

"But Wayne, what are you going to do to them? Shoot them all with your death-ray hands? I mean, it's crazy. The Order is a professional killing machine. It's like a private army, a regiment of assassins. One sixteen-year-old boy is not going to stand a chance!"

Wayne Higginbotham took a deep breath. "At the risk of sounding arrogant and stupid, James. I am not just any old sixteen-year-old boy. I am the Slanaythe Moor, or whatever it is."

James Malone's face cracked into a grin, and then he laughed. "I think you mean the Slanaitheoir Mor. If you're going to be it, you should learn how to say it." Wayne laughed too.

It took a few minutes for the two patients to settle down. James sat on his bed.

"I will not help you to do anything that puts you in danger, Wayne. I came to England to rescue you...not help you go get yourself killed."

Wayne nodded sadly. "Looks like I'm on my own, then."

James' face hardened. "Did you not hear anything I said before, Wayne? You are being arrogant again. You are ignoring sound advice. Are you actually capable of listening?"

Wayne was about to answer, when the ward sister approached James' bed.

"Mr. Malone, there are two men to see you. I said you weren't well enough - but they went above my head, I'm afraid. They're waiting for you in Doctor Howarth's office."

James scowled. "Who are they?"

The sister screwed up her nose. "Special Branch, or so they say. It's getting just like the telly in here!"

James Malone closed his eyes."You know what you were saying about avoiding police involvement, so that I could get back to the States as soon as possible?"

Wayne nodded.

"Well, looks like you failed on that count...and if my hunch is correct, this one is entirely my own fault." He picked up a dressing gown from the chair beside his bed to cover his pyjamas. Wayne looked puzzled.

"Why? Why is it your fault? What is the Special Branch?"

James began to walk towards the doors leading off the ward. "Whose big fat stupid idea was it to go and mention the IRA?" he called over his shoulder, as he marched off through the double doors, behind the ward sister.

Wayne ambled back towards his own four-bed section of the ward and almost bumped into Doctor Howarth, who bumbled out from behind a curtain surrounding a bed adjacent to the main ward.

"Ah, young Mr Higginbotham!" he declared: "I was just looking for you. I've examined your notes and - all being well, and with a bit of luck - you'll be able to go home on Wednesday. That was quite a bump you had on your head!" The doctor re-checked Wayne's notes on the clipboard. "Yes...jolly good!" He wandered off, a junior doctor in tow.

"Wednesday...that's tomorrow!" Wayne realised out loud, and punched the air in delight. The sudden realisation, however, that he was then going to have to go and face the music with Doris, soon dampened his spirits.

He slumped back down onto his bed, and a nagging thought crept into the back of his mind. If he was being arrogant and stupid then he would probably fail the tests that his real father, Aillen Mac Fionnbharr, had said were to be put before him. Maybe it was time he stopped thinking just about himself.

Maybe it was time he did something for somebody else.

Wayne leapt off the bed, and headed straight for the ward exit.

Seventy-Six

"So, who we seein' first, then?" D.S. Dean wondered aloud, as he looked at the street map of the small market town of Shepton. "The teacher, the mother, the kid, or this Malone geezer?"

"Let's hit the big fish first," D.I. Thomas snarled, as he started the Rover and spun the wheels in an aggressive reversing motion. Smoke billowed out from behind the car as it sped off out of the police station car park.

"You trying to be like Bodie and Doyle, Sir?" D.S. Dean grinned, referring to a popular television series of the late seventies, as the Rover accelerated down the long strip that was Newmarket Street. D.I. Thomas gave a lopsided smile.

"Nah, just impressing the local yokels. Let's do Malone first. If he is any relation to that IRA-sympathising lawyer git, I reckon we might just be onto somefing here. Gerroutatheway!" he snarled, at a Land Rover that had just crossed in front of him. "Bloody peasants!"

Some ten minutes later, the two Special Branch Officers marched purposefully into Arnedale General Hospital. They flashed their badges at a receptionist.

"We need to speak to a patient here...one James Malone." D.I. Thomas informed the young brunette, giving her a cheeky smile as he leaned on the counter.

The girl nodded politely and checked a long list in front of her. The list was on a piece of green striped computer paper, and she rolled it almost like toilet roll as she scanned the names.

"Ah, yes...Malone, James. He's under Doctor Howarth in the burns unit. That's ward 24." She smiled sweetly at D.I. Thomas.

"Think you're in there, boss." D.S. Dean commented over his chewing gum, as the two policemen followed the girl's instructions through several sets of blue double doors. The white-tiled corridors smelled strongly of bleach and antiseptic.

"Not my type - too bloody Northern!" the inspector grunted, before stating how much he hated hospitals.

The two soon found their way to a second reception desk at the entrance to the burns unit. Again, they went through the badge-showing routine. The ward sister was called and expressed her unwillingness to allow a patient to be interviewed while still unwell, but when Doctor Howarth was called he overruled her, and allowed his office to be used while he continued his rounds.

"These men are Special Branch," he informed the sister in a whispered aside, while the two policemen admired a young student nurse as she walked past the ward reception desk. "You don't mess with them."

Less than five minutes later, James Malone found himself sitting opposite two of the biggest, meanest-looking policemen he had ever seen.

"You haven't got a brother down in the smoke, have you?" D.S. Dean asked Malone, before any pleasantries had been exchanged.

James pondered the question for a moment. "My brother, Dan - Daniel - is a barrister in London. Why...do you know him?"

The policemen looked at one another. D.S. Dean grinned, while D.I. Thomas merely raised his eyebrows.

"Let's just say he's known to us. So...tell us what you know about this active service unit then, Paddy?" D.S. Dean demanded, leaning across the table in the corner of Dr. Howarth's office.

"And why they were up here in the bleeding sticks?" D.I. Thomas added.

James Malone hadn't faced a questioning like this outside the inner sanctums of the Order. His Gardai interview had been almost friendly in comparison. Every answer he gave to every question was twisted. Detective Sergeant Dean, the bullet-headed cop, was aggressive and sarcastic. D.I. Thomas was more empathetic, but sceptical. Every second answer was matched by James having a coughing fit, as his sore throat and lungs protested at the amount of talking that he was having to do. Eventually, he had had enough.

"Look...okay!" he almost shouted. "There was no active service unit. The IRA, as far as I know, have never been anywhere near Shepton. The people trying to kill the boy..." - he gestured out to the ward - "...are part of a Roman Catholic secret society. A Vatican hit group, if you like. They believe the boy is a demon and one of their priests was sent to kill him. He had a banshee with him. She was the one who stripped the girl at the Youth Club. It was the priest - and I can supply his name, if you like - who set the boy's house on fire. The boy was tied up, and had been left to die when I pulled him out of the house. I'm sure you've seen the statements corroborating that fact. The banshee actually did die in there!"

For a moment, D.S. Dean stopped chewing his gum. He sat transfixed, staring at the ex-priest as though he'd just stepped off a flying saucer. He turned and looked at his boss. "Bloody hell..I fink he's gone and lost the plot, Sir."

D.I. Thomas spoke into his cassette recorder. "Interview terminated, two-thirty pm." He pressed a button, and the cassette ground to a halt.

D.S. Dean shrugged. "I fink a further interview down in the smoke might be in order. What about you, boss?"

D.I. Thomas licked his lips: "I think I need a coffee. Did you get this information about the Provos from your brother, then, James?"

James Malone sighed wearily. "I just told you. It wasn't republicans..."

"Yeah, yeah, sure...it was the 'fairy folk', wasn't it, Paddy? The 'little people'?" D.S. Dean interrupted him.

"The leprechauns are revolting!" D.I. Thomas mused sarcastically.

At that moment there was one sharp knock on the door and Wayne Higginbotham, wearing one of Cedric Houghton-Hughes' best Marks and Spencer's dressing gowns, walked straight into the office, without waiting for a reply.

"What the...?" D.S. Dean muttered.

"I specifically said no interruptions!" D.I. Thomas barked, as he moved to brush past Wayne in search of the disobedient ward sister, who had promised to put a DO NOT DISTURB sign on the door.

Wayne barred his way, and held out his hand.

"I'm Wayne Higginbotham. I think I might have something to do with you gentlemen being here." With his other hand, Wayne tossed the DO NOT DISTURB sign onto the desk in front of them.

Detective Inspector Thomas glared at the boy; but as he looked into the boy's eyes, instead of bellowing at him and bundling him of the office, as he had intended, he found himself taking the proffered hand and shaking it. He was surprised by the strength of Wayne's grip, as he only seemed to be a slip of a lad.

"D.I. Thomas, Special Branch," he murmured, almost drowsily.

Wayne turned to the meaner-looking cop, and held out his hand. The bullet-headed policeman glowered at his superior, and then at Wayne. He held out his hand in a reluctant gesture, and as he looked up, his eyes met Wayne's.

"D.S. Dean, Special Branch," he whispered, as his menacing glare softened.

Wayne stepped back and waved his hand across the office, in front of the Detectives.

"This investigation is a total waste of your time," he said, quietly and firmly.

"This investigation is a total waste of our time," both policemen repeated, in perfect harmony.

"Special Branch has much better things to do," Wayne stated.

"Special Branch has much better things to do," the policemen repeated.

"This whole IRA thing is complete and utter nonsense," Wayne insisted.

"This whole IRA thing is complete and utter nonsense," the policemen repeated, in an almost mantra-like fashion.

"Mister Malone, we are sorry to have taken up so much of your valuable time," Wayne dictated, with a slight smile curling on the edge of his lips.

"Mister Malone, we are sorry to have taken up so much of your time," the police chorus repeated obediently.

Wayne looked directly at Detective Inspector Thomas. "Sergeant, these are not the droids we are looking for."

"Sergeant, these are not the droids we are looking for," Detective Inspector Thomas repeated mechanically.

"They may go about their business," Wayne stated.

"They may go about their business," Detective Inspector Thomas murmured, robotically. Wayne made a dismissive sweeping motion with his hand, and the two policemen stood and walked, like zombies, straight out of the office.

James Malone's mouth was hanging open as he watched the burly policeman shamble out of the office. He gulped.

"Did you really just do what I think I just saw you do?" he asked, timorously.

Wayne grinned. "Oh...just a little trick I learned at the Jedi academy."

James screwed up his eyes. "The what?"

Wayne shrugged. "You didn't catch Star Wars then? Never mind..."

"Nice bloke, wasn't he?" D.S. Dean grinned amiably, as he climbed into the streamlined black Rover 3500 SDi.

"Yeah...just like his brother." D.I. Thomas agreed. "Clever bloke, that Dan Malone. The kid was nice too. Strange, though...I can't seem to picture his face, now."

Some hours later and over a hundred miles down the M1 motorway, D.S. Dean rubbed his forehead.

"Jesus, 'ave I got one 'ell of an 'eadache!"

D. I. Thomas rubbed his head in turn. "Yeah, me too. Funny business that, wasn't it? It was all so straightforward. Why the hell were we up there, anyway?"

D.S. Dean shook his head. "Search me, Sir...I really don't know, Somefing to do wiv the IRA, wasn't it?"

He watched the scenery pass by for a few moments, and then turned to D. I. Thomas. "So, er...there's something I've been meaning to ask you, Sir."

D. I. Thomas nodded. "Sure. What is it, Sergeant?"

D.S. Dean looked bemused. "Well, I don't want to sound fick or anyfing, Sir...it's just a fought that came into me head."

D. I. Thomas nodded encouragingly.

"Well, Sir...er...what's a droid?"

Seventy-Seven

Father Pierre de Feren sipped a glass of water as he waited to see Bishop Donleavy, recently returned from Rome. He looked around, admiring the ancient grey stone walls of St. Patrick's Cathedral in Dublin; the sweeping medieval flying buttresses, the solid, imposing columns and the graceful arches, the colourful emblems and gruesome gargoyles. It was quite different to the churches in his native Belgium, yet no less impressive for that. The Cathedral had been built in the early thirteenth century to replace a wooden church that had been built near to where St. Patrick had baptised Christian converts in the fifth century.

De Feren had a great deal of pride in being a member of such a timeless organisation as the Roman Catholic Church. Mother Church transcended the ages, like a colossus bestriding the ocean. Such monuments as the Cathedral in which he now sat were living testaments of that timeless majesty. This very building had seen millions of insignificant mortals pass through its portals, all now less than dust. Yet the edifice of the Church remained unblemished, its spire reaching out, stretching up towards heaven, like de Feren believed all men should.

Being a member of The Sacred Order of Saint Gregory was icing on the cake for a sinner like Pierre de Feren. He had sinned in the past and had almost been cast out of the Church for his misdemeanours, but the Order had proved to his salvation. The Order had allowed him to be redeemed, to be reborn, just like his Saviour. The Order was the epitome of all that was good in the Church: unswerving in its devotion, unquestioning in its faith, merciless in the execution of its Holy mission.

That was why de Feren took such pleasure in his work. Destroying those monsters that felt that they were above God's plan, by living beyond the allotted lifespan of God's natural creatures. That was his life's work. Only Mother Church could be immortal. Even the Son of God, Jesus Christ himself, had shown himself in mortal guise and had suffered the ultimate pain; the sting of death. Why should these creatures feel that they were better than that?

De Feren smiled at the memory of his second salvation, how The Lord in the form of an innocent child had rescued him from the coma that the banshee had locked him in. He had certainly had his revenge. How he hated the immortals!

Father De Feren had worked himself into quite an evangelistic fervour by the time Bishop O'Leary passed on his way from his own office into Bishop Donleavy's.

"Come, Father. His Grace will see us, now."

The two men walked into Donleavy's office, marched over to the desk, and kissed the Bishop's ring in turn.

"Please sit," Donleavy croaked.

De Feren thought the old bishop looked tired. Every single one of his eighty odd years seemed to be deeply etched on his face. Donleavy's Adam's apple moved up and down in his throat like an out-of-control elevator.

"These are momentous days, my friends," Donleavy whispered.

He looked up and waved an acknowledgement as his assistant, Father Logan, entered, and busied himself pouring wine from a carafe for the three clergymen.

"We are come almost to the end of days."

Bishop O'Leary shifted nervously in his chair.

"Such times can test any man's faith, but we are the Order." Donleavy, paused and seemed to reflect for a moment. "For what are we, if we do not have faith?"

De Feren actually thought he sounded somewhat unsure.

"Amen." Bishop O'Leary blurted, as Father Logan passed him a glass of wine. Bishop Donleavy appraised O'Leary and de Feren in turn.

"Our Lord is alive, and walks amongst us again."

De Feren noticed that Donleavy's eyes actually looked worried.

"'God's Assassin' is dead," the ancient priest continued. "Nothing can now stop Judgment Day."

Bishop O'Leary turned and grinned at de Feren, like an excited schoolboy who had just been promised an extra day's holiday.

"Therefore, in his infinite wisdom, Cardinal D'Abruzzo has ordered the demobilisation and termination of The Sacred Order of Saint Gregory."

"No!" De Feren shouted, and stood so sharply that his heavy oak chair fell backwards and hit the floor with an almighty crash. Donleavy looked up at the Belgian in surprise.

"The Order has gone on for hundreds of years. It would be madness, folly of the highest order, to disband it at the eleventh hour!" De Feren shouted, waving his arms in the air. Bishop O'Leary looked like he was about to die of shock.

"Father, Father de Feren..." he pleaded, but the Belgian Priest was not listening. De Feren leaned over Donleavy's enormous desk, towering over the ancient bishop.

"I will still be a member of the Order, when the crack of doom swallows us all up and signals our rebirth in the Kingdom of Heaven, Your Grace."

Bishop Donleavy remained motionless behind his desk; only his undulating throat betrayed any emotion.

De Feren, his outburst over, panted for breath. He looked around at the shocked faces of O'Leary and Father Logan.

"I am sorry, Your Graces," he muttered, as he picked up the chair and slumped back down onto it.

"There has not been such an outburst in this office in very many years, Father." Donleavy whispered his rebuke. "But in the circumstances - and, given your service and devotion to duty - I totally understand your reaction. You must realise, however, that as far as the Order's mission is concerned, we are long past the eleventh hour. The hour of our destiny is upon us. Bishop O'Leary, you will please inform all of your field operatives that the Order no longer exists. Convey our sincerest gratitude and state that the Cardinal has blessed every single member of the organisation."

He sipped his wine and stared into the crystal glass for what seemed like an age. Then he looked across his desk at the two priests. The fat bishop with the stupid, self-satisfied grin on his face and the tall, bald, bespectacled Belgian, who looked as though his own world had just ended. "We will reconvene after prayer, meditation and contemplation."

He glanced again at de Feren, who sat forlornly in his chair with his head bowed.

"We will meet again on Friday morning at eleven am to celebrate the achievements of our Sacred Order. Thank you, gentlemen." De Feren and O'Leary stood and left the office, along with Donleavy's aide, Fr Logan.

Donleavy heaved a huge sigh when Logan closed the office door behind him. The old bishop took the stone from his pocket, and examined it carefully.

"So...that is that. I should be ecstatic...and yet, perhaps, I am hoping you will glow just once more," he whispered. "Perhaps."

Seventy-Eight

"The smoke damage is appalling," the fire officer said, with a practiced, sad, understanding smile. "Most of the rear of the house is badly damaged. The kitchen floor is definitely unsafe. The front isn't too bad, except for the water damage from the hoses."

"What about the upstairs?" Wayne asked hopefully. The fire officer scratched his head.

"Lotta smoke damage, but nothing is actually burnt. The stairs are okay - solid stone, you see."

Wayne heaved a huge sigh of relief. He, Doris, and the fire officer stood in a cordoned area to the back of the old front room of 18 Cavendish Street. They could see straight down into what had been the underground rear of the basement, through a gaping hole in the floor where the floorboards had collapsed. Doris wiped her finger sadly along the edge of the sideboard behind her. Everything was covered in soot.

"Will it have to be knocked down?" she asked, her eyes bright red from all the crying she'd done and from the smoky atmosphere in the house, a full week after the fire. The fire office blew out his cheeks.

"I'm no builder, but when these houses were built, they were put up with good Yorkshire stone. New floorboards are needed in the kitchen. A total re-build of the back wall and the basement." He stroked his chin.

"New windows?" Wayne suggested.

"Aye, new windows, and full redecorating throughout," the fire office nodded. "Aye, it'll be as good as new in no time. They built these houses to last."

For the first time in nearly two weeks, Doris actually smiled. "Could have been a lot worse, I suppose," she sniffed.

"Can I get some stuff from upstairs?" Wayne asked.

The fire officer nodded. "Aye, but I'd better go with you, just to make sure everything's alright."

Wayne agreed. He looked encouragingly at Doris, but she ignored him. In fact, she had hardly spoken to him since the taxi had dropped him off at the Houghton-Hughes' house earlier that afternoon. Wayne grimaced and then followed the fire officer upstairs, stepping gingerly on each step, just in case it gave way.

Once in his darkened bedroom, Wayne sadly appraised the mess. Everything he possessed was covered in a thick layer of greasy soot. He had taken his best clothes to the Houghton-Hughes' house when he and

Doris had sought the sanctuary of his aunt's house following Frank's death, but his prized New Wave record collection and his painstakingly constructed 'Airfix' models were ruined. Wayne wiped a smear of oily soot off the window, and a stream of light poured into the room.

"Oil-based fire!" the fire officer remarked, nonchalantly. "The soot's greasy. It's the same with chip-pan fires. We see a lot of them around here."

Wayne nodded. He walked to his old wardrobe and stared up at the blackened model of the Starship Enterprise.

"Looks like the Klingons got'em," the fire officer laughed, sympathetically.

Wayne almost laughed. He reached up and picked up the old tin pencil case, hidden under the damaged model. He opened it, took out the stones, and examined them. They were in perfect condition. Wayne put them in his pocket. He then crossed to his chest of drawers and pulled open the top drawer. He pulled out a small drawstring bag, which he also slipped into his pocket. He looked up at the Fireman.

"Okay, that's it!" he said, with a shrug.

"Is that all you want?" The Fire Officer looked surprised. "Alright, then."

He was about to turn to walk to the stairwell, when he suddenly exclaimed, "Oh, by the way...I nearly forgot."

Wayne cocked his head to one side expectantly.

"We found this in the basement. It was a bit black, having been in the hottest part of the fire, but it cleaned up quite nicely."

The fire officer held out a shiny gold ring.

"Somebody must have dropped it down there," he suggested. "It looks like a real antique. Strange jewel, though."

Wayne took the ring. Set in a clasp was a small plain pebble.

The ring must have been Aoibheall's. The stone was her own fragment of the stone of Falias.

"There was nothing else?" Wayne asked, plaintively.

The fire officer shook his head. "No...nothing of any note."

Wayne sighed.

"Is that everything you want from up here, then?" The fire officer asked.

"It's all I need," Wayne whispered, as he took a last look at his old bedroom.

Seventy-Nine

Elizabeth Ball shook her head. It had been a most surprising fortnight, to say the least. In the week and a half since she had heard that Frank Higginbotham had died, so much had happened that she had hardly been able to concentrate on running Gas Street Primary School. In fact she believed that she must have lost over a stone in weight, purely due to stress.

Firstly, she had found out that dear little Wayne Higginbotham, who she had taught in year three, was not entirely human. That had come as something of a shock, especially when she heard about the predicament that he was in. That the Order intended to have him killed and that James Malone was determined to save him.

Secondly, she had heard about the fire at Wayne's house and had heard that someone had been rescued by some Irish bloke, but had initially been unable to find out exactly what had gone on. She had tried to ring the Houghton-Hughes' several times, but the phone seemed to have been taken permanently off the hook. It wasn't until the Saturday that she had managed to get hold of Margaret Houghton-Hughes, who had assured her that both Wayne and James were all right.

Thirdly, she had been required to give a statement to a local police sergeant corroborating James' fictional IRA story. She had hated lying to the police, but couldn't help thinking that the lie was much more credible than the truth. She instantly regretted that decision when she had been informed that some Special Branch policemen from London wanted to interview her about the IRA story. She had never been more nervous in her life and had been close to a nervous breakdown by the time the appointed interview had been due to take place. It goes without saying that she had been massively relieved when the Special Branch had simply failed to turn up.

John Ball had blamed Elizabeth's moods on PMT, but even he had been shocked by how stressed she had seemed. It was with some trepidation, therefore, that she picked up James' message on her answering machine as she had arrived home on the Wednesday evening.

"Hi, Elizabeth! Sorry you got left outside the loop. I hope you haven't had any problems with the police or anything. Wayne and I are both well and are out of hospital now. We believe that the Order think Wayne is dead, so hopefully it's just about all over. Wayne has some wacky notion about going to Ireland and then on to Rome, to kick the

Order's collective butts. I'm trying to persuade him otherwise. I'll be in touch."

"What?" Elizabeth shouted at the machine. "All this stress, and you'll be in touch. Oh no, Mr. Malone! I think I need to be a bit better informed than that!"

She rushed out of the house, and jumped into her car.

Eighty

"This is absolute madness, Wayne!" James Malone repeated, for perhaps the twentieth time since he and Wayne had left the Houghton-Hughes house a couple of hours earlier. "I mean...okay, I saw what you did to those Special Branch boys and to your family. I have no doubt now that you have some pretty special skills...but we are talking about The Sacred Order of St. Gregory, here."

The express train rattled and rolled at full speed as it hurtled towards London. Wayne shrugged his shoulders.

"Call me arrogant if you like, James. I know I've made mistakes." He turned and looked directly into the ex-priest's eyes. "But this isn't one of them. You kill a snake by cutting off its head - and that's just what I intend to do."

Some three hours earlier, James had arrived at The Houghton-Hughes' house with every intention of leaving for London and then California; with, or without, Wayne Higginbotham. As far as James was concerned the Order would realise, sooner or later, that Wayne was still alive and would be back to finish the job. What he had accepted, however, was that Wayne could not just go off to California and hide forever. That plan had been good before the Order had struck, but now it was akin to locking the stable door after the horse had bolted.

The Irishman had found his welcome at the Houghton-Hughes house slightly less than cordial - at least, from Doris Higginbotham.

"Thank you very much for saving our Wayne," Doris had sniffed. "It was very brave of you, but all this trouble only started after you got here. I reckon these R.A.C. blokes followed you...that's how they knew where our Wayne was!"

"IRA," James had corrected her, patiently.

"I don't think you can say that, Doris, love," Margaret had asserted. "I think Mister Malone has been very brave. Without him, Wayne would be dead...and you can't blame Mister Malone for what happened to Frank." She had smiled at James.

"Would you like some tea, love?" she had asked the somewhat dishevelled Irishman, as she rose to go to the kitchen. Doris had crossed her arms defensively across her ample bosom.

"She can say what she likes...the Irish are trouble. Always have been," she had mumbled. James had flinched.

"Don't forget your own son is Irish," he had said, his voice edged with anger.

"Aye - and don't I know it!" Doris had grumbled, curling her mouth in disgust.

James had let out a sad sigh. "I came to try and help Wayne. Maybe it wasn't the Order, I mean the IRA, that I should have been worried about."

It was at that moment that Wayne had entered Margaret's drawing room, a holdall over his shoulder.

"And where do you think you're going?" Doris had asked him, incredulously.

"London initially, then Dublin, then on to Rome," Wayne had replied, just as easily as if he'd just asked for baked beans for tea. "Are you ready, James?" he had asked, pleasantly. James Malone had screwed up his face in disbelief.

Doris had then jumped up, and had sprung out of her armchair in a manner that had belied her rotundity.

"London? Dublin? Rome? Oh no you are not, young man! This time, you are going to do as you are told!" she had shouted, puffing out her chest like a bullfrog to emphasise the point. Wayne had calmly put his bag down on the carpet.

"I really can't be bothered to argue, and I don't have the time, anyway," he had stated, in a matter-of-fact tone. He had looked Doris straight in the eye, and touched his hand to her right temple.

"I have a little job to do. I'll be back at school next week. There's no need to worry. James will look after me."

Doris Higginbotham had visibly sagged.

"Have a good time Wayne, and do be careful," Wayne had suggested, with a smile.

"Have a good time Wayne, and do be careful," Doris had repeated obediently, with a smile.

"Come on...let's go!" Wayne had beckoned to a totally stunned James Malone. "Oh, hang on," he continued, as Margaret had entered with a tray of cups, saucers and tea. Wayne had strolled calmly to his Aunt, smiled, looked her straight in the eyes and whispered, "I'll be back after the weekend, Aunty Margaret. James and I have a little job to do. We have to go and save the world."

"A little job to do. Save the world. That'll be nice. Okay, Wayne, love," Margaret had beamed, as she had stood motionless, seemingly rooted to the spot. Wayne had picked up the holdall, waved cheerily, and went out of the front door, closely followed by James.

"I mean...just what do you intend to do, you know, when we get there?" James asked, as he ran his hand through his long dark hair. White and orange lights flashed past the train window as it hurtled through the fading light. "Do you intend to brainwash the entire Order as well?"

Wayne smiled, a little smugly. "No, James. Like I said, I'm going straight for the head. As for how...I liked your idea. The one that you came up with in the hospital."

James frowned and screwed up his face. "Which one was that?"

Wayne Higginbotham grinned. "It was something you said when you were really angry with me. You mentioned a certain actor, and you said that even he wouldn't be stupid enough to take on the Order."

"I did?" James asked, scratching his head.

Wayne whistled the opening bars of the theme tune of The Good, the Bad and the Ugly. James Malone sighed.

"No, no way...you're as mad as a bloody hatter, Wayne Higginbotham!"

Eighty-One

Carrie Horden snatched up the phone as it rang, rattling and rolling angrily on its cradle. "Hi, Carrie Horden...can I help you?"

The other girls in the real estate office jumped, as she squealed, "James, what's happening? You're out of hospital?"

The voice on the other end of the line laughed. "Yeah, finally. Guess what?"

Carrie shook her head as the other staff settled back down to work. "No idea...tell me honey?" She could almost see the grin on James face.

"I'm coming home on Monday, with a little bit of Irish luck."

Carrie clapped her hand on the desk in delight.

"Wow, that's great!" Then disappointment clouded her well-tanned features. "But honey...I was hoping you'd be coming home as soon as you got out of hospital."

James sighed. "I'm popping back to Ireland, briefly. You know...to see the old man, see how he's doing and all that. Make my peace with the family."

Carrie could tell there was something that he wasn't telling her.

"And...?" She left the word hanging.

James sighed deeply. "Oh, I've just got a little tidying up to do, with Wayne."

Carrie sat back down behind her desk. The heat of the Los Angeles late summer blasted into the office as a customer walked in off the street. He made straight for Carrie's desk.

"Yeah...it's nothing much. I don't think Wayne is going to be coming to California, by the way."

The Irish voice coming from the phone's speaker sounded very calm, but Carrie knew he was holding something back.

"Look, James honey, I love you, but I've got to go - I've got a client," she said, desperately hoping her client would go to another member of staff; but the customer was by now standing at her desk, smiling expectantly.

James said his goodbyes and, although Carrie felt massively relieved that James was well, she knew that what he hadn't told her was far more important than what he had. An uneasy feeling nagged at her stomach, and just wouldn't go away.

She replaced the receiver and flashed the whitest of smiles.

"Hi - how can I help you today?"

Terri Thorne felt much better. She had got out of bed for the first time in days.

"Hi, honey," Dean smiled at her, as she entered the kitchen. "How are you feeling?"

"Good," Terri lied. She had been feeling more miserable than she could remember feeling in a long, long time.

"Good!" Dean replied, lazily leafing through the mail. "A Doctor Van Groningen will be calling to see you this afternoon. He's real good, I'm told."

Terri frowned, bewildered by her husband's off-the-cuff statement.

"I've seen a doctor, baby. I'm fine - the baby's fine. What's the point of seeing another?"

Dean shrugged as he bit into a piece of French toast. "This one's a specialist...one of the best."

Terri shook her head. "Dean, I'm pregnant - it's not a unique condition, you know. There's nothing to worry about. The baby is fine."

Dean stood, grabbed the last piece of French toast, threw his designer jacket over his shoulder and pecked Terri on the cheek.

"It's not the baby I'm worried about honey - it's you," he stated as he walked towards the door.

"He's a shrink, isn't he?" Terri called after him. "You think I'm nuts, don't you?" she screamed.

Dean swung around.

"Hey, this is L.A. What passes for nuts round here? I just think you could use a little help...that's all."

He jumped into his car and sped off in a roar of engine, burning rubber and spitting gravel.

Terri took a deep breath."How am I going to convince a shrink I'm not nuts, if I'm not so sure myself?" she muttered.

Eighty-Two

Dan Malone ran both hands through his hair.

"I think you're both as mad as hatters. Why don't you just go and take on the Provos, the INLA, and all the rest of 'em while you're over there?"

"I just need another loan, Dan...just to get us over there," James stated patiently, for perhaps the fourth time.

"Another loan? Jimmy, for the love of God, I gave you a load of money back in Shepton. Two hundred notes, if I remember correctly."

James coughed and put his tongue in his cheek. "I only remember four." He rolled his eyes, and began to whistle cheekily.

Dan sighed heavily. "Jimmy, that is just..."

Wayne held up his right hand right in front of Dan, and looked into his eyes.

James was sure he saw a flash of light, but couldn't be quite sure. What he could be sure of was that his brother Dan was frozen to the spot, totally motionless, as stiff as a corpse.

"What have you done?" he gasped, as he waved his hand in front of Dan's motionless eyes. "More stuff you learned at that Jedi School?"

"Sort of. Let's just say I'm learning to improvise," Wayne responded, with a twist of his lip. "How much do you trust your brother, James?"

James Malone cast Wayne a dismissive glance. "He's my brother. I'd trust him with my life."

"I mean, really...look beyond blood," Wayne demanded.

"With my life," James repeated firmly.

Wayne clicked his fingers, and Dan was shaking his head as though nothing had happened. Wayne pulled a small drawstring pouch from his pocket.

"Do you know anyone interested in expensive jewellery?" he asked Dan, as he pulled the bag open. Dan Malone rubbed his forehead.

"Yes...why? Stolen your mother's wedding ring have you?"

The jewel that Wayne pulled out of the bag caused both of the Malone brothers to take a sharp intake of breath.

"Your Father's?" James asked, recognising the piece as being from Aillen's horde.

Wayne nodded. "I was keeping it for a rainy day. It should help to balance the books a bit, I hope. Now, then...what about those tickets to Dublin?"

Eighty-Three

Elizabeth Ball couldn't believe her ears.

"Aye," Doris stated flatly, "Wayne's gone off to London with that nice Irish chap."

"James?" Elizabeth asked.

"Aye, that's him." Doris concurred. "Well, they'd both been cooped up in hospital for a week, or as near as - makes no difference. I thought it'd do 'em both good to get away. I mean, Wayne's going back to school on Monday."

Margaret Houghton-Hughes walked into her drawing room clutching a pack of ice to her head.

"How's your migraine?" she asked Doris. "Mine's still killing me. Hello, Mrs. Ball. We've both got terrible migraines, you know!"

Elizabeth Ball frowned. "Did you know that Wayne has gone off to London with that James Malone, Margaret?"

"Oh, aye," Margaret answered nonchalantly. "They'll have a good time. Something to do with saving the world, so Wayne said."

Elizabeth was almost bursting with frustration.

"So what's been happening? The fire? The IRA?" she suggested the latter, knowing that Doris and Margaret were unaware of the true threat to Wayne. "Did the Special Branch men come and see you?" she continued.

Doris frowned. "No, no - they didn't. We were told they were coming, weren't we, Margaret? But they never turned up."

Elizabeth nodded eagerly. "Same with me. I was told I was going to be interviewed, and then nothing happened. Anyway...so what has been going on?"

Doris looked at Margaret. Margaret looked at Doris.

"I'll make a cuppa," Margaret sighed, standing up - icepack still pressed firmly to her forehead - and wandering off to the kitchen. Doris clasped her hands, and looked to be in pain.

"Do you know, it's all been a bit of a blur...what with our poor Frank and what-not. It all started last Thursday, when our Wayne was told he couldn't go to the Youth Club. I said he couldn't go, after what you and that Irish chap had said. It wouldn't have been right, anyway, just a day after his father's funeral." Doris leaned forward as if to speak in confidence.

"But you know what kids are like, and I think he has a bit of a fancy for some girl at the Youth Club. Anyway he sneaked out. How he did it, I'll not know until my dying day, but out he got. Next thing we heard the police were here, and he was in hospital. Eeeh...when that policewoman came to our Margaret's door, I could have died! It seems Wayne never got to the Youth Club, anyway. He went back to our house for some reason. That's where then it all gets a bit confusing. Wayne says he were tidying up and he spilt some paraffin which set alight, and that he passed out. Yet, some say as how he were all tied up and, er, in the nude, and that there'd been some funny business going on. I don't know if it were him or that IRA lot who set the house on fire. Any road, that nice Irishman saved him by diving through the cellar window, so they say. He should get a medal for that."

Elizabeth listened with rapt attention. "How did James know he was in there?"

Doris scowled. "Again, that's one of them funny do's. Seems some strange woman rang him. Mind you, talking about funny do's, it seems that on the night our Wayne was getting the house burned down, there was this American lad pretending to be his cousin at the Youth Club. Aye - it seems him, and an Irish girl that no one had ever seen before, stripped some lass." Doris mouthed the next few words, as if to prevent anyone overhearing from being offended: "Even her pants..."

She inclined her head sharply, her chin on her chest, her lips pursed in a subtle, unspoken implication of impropriety.

"Aye, our Stanley and Cedric found her in the toilets at that Youth Club Wayne goes to on Westmoreland Street. Naked as the day she were born, she were. The police found her clothes in our bin on Cavendish St. Wayne says he knows nowt about it. Some even say that the self -same lass was seen leaving the club with this Yankie lad. Well, I don't know. I'm right flummoxed by it all. You just don't know what to believe, do you?"

Margaret emerged from the kitchen with the tea, and Elizabeth tried to digest the confusing torrent of information. She just couldn't see the connection between the girl in the nude at the Youth Club, Wayne's supposed bondage nudity, and the girl's clothes being found in the Higginbotham's dustbin. She stroked her chin thoughtfully.

"And you say no-one has seen the Irish girl since?"

The sisters both shook their heads.

"What about the American boy?" Elizabeth asked. Doris picked up her tea.

"Disappeared into thin air. It's like he'd never existed," she exclaimed, with relish.

Elizabeth realised that the only way she would ever be able to make any sense of what had actually happened would be by asking Wayne himself.

"So...where did you say Wayne and James have gone?" she asked, after taking a sip of tea.

"London. The Irishman has a brother down there, or sommat," Doris stated, as though it was a daily event. Elizabeth smiled.

"Ah yes...I know about him. He's a lawyer. You seem remarkably sanguine about Wayne being away, Doris, after all that's happened."

Doris shrugged. "Well, what can you do? Boys will be boys, and he has got the world to save." Elizabeth agreed, but her expression belied her disbelief in the way Doris was behaving.

"And, er, how bad is the house on Cavendish Street...you know, after the fire?"

Doris shrugged again. "It's a right mess, but it's no good crying over spilt milk. Wayne's okay, and that's the main thing. Our best clothes were here, so it's not like we've only got what we're standing up in," she giggled.

Margaret smiled admiringly. "She's such a trooper, our Doris."

Elizabeth Ball smiled back. Had she not known better, she could have been convinced that the sisters had both been brainwashed.

Later that night, lying in bed, trying to ignore the sound of John snoring, Elizabeth went over the events again and again in her head. None of it made any sense.

Why had Wayne sneaked back to the house on Cavendish Street, knowing he was in danger? Who was the American pretending to be his cousin and who was the Irish girl - and why had she stolen another girl's clothes, only to dump them in the Higginbotham's bin? Why were Doris and her sister behaving as though they'd been very heavily sedated? Had Wayne gone off to London to hide from the Order?

Whatever had happened in Shepton, Wayne was at the centre of it all; and after what James had told her about Wayne and about the ancient Irish magic, Elizabeth Ball began to wonder just what the boy had been up to, and what he was capable of.

Wayne Higginbotham, or James Malone, had a lot of questions to answer, if she ever saw either of them again.

Eighty-Four

Friday, September the twenty-second, dawned unusually warm for so late in the Irish summer. Even by ten in the morning, Bishop O'Leary was mopping his brow with a white silk handkerchief, as he walked the short distance to Bishop Donleavy's office. Father Logan was knocking on the senior bishop's door as O'Leary approached.

"Come!" Donleavy croaked, as loudly as he could manage.

Logan held the door open for Bishop O'Leary, who breezed past the young priest in as supercilious a manner as any human being could possibly manage.

"Welcome, Bishop, welcome!" Donleavy croaked. "Today is a day that will go down in the annals as the most momentous in the long and illustrious history of the Order. The day that it ceased to exist!"

Donleavy laughed and coughed at the same time. After several seconds he composed himself, and pointed at a carafe. Father Logan inclined his head in a barely perceptible acknowledgement, and poured two large glasses of a rich amber liquid.

"This is a special, aged, cognac, that is generally kept for the personal use of our glorious Primate of All Ireland and His Holiness, should he ever set foot in Ireland." Bishop Donleavy chuckled. "Let us thank Our Holy Father for his benevolence."

O'Leary smiled idiotically."Father de Feren will be joining us shortly," the rotund bishop stated, with a flourish of his hand.

Donleavy nodded. "Today is so momentous, that I will confess before my peer, that I am, in fact, already a little inebriated."

Bishop O'Leary smiled conspiratorially. "How very decadent, Your Grace!" he tittered girlishly. Donleavy seemed to think for a minute.

"Have you ever taken the time, my friend, to consider exactly what we have achieved?" Bishop O'Leary swirled the delicious amber liquid around in his glass.

"We have cleared the entire world of evil, Your Grace," O'Leary declared.

Donleavy laughed, but this time the sound was caustic, bitter. "Ah, but when we say that we have destroyed 'God's Assassin', have we killed the assassin who was to kill God? Or...the assassin who kills on behalf of God?"

O'Leary looked confused.

"I'm sorry, you've lost me, Your Grace..."

Donleavy took a large swig of the Cognac.

"No matter, my friend. I fear my old brain is not working as well as it once did. Has the order gone out for the Order to be demobilised?"

"To a man, Your Grace."

Donleavy nodded slowly. "Excellent," he whispered, his Adam's apple moving up and down as usual. He stuck out his bottom lip like a child who is about to have a tantrum. A solitary tear ran down his cheek.

"It is a sad day, as well as a joyous one, is it not?" O'Leary blustered. Donleavy merely smiled sadly at the bishop.

O'Leary mopped his brow. "It is unnaturally warm today, is it not, Your Grace?"

"These are the fires of hell, in which we have surely condemned ourselves to burn." Donleavy whispered.

O'Leary, in the middle of a large swig, allowed his glass to drop below his face. "Your Grace?"

"What if we are wrong?" Donleavy whispered, staring at his Cognac. "Have you considered what it would mean if we have been the Devil's stooges all these years? What if we have been playing at being God's elite warriors and have been slowly, but surely, killing God's own servants?"

Bishop O'Leary peered over the rim of his glass.

"I don't understand, Your Grace," he bleated. "The 'fairy folk' were not Christians; they weren't even as fickle as Protestants."

Donleavy smiled, and O'Leary began to giggle.

"Oh yes, ha ha!" he snorted. "We've been killing the wrong people for going on nearly two millennia, ha ha! That's a good one, Your Grace."

Donleavy sighed. "From what I have seen of our Messiah, so far, I think that might be the case..."

The old bishop stared at the pebble on his desk. He reached out a long bony finger to touch it.

The stone suddenly began to glow.

"How the...?" Donleavy gasped.

The stone seemed to light up from the inside as though a small bulb had been switched on. Slowly, in the dark confines of the candlelit room, it grew brighter and brighter, until the stone had stopped looking like a pebble, but had taken on the appearance of a crystal; like a diamond with a tiny green sun, frozen deep inside. Both bishops' mouths dropped involuntarily open, as they shaded their eyes. Bishop O'Leary inadvertently tipped his brandy glass, so some of the precious liquid poured unnoticed to the ground.

There was a brief shout from outside the bishop's office, and - almost in the same instant - the heavy ornate oak door exploded into a hundred, million splinters, as though a huge bomb had been detonated behind it.

Eighty-Five

Wayne Higginbotham strolled into the hallowed grounds of St. Patrick's Cathedral, Dublin, like a tourist on a leisurely sightseeing vacation.

"Pretty isn't it?" he said appreciatively. "So, exactly where do I go?" he asked James Malone in hushed tones.

"Look, Wayne, this is utter madness. Will you not please reconsider?" Malone whispered, as he looked around nervously.

"Which way?" Wayne insisted.

"Follow that path around the corner of the building. There's an unremarkable black door on your left; open it, and pass through into the waiting area. Bishop Donleavy's office is the one to the far left."

Wayne nodded, and held out his hand. "If I don't make it...well...you know!"

James smiled, and shook his hand.

"You'll make it, I hope. Though do you know exactly what you're going to do yet?"

Wayne raised his eyebrows. "Make it up as I go along, I suppose. I'm getting pretty good at this improvisation lark," he shrugged. "I'll only kill in self defence - so I hope they attack me!"

He grinned evilly. James gave an exasperated groan, and punched Wayne's shoulder.

"For goodness sake, just get on with it - oh, and good luck!"

Wayne, dressed in a plain white tee shirt, drainpipe jeans and Doctor Marten boots, nodded, turned, and walked away, towards his destiny.

The boy followed the ex-priest's instructions into the building. He found himself in a typical church-like area, with lots of emblems and gargoyles strategically placed on gargantuan columns and arches.

A young priest walked slowly out of the office, which James had said belonged to the head of the Order in Ireland. The priest turned, and saw Wayne.

"Oi! Who are you? What are you doing in here?" the young priest demanded, rather aggressively.

"I was just, you know, like, looking for a restroom?" Wayne replied, in his best Danny Finn, American, accent. The young priest clucked in exasperation.

"Americans!" he grunted, as he attempted to take Wayne forcibly by the arm. Wayne did not move.

337

The young priest looked up at Wayne, straight into his eyes. Wayne decided that he didn't like the priest enough to just deal with his mind; he smiled, and delivered a vicious uppercut. The young priest started a shout, which died in his throat as he fell backwards, unconscious, to the ground.

Wayne stepped over him, shook his sore fist, and marched the few steps towards the ornate solid oak door of Bishop Donleavy's office, briskly.

The priest who had ordered his real father's execution, who had ordered James Malone's execution and who had ordered Wayne's execution - and that of anybody else who just happened to get in his way.

"This one was your idea, James. Thanks!" Wayne muttered. He morphed into a totally different person, raised his hand, and gritted his teeth. The enormous door before him flew off its hinges and exploded into a million splinters of wood, shattering the quiet, monastic calm of the church buildings.

Bishop Donleavy, who had ducked behind his large oak desk as the door exploded, slowly raised his turtle-like head above the surface of his desk and opened his mouth, his Adam's Apple rising and falling like a bouncing ball. Bishop O'Leary had fallen off his chair and was on his knees, vigorously crossing himself, his mouth and eyes wide open.

The entire room was filled with pungent clouds of thick, rolling smoke. The few candles that remained alight in the elaborate glass chandelier that hung in the centre of the room cast a faint, flickering glow in the smoky darkness. The only real light in the room came from the hole in the wall where the door had once hung.

Neither cleric expected the sight that next greeted their eyes. A tall cowboy, straight out of a western movie, emerged slowly through the thickest of the smoke, silhouetted by the light behind, his head down, his face concealed by his hat.

As the smoke and the dust settled, the priests saw that the cowboy was wearing a long Mexican-style poncho, blue jeans and cowboy boots. His spurs jingled like small bells, as he slowly and deliberately walked into the magnificently adorned room.

The cowboy slowly raised his head. His face was unshaven, his eyes no more than menacing narrow slits. In the corner of his mouth, a small cheroot cigar glowed through the smoky gloom.

"Hello, boys!" he muttered, in a low, menacing voice. "I think you punks have been looking for me."

The cowboy took the cheroot out of his mouth, leaned, and spat on to the shining polished wood floor.

"C-C-Clint Eastwood?" Bishop O'Leary gasped, in disbelief.

The cowboy tossed his poncho over his shoulder, revealing a gun belt and a large pistol in a holster strapped to his thigh. He slowly and carelessly tossed the cheroot on to the polished wooden flooring, where it immediately began to smoulder and burn a black stain in the varnish. He slowly and deliberately crushed it with his heel.

Cardinal Donleavy opened his mouth to speak but it flapped uselessly, silently, three or four times.

"Wh-wh-wh-who are you?" he finally managed to stammer. "Wh-wh-wh-what is the meaning of this outrageous and offensive intrusion?"

The cowboy shrugged.

"When you boys have apologised to me - like I know you're going to do - for everything that The Sacred Order of St. Gregory has ever done in its long and disgusting history, and when you've written out full a confession for every murder you've ever committed, or authorised...well, I might just think about telling you boys who I am."

Cardinal Donleavy reached for the phone on his desk; it exploded in a shower of shards of broken black plastic and electronic components. Donleavy jumped back in his chair, his eyes wide, horrified. The cowboy stood with his hand pointed at Donleavy's desk, his hand arranged in the shape of a gun with his forefinger and indexed finger stretched out and his other fingers and thumbs curled, exactly in the way that small boys pretend when they're playing cowboys. The cowboy put his fingers to his lips, and blew.

"Did I say you could move, punk?" the cowboy growled. His eyes narrowed to even more menacing slits. "Go on. Do something else stupid. Go ahead. Make my day."

He stepped in to the centre of the room.

"Now, tell me where I can find the snake, de Feren."

Bishop Donleavy then did something most unexpected. He actually smiled. The cowboy squinted even more.

"What's so funny, punk?" Donleavy actually began to laugh.

"For nearly seventy years, I have dedicated my life to killing such as you," he croaked. "Yet now, here you are, in my very inner sanctum, and I must confess, I am pleased - nay, delighted - to see you. You do not need to tell me who you are, young man. I already know."

O'Leary glanced at the bishop as though he'd just admitted to being a Satanist.

"I am so pleased to see you, that I am going to warn you that the person you seek is standing right behind you."

"Do you really think I'd fall for the oldest trick in the book?" Wayne asked, in his best 'man with no name' voice. Even so, some deep inner voice told him to move...and to move quickly.

La petite blasted its deadly projectile into the air with a sharp cracking noise.

Wayne instinctively shifted to the right. He watched the tiny poison-filled projectile traverse the room as if it was travelling in slow motion, like a replay of a striker's goal-bound shot on "Match of the Day."

He saw it cut a track through the smoke and felt a faint draught as it passed close to his cheek, and then - seemingly instantaneously - he watched it slam straight into Bishop Donleavy's shoulder.

Father Pierre de Feren, standing in the blasted doorway, opened his mouth in shock and horror. He saw the cowboy move so fast that he actually seemed to disappear for a split-second. His eyes almost popped out of his head when he saw the bishop jerk violently in his chair, as the bullet pierced his flesh.

Eighty-Six

James Malone was fidgeting like a cat on a hot tin roof. He was standing on the street outside the grounds of St. Patrick's Cathedral. The usual Dublin weekday traffic mayhem seemed to be exacerbated by the heat, and James had to run his finger around the collar of his shirt to stop it sticking to his neck. Even the large numbers of pretty, scantily clad girls, enjoying what was probably going to be the last gasp of a sudden Indian summer, couldn't distract James' attention.

All he could think about was what had happened that night at Mickey Finn's cottage, when the eleven year old Wayne - or Michael Sean O'Brien, as James had known him then - had walked bravely towards the Order's immortal assassin, Francisco Pizarro, trading energy bolts blast for blast. James could still see the gritty determination on Wayne's face in the flickering light of the blazing cottage.

He thought about Wayne facing down the banshee, a creature that had been held as one of the most terrifying monsters in Irish legend. Yet, Wayne had survived. He thought about Wayne facing the two burly Special Branch men and persuading them that they were wasting their time. That took a lot of guts.

Here was James Malone, however, standing outside in the sunshine, watching mini-skirted girls pass by, while a sixteen-year-old youth took on the most insidious organisation in the history of Christendom.

James snorted. "It's alright for him...he's got superpowers! Probably has a big S in the middle of his pyjamas..."

A girl giggled to her friends as they walked past, hearing James talking to himself.

"You know, I used to be a priest, until I hit the bottle!" he shouted. The girls broke out into open laughter, but quickened their pace, just in case.

Wayne might have special powers, but none of the remaining members of the Order did, as far as James knew. All they had was superior numbers.

"The kid'll be alright," James muttered.

The leaves on the trees swayed in the sunlight, and a beam of sunlight hit James' eye as he looked up for inspiration.

"Alright, alright - I get the bloody message!" James shouted.

He began to walk into the Cathedral grounds, quickly at first, then quicker and quicker, until he was running.

"Look out, kid, I'm coming!" he shouted, as an explosion-like noise emanated from inside the office area of the Cathedral. James Malone reached the corner of the building just in time to see the tall bald shape of Father de Feren entering the plain black door, way ahead of him.

Eighty-Seven

Wayne Higginbotham twisted his mouth into the meanest sneer he could muster and held up his right arm, his hand palm outwards. A bolt of pure energy flashed out and hit de Feren right in the middle of his chest, lifting him off his feet and propelling him through the air until he landed on his back, outside the blasted doorway.

The breath was knocked out of his lungs, but the tall, bald, Belgian priest quickly climbed up on to his knees and then jumped back onto his feet, his face set in a mask of twisted hatred.

Wayne was about to advance, when a harsh blow hit him on the back of the head. Although he saw stars for a second, he didn't lose consciousness. He turned and saw the bloated, perspiring, horrified face of Bishop O'Leary, clutching a heavy leather-bound antique bible.

"Oops - sorry!" the bishop whimpered pathetically.

Wayne stared straight into the fat Bishop's eyes. "Forget!" he commanded.

The bishop fell to his knees and then slowly turned and sank forward onto his face, right in front of Donleavy's desk. Wayne winked at the ancient bishop.

"Don't worry, pops, he's just taking a quick nap. He'll be fine."

Wayne turned back to the doorway, just in time to see de Feren running towards him with a wicked-looking dagger in his raised right hand. Wayne held up his hand, and blasted again.

This time, the blast was much weaker. De Feren was pushed back and fell to his knees, like a boxer hit by a heavy punch, but once again he shook his head and doggedly climbed slowly back onto his feet.

Wayne could feel himself struggling for breath. He couldn't do it all. He couldn't shape-shift, fire blasts of energy and use mind control all at the same time; not without using vast amounts of energy. Even the stones in his pocket didn't give him that much strength. He allowed himself to morph back into the shape of Wayne Higginbotham.

"You!" De Feren spat, as he recognised the youth before him. "How? I killed you! This is impossible."

Donleavy, still sitting behind the desk, began to laugh again; a gasping, croaking, desperate laugh.

"So much for your guarantees, Father de Feren," the old bishop croaked.

De Feren snarled, his face contorted with rage. He launched himself at Wayne, who instinctively twisted away like a matador avoiding a bull's lunge. De Feren grunted and swivelled his body in a trained, rapidly fluid motion that belied his weedy appearance, and slashed with the dagger. He narrowly missed Wayne's stomach this time, as the boy athletically twisted away from him.

As he threw himself backwards, however, Wayne's foot tripped over the comatose Bishop O'Leary's outstretched leg, and he fell on to his backside. Despite jumping back into a defensive crouch as quickly as he could, de Feren's swift karate kick just caught Wayne's chin, knocking the unbalanced boy on to his backside again.

Wayne blinked and shook his head, as his assailant grinned maniacally.

"No mistakes this time," De Feren leered, as he menacingly wielded the dagger in front of Wayne's face.

"Hey! You!" The shout caused de Feren to pause momentarily and glance around, as James Malone burst in through the blasted doorway and quickly looked around, to try and get an appraisal of the situation.

"Ah, the U.S. Cavalry. Just in the nick of time, as usual!" Wayne shouted. Donleavy laughed even more.

"It must be judgment day already, de Feren. See! The dead return in ever greater numbers."

De Feren ignored the old Bishop's jibe, and turned back to finish his kill. Wayne Higginbotham had, however, gone and disappeared into thin air. He screamed his annoyance.

James Malone charged towards the assassin; but, being unarmed. he had to check himself as the Belgian raised the wicked shining blade. The grinning priest forced Malone to step back, as he tossed the dagger from hand to hand, like a street hoodlum.

"At least I know that you cannot do disappearing tricks, Malone! This time I will make sure that you do die...scum!" the priest snarled as he wildly slashed at James, who jumped back, only just managing to avoid being disembowelled by the blade.

"Do you think I am just any old priest?" De Feren shouted. "I was personally saved by Our Lord, just for this purpose! I see that now. If you brainless fools knew any French, you would know that the name I adopted when I entered the Order is a French anagram: De Feren for D'Enfer, 'From Hell'. For I have been through Hell and I have been rescued, and born again. I have been resurrected. I am the Saviour. I am 'God's Assassin'!"

De Feren slashed out again at James, who had picked up a piece of the broken door and deftly wielded the blade away with it.

"You talk way too much," James Malone taunted the Belgian.

"And you have talked your last!" the priest hissed through gritted teeth as he lurched towards James, who only just managed to jump back out of the way of the blade in time. The priest laughed; a harsh laugh that took away any doubts that Wayne, James or even Donleavy might have had left. Pierre de Feren was insane.

Wayne had by now re-materialised, just in front of Donleavy's desk, his face fixed in a mask of grim determination.

"What do I do now, Wayne?" James shouted as the Priest closed in on him again. "I'm a bit of a beginner when it comes to this superhero business, you know..."

"Just hold him off for a second, James! I'm sort of recharging my superpowers." Wayne bellowed, in the hope that de Feren might lose concentration.

"Er, like what superpowers exactly are we talking about, here? Because I'm not seeing them at the moment!" James gasped, as de Feren swung the blade and, this time, nicked his arm. The priest grinned maniacally.

"I can smell your fear," he hissed.

"No, that would be my bowels," James replied through gritted teeth, as he covered the wound with his hand and tried to dodge past the crazed de Feren. The Priest jumped sideways to block his path.

"Wayne, isn't it time you, you know...cast a web, or used the laser death-rays from your eyes? You know, some of the more mundane stuff?" James shouted, his desperation clear in his voice.

"I think I'm all out of web juice at the moment, and my lasers are on the blink!" Wayne replied acerbically, as he flexed his fingers, feeling waves of fresh energy coursing through his body again.

"Baterang?" James suggested.

"Robin lost it," Wayne quipped, as he glanced rapidly around, looking for a weapon of some sort.

De Feren finally trapped James in a corner of the room. "Wayne, I think like now might be a pretty good time." James called, as de Feren closed in for the kill.

Bishop Donleavy pushed the carafe of expensive Cognac to the edge of his desk with an anguished gasp of pain.

"Thanks, Bish, Who needs superpowers?" Wayne stated quietly as he picked up the carafe, realising immediately what Donleavy intended. "Oi baldy!" he bellowed, hurling it, with all his might, straight at de Feren.

De Feren turned, and from the corner of his eye saw the carafe flying through the air, aimed precisely at his head. His reflexes were uncannily fast and he managed to raise his elbow, just in time. The crystal carafe shattered on de Feren's elbow in an explosion of glass and orbs of golden liquid, glistening in the gloomy mixture of candlelight and smoke. Some of the glass cut into the Priest's face, and his black cassock was soaked.

De Feren's attention turned back to Wayne, and he sneered, "For that, I'm going to get you first, demon spawn. Let's see if you have the courage not to disappear again!"

He began to advance slowly and ominously towards Wayne.

"Oh good. I was hoping you'd say that." Wayne grinned. He waited until the priest was directly underneath the huge, ornate, chandelier, where a few candles still flickered and burned.

"You tried to burn me to death in my own home." Wayne hissed, through gritted teeth. "Please allow me return the compliment, baldy!"

Wayne raised his hand, and pointed at the chain suspending the chandelier; there was an almighty crack, like the report of a gun, as the chain snapped.

De Feren looked up, his mouth agape and his eyes wide in shock as the entire chandelier tumbled down towards his head. Even then, de Feren's instincts were far sharper than any normal man. He threw himself sideways, as the chandelier crashed to the ground in a huge explosion of glass and metal.

De Feren painfully pulled his legs from the mangled wreckage, looked up at Wayne, and grinned. His teeth gleamed from his dark, blood-splattered face.

"Is that it?" the Belgian hissed."Is that the best of your so-called powers, demon?"

Wayne raised his head, and his mouth curled in a half smile. "It'll do!"

The candles had set the spilled Cognac alight and the flames rapidly spread across the few inches of floor between the wrecked chandelier and the insane priest. Flames rapidly licked up de Feren's alcohol-soaked cassock. He looked down in horror, screamed, and started flapping uselessly at his clothing as the flames spread up his body.

Wayne closed his eyes, and made one last, huge, effort. He held out his hands towards the blasted door and drew in the deepest breath he had ever managed.

The room was filled with a sudden gust of warm wind from the summer day outside. The strong breeze whirled around de Feren, fanning the flames, which - instantly, totally - engulfed the priest. Father Pierre de Feren writhed and twisted in agony as he ran, screaming, out through the blasted doorway, like a human torch.

"Follow him, James," Wayne commanded. "Make sure he doesn't manage to jump in a fountain, or something."

James Malone nodded curtly, and did as he was told without even thinking about it. Wayne stamped out the small puddles of flame that remained on the wooden flooring.

"Sorry about the mess," he said apologetically, looking up at Bishop Donleavy. "And thanks for the Cognac tip...that was cool."

Donleavy's breath was coming in short sharp gasps; Wayne frowned.

"Although...I don't really know why I'm apologising to you. I did intend to kill you, as well as de Feren, you know that?" Wayne stated. "Not that I could have done it, I suppose...not when I come to think about it. So, come on - why did you help me?"

The old man smiled, weakly.

"The Lord moves in mysterious ways, my boy; and my demise is, ironically, at the hand of my own Order." His voice was little more than a whisper.

"I couldn't have killed you in cold blood, anyway. Not even you. You, who gave the order to kill my father and me." Wayne shrugged. The old bishop laughed, a gasping, croaking sound.

"This is what I feared the most. Your words are not those of a demon. You are not the 'God's Assassin' we feared, are you? All the work of the Order has been..." - he paused to catch his breath - "...misguided."

Wayne nodded knowingly. "We all make mistakes. Look...I'll go and get some help for you."

Donleavy smiled sadly. "It is too late to help me," the bishop groaned. Wayne noticed the peculiar way his Adam's apple bounced up and down like a ball in his neck. "Pass me that paper and the pen, my son."

Wayne reached over the desk, and did as he was asked. The bishop scrawled a few words on the paper, picked up a small jar of wax which he held over a candle for a few seconds, then dabbed his ring into the wax, folded the paper, and sealed it. Wayne stared at the bishop, inquisitively.

"This will ensure that the authorities and the Order are not suspicious about the circumstances of my demise," Donleavy croaked, waving the sealed note. Wayne snorted.

"I don't care about the Order. I'm getting you some help."

"Stay!" Donleavy croaked again, still with a surprising amount of authority in his voice. "De Feren's poisons are always lethal. There is no antidote. You cannot save me...not my body, anyway. I am old. I have lived well and, at the end, at least my soul will be redeemed. Do you believe in Our Blessed Lord?"

Wayne shrugged. "No, not really."

The old bishop smiled sadly. "Not a servant of Satan, but sadly no angel either. So be it."

He took the stone from his desk.

"This should be yours, I think. You may need it in the dark times that lie ahead. There are more like it in a vault in the Vatican City in Rome. If you need them, ask for Father Giuseppe Bianco, and tell him I sent you," he coughed, as Wayne took the stone. "Show him this!" Bishop Donleavy took a ring off his left hand and gave it to Wayne.

"Thanks!" Wayne whispered, as he glanced at the gold ring. A small white sword emerging from a flame decorated its front. Wayne slipped the stone and the ring carelessly into his pocket.

"What do you mean by dark times?" he asked the old man, quizzically. The bishop coughed violently, then wiped his mouth with his sleeve. Traces of blood were smeared across his face.

"I have little time left, my son, so listen well," the bishop wheezed.

"There are those in the Vatican who believe that the Christ has been reborn. They believe that they have engineered the Second Coming and will do anything to protect the child. I myself have seen him. I will confess that for some weeks, I have had my doubts about the child being who they say he is. So...as I prepare to leave this mortal shell, and as I have now looked upon the face of he that is supposedly the truly evil one, I have a judgment to make. It is...it is..."

The bishop's eyes rolled and his head fell forward, his chin on his chest. Wayne sighed, and began to turn to leave; but Bishop Donleavy opened his eyes.

"I am not done quite yet, boy. Hearken well to me now..." he whispered, his voice barely audible. "It is my belief that the child who we, the Sacred Order of Saint Gregory, have invited to our world, is the son of the devil himself. The Order is not a threat to you any more, for it has been stood down. I now believe that you are God's Holy weapon. You are 'God's Assassin', but not as we understood it. We have always thought the prophecy referred to the one who would try kill Our Lord - not kill on his behalf."

"I don't get it," Wayne muttered. "Anyway, I'm not sure I want to be anybody's weapon. God's or anybody else's."

The bishop closed his eyes again, as he held out his bony hand and firmly grabbed Wayne's wrist.

"I have seen the error of my ways and I am truly sorry for all the harm I have done to you and your people. Will you find it in your heart to forgive this repenting sinner?"

Wayne took a deep breath and nodded. "Yeah, I suppose so."

Bishop Donleavy smiled. "Hardly the most gracious pardon, but if the child in Rome had had a quarter of your compassion and mercy, I might still have believed. It is your destiny to rectify our mistake, boy. It is you who must kill the demon that we have brought to God's green earth, before he enslaves the entire world."

The head of the Sacred Order of St Gregory in Ireland looked imploringly at Wayne, his grip on Wayne's wrist tightened.

"Go now," he sighed, "fulfil your destiny, God's true assassin. May Our Lord God and the Blessed Virgin Mary be with you."

The bishop raised his arm and made the sign of the cross. Then with one last huge exhalation, he released Wayne's wrist and slumped back into his chair, his eyes glassy and unfocussed. Bishop Donleavy was dead.

"So...I don't get to hear the prophecy, then?" Wayne sighed. "Oh well. Probably a load of codswallop, anyway."

Wayne took a few deep breaths and turned to leave the office, almost tripping over the prone form of fat Bishop O'Leary again, when he heard a shout.

"Hello?" a voice called from outside the blasted door. Wayne suddenly became aware of a torch being shone into the room. Two Gardai entered the ornate office and gasped at the sheer opulence and the weight of destruction evident before them. Luckily, Wayne had made enough of a recovery to be able to make a silent and invisible exit.

He found James standing by the main road outside the Cathedral. There was quite a commotion going on. Police sirens wailed, and blue lights seemed to be flashing everywhere. James glanced at the teenager, and smiled.

"Ah, something terrible has happened. Some priest seems to have lost his marbles. It must have been some sort of protest, or something...anyway it looks like he set himself alight and charged out into the main road without looking. The poor bus driver must have had a hell of a shock. Those double-deckers make a hell of a mess when they hit you."

Wayne grinned. "You get nutters everywhere, nowadays."

Malone nodded. "Donleavy?"

Wayne shook his head. "A convert at the end. I can't believe he actually helped me."

"O'Leary?"

Wayne shrugged. "Big headache, tomorrow."

James made an approving grimace. "So, are we off to Rome now then?" he asked. "You know, we've won at home, but next comes the tough away leg, in a steamy Italian cauldron. Hostile atmosphere, crowd against us, backs to the wall, and all that."

Wayne shook his head.

"Nah...maybe you were right. Maybe I do need to strengthen my team before that leg. Had the star substitute not made an appearance at just the right moment, I think the result might have been very different. The old bishop seems to think I'm some sort of holy warrior - but firstly, I'm an atheist, and secondly, when I got into that room, I just sort of knew I couldn't kill them. If it hadn't have been for old Baldy, I think it all might have been a bit of a mess. I know now I couldn't kill anybody - not in cold blood. Not much of a holy warrior, am I?" He shrugged. "And anyway, the old man reckons the Order has disbanded, so it looks like we're through on a bye."

James Malone ran his hand through his hair.

"For once, I think you've actually gone and made a smart decision, young master Higginbotham. Now I better get bandaged up, before I bleed to death."

"Just one thing..." Wayne scratched his head as he spoke. "What do you know about the a prophecy? The one about 'God's Assassin', or some such nonsense?"

James Malone raised his eyebrows.

"It's supposed to be the entire raison d'etre of the Sacred Order of St. Gregory - or was - but to be honest, I've never heard it. Now, come on! I've lost at least a pint of blood already, and I've only got seven left!"

Eighty-Eight

Sergeant Hartley shook his head and placed the buff folder back in the grey metal filing cabinet, pushing the drawer shut with a resounding thud.

"I just don't get it!" he said, for probably the fifth time. "They didn't even bother to let the Higginbotham woman and that Headmistress, Mrs. Ball, know that they weren't going to interview them. A few minutes at the hospital with the Irishman and the boy and they just got up and buzzed off back down to London, without so much as a 'by your leave'!"

Inspector Harrison slammed a pile of paperwork onto her desk.

"That's Special Branch for you," she said, dismissively. Sergeant Hartley picked up his mug of coffee.

"I still think there's an awful lot more to this whole Higginbotham business than meets the eye, you know."

Inspector Harrison looked up momentarily. "Listen, Bill, until the Higginbotham boy chooses to tell us why he just happened to be found, tied and bound, in a burning house and decides to press charges...then there isn't much we can do. As for the Fleming girl, she insists it was the Irish girl who assaulted her, not the American boy - and as there's absolutely no trace of either of them, once again, there is very little we can do. Obviously Special Branch decided that the whole IRA story was a total waste of time, and the reason we haven't heard from them is probably that they are pretty cross about it."

Sergeant Hartley noisily slurped his coffee.

"But how come I have sworn statements by that Ducket girl and two others saying that they definitely, absolutely definitely, saw Stephanie Fleming leave the Youth Club with that Yank, an hour before she was found in the toilets?"

Inspector Harrison shook her head, and returned her attention to her paperwork.

"It's all quite beyond me," she muttered. "Some things, Bill, are beyond explanation."

Sergeant Hartley scowled. "One day I'll get to the bottom of all this...if it's the last thing I do!"

Inspector Harrison cast him a furtive glance. "Good luck with that one, Sergeant!"

Eighty-Nine

The pub was busy, noisy, smoky and uncomfortable, but the Coke that James passed to Wayne tasted as good as any drink he had ever touched. James obviously thought the same about the pint of Guinness that he seemed to sink in seconds.

"Thirsty work, saving the world," James sighed gratefully, as he wiped his white, foam-fringed mouth with the back of his hand. "Ouch - these stitches hurt! So, are you going straight home now, Wayne? You're welcome to stop at my mother's tonight."

Wayne shook his head. "No, I've got until Sunday. I'm back at school on Monday morning. I thought I'd go over to the West. I'd like to see my grandfather, and the rest of the family over there."

James nodded, but seemed distracted for a few moments. Eventually, he looked up.

"I'll take you over. I can fly from Shannon, anyway. There are a few ghosts I want to exorcise in the village of Finaan."

"How do you exercise a ghost?" Wayne asked, screwing up his nose.

"Have you seen the papers?" James demanded, as Wayne emerged downstairs at the Malone house on the Saturday morning. James' mother, busy slaving over the cooker, turned and laughed.

"Would you be leaving the poor lad alone...he's only just woken up! How can he have seen the papers?"

Wayne pulled out a wooden chair and sat sleepily at the breakfast table in the large, warm, kitchen. James threw a copy of The Irish Independent over the table.

"RETIRED BISHOP, DEAD IN CATHEDRAL SCANDAL!" the headline screamed. Wayne read on:

Retired bishop, Conal Donleavy, was shot dead in his private office in Saint Patrick's Cathedral yesterday morning, and Bishop Desmond O'Leary of Knock injured. The assailant was reported to be a deranged Belgian priest, later identified as Father Pierre de Feren. De Feren had a history of mental illness and had been expelled from his Parish in Belgium in the mid Sixties.

Bishop Donleavy was a popular figure in the Church in Ireland and was a good friend of the Primate. A spokesman for the Cathedral said that the bishop had continued to work hard for charitable causes ever since his official retirement, and that his contribution to Church life would be sorely missed.

According to witnesses at the scene, the assailant set fire to himself within the Cathedral in an apparent act of contrition, and then ran under a bus.

Bishop O'Leary is expected to make a full recovery.

Wayne raised his eyebrows and carried on reading, his drowsiness evaporating faster than water in the Kalahari.

"Charitable causes?" he exclaimed.

Mrs Malone carried a huge white plate over to the table and plonked it down in front of Wayne.

"Look at you - you've no weight on you at all! It's fading away, you are. There's bacon, egg, sausage, tomato, white pudding, black pudding, potato farls and fried soda bread. If you want any more, just shout."

Mrs Malone bustled off, and James laughed when he saw Wayne's bemused expression. "I don't know how I'm not twenty stone!"

Wayne devoured the breakfast platter hungrily, and was suitably effusive with his praise.

"Ah, away with you, it was just a normal breakfast!" Mrs Malone beamed.

James Malone said his goodbyes to his family later that Saturday morning, promising them that he would soon bring Carrie over to see them all. He gave his father a huge hug, and slapped his back.

"Take care of yourself, Da. Don't go ending up back in hospital," James whispered.

"It's good to have you back from the dead, Jimmy," his father said as he held his son by the shoulders. "Is this the lad you told me about?"

James nodded, and the elder Malone studied Wayne carefully. Eventually, he nodded too.

"So, now I can go to my grave saying I've really seen one of the 'little folk'!"

Wayne looked slightly upset.

"I'm five foot eight," he protested, "and a half!" he added, as an afterthought. Both James and his father laughed.

Wayne thanked the Malones for putting him up for the night, and for the monster breakfast. "It was a pleasure," he was told.

It was almost as soon as James had driven away from the house in the Ford Fiesta hire car that he announced to Wayne that Dan had telephoned him the night before.

"Well, now, it seems you're a very rich young man," he said, a note of mischief in his voice.

"How rich?" Wayne asked, gravely.

"Rich enough," James said quietly.

"No, come on, James...what did he get for it?"

"Only half a million," James said, trying to sound as unimpressed as possible.

"He was robbed. I was expecting at least twice that," Wayne grumbled miserably, before casting a furtive glance in James' direction and cracking into a smile. The pair laughed like drains most of the way to Oughterard.

Ninety

"So, Terri...tell me about your childhood, where you grew up. Tell me about your parents and friends."

"You've gotta be joking, right?" Terri demanded incredulously. "I mean, that's what they say in the movies!"

Doctor Van Groningen smiled, condescendingly.

"That's because that's how we do things," he said, with an open-handed gesture. "I will not be taking notes. I just want you to talk to me. Tell me about your life."

Terri told Van Groningen all about her childhood in Ireland. She told him about her relationships with her parents and siblings, her childhood ambition to be an actress. She told him about her relationship with Danny Finn, and how she had ended up pregnant and alone in London. She told him about how she had had to give up the twins for adoption, and how the nuns had made her feel cheap and unworthy.

"That must have been quite a trauma," the doctor stated sympathetically.

"I had a breakdown," Terri confessed. "To surrender a child, no matter how much they try to convince you that it is in the child's best interests, is the hardest thing any woman can ever do. To surrender two is beyond any woman's capability...even mine," Terri laughed. "That's why I went a bit nuts, I guess. You wouldn't believe the things that I thought I saw and heard."

The doctor smiled. "Tell me what you think you saw and heard," he commanded.

So Terri did. She told him about Danny morphing into a medieval warrior; about his claim to be immortal, and about how he could perform other magic tricks.

"Man, I must have been so far gone," she sighed.

The doctor smiled again, and nodded thoughtfully.

"And have you seen this, this, being, since?"

"No," Terri lied.

"I believe you were recently reunited with one of your children," the doctor prompted Terri. "Did this not cause any stress?"

Terri shrugged. "Recently? It was five years ago. Of course it was stressful, but it was also quite beautiful. Getting one of my babies back was more than I'd ever expected - and then...and then I went and blew it."

"Blew it?" the doctor pounced on Terri's confession, and Terri took a deep breath.

"Things had been going real well, right up until a couple of months ago."

She hesitated. "Mmm...?" Doctor Van Groningen prompted her.

"Oh, well...Dean thinks that if the media get hold of my 'missing children' story, well, then that's my career over. Wham, bam, thank you, Ma'am."

"And what do you think?"

Terri screwed up her nose.

"I think that maybe he just wants me to be the mommy of his baby, you know? To like, forget everything that happened before him. Dean's a bit of a control freak."

The doctor scribbled a note on his pad.

"I thought you weren't taking notes," Terri sighed.

"Just one," Doctor Van Groningen replied dismissively. "And so, what happened a couple of months ago?"

Terri blew out a huge, regretful sigh.

"I wrote to Michael, my son, and said that it would be better if we didn't contact each other for a while."

The doctor raised his head and pushed his spectacles to the end of his nose. "For a while?" he repeated inquisitively.

Terri wiped a tear from her eye. "Yes...I went and pushed him away in a letter. I wrote back asking him to forget what I'd said, that I was stressed...but I haven't heard anything. He probably just threw the letter in the trash."

Doctor Van Groningen took off his spectacles and wiped them on a clean white handkerchief.

"And there has been no trace of your daughter at all?"

"No," Terri replied, sadly.

The doctor nodded thoughtfully. He looked at his watch.

"Goodness, is that the time?" he exclaimed. "Terri, the root of the problem is already apparent to me. I am going to save you and your husband an awful lot of money by saying I will only need to see you one more time. The trauma of what happened to you sixteen years ago is still very fresh in your memory. The reunion with your son brought back a lot of bad memories, but being pregnant has resurrected all of the pain of losing both of your babies. To make matters worse, you have taken your husband's warnings about the press and have, in your own mind, repeated the mistake you made sixteen years ago by abandoning your son - only this time purely for selfish reasons."

Terri nodded. Doctor Van Groningen smiled sympathetically.

"I am personally surprised that you are not wearing a Georgian dress and claiming that you are the Empress Josephine. The human mind can only deal with so much. Your mind has had to deal with more than anyone I've spoken too in a very long time. I'm going to prescribe some medication that will help, until we get together next week. You are a very level-headed woman. What you have been through would have destroyed most people. I think hearing voices - in your imagination, or not - is a very low-key reaction, after what you've experienced."

Terri shrugged. "Is that what you are going to tell Dean?"

The doctor frowned. "Mrs Vitalia...I am a professional. I will not discuss your case with anyone else, including your husband. Like an MD, I am bound by the Hippocratic oath. All I can say is, you are as sane as anyone I have met in this town, and a damn site saner than most. I will see you next week."

Terri closed her eyes, and sighed deeply.

"Well that's one thing. At least I'm not going nuts," she whispered.

Ninety-One

Cardinal D'Abruzzo surveyed the damage in Bishop Donleavy's office, without any discernable emotion.

"And there was absolutely nothing you could do?" he asked Bishop O'Leary, who, despite the cool late September breeze that whistled through the blasted door, was perspiring and wiping his brow. The Indian summer had not lasted long.

"Not really, Your Eminence. I would have given my life for the Bishop, of course."

"Of course," the Cardinal repeated, with only a mere hint of irony in his voice.

"I mean, I know a few tricks - my Masai bodyguard in Africa taught me some useful self-defence techniques - but de Feren was a professional assassin. He must have crept up behind me while I attended to the Bishop, and bang! I was knocked out. I saw nothing," the plump bishop babbled, as both men watched workmen carefully pack valuable 'objets d'art' into packing cases.

"I'm sure, had he not been so unsporting, that you would have put up quite a fight," D'Abruzzo stated. His left eyebrow rose sceptically.

"It was the dissolution of the Order, of course. He just couldn't accept it," O'Leary gushed. "Oh yes...the Bishop left this for you, Your Eminence."

Cardinal D'Abruzzo ripped open the sealed note, raised both eyebrows, nodded and re-folded the piece of paper. Bishop O'Leary stared at him in anticipation, and the Cardinal nodded.

"The late Bishop states that Father Pierre de Feren had gone mad and attacked him, in revenge, for taking away the meaning of his life. He also states that it is fitting that he himself passes with the Order." Cardinal D'Abruzzo frowned thoughtfully. "He also tells me, personally, not to despair, that the Lord is with us; his sword hand lives." The Cardinal frowned again. "I wonder what he meant by that?"

He shrugged, and walked over to the Bishop's ornate desk. "You said that he had destroyed all the files?"

O'Leary nodded, rubbing his hands together in a desperate desire to be seen as diligent. "The Bishop destroyed everything on Thursday."

The Cardinal nodded approvingly. "So there is absolutely no trace of the Order, or any of its activities?" he whispered. Bishop O'Leary shook his head, making his cheeks and several chins wobble in unison.

Cardinal D'Abruzzo watched a workman pack a painting into a crate."Please be careful...that is worth more than half of this city," he ordered. He turned back to O'Leary.

"Well, Bishop, we have a funeral to attend. Let us leave this place."

Bishop O'Leary bowed his head.

"Yes, Your Eminence...but I have one question."

Cardinal D'Abruzzo raised an eyebrow in anticipation. "And what is that?"

O'Leary looked concerned. "If the Order has been totally disbanded...."

The Cardinal waited patiently, as O'Leary seemed to hesitate in asking his question.

"Then...who is now to protect the Holy Child?"

Cardinal D'Abruzzo sighed; a deep, heavy sigh, that betrayed his complete and utter frustration.

"The child...ah yes, the child. He has decided that his future would be better served in the hands of those whose business is, for want of a better word...protection."

O'Leary frowned. "So he is no longer under the protection of the Holy Mother Church?"

Cardinal D'Abruzzo shook his head.

"Our Lord moves in mysterious ways, Bishop; sometimes very mysterious ways."

Ninety-Two

When Wayne and James eventually arrived in Oughterard, they were almost overwhelmed by the effusive greeting that Wayne's Aunt Molly gave them.

"What a surprise! It's great to see you," Molly had gushed when Wayne had knocked on her door, and, after hugging him almost to death, she had immediately set to work on preparing copious amounts of tea and sandwiches.

Wayne had been amazed at how much his cousin Patsy had grown, and how much the boy actually resembled him at a younger age - without the ears, of course.

"I'll be taking you to see Daideo as soon as you've finished eating," Molly had insisted. "He's on his own, now. Our Katie has gone off to join your Uncle Colm in New York. Will you be coming, Father?"

James had smiled, somewhat embarrassed. "I'm not a priest any more, Molly. I gave it up, after all that we went through up in Mayo that night. No...I'm going on up to Finaan...I suppose just to see the old place and say some goodbyes that I never got the chance to say before. Then I have a plane to catch, first thing tomorrow morning, at Shannon."

Molly nodded. "Oh well, never mind. Have you got somewhere to be staying tonight?"

James nodded. "I have - I'll be staying by the airport, thanks."

"And how long can you stay, Michael?" Molly asked.

"Just until tomorrow, if that's okay?" Wayne answered. "If someone can get me down to Galway, tomorrow morning, I'll take a train across to Dublin and then catch a ferry home to England, and then the train again. I've got to go back to school on Monday."

"Sure, that'll be no problem at all. Now, how's that lovely Da of yours?" Molly chirped.

Wayne told her about Frank's recent and untimely death, about the Order's attack on him in Yorkshire, and about how he and James had finally defeated them in Dublin.

"Good Lord. Let's hope that's the last we ever see of them," Molly said. She visibly shivered at the memory of how the Order, in the shape of Francisco Pizarro, had so nearly condemned her and Patsy to a fiery death in Mickey Finn's cottage, five years earlier.

"John is in Galway, himself," Molly informed Wayne. "It's a shame you won't be seeing him this weekend, but it's the big game tomorrow: Galway against Kerry."

Wayne grinned. "Never mind. I guess it is Daideo that I was really hoping to see while I was over here."

Molly smiled. "Ah, he'll be delighted, so he will."

James finally stood and said that he'd better be going, if he was going to do what he had to do in Finaan and then get down to Shannon. Molly said her goodbyes, and then set about clearing up the dishes.

James shook Wayne's hand, gave him a hug, and slapped his back.

"It's been sort of fun," he said, after a moment's consideration. "But I better get my crazy, alcoholic carcass back to L.A."

He grinned mischievously at Wayne, who snorted in derision.

"You know why I had to say those horrible things!"

James laughed. "So, you're definitely coming over to California in your Christmas holidays? Carrie's desperate to see you. I've told her all about you and your abilities. I even told her about the ears."

Wayne punched him on the shoulder. "That'd be great," he said. "I'll have a reasonable excuse to get past Doris and visit my mom."

"Ah...so you'll only come as an excuse to visit your ma, will you?"

Wayne shook his head in exasperation. "You know what I mean. I've never been able to say to Doris 'hey, I'm just popping over to L.A. to see my real mom.' Now she'll just think I'm visiting you!"

James turned around, with a laugh and a wave.

"Look after your mother...you could have done a lot worse."

"Which one?" Wayne laughed.

James' hire car sped off into the distance.

"He's a good man. He should have stayed in the priesthood," Wayne heard Molly say from behind him. "After what we saw five years ago, and after what you've just told me, they need a few good ones. Come on, then...let's go see your granddad."

Ninety-Three

Rupert William George Digby Hetherington had discussed the matter at length with his wife, Melinda. That did not make what he had to do any easier.

"Look, Darling," he began to address his daughter, as the family sat down to dinner on the Saturday evening.

Lucy Hetherington's weekend home visit from school had been quite unremarkable, up until that point. She had been collected from the airport near St. Helier by Brown, the family chauffeur, on the Friday evening, and had promptly been whisked to the family home near St. Ouen. Saturday morning had been spent riding and grooming her horse, Flick, something she missed terribly while away at school, while the afternoon had been spent walking on the beach with her mother and the family's two golden retrievers: Spick and Span.

Her Father's announcement, therefore, as the three of them settled down around the table, was quite unexpected.

"Mummy and I have something terribly important that we've been meaning to tell you, Poppet. We were going to wait until you were eighteen, but this business at school, well, er...well, frankly, it's been something of a catalyst."

"Oh God, you're not getting divorced, are you?" Lucy gasped, aghast.

"Good God, no!" Rupert laughed. "Don't be silly, Poppet." He'd called Lucy 'poppet' for as long as she could remember. "No, it was when Mrs. Barrington, the headmistress..."

"Oh Daddy, please, not that phone business. I was sleepwalking," Lucy interrupted him.

Rupert held up his hand.

"Look, Poppet, Mrs Barrington told us that you'd referred to a...well, er, a brother...a twin brother."

Lucy rolled her eyes, and made a face.

"It was a dream, Daddy, just a silly dream. I also referred to my having been adopted, didn't I? I mean - how ludicrous?" Rupert glanced at his wife. He had known that what he had to say would be difficult, but it was proving impossible.

Melinda reached out a hand across the crisp white linen tablecloth and grabbed Lucy's hand.

"Do let Daddy finish what he has to say, Lucy darling," she gently chided her daughter. "It really is frightfully important."

Lucy couldn't help but notice that her mother's eyes were brimming with tears.

"Oh God," she whispered. "We're broke, aren't we? I'm going to have to leave school, aren't I? We'll have to sell the Range Rover and Flick."

Rupert laughed nervously. "Good grief - no, Poppet, it's nothing like that at all. It's just that...well, you're..." He coughed, and looked at Melinda for encouragement. "You were, er..."

Lucy had gone quite white.

"Poppet, you do know you're terribly special, don't you?"

Lucy smiled a puzzled smile and grasped her Father's hand.

"Of course I do, Daddy." Rupert shrugged.

"You see...you're special, because you were chosen."

Lucy looked at Melinda with a Daddy's gone mad! expression on her face. Melinda smiled reassuringly.

"What?" Lucy asked, her voice a mixture of incredulity and annoyance. "What do you mean, chosen?"

Rupert took a large swig of his Cabernet Franc.

"We adopted you, Poppet. Frightful bad luck, but Mummy couldn't have babies. We didn't tell you sooner, because..."

There was an almighty crash as Lucy Hetherington fainted and fell sideways off her chair.

"...it might have come as a bit of a shock." Rupert hesitantly and robotically finished his sentence, as Melinda knelt and cuddled her daughter, tears pouring down her face.

"I don't suppose I should mention the twin brother yet, then?" Rupert asked, sort of rhetorically.

Ninety-Four

From the top of the mountain, Wayne Higginbotham felt like he could see to the ends of the earth. It was a beautiful late summer's evening in the West of Ireland, with the first chills of Autumn just beginning to make themselves felt, as the sun disappeared behind the wall of mountains opposite.

Wayne loved the view from the top of what he called 'Daideo's Mountain'. It was the second time he had climbed up to the cairn beneath Buckaun, and the view was no less breathtaking for having been seen before. Lough Mask, with its tiny, tree-crested islands, was spread out in front of him like an enormous mirror, faithfully reflecting the ever-shifting clouds. Beyond the Lough he could see maybe thirty miles, probably all the way to Sligo. He could see his grandfather's cottage way down below, and Molly's Ford Escort parked outside, looking like a matchbox car. Everywhere else he looked, he could see mountains.

The Yorkshire Dales were beautiful, but Connemara was beyond beautiful. It was spectacular.

Tom Mick a' John O'Brien had been overjoyed to see his grandson, after a gap of over three years. Frank had managed to get Wayne over to visit his family just once since the Pizarro incident, pretending that he was taking him fishing. Doris had been suspicious - Frank and Wayne had never fished - but Wayne had 'persuaded' her to let them go. Tom, - 'Daideo', as Wayne called him - had been devastated to hear of Frank's death.

"He was a fine man, your da," he had said sadly, offering Wayne a large glass of whiskey, which Molly had quietly and promptly confiscated.

Wayne had asked if he could pop up the mountain before it got dark. Tom had readily agreed, although Molly had urged him to be as quick as possible, as the mountainside was steep and treacherous in the dark.

Wayne wasn't at all surprised when a sudden mist descended on the mountain-top and quickly surrounded him, blocking out the spectacular panorama that he had been appreciating.

"Hi, Da!" Wayne laughed. "You haven't been much help, lately."

Aillen Mac Fionnbharr slowly emerged from the mist, grinning from ear to ear.

"So, Michael Sean Mac Aillen. You have become a true Tuatha warrior, at last."

Wayne smiled shyly. "Thanks."

Aillen, wearing his ancient robes, folded his arms, and his forehead creased into a serious frown. "You have made many mistakes, my son, many foolish mistakes...but fortune has favoured you."

"Mistakes?" Wayne repeated incredulously, his eyebrow raised quizzically. "I don't know what you mean. It was all planned, you know."

Aillen nodded sceptically.

"Hmm. It is not of consequence now. You have succeeded in passing two of the great tests that were set before you."

"Two?" Wayne repeated, shocked. "Only two?"

Aillen motioned for Wayne to sit down on a nearby rock.

"This surprises you?"

Wayne nodded, disappointedly. "I mean...in the course of the last few weeks, I thought I'd lost my real mother, been rejected by the only girl I love, lost my dad, lost my house, had people try to burn me alive, had to brainwash my mother, and I've had the bloody police and Special Branch on my tail. And, after all that, I went and smashed the Order. And you say I've only passed two tests?"

Aillen raised in hands in a gesture of capitulation. "You have succeeded in two of the trials we foresaw. You survived Pizarro's attack, and now you have overcome the Order's new assassin and his pet banshee. The rest are the normal trials and tribulations of mortal - and, in some cases, immortal - life. Love and death are always around us. You will find love, Michael, many times. You will see many people that you love die. So it is now, so it has always been, so it will ever be. It was thus, even for the Tuatha De Danaan, in our earthly days."

Wayne sighed, and nodded. "I suppose you're right, although I've been bloody lucky both times. It was my dad, Frank, who really dealt with Pizarro, and there is no way I would have defeated de Feren if James, and even the Bishop, hadn't helped. I'm not that brilliant, really."

He sighed again, and looked thoughtful for a minute. Aillen nodded.

"Every warrior needs good fortune. Was it not Napoleon who said that he only needed lucky Generals?"

Wayne nodded. "And things are picking up. Mom has written and apologised, so I suppose I haven't really lost her."

"You will never lose her," Aillen smiled sympathetically. "Your chosen paths will come together, and she will soon play a much greater part in your life."

Wayne pondered for a second.

"Do you foresee me getting off with Stephanie Fleming?"

Aillen scowled, bemused. "Getting off? What is this? Who is Stephanie Fleming?"

Wayne shrugged. "That sounds like a 'no' to me."

Aillen shook his head. "You sometimes baffle me, my son."

Wayne smiled. "Sometimes I baffle myself."

Aillen looked serious again. "You have a judgment to make."

Wayne looked surprised. "What's that, then?"

Aillen seemed to think deeply for a minute and then addressed the boy.

"Aoibheall the Banshee, who was exiled and cast out into the mortal world many centuries ago, has passed into the realm of mist and darkness. You were the last human that she transgressed against. By your word, she can return to her people and to redemption. It is either that, or for her sins, which are beyond count, she can stay confined in the Never World for all of eternity. What is your judgment, my son?"

Wayne scratched his head.

"James said she wasn't all that bad. She just wanted the stones, not me. So I guess I forgive her. I mean...mercy and compassion are signs of strength in every book I've ever read."

Aillen nodded, serenely. "Your wisdom is pleasing. Aoibheall was always misguided, but never truly evil. Your mercy will allow her to join us in this realm."

Wayne pondered for a few moments.

"So first Pizarro, then de Feren, and a banshee. The Order supposedly doesn't exist anymore, so what's the third trial going to be? The bishop mentioned a demon that it was my destiny to kill, because I was 'God's Assassin'?"

Aillen smiled sadly.

"A great and powerful evil has entered the world, and even now it grows in strength and power. Soon it will make itself known and you shall have to face it, my son. Succeed and you will save the world of mortal men from a horror that defies the imagination. It will be a far, far greater trial than you have faced so far. Such is your destiny as the Slanaitheoir Mor."

"Oh, great." Wayne gasped. "No pressure there, then?"

Aillen nodded. He reached out, and touched Wayne's cheek.

"You have left childhood behind, my son. The first two tests have made you a warrior of the Tuatha. It will hopefully be a few more summers before you have to face the final test. You are already wise beyond your years, but your years are still tender. I will always be here for you, my son. You have made me very proud."

Wayne smiled sheepishly.

"Thanks, Da," he said pensively. "Da, there's something I've been meaning to ask you. You know...a clarification sort of thing?"

Aillen slowly inclined his head. "And what is it you wish to know?"

Wayne twisted up his face. "Am I immortal?"

Aillen smiled, sadly.

"Fortunately, no. Trust me in this, for to us, the endless sleep is a blessing. You have not been cursed with the endless passage of time. You were born of mortal woman. Only those born of the immortal womb are doomed to live forever."

Wayne nodded, his father's words tempering his disappointment a little.

"Pity, though," Wayne mumbled. "I would have loved to have lived long enough to see starships for real."

Aillen turned, as though to disappear into the green mist which surrounded them; but before he could move the familiar figure of Aoibheall the Banshee emerged, dressed in a long, green, low-cut gown, with her raven black hair now worn long and plaited.

Wayne's mouth dropped open. He had to admit that she now looked more beautiful than any woman he had ever seen, even Stephanie Fleming. She smiled demurely at Aillen.

"I have come to thank the boy," she stated simply. "As he has found it in his heart to forgive me, I forgive you for the killing of Culhainnein and for placing me in exile."

Aillen nodded gravely. "Forgiving is second only to loving in the eyes of the goddess. I too, in turn, forgive you the folly of your youth."

Aoibheall bowed and kissed Aillen's hand. She then turned to Wayne, and planted a ghostly kiss on his lips.

"You forgave me my intent, and you avenged my death, I thank you, Slanaitheoir Mor. I also forgive you for spurning my advance. See now what you missed!"

She winked mischievously, then smiled at Wayne, and her beautiful green eyes seemed to mesmerise him. She bowed her head, curtsied, turned and disappeared.

"She always was comely," Aillen muttered.

"I've seen her when she's not looking her best...you know, the rotting, zombie corpse look," Wayne said, with a grin. "But hell - she really does scrub up well!"

Aillen raised one eyebrow.

"Stay well my son, until we next meet."

The mist thinned and disappeared, leaving the view before Wayne.

The light was now fading quickly, so Wayne galloped down the steep incline as fast as he could. As he reached his grandfather's cottage, he could hear the telephone ringing. Tom picked it up as Wayne entered.

The old man spoke a few words in Gaelic and then, with a twinkle in his eye, looked at Wayne, who was panting from his recent exertion.

"There's somebody here you might be wanting to speak to..."

He passed the phone to Wayne. His eyes widened.

"Mom!" he shouted.

Ninety-Five

Carrie Horden squealed with delight when she saw a rather dishevelled-looking James Malone emerge from the International Terminal at LAX. He had a few days growth on his chin, he looked pale, and his long hair was greasy and untidy. Even so, she ran up to him and threw her arms around his neck, smothering him with kisses.

"Thank God you're safe!" she whispered, as she grabbed James' face and stared deep into his eyes. "There were times when I felt sure you weren't going to make it. I thought I might never see you again."

James put down his bags, and hugged his girlfriend as tightly as he could manage.

"I can tell you there were times when I thought I wasn't going to make it," he laughed. "But it was all worth it, to get back home to you."

Carrie pushed him back. "Ah, you've been refreshing your blarney, I see." James grinned.

As he looked around the airport terminal, with its thronging crowds of arrivals and happy friends and relations screaming, hugging and kissing their loved ones, he really felt as though he'd come home. Ireland and England seemed so dark, and the bright sunlight streaming into the terminal building reminded him why he loved being in California. In California, he felt alive.

As Carrie drove him home to Box Canyon along the San Diego Freeway, he thought back to his short trip to Europe. Had he really only been away a little over three short weeks?

Carrie was chatting happily, but James was reflecting on his survival in the River Liffey, the inferno in the Higginbotham's basement, and the maniacal stare of the knife-wielding de Feren as he had tried to slice open James stomach. The worst bit of all, though - the bit that had caused James the most pain - was seeing the moss on Father Dermot Callaghan's tiny gravestone in the churchyard in Finaan. James had found the grave after a long search, hidden away in an unconsecrated, weed-ridden corner of the churchyard. The corner reserved for those who had not been christened, and for those who had committed suicide.

James had been furious. Dermot Callaghan had been a good priest, and had deserved better. He had defied the Order, and his eternal reward for standing up for what he believed to be right was a mouldy old stone hidden in the weeds.

"Have you been listening to a word I've said?" Carrie demanded, although her face was creased in an understanding smile.

"Most of it," James lied. "I'm just worn out, I guess. It was a long flight after an eventful trip - and I've still got the buzzing in my ears from hearing the very last cry of a banshee." Carrie nodded sympathetically.

"You get some rest, and then I want to hear every last single detail. A banshee...woah! You know, from what I've heard so far, you should so write a book about all this stuff."

James stared reflectively out of the window, watching the palm trees and the brown burnt earth pass by. The lines of cars crawling along on the other side of the freeway glistened in the afternoon sun, and James had to shield his eyes.

"Normal people, leading normal lives. If only they knew." He thought to himself before responding to Carrie's suggestion.

"Perhaps I will...perhaps I will," he whispered, before turning and giving his beautiful girlfriend a broad, beaming, smile.

"It really is just so good to be home."

A couple of days later, James found Carrie staring wistfully at the huge rocks that seemed to hang precariously from the high rock walls above the Canyon.

"A penny for them?" James laughed.

Carrie glanced at him, and smiled forlornly. "Oh, I was looking forward to you bringing this Wayne kid home. I've always wanted to meet someone mystical, I guess. You know...one of the 'fair folk'?"

James frowned. "'Fair folk'? He's not that mystical, you know. He doesn't come out with life-changing profound statements every five minutes. He's a sixteen-year-old kid with English teeth, bad hair, a touch of B.O, spots, and the typical punk attitude of the average global teenager." James laughed. "He's a good kid though, even if he is a little self-centred. Oh yeah - I forgot to mention he's also got pointy ears, and he can do a few impressive tricks. You'll see them when he comes to visit after Christmas. That is, if you don't mind?"

Carrie clapped her hands gleefully, and laughed. "I look forward to it. Though it sounds like with friends like you, he doesn't need too many enemies."

James grinned. "Funny...that's what I said to him. Well, he did tell the cops I was a washed-up, delusional, alcoholic old ex-priest."

Carrie frowned coyly. "So, did he say anything that wasn't true?" She skipped off, after sticking her tongue out at her boyfriend. James chased her around the yard.

"I'm so lucky to have found you," he said, after catching, holding, and tenderly kissing her. "Are you disappointed because you were excited at the thought of having a young person around the house?"

Carrie pressed his nose affectionately.

"Yeah, okay...a little disappointed, I guess. I'd sort of gotten used to the idea of a kid...well, okay a younger person...hanging round the place for a while."

James grinned.

"Well, if you want a kid hanging round, I guess..."

Carrie opened her mouth wide in astonishment.

"James Malone, if you are suggesting what I think you're suggesting, you better get down on one knee, right now!"

James laughed and knelt in front of the beautiful Californian girl.

"Carrie Horden...I would be delighted and honoured if you would deign to take my hand in marriage."

Carrie grimaced.

"Let me think about that...okay, yeah, sure! I thought you were never going to ask, you slippery sucker!"

James took off his own Claddagh ring, and slipped it on to Carrie's finger.

"Consider yourself engaged to be married, Carrie Horden."

Ninety-Six

Terri Thorne felt so much happier. The shrink had gone and put her life in perspective, so Dean had probably done the right thing in calling him in. All the grief and pain that she had suffered sixteen years earlier had been stirred up by her reunion with Michael; she knew that now. However, it had been worth it, just to have Michael back in her life.

Her pregnancy with Dean's baby had had a similar effect, evoking memories of the last time she had carried a new life inside her and what had then subsequently happened. The fact that she knew that Dean was already cheating on her, after just a few months of marriage, just exacerbated the situation.

Instead of feeling down or worried, however, she now felt great. Terri knew that, despite occasionally hearing voices - well, one voice, at least - she was not only normal, but was a superwoman. Who else could have gone through what she had and not gone totally gaga? "Thank you, Doctor!" she had said at the end of her first session; and she really meant it.

It was the icing on the cake for her, therefore, when she called her dad on the Saturday lunchtime, her time, and ended up speaking to Michael.

"Mom!" he had squealed excitedly. Terri had screamed in delight.

"Michael! Oh my God - Michael! What a fantastic surprise. I thought I'd lost you again...thank God you're still speaking to me," she had gushed, through tears of happiness.

Wayne, as everyone but his Irish family knew him, talked to her for ages. He told her about his adopted dad dying, which upset Terri, as she had met him and thought him 'sweet'. Wayne did not tell her about his adventures with the Order, however. He felt it best not to bother her with all that stuff. The best bit came right at the end of the call, when he told her that he would be visiting Los Angeles straight after Christmas, to link up with his buddy, James.

Terri had squealed excitedly. "You've gotta come and stay with me, you've gotta!" So, Wayne had agreed.

As she replaced the receiver, all the fear that she had felt about losing him because of that dumb letter just evaporated, and she started to make plans for his visit.

When Dean did come home and she told him about it, she was in such a good mood that her enthusiasm was infectious.

Dean just shrugged, and said. "Well honey, if he's so important to you, I guess we better make him as happy as possible." Terri thought he'd almost sounded sincere.

Terri Thorne's life seemed to be on the up again. She looked out over her view of Beverley Hills, and smiled.

"All I need now is an Oscar on the mantelpiece!" she laughed.

Ninety-Seven

"So, boy...you're back at long last!" Dai Davies' booming voice echoed ominously around the physics lab. "Had enough of a holiday, have you? Summer holidays not long enough for you, eh?" The boys of 6A giggled nervously.

"I was beginning to think that you was not coming back until after Christmas!" Mr Davies continued, leaning on Wayne's desk in his most imposing manner. "Thought that you might have better things to do than come to my Physics lessons, did you?"

Wayne was about to protest his innocence and refer to his compassionate leave and spell in hospital, when Dai Davies - the deputy Headmaster, Physics teacher, and scourge of the errant pupil - whispered, "I know about your father, boy, and I'm sorry. He was a Desert Rat, Eighth Army, like me. He must have been a fine man...a very fine man." He nodded respectfully and gave half a smile, before turning back to the class.

"104 in the shade, and no shade. That's what we had to put up with. We could fry an egg on the bonnet of a Jeep, and you - you bunch of Nancy boys! - complain if it's a bit cold out on the rugger pitch. We dreamed of being cold. Harland, explain the principle behind being able to fry an egg on the body of a motor vehicle in the desert?"

Wayne grinned; life was almost back to normal. He and Doris were still staying at the Houghton-Hughes', but the cheque that he had received from Dan Malone would mean that Doris would not have to be jealous of her younger sister for much longer.

The days passed and Thursday evening rolled around, seemingly in the blink of an eye. Wayne rushed to the Youth Club that evening as fast as his legs could carry him. He had spent ages thinking about how he was going to explain about his alter ego Finn's disappearance to Stephanie, although he wasn't too confident that she would react in the way he hoped. That was the problem with girls; boys just never knew how they would react in any given situation.

Wayne felt David Smith eyeing him suspiciously as he entered the Youth Club. "Oi!" The Youth Club supervisor shouted, before Wayne had even crossed the threshold. Wayne sauntered innocently up to him.

"Yes, David?"

David Smith narrowed his eyes. "There was a Yank here, claiming to be your cousin, but your uncle knew nothing about him. Can you explain what was going on?"

Wayne shrugged his shoulders. "Michael Finnegan is my cousin, and he came when I couldn't. My dad was killed, you know?"

David coughed."Oh I...er..."

"The reason Uncle Stanley doesn't know Michael," Wayne interrupted him "is because Michael is a cousin in my birth family - you know, my blood family - and Uncle Stanley is my adoptive mother's sister's husband. So he's never met him."

"Oh I...er..."

Wayne shrugged. "Am I my cousin's keeper?"

David Smith took a deep breath, and his face coloured from red, to purple. Wayne grinned, and continued.

"I've heard that there was some funny business going on here, according to my Uncle Stanley and my adoptive cousin, Cedric, involving naked girls and all that sort of stuff. Well, I can tell you that at the time all that was happening, my cousin Michael was on his way to catch a connecting flight from Yeadon airport. You know...my mother is quite worried that I might get corrupted, coming here."

"Oh I...I see," David Smith stammered. "Adopted family, eh?"

Wayne smiled sweetly., and David Smith waved him in.

"There's something funny going on here," he thought to himself, before sniffing and muttering "Lucky bloody Yank," under his breath.

Wayne noticed the girls hanging around near the stage. He approached Anne Ducket, initially.

"Hi, Anne," he greeted her, just a bit apprehensively. She glared at him.

"Oh look...the rat's cousin," she spat, venomously.

"Rat?" Wayne repeated, somewhat taken aback.

"Well, the Yank was your cousin, wasn't he? Or is that a lie, as people have been saying?"

Wayne nodded vigorously. "No, Finn is my cousin, really."

"Well, tell him from Stephanie that she hopes he never comes back to England -ever!" Anne sneered.

"Is she here?" Wayne asked, as Anne turned her back on him.

She snapped around.

"What, having been seen in the nude by half of Shepton? She says she'll not show as much as her face here ever again." Anne turned away.

"Where does she live...I've got something for her!" Wayne almost shouted in desperation. Anne turned, and glowered at him.

"59 Greenacres." She turned away again, and Wayne dashed to the door.

"Where are you going?" Paul Harland asked, Wayne bumping into him as Paul entered the Youth Club.

"I've got to go and see Steph!" Wayne cried, already running out onto Westmoreland Street.

"Some people have seen quite a bit of her here, by what I've heard!" Paul giggled as Martin Taggart and Liam Riley arrived, just behind him. Wayne knew that, from what Uncle Stanley had said, that Uncle Stanley had been the only one to see Stephanie naked - but to hear them all talk, half of the Youth Club had seen her! That was the way these things went.

Twenty minutes later, Wayne knocked on the door of 59 Greenacres, his heart pounding nervously in his chest. A middle-aged man opened the door, and peered myopically at Wayne.

"Yes?" he asked brusquely.

"Is Steph - I mean, Stephanie - in?" Wayne asked, as routinely as he could manage.

"Who's asking?" the man demanded.

"Wayne Higginbotham," Wayne replied.

The man grunted, then disappeared. Wayne waited and waited, hopping nervously from one foot to the other.

Eventually, the door opened and Stephanie Fleming appeared, looking more gorgeous than Wayne had ever seen her.

"Hi, Wayne," she said, shyly.

"Hi," Wayne whispered, averting his eyes from the beauty that his alter ego had kissed.

"Look," Stephanie began. "If it's about Finn, I don't..."

"He gave me this, to give to you," Wayne handed her a letter, before she had time to dismiss him and cruelly slam the door in his face.

Stephanie looked at the letter and then at Wayne, thought about it for a few moments, and then ripped open the letter:

My Dear Stephanie,

"I do not know what I said, or did, but obviously you decided to sneak out of the Youth Club, pretending you had to go to the bathroom. I waited for you for ages, but I had a train to catch if I was ever going to get my flight, and you just didn't show up again.

I'm sorry if I did something wrong. I guess five thousand miles is a long way, and you do things a little different over here. Whatever I did to offend you, I'm real sorry.

I've never met anyone like you before and I know I never will again. Write me if you ever change your mind about me.

I love you

Finn

P.S. Wayne loves you too, but he's just a kid, I guess.

Wayne watched as Stephanie's eyes filled with tears. Her chin crumpled, and she wiped her nose on her sleeve.

"I did not sneak out!" she groaned. "I didn't! That Irish cow did something to me and took my clothes. I didn't sneak anywhere. He should have come and found me, or sent someone in to find me."

She looked defiantly at Wayne. "You tell your stupid cousin that I did not sneak anywhere. I do not sneak, and I did not dump anyone!" she stated angrily, as a solitary tear rolled slowly down her cheek. She sniffed, and carefully folded the letter.

"Thanks for bringing this, Wayne," she whispered, after taking a moment to compose herself. She leaned forward and kissed him on the cheek. It was only a small peck, but Wayne's heart soared. Stephanie then turned away slowly, and closed the door in his face.

Wayne stood, dumbfounded, on her doorstep. His emotions were a weird mix of elation, disappointment, and the sense that he'd totally failed - either to set the scene for a repeat visit by his alter-ego, or to convince her that he, Wayne, was a nice guy. He could defeat the Order...but he couldn't get the girl.

Somehow, he didn't feel like returning to the Youth Club, so he mooched slowly home to the Houghton-Hughes' house.

"Maybe I should have just gone and bloody well used mind control!" he thought bitterly, before going to sleep that night. Suddenly, all his achievements in defeating the Order and setting up his first trip to Los Angeles paled into insignificance. That night, for the first time since Frank Higginbotham had died, Wayne cried himself to sleep.

When Elizabeth Ball managed to pin him down a few days later, so that he could explain everything that had happened to her, she had explained to him that the reason he had cried so much that night was because it was the first time he'd really had the chance to mourn his dad. Wayne knew that she was sort of right, but the tears weren't just for Frank, the man who had raised him; they were also for Stephanie Fleming. The girl he'd lost, twice.

Elizabeth had been amazed by his relation of events and couldn't believe that he had travelled to Dublin to take on the Order in their own base. Wayne couldn't help but cry again when she had hugged him at the end of his story, and she had said, "Your dad would have been so proud of you, you know. That's the sort of thing he would have done, when he was younger."

Some weeks later, Wayne heard that Stephanie Fleming had been down to Oxford to visit her old boyfriend, Martin Berenger. He was a little upset, but by then he had heard that Caitlin O'Rourke fancied him and she was really pretty, even if she was only in the fifth form.

Wonder if she'd like to go to L.A? Wayne thought...

Ninety-Eight

The small, angelic-looking, boy looked out of the window of the plane as it made its final approach into Logan airport, Boston, Massachusetts. The late Cardinal D'Abruzzo had often told him of his favourite city in the United States, where he had been a simple parish priest, many years earlier. It was such a pity about his recent tragic, fatal, heart attack.

"Are you alright there, son?" The boy's new father grinned as he patted the boy's knee, while his mother smiled at him indulgently.

His mother's affair had been something of a whirlwind romance. She had only met her new husband several weeks earlier. It had been one of those 'love at first sight' spectacular events, and the girl had accepted the man's proposal without even having to think about it. After all, it was so much better than being a Sicilian nun.

Now the boy had a nice, proper, nuclear family. A huge, and close, extended family. A very, very wealthy family. He didn't have to live in a stuffy old Church building any more.

Aurelio Vitalia was from one of the richest and most influential Italian-American families in the entire United States. Aurelio's profession had been a lawyer, and although rumours of Mafia connections had followed and plagued him for years, mainly based on his successful defence cases for several major Mafia figures, nothing had ever been proved. Indeed, in recent years, his ever-closer contacts with the Catholic Church and his move into Right Wing Republican politics, had meant that any such rumours had humorously contributed to his nickname - 'The Holy Don.'

The boy's new father turned to his neighbour across the aisle of the private Lear jet, as it prepared to land.

"So, cousin of mine - when's that beautiful wife of yours going to give you that son and heir, and playmate for my boy here?"

The neighbouring passenger laughed. "Any day now, Aurelio. That's why she couldn't make it to the wedding. She's gonna pop any day now."

Aurelio laughed. "Good job that blonde could come, huh?"

The cousins laughed uproariously.

"You going straight back to the fantasy factory?" Aurelio asked, as he glanced out of the window.

"Oh yeah...she'll whine and whine if I don't get straight back to L.A. She's been on the verge of a breakdown for most of her pregnancy. I had to get a shrink out to see her. He said it was depression. I said to him, what's she got to be depressed about? She's married to a rich and gorgeous guy and has a house that most women would kill for. Pah!"

"Deano, Deano, why'd you go marry an Irish, anyway?" Aurelio motioned expansively. "A good Italian girl would've been more robust." Aurelio patted his new bride's knee, and she smiled lovingly at him. "Anyway, these Hollywood actresses are all so flaky."

"I know, I know," Dean Vitalia laughed. "But I'm a sucker for good looks, you know? And at least she's a good Catholic. Mind you, she's put on an awful lot of weight during this pregnancy. If it wasn't for my girlfriends, I'd go insane." The two men laughed and laughed.

The boy smiled beatifically at his mother.

His mother smiled back.